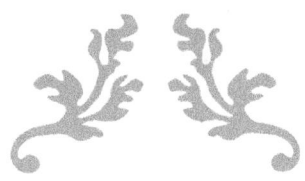

The Basilian

A Clash of Cultures

Fiore L. Cianflone
CianfloneBooks
www.opusw.com

Warm and noteworthy thanks go to my wife Mary Alice for her silent patience in this endeavor.

Acknowlegements

Since it is historical fiction that takes place during a time of turbulence and destruction and the written record is scarce, I would be lacking to not mention my reliance on others whose arduous and grueling research combined with extraordinary insight shed a realistic light on the period in question. Though there are too many contributors to list here, the deligent analysis of the conflicting and vague chronicles made by such serious scholars as Giovanni Saladino, Michele Amari, Luigi Cunsolo, and Enzo Agostino was invaluable for rendering a cogent picture of the events and daily life created in this book. Not to credit only foreigners, I also benefited by the lifetime research of John Haldon and Warren Treadgold, who have conducted worthy studies on the Byzantine world.

Map

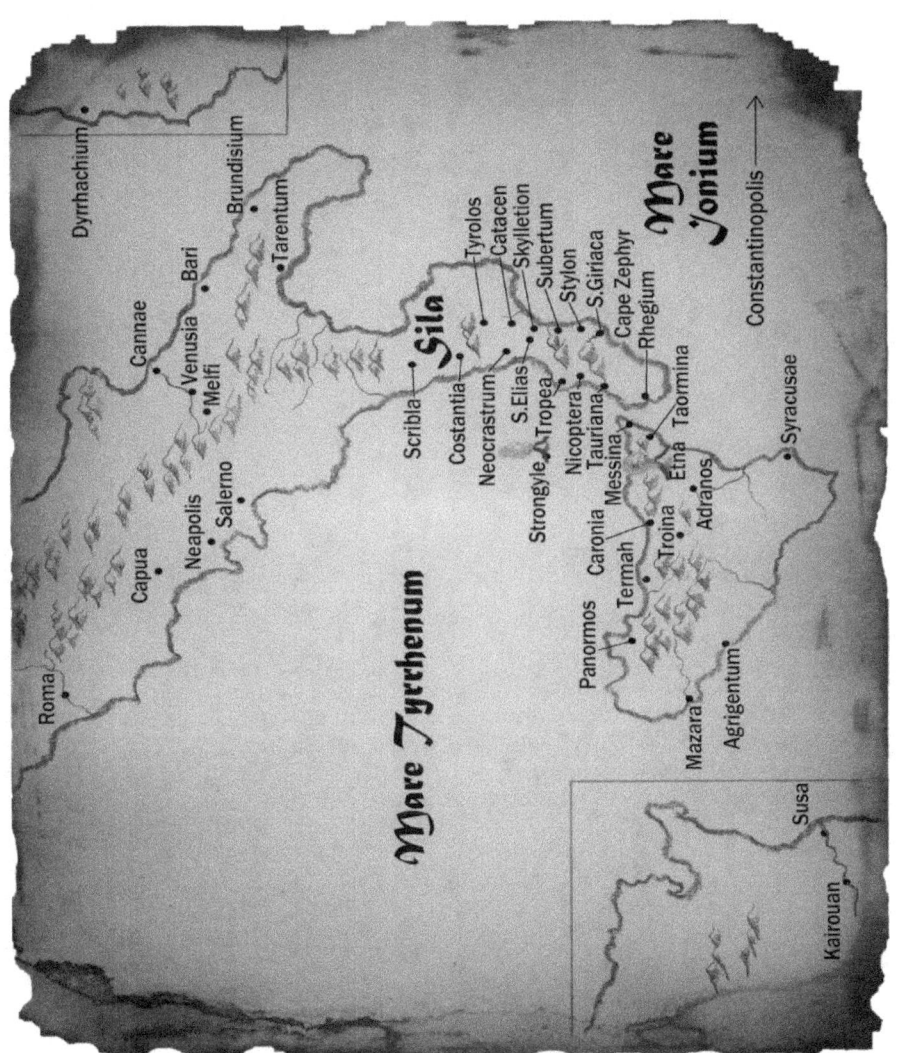

Preface

On June 14th, 827 AD, from the ancient port of Muslim-held Susa, Ifriqiya, today called Sousse, Tunisia, a human wave came to life and headed toward the coast of Sicily. The wave hit the shores of Mazara first, bloating with more than ten thousand Arabs and Berbers. Then it proceeded to inundate the rest of the island, drowning a good part of the Christian culture.

The higher ground of the eastern terrain was last to be submerged; Syracuse remained above the drowning water until 878 AD and Taormina stayed afloat until it, too, sank in 902 AD. From then on Southern Italy was never the same. The island now became a Muslim springboard for assaults and constant pirating of helpless Christians within its reach on the shores of the mainland. Although the neighboring mainland was a natural breakwater, the destructive wave, once even struck Rome itself.

Few escaped the carnage or enslavement. Whole populations vanished in its path. In Calabria, they spoke of monks being decapitated and churches sacked. In this hellish turmoil the Basilian monks fled Sicily to Calabria to preserve the culture and faith of the people in their path. There, the monks endured with their extraordinary stamina and spiritual convictions until confronted with a new wave from the north, nailing their final demise in Italy. These were the Normans and the cycle started anew.

Bruttium is the historical name for Calabria, and history has blessed Bruttium with earthly borders contiguous to heaven as well as hell. This is a story of a people whose genes have sprung from its womb. They are polished, yet crude; good, yet evil; victims, yet perpetrators; one people, yet many—they are God's people.

Table of Contents

PART ONE

Chapter I: Palermo
Circa 1010 AD

Frankly, his young years are not at all difficult being the stepson of a Berber merchant whose small palace, located near the entrance of the Arabic wall, is his home. The palace is in the new quarter of the city called Harat-al-Hadid situated south of the neighborhood containing the mosques, and east of that neighborhood is the al-Khalisah or Kalsa, with its splendid, royal palaces. The city is the lad's world, at least for now.

The present rulers call this city Bal'harm and it is home to thousands of people of diverse races, the majority of whom live in the suburbs. The city is a Mediterranean pearl, lying in a golden basin and acting as a commercial and cultural hub. Its spokes extend outward to Italy proper, Spain, the southern shores of Gallia (France) and coastal Africa.

Pleasant weather frequents it as a suitor serenades his lover and brightens up her spirits. The main paved street called simat al balat, "the marble street", leads to the sea and crisscrosses another street, equally important, that connects the Kalsa to the Slavic quarters. Everywhere sculptured columns uphold the shiny domes of mosques, painted inside and out, and flanked by towers that call the faithful to prayer.

Splendid baths and gardens nourished by fountain waters embellish the noble palaces adjoining them. Countless shops bustling with all sorts of worldly goods flank every street, and the wall-to-wall markets *suqs* invade any available space, ripe with the odors of fresh fish, grain, meat, herbs and spices from every corner of the world. To these charms, Bal'harm adds one school of medicine, one for mathematics, and others for law and the arts. It was a rich, learning environment for our lad in the present darkness of Europe.

When born in that small palace, the merchant who had bought his pregnant, Greek mother for his harem, accepted him as his son. During his adolescent years and before his Christian lessons, he relished this city with its flowering culture, splendid and growing, although in his youthful inexperience and ignorance he was not aware of the ancient, layers underneath, sacrificed for its growth.

As one of the master's children, natural and adopted, he enjoyed a Muslim identity and dressed accordingly in the Berber attire that offered freedoms denied to infidels. The master would often bring him along when he went about his business, mostly to the Slavic quarter, where the foreign merchants unload their goods for sale.

The Berber always dressed appropriately to his class, his long, white breeches held by a rope-like belt, interwoven with golden threads, a white shirt under a blue mantle, and upon his head sat a turban cap. He sported a well-groomed bushy beard, outdone only by the careful application of kajal around his eyes. Never did he forget to fasten the sheath containing the dagger, its handle inlaid with gold, a privilege granted only to Muslims.

His customary stance of making fists and resting them on his hips in the proud and arrogant fashion of the culture exerted an influence on the boy. Similarly dressed, save the makeup and dagger, which was gifted to him later, both would trek to the Slavic port where his stepfather needed him as an interpreter since Greek was still common among the foreign merchants and the child had been taught the language by his mother. They passed through the Gate of the Jews, entered the old section, walked north, exited the Gate of the Fountain of Health, and made their way to the piers by a route parallel to the outer wall.

They would pass private palaces, markets, synagogues, mosques and more mosques. When the two rivers, Kemonia and Pepyritus, which flanked the city ran high with water, scantily dressed lads of many races, Greek, Latin, Berber, and

Arabic splashed about in its waters. But the two had their own private bath fed by underground waters coming from these very rivers via the qanats or trenches that led to the noble palaces, an engineering feat equaled only by the Romans.

But the boy's fascination for this Arab world together with the merchant's influence was problematic for his mother. The Arabs had taken away her beloved husband and now they were taking away her son which weighed on her mind with the mass of an anvil. One day when her son was close to fifteen, she fell on her knees before the master, calling on his benevolence and worldly tolerance.

"Sidi! Sidi! Let my flesh and blood, begotten from Christians, be also a Christian."

It was not long afterwards that the youth ceased his studies of the Quran in the local mosque. The Greek Bible became, instead, his spiritual nourishment when not accompanying the merchant to the piers.

Outside the outer city wall, where the Christians were huddled in self-preservation, lived a devoted family that his mother entrusted for his emersion into the Christian world. Being designated *dhimmis* by the authorities, this family was permitted to exercise its religious duties, but only in private and with the burden of the tax. Every day spent with this family, or their neighbors rendered the youth more aware of the other culture beneath his feet.

Though he walked in two worlds, Christianity enjoyed an advantage by the name of Helena, the daughter of the mentor-family, whose devotion to Jesus and the Virgin Mary matched his mother's. A glow surrounded the pious girl, illuminating his heart and weakening the Arabic rock he stood upon as she opened the door to a world he had not seen before.

In Greek, the name Helena evokes splendor witnessed by her sparkling black eyes, long eyelashes and a constant smile. The palaces and mosques glittering under the Palermitan sun were dim before her radiant face and left him breathless at every gesture or expression in her possession. They wandered about the streets, hand in hand, with the freedom that his attire offered the two enamored Christians.

Little by little, these aimless walks achieved a pilgrimage-like tone as Helena's comments and observations unveiled a Christian subsurface that rarely entered the Arabic public discourse. He learned, for example, that the Grand Mosque—Gami—had been at one time the Palermitan Church of the Virgin Mary.

Through Helena's eyes, the city he had seen a thousand times now shone a different light. She peeled away their façades, one layer at a time, to reveal a rich past. The Halgah quarters became once again Paleopolis, the Qasr, Neapolis, and the two rivers became once again the Kemonia and the Pepyritus.

The girl had planted a seed of love in his heart, nurtured by her warm presence making the days too short for this courtship. The couple stretched every moment, often returning to her apprehensive Christian parents in darkness. Under this umbrella of bliss, the youth continued to brush aside his obligation to his mother, a promise made before the beautiful Helena had stolen his heart—be baptized in Calabria.

Several more years passed this way until it happened. Once, at her home, after the Bible lesson, Helena avoided our youth for some unknown reason—refusing to talk, and insisting he go home. Upset, her eyes avoided his and looking down she tried to hide her trembling hands. Baffled he swore to return, but before leaving, her Christian mother took his hand and implored, "Please, return later, give her some time."

A week passed, which seemed for him an eternity, barely sleeping and eating little. The mother's words repeated in his mind. Time for what? Is she sick or does she have doubts of our relationship? When he could not take it anymore, he found myself knocking insanely at her door. The door creaked as the mother opened it slowly, and cautiously, not knowing who so persistent was at the door. "Thank God, it is you. Come in, she is waiting." Her words creaked like the door she closed behind me. Helena appeared without the lively sparkle in her eyes, nor the facial splendor demanded by her name. However, she was calmer than before.

"Let's go outside. I need some air," she said in a matter-of fact tone. Obediently, he followed.

Helena led him on the road next to the river Pepyritus, and they walked in its upstream direction. They did not speak, for Helena did not know where to begin and he was too confused and overwhelmed to articulate sensible words. They remained silent, even as they passed through the gate called Bab-al-Sciantagath or the Saint Agatha Gate to take the road leading to the Grand Mosque.

The sun, that day, made no attempt to battle against the heavy clouds. The air was dense with humidity. It was difficult to tell if it was ever-so-lightly raining or if the pregnant clouds merely hovered over their heads and condensed moisture on the skin.

She stopped before the Grand Mosque, which for her would always be the Church of the Virgin Mary, where that celestial being dwelled and protected helpless Christians like herself. Retaining its Christian structure but Islamic in use, the people of Jesus, who were not allowed entrance, would approach it silently making the sign of the cross. When the couple arrived, various Muslim groups were scattered here and there as they waited for the next Muslim prayers. They loitered about in the open space, now partly sunny, to update each other on the latest.

"My mother says, if one listens carefully, one can still hear Mother Mary weeping for her Son. Even the Muslims attest to this and kept the church more or less the same." Her fiancé remained quiet, hoping Helena would explain her ill mood. "My ancestors arrived from outside of Panormos, where their land was confiscated because they refused to convert. Since the city was depopulated due to extermination and imposed slavery, the Muslims sought to repopulate it, allowing Christians and Jews a place within its walls. Of course, they could not escape that personal hideous tax."

The fiancé, who lived as a Muslim, had not paid much attention to this fact, and although he knew of it, its reality now took on a more sinister hue. "It seems strange that the non-Muslims are taxed for the air they breathe, given free to all by God. They think they own the air. What arrogance," he commented.

Suddenly they heard the Muslim call to prayer, *zuhur*, originating from the mosque tower, and Helena started trembling and it worsened with the growing crowd of Muslim faithful funneling into the mosque. Something was tormenting her, something ominous that hanged over her head like the heavy clouds that had followed them but then Helena's agitated state settled with the winding down of the zuhur.

"I do not understand, Helena," her fiancé said, now embracing her tightly. "What is wrong? With all these mosques, I would think you were used to them by now."

She began to sob violently, like trying to catch her breath when recovering from drowning. Her nightmare buried deep within, was sporadically coughed up and intermingled with barely discernable words. Her torment finally exploded into an anger her Christian heart had never felt before, an anger that conquered her sobbing.

"On an errand for my mother, ruffians stopped me, those people from the marches." She now felt the Virgin Mary by her side.

"Those brutes that loiter in groups and harass Christians?" He guessed.

"Yes!" and the sobbing began anew. Stunned, he could make out only one word from those trembling lips—violated.

"It is okay, okay, you need not say more," he said embracing her tightly.

In his embrace, she replied, "I feel dirty, ugly. You will not love me anymore."

"No, no; do not talk that way. God loves you; the Madonna loves you; I love you. Just tell me who it was," he demanded in his flush of anger.

"No, they will hurt you." She pleaded for his safety.

"They are not going to get away with this. It is simply wrong!" His tightening muscles said more than the words.

They turned around for home, walking slowly and saying nothing other than the sporadic objections coming from Helena, who had guessed her fiancé's intentions.

"It will end badly for both of us," she said. The farther they walked, the less the couple spoke, absorbed in them selves as they pondered their future.

The Kala bay had given birth to the north wind; it challenged their hopes and dreams, and the hate grew in his young mind. His focus became singular, his muscles stiffened even more, and he lost that gentleness Helena desired in him. Sensing this, she squeezed his hand even harder, hoping to draw out the irrational poison that would ruin everything. When they arrived at Helena's door, they found comfort in each other's arms and stretched the moment as much as possible.

"Please! Don't pursue them," Helena warned, enunciating the word please. Then as he reluctantly loosened his embrace to depart, she added, "Let things be. God wills it so, good-bye."

The young man took the usual street home, now dark except for the occasional dim lights flickering gently from open shutters that helped show the way. The dwellings that held the clothing shops and various mercantile activities were silhouettes against the sky.

When he passed through the Jewish Gate, the Jewish quarter before him gave assurance he was on the proper path home, but instead he turned left, attracted mysteriously toward the marshes. The Greek stepson wanted to un-mask the city, to find out where the lowest of the low lived, where those paid to do Islam's unspeakable deeds had their lairs.

Always with one hand on the dagger handle, his eyes probed the shacks lining the muddy pathways. Each shadow was an attacker. Nothing! It was too dark. He must return the next day to make inquires. Maybe encounter the perpetrators themselves. Turning around, he retraced his steps to the Jewish quarter, where he released the firm grip on the dagger handle and gave a deep sigh of relief. Within the vicinity of home, he relaxed, walked more slowly, and tried to make some sense of the confusing day.

He had no sooner arrived at his door when he heard the *isha*, the midnight call to prayer. Prior to this day it had been delightful and pleasant. Now, the screeching noises unraveled the few thoughts he had managed to put in order. Quietly entering, he headed for the bedroom, and threw myself on the bed.

Helena's words returned as echoes and put, once again, into question his intentions. His love for her certainly had not waned. It had taken flight. Of course, Helena would not approve of any physical confrontation. She was too good, but this shame consumed his honor and dignity. Honor and dignity come with a price, however, and what value can honor have away from her as he rots in a dungeon for the rest of his life? Would it not be better to prostrate before the yoke of humility, carry the cross, as Jesus did? At least he would be by her side.

The next day, the youth was taken again by that strong urge to know who the perpetrators were. He hastened for the Kala marshes to meet the disgusting bullies. He wanted peace and that could only happen when this ineffable injustice surfaced to the light of day with its authors rightfully punished.

But the walk gave him time to contemplate Helena's warnings. His fury subsided, and better judgment filtered in his troubled mind. Filing a complaint, *mohtesib*, with the authorities was still an option, although when Christians are involved, there is usually no result. On the other hand, his stepfather, who participated in the senate of the nobles, *gema*, could possibly help, for he knew the city officials and other nobles. He flirted with this thought, but for now, he stayed the course wanting desperately to find these brutes, stare into their eyes, and yell, "Why! Why!"

The paths became more rutted, uneven. At one point, the road turned into a furrow-like path of dried-up mud flanked by decrepit shacks, their walls eaten by the saltwater of the Kala. His mind was unmoved by the squalid neighborhood. It was fixed on images of his suffering Helena, images that encouraged and emboldened him. He was after all in Saracen attire and appeared as a convert cut from Latin or Greek cloth.

The people living here occupied the lowest run of the Palermitan ladder. They aspired to the *mujahidin*, a man of the cloth or a soldier protecting the frontier. In Panormos, however, there were already security squads under a central command. These people here had another purpose, one more sinister. They were illiterate charlatans peddling the Quran and earned their living as paid lackeys to the unscrupulous nobles who preferred to settle scores illegally, often violently, eliminating obstacles to their most base of ambitions.

"Ahee! What do you want here?" a menacing voice echoed from the shadows which hid its origin from sight.

"I am looking for some youths who were in the Slavic area a few weeks ago."

"Who are you?" the shadow asked.

Not wishing to reveal his identity, he replied, "I am here on behalf of a noble who lives in the Gadid and needs a favor."

"Further down, you will find some lads; perhaps they know something," came an unwelcoming voice, then he heard the slamming of window shutters.

The narrow dirt road could have served as a shortcut toward the Slavic area but was rarely used. When the road turned left to avoid the shallows of the Kala, there appeared a small square, open to the light of the early morning sun in which several youths were gambling with dice, shamelessly defying the rule of Islam.

The poverty of their attire contrasted sharply to the wealth they used in their gambling. Almost grown up, they seemed to be waiting their turn at the hardened criminal life led by their elders with this mischievous entertainment. The youth greeted them cheerfully to prevent them from scattering from a suspicious stranger, but they stood firm at their activity, and maintained a brazen energy that denied him any recognition.

He felt invisible to them, "Are you available to do a simple task for the noble ....?" He made up a name. He still received no response nor any subtle gestures, purposely or inadvertently.

They distrusted strangers, these people of the street living in the shadow of the law, he soon realized. He watched them attentively hoping to learn more as he allowed his presence to become familiar to them. There were three of them. The older had a recent scar on his cheek, an ugly complement to his hideous huge jaws, which helped in his behavior as leader. The others were less hideous but had rugged, leather-like skin common to desert life.

The ringleader feigned interest in the game while he sized him up carefully with the corner of his eyes. Occasionally, the younger ones glanced at their leader to catch the subliminal commands darting toward them in the matter of the stranger.

All this told him whom he had to deal with to illicit some meaningful response.

"You, there, with the scar, don't you want to make some money?" He challenged the leader.

"Talk!" yelled the scarred face.

His fear did not hold him back as he lured them to break their criminal code of silence. "I see you are not chatterboxes. Okay, Sidi— has a business rival, a Christian that has a very profitable tailor shop. He would like to buy him out, but the man refuses to sell. There are ways of persuasion I know are familiar to you."

"Sidi—! Never heard of him." The bandit was puzzled.

"You don't have to know him. I represent him."

The bandit lowered his brow, nodded, and remained coy, offering little.

The fiancé then extracted, from the folded section of his breeches, a recently minted gold coin called a ruba'i, waved it before them, and said, "Do you want to earn this or not? If you do not have the stomach, I will go elsewhere."

"One ruba'i, ha! Ha! As you see we have more just for our entertainment," boldly yelled one subordinate who was permitted to interject by the acquiescent look received from his hoodlum boss.

"Do you have more? At least one dinar, or just go away," protested the ringleader, his chest heaving with pride.

The youth pulled out three more ruba'i, which totaled precisely one dinar.

After the three searched each other for objections with their eyes, the ringleader replied, "We work in our own way, if we do it."

"Of course, but no bloodshed," The fiancé insisted, as his voice began to crackle nervously in memory of the incident. "Theft and rape, yes. I have heard there are experts in this matter."

"Do you mean this Christian has a daughter?" the leader asked after he mulled it over.

"But you are only braggarts, petty thieves who settle for crumbs at the feet of real thugs," he hesitated, thinking they should know something. "I may have to go elsewhere, for you seem to have no experience." He prodded their criminal pride and threw the bait back into the water. "Have you ever really done anything?"

Now truly offended, the scarred face barked, "What did you call us? Petty thieves?" while approaching him to intimidate or, worse, throw the first blow. Ferocious eyes now froze on the fiancé. "Do you want to know what we are made of, Greek swine?" The thug, menacing and ready for conflict, had nibbled on the bait.

"Well then, do you have the stomach as those who violated that girl? The noble will pay well." He tugged on the line to deepen the hook. They know something, he surmised. Such deeds travel faster among criminals and become common knowledge in their midst.

"We did her. We took turns with that Christian pig. She is pretty, and this scar was worth the price." His boasting, like a hammer, shattered the fiancé heart.

The ringleader's biting tongue, controlled by a sick pomposity and hoodlum-like arrogance, held back nothing. The fiancé's blood began to boil, and his temples pulsated with his racing heart as the prudence he hitherto maintained gave way to raw rage. He had not yet learned the Christian act of forgiveness. Even if he had, it would not have penetrated that vengeful mind in this marshy hell.

He then raised his clenched fists, delivered a blow square on the scarred cheek, and its owner fell backward. Meanwhile the companions ran to help their disgraced leader. They surrounded, grabbed the fiancé, held him in place as the fallen brute recovered from his fall who then lunged for his neck. He could not breathe; the arms of the companions held his arms tight against his torso. Nevertheless, he succeeded to free the one arm closest to the dagger.

It was not his hand that plunged the dagger into a soft belly but the hand of Lucifer himself. The hand was possessed. Suddenly he felt a blow on the head, and everything became dark.

The fiancé came to, stretched out on the damp, packed earth of a dungeon, barely lit by a hole in one of its thick stonewalls. The only fresh air was the sultry air of the sea flowing through its two crisscrossed rusty bars. His shirt was drenched in blood, the dagger had been stripped away, and his body ached all over. A horrible smell of excrement from a hole in the ground, used for bodily relief, assailed his nostrils. The only means of communication was a miniature door in the center of a larger wooden door used to pass the pig-like fodder they called food.

He recognized the place. It was the Kalsa prison, and he would have to wait for the judge *cadi* to administrate a trial. A condemnation to the gallows or worse yet, rotting forever in this infernal cage without a trial, would be a normal Christian lot. He was dead, yet alive, dead in spirit, but the body still contended with some life.

With the rising sun, the dim light traversing the crisscrossed bars became more brilliant, a sort of beacon in the darkness. When it struck the earth at his feet, it imprinted a shadowy image of the crossed bars it left behind. He fell to his knees before the light and the cross it made, imploring God Almighty for absolution and salvation.

His senses yielded to fits of delirium in which succeeding images and visions of Helena, his mother, and Christ flashed repeatedly in his mind. They guided him to the heavens and showed him the whole city from that advantageous place. The main street via al-qasr formed a shiny, huge cross with the other street, equal in stature and going northeast to the Slavic quarters. Panormos was brooding a Christian cross, destined to resurface, and he would rise with it, he was sure of it. The delirium vanished into nothing, taken over by a profound sleep, needed badly.

The next day there was a ruckus outside the cell, which then subsided into a low, quarreling chatter that disturbed his sleep and gradually brought him to full consciousness. Dragging feet approached the wooden door, which was flung wide open, and accompanied by a huge bang. His Berber stepfather appeared.

"I paid dearly to those filthy Arabs for you." (Arabs controlled the government.) "Quick, hurry up, your mother is waiting."

They hurried for the palace to avoid further danger. He had to make his last good-bye to his mother and, of course, pack. He was a wanted man, if not by the law, at least by the thugs of the marshes who thrived on revenge.

"I have prepared a voyage for you on a Pisan ship, which is scheduled to stop at Tauriana (Gioia Tauro). From there, through the mountains lies your family's precious Saint Giriaca. I cannot do more; a civil war is churning in the belly of the city. As a Berber, I have my own problems with the Arabs."

"When will I leave? Can I also see Helena?"

"No, to be honest, I don't know if you will ever see her. The ship sets sail tonight." His young heart sank to a depth only Christ could lift. He embraced his tearful mother, said good-bye, and left.

Chapter II: Calabria
25 Years Later

The monk had grown thin with the weight of his vows given to his God. His curly hair, once charcoal black, was now, together with his beard and mustache, speckled with the early whiteness of his forty years. No one in Saint Elias knew Nicholaos' family name; they simply accepted him as God's gift, for it was unseemly for the common villager to question the authority of the church. His laity nicknamed him Father Nicholaos the Gatherer, based on one of his passions, gathering orphans wandering about the countryside in need of nourishment and spirituality.

He had been a wanderer, betrayed by fate and pursued by a dark shadow from his youth that seemed to be always at his back. His last refuge, before this little village was the Valley of Salt, an area settled by hermit monks like himself. It was a place of Basilian sanctity, consisting of an ascetic and coenobitic life initiated at least a century before his arrival by saints such as Elias Speleota and Elias of Enna. They lived in grottos and hovels and rendered the area noble by sowing God's word. There in the year of our Lord 1025, when Nicholaos was twenty-nine, after four arduous years of vocation, they shaved his head, laid the schema over his shoulders, and proclaimed him Father Nicholaos with their benediction.

From that day forward, he ceased to dress formally, never covered his unruly hair, and wore only his inner garment, *Anteri,* soiled and torn by toil and neglect. The rest of his holy clothing, the exterior garment *exorason,* last vesture schema, and cylinder cap *skoufos,* he had diligently folded and stored away in his worm-eaten chest. Buried underneath was other clothing, remnants of his past, a past whose pain he shared only with that shadow and one special lad, Iohannes. Now a Basilian monk and addressed as Father by orthodox tradition, he humbly took on his new responsibilities.

Prior to his vocation, however, he had pounded the tortious paths that furrow a stretch of mountains running northeast from Rhegium to the Catacen Isthmus and called "Le Serre." He immersed himself in the people and their land, whose mountain range resembled a viper common to its forest. The highest terrain, the massif of Aspromonte (6,414 ft.) which challenges Arabic Sicily, could easily be mistaken for its menacing head. The rest of the ridge with its crisscrossing distinctive ridges and gullies, narrows, twists, and finally descends at the isthmus, where it eerily resembles the viper's curved tail.

And just before the isthmus, the little hamlet of Saint Elias rests on a plateau, and is overlooked by the orphanage, which snuggles against the mountain as a pup to its mother. Father Nicholaos fulfills his vows here by assisting the guardian reptile to hide and protect his people.

His main mission, the orphanage, requires many roles: provider, father, and teacher in which he also taught Iohannes, from the circle of his laity, now seated before him. The monk taught him Latin and Greek by reciting the Aeneid and the Odyssey, a method of teaching in those days, but sometimes he digressed. Spurred by his love for the land and its people, he would transform himself into an epic poet, mixing real life with the lessons and, like any good schoolmaster, he captured the pupil's undivided attention. The lad's mother, Maria, like the town's folk, praised the monk for his work with the orphans and many contended for his precious time to teach their sons.

"This land is graced by the muses." The erudite voice of Father Nicholaos, in contrast to his feral hair, met Iohannes. "It conveys its story through the mouths of its inhabitants rooted in its bosom, who apart from their wails and anguish also sing of joy and its beauty. They give thanks for its rutted paths that offer safe passage and its rushing waters that turn mills and irrigate their fields." These words resonated in his pupil's mind with a godly authority, even though he had heard them many times before, issued through that burly mustache and beard.

"Where have you gone, Father?" asked Iohannes, seated at the kitchen table, whose imagination rested on the wings of the idyllic narrative. Clad in medieval attire of leather socks for shoes and a wool skirt, tied at the waist, for a shirt, the youth was lucky; most went barefoot.

"In my youth, I travelled from Seminara to Saint Giriaca and finally to Tryoros and back—prosperous towns reduced to little defensive units, *choria* after the destruction by the Saracens. I have witnessed snowy peaks dressed in skirts of coppice trees and pine, and, descending a bit lower, chestnut, oak, and beech embroider their skirts. When in season the lower trees wear an undergarment of ferns. To the traveler on these numerous paths the mountains offer the serene beauty of lush meadows sprinkled with heather, broom, and holly." The monk took a pensive breath to recapture his poetic spirit.

"Torrents everywhere greet you, demanding your attention as they noisily cascade into pools that harbor mossy rocks. Some trails barely adhere to the not-so-solid ground of a precipice and dare the passerby to stop and marvel at the ravine below. The ravines bear rushing streams and waterfalls with bewitching mists that hover over the water and rocks only to be banished by the noon sun. This land is enchanted and populated with elves and all sorts of strange creatures." The monk put on the face of a Greek tragic actor. "This is God's world." Iohannes' green eyes were frozen on his master.

The boy's father, a local patriarch of Latin tradition, had entrusted his son to Father Nicholaos in exchange for favors to the orphanage. And every Monday and Thursday, excluding the winters and the farming season, Iohannes arrived here in the high ground for his lessons, which had started at age eight. As the boy got older, the monk would unwittingly release more tidbits of his former life, intermingled with the lessons.

The classroom comprised of a crude table chiseled by an axe-wielding maker and centered in a hovel whose thatched roof was held up by three stoned walls. Missing the fourth wall, the hovel was an add-on to the Father's hermit cave and built to accommodate the growing number of little souls that needed his expert hands for their molding.

The hovel-like dwelling was nestled into the natural surroundings of the remote high country like a bird's nest out of sight from its prey. The place, together with the hovel and the cave, the neighbors conveniently named, "The Grotto."

A narrow clearing that turned into a precarious incline not far from the hovel's doorstep presaged the life awaiting the occupants of the nest. Functioning as its farmyard, it stretched to each side of the hovel and nicely supported a stable, and a sheepfold. In the other end sits a fire pit for deshelling chestnuts, social gatherings and a favorite play spot for the littlest, barefoot orphans, Leonellus and Iulia who have yet to learn to fly.

Becoming concerned, the Basilian monk rose from the table, strolled toward the open door, and paused there for a moment to observe the children who began arguing in their play. He gently scolded them, then he drew into his lungs God's beautiful country to quench the lingering fires in his soul, fires, that dwelled in all men's souls except his orphans before they learned to fly. Iohannes, at fifteen, had just learned to fly, with wings strengthened by curiosity and the beauty of Flavia, another of the monk's barefoot orphans.

A chaotic twitter caught the monk's ears as the incoming swallows perched on a nearby beech tree to recover from their annual stressful voyage toward Africa. "This land is a sanctuary for these birds just as it is for us. We can rest our aching bodies here as well," he half whispered on his common theme not knowing if Iohannes inside had heard. He then returned to his student who made no immediate comment.

"Where did you acquire your knowledge, Father?"

"Before I answered the spiritual calling near Stylon, for my heart was not ready, my quest for knowledge was greater than my need for spiritualism. Staying in various monasteries, I increased my knowledge until my heart was ready for God." A subtle smile ended his words.

The late autumn sun, busted obliquely through the windows and doorway and landed on the dirt floor, highlighting the dust specks on its travel. Father Nicholaos sweated a bit. "My son, notice the swallows outside, they are now quietly feeding." He wiped his sweaty brow with his arm. "Their scanty bodies will gain their fill for their long journey south."

Iohannes maintained his respectful attention.

"This land also fills our bellies while the monks quench the mind with the culture they preserve in their manuscripts. It is my honor to be one of them." He thought of his vows that had battled the raging flames within, at a time he screamed for redemption.

"Father, is your family from Saint Giriaca?" Iohannes' inquisitive eyes fell on the table, hesitating to peer into the Father's personal past.

"Yes, but my father is dead, and I have no siblings" said the monk, flatly, His student was bringing out those former fires, in Nicholaos' youth.

Iohannes, now playing with his satchel resting on the table, timidly continued, worried the monk would return to the lesson. "But what happened to him?"

"I never knew my father." The monk acquired a distant gaze, and Iohannes waited patiently for the monk to collect his thoughts wondering why Father Nicholaos was so hesitant.

"I mean how did he die?"

"You are persistent, my son," the monk paused to clear his throat for a second. "My mother told me that the Saracens had killed my father, but he valiantly took down two of theirs before those demons cut him down.

The boy's inquisitive expression froze in disbelief, his eyes widened. The world cannot be that awful, he thought.

The monk had read his mind. "But son, we live in turbulent times." The monk was now fighting the lump in his throat and could not continue. Iohannes swore he saw a tear roll down Father Nicholaos' cheek and disappear into his wild beard.

At the same time, Iulia and Leonellus began bickering outside which gave Father Nicholaos an opportunity to deflect from having opened-up his heart. "Darn it," he said, turning to the source of the noise, hoping to have pushed aside his student's attention on himself. Then he turned back to Iohannes, outlined a smile showing embarrassment and waited for the fighting to stop. When the silence returned, the monk had lost his train of thought, something he rarely did.

Iohannes gave one last tug at the monk's personal life against his better judgement. "But, Father, you have not told me everything? Where was the militia?"

"Perhaps some other time, son," said Father Nicholaos. "In the next lesson."

Father Nicholaos paused to regain his breath and began to unwrap a small parcel within his reach. A brilliant blue spinel-stone from Tryoros appeared, which he offered to the lad. "This gemstone reflects all the beauty my eyes have seen. Should you ever find yourself away and homesick as I have been, just gaze into its blue glitter; it will warm your heart." Father Nicholaos knew what was in lad's heart, it was those blue, sparkling eyes of Flavia.

The Father's tale had meandered; it had no conclusion, and left Iohannes wanting to know more of Nicholaos, the man. His instincts told him the traumatic flight from Sicily was related to Father Nicholaos' divine calling. A calling by which Father Nicholaos had pierced some of life's eternal secrets.

A stillness had descended both inside and outside the humble shack. The swallows were silent, and the sun, tired of beating down on the roof, began to rest lower in the sky. It was getting late for Iohannes. There was a two to three-hour brisk walk waiting for those young feet on paths and trails with loose rocks and overhanging cliffs. Their ruggedness can threaten even the surest feet. One spot conjured up adolescent fears of tumbling down into an abyss of unspeakable horrors. Avoiding this treacherous precipice meant adding time to the already overwhelming trek home.

"Father Nicholaos, it is time for me to leave," Iohannes sadly reminded his mentor.

Father Nicholaos thought for a second, picked up the scroll on Vergil, toyed with it, and said, "Yes, of course, Your mother must now be worried. In the dark these forests harbor thieves and cutthroats."

The youth, slightly older than Iohannes, was awakened again, as often happens every time he tends to the monk's goat in the high country. The fire in the shepherd's shack had died down to ambers and the cold, night wind outside had worked its way inside to penetrate his bones and reminding him how much he hated to be here. Quivering, he cursed his way outside to obtain fuel for that damn fire. "That crazy monk must hate me," he mumbled. "Why not Peter?"

With his bare feet he walked carefully over to a small pile of logs easily seen in the starry night which he had set aside during the day and picked up three in his arms. When he turned around, he was struck by a feeble light which he took to be a campfire coming from the yet higher ground. It was mimicking signals as it made its way through the wind-agitated foliage, a wind which carried with it a wolf's howl. To his surprise, he experienced no fear just a strange curiosity for it appeared to him as an implied invitation of some sort.

Back inside, he revived the fire, laid down on his straw mattress and tired to fall asleep to the crackling lullaby of the fire, but his thoughts denied him sleep. They took him back to his youth when his father had him by his side, but the memories were foggy. He remembered that his father was referred to as an *iman* and a *murabitum*—whatever that meant.

The monk, however, seemed to have some of the answers. He spoke of an endless cycle of destruction, Muslim violent incursions into Calabria, made right on Christian doorsteps forcing the inhabitants into the safety of the mountains. But with local resistance and help from Constantinople the locals would regain their homes and land dispersing the invaders that formed small bands as thieves, and murderers. Your father, he had concluded, headed one of these and was killed when mounting a raid on local Christians.

What Father Nicholaos had not told the youth was that he had convinced the militia to spare the lad, vowing that he would tend to his welfare and education. "Although conceived in an act of violence," he had argued before the militia, "he was born from a Christian womb." The youth fell asleep in a cloud of questions whose answers he would eventually glean here and there from the community."

Chapter III: Orphans

The eastern face of Mount Elias that cuddles the grotto looms over the river Alessi, which runs east and cuts the little hamlet of Saint Elias in two. Both the town and the grotto, the sun greets early, but then vanishes quickly behind the mountain; daylight comes early as does dusk.

Inside the humble structure Father Nicholaos squinted to read The Odyssey in preparation for the next lesson; however, his heavy eyelids fell with the approaching twilight. When he was deep in his nap, the orphan Flavia emerged from the wooded area above, making her way cautiously down the steep slope.

The more audacious children had nicknamed her the Naiad, the goddess of streams and springs, and rumor had it that she was found swimming in a river pool shrouded in mist and fed by torrential streams. In truth, Nicholaos, the man of God, had come across a creature of God, a rag doll covered in Naias plants and trembling in fear.

She carried on her honey-blonde tresses, in perfect balance and supported by a graceful form of fourteen years, a basket of blackberries and raspberries, gathered for the evening meal. As soon as she saw the two little ones playing nearby, she yelled their names, and the three collided into a joyful embrace.

They made their way to the grotto, where she placed on the table her day's gatherings before the napping monk, whose bristly chin rested on his chest and whose outstretched arms seemed to reach for the fruit in his sleep. Placing her index finger to her lips, she motioned the children to be silent as she quietly prepared the table. Then she grasped Father Nicholaos' sturdy arm crisscrossed by bulging veins and gently shook it until she saw his head slowly rise. The children giggled, and Flavia smiled back as Father Nicholaos slowly raised his eyes.

"Do you think the others will return before dark and bring the vegetables?" she asked of him.

"They should, my child," he stammered, still groggy from his nap. "The older ones know better than to return in the dark."

She was his favorite child, and he was beginning to sense in her a hidden astuteness unique to womanhood and reflected in her whole-hearted commitment to her chores. Along with that, he knew her playful innocence, still there in certain times, was being replaced by flames of the heart.

Father Nicholaos allowed Leonellus to jump on his lap while Iulia clung to Flavia's side. "I know we do not have white bread and meat," he said. "Use the chestnut bread. God will provide."

"The children hate that bread, Father." Flavia was already slicing it.

"Hm." The monk nodded slowly. "By the way, you remember Eugenius, the father of my student Iohannes? He has promised me some dried pork and a piglet this spring for us to raise. Also, with donations from the neighbors, we can begin to raise sheep as well."

Flavia's heart skipped a beat and her face blushed at the mention of Iohannes while Father Nicholaos smiled contently at her. He knew his flock well and her feelings were no exception. A handsome prince had entered her heart and since his words would only add to the girl's bashfulness, he remained silent, pondering on the young couple who rarely were alone together and mostly in his presence. Lacking the courage to engage with each other directly, they would exchange furtive glances and utter awkward words of little sense. Oscillating between shyness and a hidden maturity, their encounters harbored a seed of desire, not fully recognized by each, but, nonetheless, sprouting between them.

The others arrived together, chattering, joking, and jostling each other as they carried the produce from the garden they attended. After making their greetings they placed figs, lettuce, and onions on the table. They sat quickly in their usual seats and waited for the blessing before attacking the food, already washed, and prepared by their little hands in the nearby stream. A dozen orphans comprised Father Nicholaos' flock, and it was still growing.

Only the sixteen-year-old Alphaeus was missing, for his required chore was the pasturing of the goat farther up the mountain, an hour's walk from the grotto. That day he was due to return in with the goat. Able but cocky he sometimes returned late as if to challenge the monk's authority.

Exceeding in confidence more than his wit could justify made him disagreeable to Flavia and tested the monk's patience as well; however, it entertained the others. Flavia found him somewhat handsome, with his brawny form and chiseled facial features, but he was no match to Iohannes' fairer visage. Alphaeus had a permanent rusty tan and curly black hair, but Iohannes had long brown hair and was tanned only by the sun. Alphaeus seemed aggressive and boorish; Iohannes was intelligent, mild, and closer to her age.

"Where in the world is he?" yelled the monk. "He was to graze the goat on the nearby meadow, not the far one." He stared at the onion that would later burn his stomach. "These are dangerous times. Skylletion is still not completely refortified." He pushed aside the onion and settled for plain bread. "We can't wait any longer. Let's eat, children; I will get some wine."

Now muttering to himself, he stepped into the cave section of the grotto, which served as the summer sleeping quarters and storage space, to draw cool wine from a large clay jug. When he returned, Alphaeus had entered, having secured Browny in the fold and milked her. The brown nanny had yielded a jar of milk Alphaeus held in his hand, projecting a large grin.

"Well, finally!" Father Nicholaos took his seat opposite Alphaeus. "At least you can pour the milk you brought for the children before sitting down."

Flavia sensed the approaching tension and poured the fresh goat's milk into the wooden cups herself. Then the children burst into giggling in reaction to Alphaeus' deflated bravado and stopped abruptly when the Father cleared his throat to give the blessing. They resumed their snickering and jeering while they shoveled in their portion of chestnut bread and washed it down with the warm milk, which gave them a white mustache.

"Iohannes today brought word from his father Eugenius that the Saracen pirates are in the mountains, raiding farms and kidnaping Christians. News of last year's peace treaty (1) with the Arabs apparently has not reached these demons," volunteered Father Nicholaos, who wondered if the news would frighten his orphans.

"Blah, blah, I am not afraid," interrupted Alphaeus.

Ignoring this, Father Nicholaos turned to the others.

"My children, even fear can be good; it keeps us alert. Alphaeus, when you graze Browny on the high meadow, scan your eyes over the land below for any unusual activity. The rest of you, always be on the lookout. We have a decent view from here as well. On a clear day, we can see the Ionian."

The children fell into a frozen obedience while the monk's words buzzed and whirled in their minds and finally digested.

"I don't want to frighten you, but you must know how to react when the pirates come. Flee into the woods; hide or head for the Florus farm. I will remain here; they will not harm a withered old monk."

The monk stole a pensive moment. Life is cruel, he told himself, but my little robins must learn to fly.

Iulia immediately burst into tears with all this talk of pirates. Flavia hugged her, kissed her on the cheeks, wiped her tears. "You can come with me, dear," she said. "You will not be alone."

"Until we can construct a hiding place, this will be our plan," said Father Nicholaos, now becoming reluctant to continue.

"But where?" A tongue was loosened from its frozen state.

"Past the stable. There is a shallow cavern at the foot of the hill. We can expand it to accommodate all of you. We will cover the opening with branches and foliage so it will appear natural," replied the monk, sensing the fear hover over their little heads.

"Anyway, this is all for tomorrow," he continued, falling into his own thoughts, as the table began to pick up its own tempo. He observed the children in tattered rags, partially clad, still gaunt from a prior hunger, and recalled rummaging for their clothes in the towns sacked by the Saracens. Clothes left behind by a people swept away into slavery or left lying lifeless.

Acquired in his travels and circulating for many generations, the stories of these Saracen tempests were not meant for their innocent ears. Like diabolical whirlwinds from nowhere, they left nothing but ruins behind. Real pirates that destroyed real towns, Saint Giriaca, Stylon, Skylletion, and Tryoros. "God, help me shield them from such evil," he whispered to himself.

But the monk had a way with his orphans. He rekindled their spirits and restored the sparkle in their eyes despite their faults and childish defects. There was the restless, the mischievous, the reserved, the weak, the witty, and the braggart, but all good in his eyes. The spark of life was still intact, he reassured himself. "They are children of God, after all, entrusted to me," he often murmured to himself when losing patience.

The varied personalities crammed around the table now engaged in a multitude of conversations, one indistinguishable from the other with no understanding except to the immediate listener. This warmed the monks' heart even more than the wine. Even the braggart Alphaeus no longer worried him, and the impressionable Iulia had stopped crying, although she held tight, in her little hand, Flavia's torn dress that did not distract from her beautiful form already formidable in her fourteen years.

Alphaeus, struck by the vision, ogled her, and anxiously awaited any opportunity to converse with the Naiad. The others, aware of his mawkish stare, giggled and mocked him. But to Alphaeus, all the voices reached his ears comingled and unintelligible. Every time he focused on one voice, the others would become louder and more distracting. He stopped listening to anyone; just gawked at Flavia, making her uncomfortable. The children feigned the swooning of lovers, placed their hands on their hearts, blew kisses at one another or shared amorous whispers. The jests multiplied into a chorus and flew about the table, loud laughter now drowned all serious talk. Alphaeus was crushed.

But when the monk erupted into a guffaw and Flavia snickered, Alphaeus was jolted out of his staring stupor. He looked around and searched for an explanation but to no avail. Everyone was laughing and he, their leader as he believed, was the object of these jokes.

"Hey, people!" Alphaeus' voice cut through the others. "Let's build a bonfire at the pit."

The others shrugged, putting Alphaeus into a motionless moment of humiliation which quickly transformed into anger. "Hell, with you!" he cried, suddenly standing. He stormed outside and a dead silence supplanted the hilarity.

Father Nicholaos, whose faith in the lad's redemption rarely wavered, now saw the need of a moral lesson, a serious reprimand in private, though perhaps this was not the moment. He let it go for now.

"Children." The monk cleared his throat and sipped some wine. "Let me speak of Cassianus and Augustine of Hippo. Their writings illustrate how man can unite with the spirit."

"Oh, not again," came a protest, accompanied by sporadic murmurs of discontent and boredom from around the table. The monk, whose clever and serious nature could normally prevail, was now compromised by the stammering and other effects of the wine. The children exploded into a laughter that dragged him in as well.

"You children have given me my life back," he whispered to himself.

It grew late and Mount Elias, blessed by the sun, now lost its reddish yellow halo, the last remnant of daylight. Inside, the glow from two clay cup-like lamps on the table, along with the embers in the fireplace, replaced much of the departed light. From their beaks and immersed in olive oil, the flickering wicks of flax created dancing shadows everywhere, while the embers of the dying fireplace threw an eerie yellow glow. The general merrymaking of the children gave way to the lamp's weird show.

"Enough, my dear children," said the monk. "Let us be serious! Tomorrow will be a long day. This hiding place will not build itself. It must be large enough for all and I would like to finish it in one day. Thanks to Eugenius, God bless him, we have shovels, picks, hoes, and an axe."

Flavia yawned, and the contagion spread to the rest of the table. "Father," she urged. "The little ones are tired. They want to sleep."

The monk nodded his head in agreement, and the children, like mice, all scurried to their respective nests in the cave, one by one. With rags laid over a pile of straw, the beds were indeed nests, haphazardly arranged in any convenient spot on the cool cave floor. In winter, if cold they would move them closer to the warm fireplace in the hovel proper.

"Hurry on. It's late," insisted Flavia.

The monk slipped outside to meet Alphaeus at the fire pit.

Alphaeus busied himself gathering brush wood for his bonfire, hoping to get attention from the others. With the dry branches lit, he brought in logs, the biggest possible, to feed the beast. All the while, he threw glances at the hovel, sometimes coquettish, sometimes sinister, depending on which mood bedeviled his mind.

The logs crackled, sending live cinders into the air, where they were captured by the updraft and flew even higher. His heartbeat harmonized with the crackling; his amorous thoughts flew with the embers; they were calling Flavia, but she was now asleep.

Father Nicholaos arrived at the fire pit. "What are you doing?" he demanded. "The whole forest will catch on fire. A small fire is enough; it is bedtime."

The stone-faced lad reluctantly stopped feeding his fire. He anticipated an unwarranted chiding and refused to look directly at the monk.

"My son, you were rude tonight. The younger ones always laugh and giggle. You should be more mature." Began, the monk, while Alphaeus said nothing as he gazed into the flames that had ceased to inspire him.

"Are you listening, son? Can you tell me what is wrong?" asked the monk, whose instincts now foretold something deeper.

Alphaeus turned the embers with a twig, agitating them until their glowing edges loosened and flew dangerously high into the darkness, unaware of the consequences and too recalcitrant to answer the monk. The monk sensed a reckless frustration in the lad, reminiscent of what had stirred in him.

"In the end, you are not different from the orphans who have fled into the woods and have no parents. The others lost their loved ones by the hands of one enemy, while you lost yours by another. All of you are my children."

"But they killed my baba," blurted out Alphaeus.

The Father breathed slowly before answering. "Your Berber father took possession of a local woman, your mother, and you are thus a product of this land, as we all are."

"My name is Hasan, not Alphaeus," cried the lad. He would not be lectured.

"Your parents are no longer here, so you have become Alphaeus in our group."

"They all reject me, even Flavia. Why can't you promise her to me?" His hurt acquired an impudent hue.

Father Nicholaos shook his head. "She has a mind of her own, which you must respect. Then again, she is still too young; she has a life to grow into before she can make such decisions. She even believes herself inspired to taking the vows. Patience, my son, patience," and he waited for a response. When he received none, the monk rose and made his way leisurely to the sleepy hovel. Further opportunities would arise, he reasoned.

Alphaeus' attention returned to the dancing flames whose cadence slowly transported him to those vague childhood memories that still needed clarification. Like the objects in the darkness, he could only discern their shadows.

Despite the circulating rumors that warned of pirates lurking everywhere, the wine-induced light-headedness and the evening beating of the semantron helped the monk sleep well that night. The instrument, a plank struck by a fellow monk's mallet down below in Saint Elias, produced hollow sounds that soothed his spirits. Its rhythm, its subtle changes of pitch with its strength in travel distance captured the souls for the usual calling of the nightly prayers. Everything was normal.

The next day, he rose from his primitive bed of planks on which lay a straw mattress. He stroked away any straw clinging to his garment, then neatly folded the bedcover to place it on top of his chest kept beneath the bed. The mattress itself, he rolled up against the wall so the orphans could use the planked bed as a bench. With short, light steps, not to awaken the others, he made his way to the dying fire. He fed its live embers with dry twigs and logs and exited the hovel to get fresh air and clear his mind.

The sun greeted him as it surfaced from the Ionian waters and begun its daily chore of disbanding the morning fog that hovered over the sleepy landscape. Its warmth exposed the shoreline first, then Skylletion, Saint Elias, and finally the grotto. He focused on the brave little oratory (2) on shore dedicated to the Blessed Mary, occupied by more of his acquaintances who assumed the responsibility of alerting the folks of danger landing on shore. He began his morning prayer, this time for Skylletion.

Skylletion had many scars. Its fortress, although garrisoned, needed repairs and the town's scattered, crumbling structures were yet to be cleared. But its proud people, endeavoring to be a village, healed its wounds and kept the Byzantine culture alive.

When done, he backtracked into the hovel, where he noticed Flavia leaning over the suspended cauldron in the fireplace and stirring a mixture of greens and chestnut bread—a soup-like meal, no different than all the others.

"Good morning. What would I do without you," he remarked cheerfully, not noticing Flavia's sulkiness?

"Good morning, Father," she muttered, refusing to turn and face him.

Nicholaos stretched his neck to see her face better. "Is something wrong, my child?"

"I don't know what you are talking about." She disguised her anxiety by stirring the soup a little faster.

She had spent the night with thoughts churning in her head which carried over into morning, and her heart was in disarray. Yesterday's gossip and incidents had hurled her face-to-face with the life before her. Her mind struggled with the new demands of the heart. She needed advice.

"My, child how come this face, red as a flame?" said the monk when she found the courage to turn her head. "There is no shame here," and, reached for the bowls hanging on the utility rack to help set the table.

She continued the stirring, waiting for those magic words that always resolved everything.

"I know the sentiments of my children, despite my age," he continued in jest.

Her sour look sweetened into curiosity.

"Your growing feelings for Iohannes are natural." The monk only wanted the children to be happy. "You need not fulfil your vows just for me."

"But you have said God is important in our lives." She tested the monk's wishes once laid upon her.

"You must remember the paths to God are many and they vary with the individual. Have faith in God; when you are ready you will know what to do."

Flavia felt relieved, free to acknowledge Iohannes was at the center of her heart. She acquired her shiny face again and Father Nicholaos smiled back. But gradually, the healthy shine was replaced with fear. "But Alphaeus frightens me," she claimed.

"His crude advances and the teasing of the others?" Father Nicholaos offered as an explanation.

"Yes, Father."

"And I am afraid for him. When I saw him outside, yesterday, his eyes shot frustration. He holds back something in his heart, something dark." The monk believed in evil. It was the nemesis of the Basilian monks.

"But, Father," she said in desperation, "what can I do!"

"This is my cross to bear, not yours."

Just then, Alphaeus entered and strutted to the fireplace to warm himself from the night outside. "Good morning, Alphè," shouted the monk.

Not answering he glanced over to Flavia while rubbing his hands over the hot embers. Flavia and the monk exchanged perplexed glances over the non-response. Alphaeus had sensed he was the object of the conversation.

The Refuge

After the morning meal, at the orders of Father Nicholaos, they marched one by one into the farmyard and headed for the stable where the project awaited them. The younger ones skipped about in front while the rest strolled behind in conversation. Sometimes the littlest would double back to hop and skip at the feet of Father Nicholaos, and then return to the front in an elated gait only to repeat the cycle.

The anticipated activity ushered in a healthy distraction, and their spirits were renewed as the orphans looked forward to the project. Along the way, the rock rose, and the yellow-gold flowers of the broom emitted a sweet scent in the air and enhanced their cheerful mood. Only Alphaeus remained unexcited, revisiting the disappointment from the prior night, and intensifying his gawking over Flavia.

"She is not for you, my son." Father Nicholaos was watching him closely.

"Father, you are her guardian; offer her to me." Alphaeus repeated his outrageous demand.

"We will talk later, son. Now we have our work before us." The monk imagined Flavia's heart crumbled and disintegrated at such a prospect. I must put distance between the two, he concluded.

With the project completed late that afternoon they found themselves on their return trip. Exhausted, the smaller children no longer frolicked around Father Nicholaos. They stayed by his side while he carried Iulia straddled on his shoulders. He firmly held her in place with one hand and with the other petted Iacobus walking at his side. Bold enough to challenge Alphaeus' bully behavior, he kept tugging at the monk's robe, trying to get his attention. "Alphaeus stole something," he finally said.

"What is it?"

Father Nicholaos put Iulia down and knelt before the lad who whispered in his ear an incident involving Alphaeus and Iohannes just before the usual lesson. He had seen Alphaeus push Iohannes to the ground, where the two wrestled and tumbled, causing something shiny to fall out from the fold of Iohannes' breeches. Alphaeus slyly picked it up in the scuffle, unbeknown to the other, who afterward believed he had accidently lost it.

This was over the top even for the forgiving monk, who forced himself to wait and see if the lad's conscience would get the better of him and return the gem. If the lad didn't, he knew God would present the proper time and method to confront the blustering thief.

Alone, Flavia and Alphaeus formed the tail end again, this time without the monk. It was an uncomfortable situation for the naiad to be paired with Alphaeus, who purposely stayed behind to be with her. But she had promised the others she would bring back blackberries and headed off deeper into the woods followed by Alphaeus who insisted on helping her.

Expert as she was, she quickly spotted the telltale thorns and fruit of a blackberry bush.

"Fla! Can I help?" In her head, Alphaeus' voice erupted like thunder from a volcano.

She just glanced at him for a second, unable to respond.

Accepting her silent defense as a "yes," he jumped into the activity and they both began extracting the berries under an awkward silence.

With her apron now filled to its max, they hurried to the hovel. The volcano was quiet now and so was the naiad; the awkward stillness lasted all the way back.

Chapter IV: A Small Holding

Having faded away as mysteriously as it appeared, the account of the Saracen pirates became old news and the semantron emitted the regular cadence of the nightly vigil. The worldly powers with their mischief became a faint memory, and the Saracen marauders and wayward mercenaries who bring chaos and suffering had not been seen or heard. Consequently, the general tension that had hovered over this corner of the world stretching from Neocastrum all the way to Saint Giriaca gave way to their normal life.

Since winter was ahead, Father Nicholaos decided to utilize the emergency refuge to better serve as storage for the yearly fodder. Every orphan assumed his or her task in preparation for that white blanket that would cover the sleepy land. The animals would have to be fed, and so would the people. They gathered what they could for the winter fodder from the natural surroundings, certain weeds, alfalfa, and oats to be mixed with crop residue offered from Eugenius.

When the refuge overflowed with fodder, the group busied themselves to store their own food stock in the cave, an ideal depot for its small cavities that could hold jars and other sundries. Donated, not only by the usual Eugenius but also by good Samaritans and others seeking blessings from Father Nicholaos, were baskets of peeled dry chestnuts, dried figs, jars of olive oil, and cereal, which the bigger lads handled. The smallest of the orphans would plot to snatch a fig or a chestnut, but Flavia, who did what she could to watch over them, let only a few vanish before storage.

It finally fell, dense and continuously, the early snow, and it accumulated on top of the stable, falling through, landing on the poor animals. Browny was not hurt by the falling debris, but frightened by the thundering noises of the mishap, she managed to escape through the breached fence. The monk assigned the little ones to retrieve the goat, but the moment they laid their little hands on what now appeared a coy, playful animal, she would leap from their grasps, causing them to tumble into the wet snow. One on top of the other, they would burst into uncontrolled laughter. Then they rose, regrouped, and repeated the scene until they managed to lasso the poor animal and return panting and exhausted.

Together with Father Nicholaos, the older children set about clearing the stable of broken roof rafters and snow, which completely covered the poultry pen occupying a corner of the stable. They discovered the white, smaller hen frozen, solid as a stone. Fortunately, the other hens were still alive. Unable to accommodate the hens and Browny outside, they decided to bring the pen and the goat inside the hovel until they could reconstruct the stable in better weather conditions.

In the following days, the east winds, which scooped up the sea moisture and carried it to the colder mountain air to dispense it as snow, disappeared as quickly as they came. Those large, wet snowflakes, gently falling, ubiquitously, in infinite amounts, would no longer be seen. Dryer winds from elsewhere pushed the clouds away, and the sun slightly melted the surface snow. Under this remaining white mantle, the extra moisture created a mud-like subsurface.

The reconstruction work became difficult. Slipping clumsily everywhere they projected a comic performance coming across as unfit for their tasks. Self-derision and spontaneous laughter reigned as they attempted to remain erect and serious. Nevertheless, the amenable weather allowed the group to make sufficient repairs and accommodate the animals for the winter. Even the reluctant Alphaeus fell into the mood, pounding posts into the squishy ground and lifting rafters in place.

From then on, the snow fell short on its visits, and the anxious children, who looked forward to the outside activity, were disappointed. More frequent was the rain and hail that threatened leaks as they belted the thatched hovel roof. Luckily, it held fast.

Children have monsters, and confinement and boredom are the biggest. When the lessons could no longer contain their bursting energy, the small children improvised war games or walked around on the stilts made by the monk. They scurried around, battling with contrived swords and spears made of simple sticks while some loner, not part of the imaginary battle, would circle the activity on his stilts.

The older ones consumed their time playing backgammon or zatrikion, a type of Byzantine chest donated by some passing good Samaritans, but Flavia and Alphaeus rarely participated. She was content in her chores, one of which was supervising the children in their infantile games and buffoonery, occasionally participating.

He, on the other hand, mostly sulked, as he sat in a corner daydreaming of the time when she would abandon her silly notion of nun-hood. He watched her every move, the playful antics, her seriousness in her chores, and above all the way those female features filled the cold spaces of the hovel. I want her for me, he thought, and I will find a way, damn that monk!

The monk, while observing the lad, came to the realization that he needed help and chewed over his recent talks with Eugenius about the recalcitrant lad, after all he had his hands full with the other children.

"Alphè, come here," yelled monk trying to hide his disciplinary tone. Alphaeus walked slowly to his side. "Why this behavior, this distance?"

"I don't know," Alphaeus grumbled, hoping for no further inquiries.

"You don't, or you don't want to say?" demanded Father Nicholaos, fishing for his next words. "Your heart is ill and nurtures something I am hard-pressed to know. And your anger, it's like the bonfire of the other night."

Father Nicholaos received only a blank stare. "Listen here," he followed, pointing his index finger toward the youth. "Must I speak more clearly? Your anger will get the best of you. Why feed this most base of human qualities? Your arrogance feeds it."

"I don't understand," snapped back Alphaeus.

"The other children have suffered too, but their humility has given them strength. Learn from them." Nicholaos believed that humility is the first step to redemption.

"You are quibbling and saying riddles," mocked the youth, still hoping for the end of what he saw as a reprimand.

"Hmm." Father Nicholaos leaned back and shifted his brows closer as he studied the young man. He wondered why the youth did not understand what had seemed so clear to him throughout his life. Nevertheless, he was pleasantly surprised when Alphaeus relaxed, and then nodded with a receptive smile that resembled comprehension.

"Let's play zatrikion." Alphaeus veered the conversation.

But doubts remained in the back of the monk's mind as they both focused on the game. He was unlike Iohannes, who accepted his consoling. This lad was crude and cunning at the same time.

"Father does Master Eugenius have honey to make sweet pastries?" asked Flavia, as she was mixing the flour with eggs and water to make the dough. She wanted to surprise Iulia, who was clinging to Flavia's dress, with something sweet.

The monk, keeping his concentration on the board lifted his eyes to Alphaeus, "I am not sure, but we can send Alphaeus to the Florus farm."

"I do not want to go. What if another storm arrives during the trip?" A sudden irritation gripped Alphaeus.

"Perhaps, but you are almost a man. Stay there for the night. Besides, you must get to know the family. Eugenius has promised me to take you in as laborer and shepherd, perhaps later, also as foreman."

"No! Send Peter." Offended and betrayed, he envisioned Peter in the high pasture while he labored down below away from Flavia.

"Not Peter. He is still young. He stays here, taking your place," objected Father Nicholaos. Peter, who was supervising the flour-making, rejoiced in his new status as shepherd and fell naturally into humming a pastoral poetry—bucolic verse.

"When is this to take place?" demanded Alphaeus, indignant by the humming.

"For the honey, tomorrow, for your service, in the spring, beginning with the cultivation. There is still time," said Father Nicholaos, while studying the board with no intention of winning.

"Checkmate, I win," yelled Alphaeus, his indignation replaced by pride.

Alphaeus now moved here and there gathering supplies for his trip. When he wandered over to Flavia, he grabbed her arm and froze the moment with a piercing stare into her soft eyes. He wanted her in the same way he owned that blue spinel, that precious cobalt stone like her eyes, but the reproaching eyes of Father Nicholaos loosened his grip when Flavia looked at the monk for help. Alphaeus let go, muttering some excuse, and then finished packing and sat near the fireplace. Later, when the others headed for their nests, he lowered his head to his knees and went to sleep. He dreamt of a mysterious figure, a man whose face he could not recognize. Yet it had a distinct familiarity.

The next day he was abruptly awakened by the monk.

"Alphè, wake up. Time to go; when you arrive there, tell Eugenius I have the Disticha Moralia for his son, and make sure you get the latest news from Constantinople."

After eating, Alphaeus put on his wool mantle, slung the saddle-type knapsack over his shoulders, and left. He had never been at the farm; nevertheless, it was along the way to Saint Elias and the route was familiar to him. The Father had once brought him to Saint Elias to rummage and beg for clothes and supplies for the orphanage.

Iohannes also took this path on his way to his lessons, but in fairer weather, not in winter when slippery, a fact that revived Alphaeus' ill mood of yesterday, distracting him in his walk. His feet broke through the surface ice of a puddle in the road, and rage kicked in as a freezing wind cut into his face like a cold knife. He wished to turn back.

Continuing, Alphaeus had walked approximately half an hour in that vexed state when before him appeared a high cliff dominating a rocky and threatening ravine, in which ran one of the branches of the river Alessi. On the other side of the river, he could see the Florus holding, which occupied a dell and was surrounded by a wooded area, naked of its seasonal foliage. His sanguine eyes from the icy wind scanned the natural expanse below, and he locked his teeth like a vise, then felt the chill no more.

He extracted from his breaches the spinel stone that sparkled like the ice clinging to the rocks below. He held it high and yelled defiantly at the distant mountain, at the ravine, and above all, at the farm below, "This is mine!"

But only the mountain replied, with a mocking echo. Alphaeus yelled back, "This cliff will help me. No one can survive a fall upon the jagged rocks below." He replaced the stone and returned to the rugged path which in spring bore rushing waters. Now winter had given birth to frozen mud.

 He quickened his pace in the final descent toward the warmer temperature and softer wind of the valley. Sweat began to trickle down his chest; it dampened the garment under his woolen mantle, and, removing it, he stuffed it in the knapsack. The foul mood now transformed itself into an uneasiness in anticipation of the encounter with the Florus family, Latin in stock but Greek in culture. Would that family see him as a dusky half-breed Saracen or a Greek by his mother, he wondered?

When he arrived at the junction to Saint Elias, the road widened, and the riverbed-like path became a packed dirt road. At a distance to his left, he could see the village of Saint Elias, which at the time consisted of a church and a monastery surrounded by stone houses, some erect, some leveled to the ground, and others partially crumbled but still inhabited. Turning right, he took the path to the farm, crossed over a small bridge, and later found himself before a small plain.

The farmyard accommodated two shacks close together, with mud-like thatched roofs and a farmhouse roofed in tiles separated from the shacks. On his left, opposite the buildings were two fields. One, seeded in late autumn, was already showing its green wheat shoots through the patches of snow, and getting ready to offer its contribution to the bounty. The other had been resting and convalescing and probably was ready for the spring cultivation.

A good portion of the crops, the Florus sold, not in the quantity of prior more stable years, but sufficient for the local market whose population had dwindled at the hands of marauding Saracens. Mostly for personal use, on the right of the farmhouse was the garden, which, in season, contained lettuce, onions, turnips, cabbage, and leek; behind that was the olive grove.

Now that Alphaeus was deep within the enclosed valley, the wind had died down to a tomb-like stillness, comfortable but eerie. He jumped when startled by an uproar of cawing and fluttering originating from the surrounding thicket. A flock of crows had announced some disturbance or mishap. Perhaps a poor unfortunate hare had ended up in the mouth of a fox after a savage and violent chase, he told himself.

The stillness returned, and no other signs of life greeted him as he approached the habitation, except for the undulating heated air emitted by the farmhouse chimney. He knocked ever so lightly on the door, fearing to break the stillness. The door opened, and a tall, formidable, older man, who still maintained the chivalrous demeanor of his youth, appeared.

"Ah, Alphè, you have arrived. Maria! Alphaeus is here. Come on in," yelled Eugenius.

"Hello, I came in the name of Father Nicholaos." Alphaeus felt the family eyes digging into him.

Amazed at the large kitchen, which was twice the hovel's size, he remained motionless while looking all around. Fresh baked barley bread assailed his olfactory senses, coming from a real bread oven, and his feet stood on, not dirt, but pavement, and it was dry and easily washable.

His eyes then sought Iohannes but saw only his sister Saverina, a shapely, buxom lass, and still unmarried. She pretended not to notice him, at first, but then her eyes teased coquettishly as she made her way to her mother with the bread dough in hand for the oven. He wondered if there was a resemblance between mother and daughter, but neither one up to now was in full view.

"We are making pastries for the children. Honey is a treat for them, and Father Nicholaos was asking….." But before Alphaeus could finish, the cordial hospitality began.

"Make yourself comfortable. About the honey, in due time," said Eugenius, with an authoritative tone left over from his days in the Illyrian expedition for his knighthood rank still lingered in his comportment. He pulled out a chair from the table in the center of the kitchen and the visitor obediently sat down.

"Genè! Give the guest something to drink. I will prepare soup and fresh bread for all. This poor messenger of Father Nicholaos must be hungry after such a journey in the cold. And let him sit by the fire for his clothes are wet," arrived Maria's compassionate voice as she was extracting the bread from the oven with her wooden paddle.

The matron, now visible to Alphaeus, resembled her daughter in face and body. Freckles were scattered on every visible part such as the face and neckline where her bodice did not cover. Her hair matched her freckles, a dull brown, and her stature was every bit her daughter's. The visitor looked for clues to tell them apart but found only an occasional white hair or a small wrinkle on the mother. Alphaeus would have to rely on the more refined clothing of the matron and the necklace that carried a cross.

"What news does the Father bring us?" asked Eugenius as he placed two chairs next to the fireplace, for himself and his guest.

"The usual humdrum. The children are fine, all are well, and the Father has a new scroll; that is all." Alphaeus was not in the mood for idle chatting; he still objected to being here.

"Come on, there is more? Winter has imprisoned us from the outside world with its gossip. How's Flavia? Are you coming for the spring tilling?" the matron demanded in a bubbly and chirpy manner, trying to pry loose the visitor's tongue.

The gracious hosts ignored his Arabic inflection as Alphaeus recalled the grotto's winter incidents, captivating the hosts, who laughed out loud at the goat's demise. After all, for the eager listeners, this involved the reverent Father Nicholaos and his orphanage. But when it came to Flavia, their interest flared.

"She is the beautiful helper to the monk." Alphaeus was caught in the moment of excitement over Flavia.

"Is she going to be a nun?" asked Maria, wishing otherwise.

"Father Nicholaos says he is not sure, but I think she is changing her mind and he knows," Alphaeus volunteered eagerly.

"Thank God!" Maria sighed.

"I like Flavia." Alphaeus sensed resistance in the air and his Arabic inflection became heavier. "I want her to be mine," blank faces now speared the visitor, "but Father Nicholaos does not approve." He had expected at least some sympathy but received pathetic looks from Maria and Eugenius.

Saverina, who was closest in age and interests to Flavia, knew that Flavia preferred her brother Iohannes, and this was good with her, for she liked Alphaeus and threw him flirtatious looks. Her parents, Eugenius and Maria, wished their son to marry the girl if she should decide to give up the vows. With furrowed brows they searched for a consensus from each other to make the youth understand. But they came up short, shown by their blank faces.

Alphaeus continued his lament, under the obligated politeness of the hosts.

"Oh my, oh my," they interjected into his grumblings.

Suddenly, the door swung open and cut short Alphaeus' lament. Iohannes was carrying an armful of logs for the oven and his frame dominated the threshold, winning over any daylight trying to get in. He had grown so much during the winter that he overtook the visitor by at least ten inches in height, and with broader shoulders he was no longer the sticklike youth of last summer. To Alphaeus, his nemesis was now a true challenge, and odious thoughts replaced the shattered complaints. He bit his lower lip, managing the shock. Their eyes squared off, neither one able to speak.

"Say hello to your friend, don't be rude," said his mother as she cut the bread while her daughter was setting the table.

But Alphaeus's attention was now drawn away from the unsettling figure of Iohannes, and he watched Saverina, who seductively leaned a little too much over the table, giving him a generous view. He wondered how far down went the invasion of freckles and he fancied the opportunity to find out. Saverina had taken his disappointment over Flavia and turned it into lust, but Flavia still floated around somewhere in his head.

Eugenius had seen that look toward his daughter before and tapped Alphaeus firmly on the shoulder to which Alphaeus slipped back into his somber state. There is no bashfulness in this lad, Eugenius thought.

"Grab your chair," Eugenius ordered, and motioned him toward the table. "Your clothes should be dry."

After the lull that usually accompanies a table setting, Saverina, content with herself for having drawn the lustful eyes of Alphaeus, asked him, "Is Flavia coming during the cultivation?"

"Certainly, almost everybody will come. Only Peter will stay behind to tend to the animals."

"Great," the mother added, "she is near your age. A little younger of course, but you will have many things to talk about."

"Yes, Mother," Saverina agreed with excitement.

"Aw, yes, the cultivation. This year the chorion will have new youths to help with the oxen and tiller. You will accompany us from farm to farm." Eugenius prepared for resistance, knowing the young man's unbending nature that seemed to follow him like a shadow.

"How's that?" demanded Alphaeus, ruing his time had come for the grueling work.

"Well, no man is alone in our little community; we are all in the same boat," explained Eugenius, who oversaw the community equipment since he had the largest farm in the area.

"The chorion is an enlarged family living under a warm blanket of Christian morality and Greek protection." Maria contributed her reflections to ease the perceived tension.

"But often we are left to ourselves..." A hackneyed phrase sprouted from an elderly woman ensconced in the shadows of the room. It was Mother Laetitia, Eugenius' mother, who was barely audible over the squeaking of her spinning wheel. "As a child, I remember when the Saracens occupied a town nearby called Saint Giriaca." The squeaking stopped for a second. "Where were the Romanoi then? They left us to fend for ourselves. Women were raped, and their men were killed. My cousin, who lived there, was violated after they killed her husband, so she came to live with us and later died of sadness. Where was the great Basileus, who had conquered Bulgaria?"

"Didn't he send Catepan Boioannes?" said her son. Eugenius had served under the command of the catepan and had witnessed his tenacity and ability in battle. Although few, there were for him some competent leaders in the empire.

"Late are the provisions when the problems have already arrived, my son," the old woman retorted and returned to her worries over the visitor since something in him had stirred her premonitions. Suspicious from the beginning, her gaze did not leave him as she addressed the whole table. Offended, Alphaeus challenged her with his bovine eyes, but she remained composed, and calmly kept operating the spinning wheel as she spoke.

Eugenius took note of the chill that had descended between the two and began with the latest news for the visitor to take back to the monk. He talked of the internal power struggle in Arabic Sicily and the intention of the present catepan, Leo Opos, to enroll militia men and form a fleet for Panormos. His mission under the treaty was to bring Greek oversight of Sicily. All this was good news and his audience listened assiduously, which gave license to Eugenius to recount his days of chivalry in Dalmatia, stories that stirred in his son the same dreams he had as a youth.

As a child, Iohannes would entertain himself with his father's armor. The round shield, hanging on the wall with the Florus coat of arms, invited him to imitate a warrior. It was too heavy then for his small body to bring down. But poking around in his father's chest, he would yank out the mail coat made with interlocking rings and put it on, only to disappear within it like a mouse in a sack. There was more in there, a pointed metal helmet with a curtain of leather straps hanging from its back to protect the nape, a sword, and a lance. All were jewels for the little ferret.

Time, favorable to his growth, however, had sculptured an Olympic statue out of that body, and his frame now filled the armor with no space to spare. The Romanos shield and sword were now an extension of his strong arms. He would be like his father and protect their land and culture.

"This Catepan Opos, is he competent?" Iohannes asked his father.

"Certainly, unlike Pathos Argiro, this general has had success over the bandits just north of here."

Triggered by the topic, the old spinner, who had seen a lot in her days, stopped her spinning to approach the table and release what was on her mind. "Opos' reputation as a lover to that whore Zoe has arrived here before him." She stood erect and firm with a fist on the table. "His possible success could be compromised from the intrigue and treachery in that mad imperial court. Zoe is wife to the emperor but still has lovers." She brought her fist to her chest. "We barely survive while they plot and weave mischief among themselves." With a mocking air she waved her hands. "They see themselves as protagonists in history while we, who are connected to the earth, pay dearly for their hubris." She returned to her spinning, firm and proud.

"That whore as you call her, Mother dear, I don't understand why she would be a factor in the war," protested Eugenius.

"The woman is vain and always hungers for power and using the status of the purple she plots to gain even more. She is extraordinarily cunning and mars the dignity of a proper empress." Her spinning activity softened her proud stiffness. "No heir exits her womb; perhaps it is as barren as the desert. In my opinion she is infertile by her own hand, so no heir can take away her purple."

"But they say she has the beauty of a Greek goddess, Mother Laetitia." Maria poked and stimulated her mother-in-law's harangue.

Emboldened by the question, the delightful but strange old woman eagerly resumed her speech. Her skillful narration could twist and pull the roving acquired in her sleep into a fascinating yarn colored with intuition, sagacity, and witch-like divining, all the while capturing her audience with outrageous remarks.

"Indeed, Venus has graced her with beauty; however, she frets over it too much, using oils and expensive perfumes from afar. Her charm draws innocents to her den," insisted Laetitia, ready to stand again but changed her mind.

"Frivolity, Mother. Our fate depends on God, the catepan, and the local troops stratiotoi in which Iohannes wants to enroll," shot back Eugenius.

"Dear son, I don't mean that her make-up and cunning ways will bring ruin to us directly. They are only food for idle chatter. Our ruin arises from what she represents. Chaotic and violent changes in the imperial power do not produce legitimate qualified heirs able to protect us." Laetitia spoke calmly; she needed just one pause. "This happens when conspiracy and deceit breed disgruntled players who, not receiving justice, seek revenge at all costs. The imperial court becomes unstable where immorality and narcissistic tyranny replace its lack of governance."

A wake of silent thoughts ensued. No one knew how to respond. They ate, quietly digesting Laetitia's words that winter afternoon. Outside, the overcast-with-just-a-hint-of-clear sky seemed to portend an uncertainty in the Sicilian expedition projected by Constantinople. Inside, Eugenius tried to ignore his mother's presentiments, but his heart wrestled over his son's safety. Iohannes would stay home and receive further training from him for the next expedition, the one with the great General Maniakes.

Attention now was given to the guest, who had to get ready for his departure. Maria and her daughter prepared his knapsack with the honey and other items in accordance with Maria's benevolence.

"Alphè, please be careful when you get to the cliff. The road up there is still icy. Also give our best regards to Father Nicholaos and the children. Remember, I will send notice of the tilling date." Eugenius sent him off.

Clutching and throwing the knapsack over his shoulders, Alphaeus could not leave fast enough. He felt abandoned, his legs were shaky, his mouth was dry, but he managed to give his farewell. On the way he tried to recover his former confidence, but his imagination made matters worse. Iohannes was now bigger and stronger. Alphaeus did not have the Florus' support as suitor to Flavia, but Iohannes did, which he had gleaned from the visit. He saw the plan to make him laborer and foreman to the farm as a plot to divert him from his wishes.

His mind buzzed with feelings of betrayal, and his usual friend, anger, returned.

⁓

The discretion displayed in the company of the visitor at the farm vanished to be replaced by family frankness and spontaneity. The old woman's tongue, which had been restrained before by decorous diplomacy, now spoke of Alphaeus.

"In my opinion, he has the evil eye," she advised her son.

"Don't look a gift horse in the mouth. The farm needs a laborer and shepherd, a gift from Father Nicholaos, a trustworthy man of God." Eugenius added some needed practicality.

But Laetitia could not hold back. "This stubborn horse will not be bridled, my dear son."

"I must say, he is somewhat handsome although a little rustic," jumped in Saverina, and, turning to her mother, "He needs a little work."

"Of course, dear. With faith in God's will, anything can be done."

Maria, now petted her son's head as if he were still a child, ruffled his hair faster when he tried to avoid her fondling by shifting his head. "Our true handsome man is our little Apollo, here, gifted with Apollonian attractiveness and a gentle voice from the muses. There is no equal to my Apollinus," she boasted.

Since her son continued to resist, she now massaged his shoulders amorously, but the uncomfortable Iohannes gracefully pulled her hand away and explained his relationship with his rival, omitting, the details of the actual scuffle.

"I used to be intimidated by his penetrating look and heavy hands. He was worse when Flavia and I would talk but now he does not seem as big and threatening as before. He is small and pathetic," boldly volunteered Iohannes.

"Be careful, Mother Laetitia may be right. Who knows what brews in his mind? I will go crazy if something should happen to you," Maria insisted with a slight tremble in her words.

Chapter V: The Cultivation

Announced by the warble of nightingales, the land finally awoke from its winter sleep, displaying a fresh green garment worn by the trees and the spongy earth of spring. The field of winter wheat once hiding under the snow at the Florus' farm was now a sea of green that undulated with the terrain. Their young stems in booting stage mimicked their distant cousin, the common grass.

They lined up like little soldiers, in the service of man, offering abundance, a blessing, since the empire had experienced grain shortages from their principal source in Anatolia. Consequently, the grain ships from Crotone ceased to arrive in Skylletion to unload their precious cargo. Instead, they went to Taranto, Bari, or Constantinople, and the locals were forced to increase their production to supplement the shortfall.

Fields would have to be plowed, and in the community the first opportunity to the oxen and plough was given to Eugenius, who decided to utilize the empty field destined for the summer crop. The crew which just had yoked the two oxen together was already working the field. Then his neighbor Matthaeus would be next.

The beasts struggled to pull the simple plow, objecting with their snorting. Matthaeus would tug on the nose rings when the oxen were stubborn and at the plow stilts Eugenius expertly battled with the handles to steady it as it cut into the necessary depth. Alphaeus prodded the animals with a stick to reinforce a straight path, a task more important for learning than an actual contribution since Matthaeus was at the lead.

As the plow cut through the earth, it also flipped the soil upside down and released an odor of decayed vegetation. The smell promised a heathy crop from the seeds that Maria flung from her basket as she followed closely behind the team. They fell neatly and consistently into the furrows, which Myrtilus, hoe in hand, covered up gently after breaking up any residual clogs.

No one talked. The distinct sound of metal cutting earth, the sporadic snapping of roots, the heavy breathing and occasional animal grunts were the only sounds. Even the orphans were silent as they worked the garden in the lower terrain, where they extracted roots of prior plantings to prepare the ground for furrowing.

"Mattè! Stop. I want to change places with Alphè," interrupted Eugenius, whose panting competed with the oxen's. "Alphè, you are young, take hold of the handles for this old man."

Alphaeus took hold of the stilts with a vise-like grip but, plowing skills the former bandit's hands did not possess. "I hate taking orders," he mumbled to himself as the share glided ineffectively over the soil; going right then left and back again. "The damn thing won't stay steady," Alphaeus cursed out loud, while wrestling with the stilt handles as if they were the horns of an angry bull. The cutting edge then dug deep, too deep for the struggling oxen and everything came to a stop.

Eugenius came to the rescue and retook the plow. "Keep a normal depth and a straight line. I'm sure you have the strength," he insisted, displaying a farmer's dexterity handed down many generations. At the end of the field, when turned around, Eugenius returned the plow to the reluctant, clumsy hands that gradually wrestled the plow into a satisfactory rhythm.

After they finished this section of the farm, they disengaged the plow from the yoke, flipped it upside down, and reattached it to the yoke to drag it to the garden, which they were to plow next. Meanwhile, Maria returned to the house to help her mother-in-law prepare the afternoon meal, which all would eat outside as was the custom.

"Genè, is there any news on the catepan's expedition?" Matthaeus asked on their way to the garden.

"I haven't heard anything, but I know that some youths joined up with the expedition when the catepan stopped at Skylletion," said Eugenius, who was leading the oxen.

"Do you think he is already in Panormos?"

"Who knows? I haven't been at the garrison lately." A visit to the garrison for Eugenius was not unusual.

When they arrived at the lower terrain, the garden group had not yet cleared the field of brush so they un-yoked the animals, which Myrtillus then led to the water trough. The others, joined by the monk, sat at the edge of the field to rest, chat, and watch the working children, who, positioned abreast of each other, chopped up unwanted growth with their hoes as well as cleared the field of the forever-present rocks. Meanwhile, the quiet stupor of the children carried over from the early reveille for the cultivation gave way to the familiar hilarity, giggling, and shouting.

"Look," shouted Iacobus, gesturing toward Leonellus and Iulia struggling with rocks that weighed more than they did. A laughter spread throughout the other children but the two were so distracted in their seriousness of their task that they did not notice.

"Don't listen to them," shouted Flavia in sympathy.

"Aw, how adorable!" interjected Saverina, who then returned to the personal talks with Flavia.

Prolific nature was busy everywhere; its handiworks were the tree buds, the fresh grass, and the crisp smell of spring. Nature mysteriously stirred within the two mature feminine bodies of Saverina and Flavia, whose vows disappeared in this mystery as ice melts in boiling water.

Naturally together and distant from Iohannes, both girls had a lot to discuss, a lot of nothing masking something. The spring sun, in the presence of the young men, warmed their bodies in a distinct way, and they hummed light tunes when they were not snickering or whispering. They sought the other's secrets once hidden by adolescent shyness but now ripe for the spring sunlight.

"Who do you like?" Saverina asked Flavia, who became flushed and tongue-tied. The inquiry appeared ubiquitous, coming from Father Nicholaos, Maria, Eugenius and, worse, the teasing children. Embarrassment and joy swirled together in her head. "I always knew it was Iohannes," her friend insisted.

"No, no," protested Flavia, in a meaningless gesture, when the shyness finally released her tongue. She tried to escape her friend's doubting eyes as she unwittingly focused hers on Iohannes, who was absorbed in his work. It was almost noon as she watched Iohannes now sweating copiously. His already toned muscles quivered with every motion of the hoe as he chopped up the dead plants and the wild growth that would become compost for the new life. For an instant, her imagination swept her into his arms.

The sun, now overhead, beat a huge thirst into Iohannes. He dropped the hoe and headed for the jar of water next to the chatting plow crew. When he had to pass by Alphaeus, Alphaeus extended his leg to create a feigned accident. Maria's little Apollo tripped, and rolled on his back, allowing his adversary to start kicking him.

This time he was no longer the younger weakling unable to react, but another, one more agile, more robust, quicker to respond. Trained properly by his father, he knew by pure instinct his next move—a move that had saved his father's life in battle. After Eugenius fell off his horse, losing his shield and lance and lying helpless on the ground, the enemy rushed to thrust his lance into his body. But Eugenius threw his foe off balance, unsheathed his dagger, and planted it in the enemy's chest, who fell dying.

Now his son would repeat the same reliable defense, a thousand times done in training and a thousand times stamped into memory. Iohannes planted his left foot on his opponent's shin, and, using his other foot, he hooked the back of the opponent's knee to collapse that one leg. He formed a type of plyers or scissors with his feet, and when he pulled back with his right foot, Alphaeus tumbled down, bewildered and confused. The instigator, now on the ground, was barely able to breathe, for Johannes had him pinned with his sturdy body.

The other children had gathered around the brawl, shouting, "Go, Iohan, go!" And the adults waited for some sign from the reluctant Eugenius, who felt the troublemaker needed a lesson. Maria, who had just run out of the house to the commotion, cried in maternal anguish, "Oh, my poor Apollinus! Enough! Enough!" Maria then turned to her husband as if to say, are you going to stop it?

Iohannes felt confident and knew he could seriously hurt Alphaeus, but instead delivered only a few blows at his opponent. Then they rolled and tumbled harmlessly, which, in the confusion, caused a shiny little object to fall out of Alphaeus' pocket, seen only by the astute Iacobus. Iacobus nonchalantly covered it with his foot until he was able to recover it unbeknownst to the others.

By now, it was realized that the tussle had no end in sight. One was too tenacious to surrender and the other too compassionate to end it with the necessary blows. A hero emerged to all, especially to his father and to the monk, both of which applauded his compassion in the fight, and then the two men sought to end it.

Eugenius walked over and tapped his son on the head who was now sitting on the unfortunate opponent that was trying to breath normally. "Enough, stop it, get up."

When Iohannes released Alphaeus, the monk helped Alphaeus up, restraining his useless and stubborn resistance. "Your eye, it's a red balloon, my son. Go and take care of it." Alphaeus shrugged, refusing to move.

"Come on, now! Get your hoes and shovels," Eugenius shouted to the garden crew. "You, Alphaeus, when done with your eye, help the children in the garden. Take Iohannes' place." And winking at his son, "Iohan! Hook up the plow with us."

Alphaeus' throbbing eye screamed of humiliation, but the pain vanished with every clog of earth held compact by dead roots that he attacked relentlessly. He saw them as a barrier to his ambitions, obstacles he madly destroyed with every stroke of the hoe. Saverina and Flavia continued their giggling in the garden and only made matters worse. "Why can't those magpies shut up?" he grumbled.

And when Saverina threw a friendly smile at the frustrated figure, Alphaeus mistook the gesture for derision. But Saverina dreamed of nursing his eye and cuddling him with her healing love. I can bring him over, she mused.

Meanwhile, in Flavia's mind, only Iohannes existed. "Saverina, does your brother like me?" Flavia whispered timidly into Saverina's ear.

"I was wondering when you were going to ask." Saverina spoke too loudly for Flavia.

"Hush." Flavia looked around in embarrassment.

"Your eyes light up and sparkle in his presence. The thunderbolt has struck him too. But he is too shy to say anything," Saverina pressed on.

"Come on, now!" Flavia's face now was red. "Others can hear!"

Saverina got closer, cupped her hand around Flavia's ear. "Guess what? I've seen my brother naked," then leaned back and looked around for listeners, "and so can you if you can stay with us at our place."

"You are teasing me," shot back Flavia extremely embarrassed; she could barely stand. "Please, don't tell anyone I asked!"

When the children completed the weeding of the lower field, they released their leftover energy in their play, followed by Alphaeus, who was not up to dealing fully with the adults. Flavia with Iulia at her side remained by the field to watch the plow crew now plowing the garden.

The bellows and snorting of the reluctant oxen resumed, but this time Iohannes was at the plow handles and quickly adapted to the task. Flavia fell into a type of trance with her eyes following Iohannes up and down the field.

"Flà! What are you doing?" Saverina woke her out of her dreamy state. "We should help my mother with the food."

Flavia grabbed Iulia's hand and followed Saverina to the house. The tilling ended shortly thereafter, and the weary plow crew eventually found its way to the edge of the field. There, the monk and Eugenius were already drinking wine and chatting.

"Father Nicholaos, that lad," Eugenius was saying after taking a good gulp of wine, "he does not listen; he is headstrong."

"You don't have to tell me." His friend also took a gulp.

"What am I to do?" Eugenius lifted his glass but did not drink. "Will it not be better that you take him back, Father?"

"You know when they grow up, they need a trade, a sense of independence." The monk marveled at the wine, holding the cup in the air. "How do you keep it so cool?"

"I placed the jar in the running water of the stream." Eugenius doubled back to Alphaeus. "It is his time, I agree, but my son and daughter......"

"Please teach him a trade," pleaded Father Nicholaos. "I have my hands full with the others."

"If he stays with me, I will have to watch him closely, especially around my son, Father."

"And if he stays with me, I'll have to watch him around Flavia," shot back Father Nicholaos.

The orphans remained at the Florus' one more day, while the tilling crew, minus Iohannes, moved to Matthaeus' field. And when they finished, they returned with a puppy they called Argus, donated by Matthaeus, who bred herding dogs. Meantime, the children, who were still fatigued eagerly went home, longing to sink their weary little bodies into their crude straw beds. This included Flavia, who was needed at the grotto. Iacobus and Alphaeus remained to help on the Florus' farm.

Iohannes displayed a new vigor working on the garden. In the scuffle he had acquired a confidence in his masculinity. As he worked, he felt Flavia's presence everywhere and this warmed his heart like the pleasant rays of the sun. His mind was suspended in the clouds, reluctant to descend. It was a dream from which he awoke only when chided by his sister and Iacobus or mocked with their laughter and giggling as they did their chores.

Planting the garden was the first phase of the long and tedious work, for the beans and cucumbers required trellises to support them. These priorities, for the anxious Iohannes, demanded they postpone the lessons into a never-arriving future where he could see Flavia. Fortunately, the plow team returned after a week or so from its community plowing. The additional hands speeded up the work.

The lesson days finally arrived, and Iohannes and Iacobus were ready for the trip to the grotto. Maria was left alone that early morning and Alphaeus was at the fold. Eugenius and the two lads were outside waiting for their sacks of supplies she was preparing. Saverina and Mother Laetitia were still in bed. Maria busied herself nervously, stuffing the two sacks with bread, cheese, and whatever else came to mind that the orphans might need. Rarely had she been apprehensive whenever her son left to be under the care of Father Nicholaos for the day.

But now things were different since Alphaeus' uncomfortable visit and the senseless fight. That empty feeling when her first Iohannes died in infancy revisited her. It was the clutches of evil that Mother Laetitia talked about that had ripped that precious gift from her arms. Her single focus, then, was to fill that void, and she filled it with Eugenius' masculinity until her stomach grew with another gift of legacy, Iohannes number two. That bundle of maleness was to be kept in the world with all her love, she swore to herself back then. She would cuddle him, suckle him, and block evil before it hit him, but now he had his own life before him and, Mother Laetitia has never erred, she said to herself as Laetitia's premonitions echoed in her mind.

Maria began to work her way out of these unpleasant thoughts by wondering when Saverina would get up. She let her sleep past normal, a gesture of appreciation for her contribution to the garden work. Saverina appeared, dragging her feet.

"Ma! Did you talk to Papa about Alphaeus?" Saverina had just left her room shared with her grandma Laetitia, bearing that burning question on her mind.

Maria had to remind herself of the matter. "We've talked about it; your father and I have agreed. There is something wrong with that lad."

"You have always fussed over Iohannes; never do you consider me." Saverina felt strongly justified in her accusation to her mother.

Maria looked past the grown-up before her and saw the little Saverina absorbed in herself as Maria tended to her second male infant. "I may have relied on you, too much before your time," she said sympathetically with thoughts of regrets.

"I am independent. Papa thinks I am simply stubborn." Saverina seemed to demand an answer as a silent tear rolled slowly down her cheek.

"Just slightly rebellious!" Maria smiled.

"Please, Ma! Talk to him."

Maria now felt obligated to her daughter. "I will talk with your father." She loved her daughter not less than Iohannes, and her daughter's wishes now had some weight.

"You will?" Saverina wiped her tear with the back of her hand.

"Yes." But Maria knew Eugenius' answer already. It was to be Peter for Saverina.

"Furthermore," she continued. "I will ask your father to talk to Father Nicholaos." This was the only comfort Maria could offer. "The Father always seems to know what to do." Saverina's face lit up and she disappeared in her room.

When Maria finished with the sacks, she carried them outside for the two lads who had been waiting anxiously, said good-bye, and returned to her chores.

"Be careful. Tell Father Nicholaos I will pass by when I acquire any political news; there still is a humdrum nothingness in the air," Eugenius said. Then, making sure the women were not looking, he promptly slipped a dagger behind Iohannes' belt covered by his mantle-like jacket.

When they left, Eugenius went to deal with Alphaeus at the sheep fold. "Alphè! Since we are caught up with the field work, in a few days you will come with me to the mountains with the sheep. There you will join up with Peter to pasture them for the duration of the summer." The lad mumbled something, which Eugenius accepted as a reluctant yes.

From the time the group had returned to the grotto, Flavia had not mentioned her vows at all. She would rise early, complete her chores quickly, and always retire to her bed late. The foliage outside appeared greener, flowers radiated more intense colors, and the sky was bluer. There was something savage in the natural surroundings, something nature wanted to communicate to her. The ties to her adolescent past had been broken. Her thoughts flew about as sparrows caught in a fickle wind, and nothing fazed her, not even the bickering of the children.

She was feeding the chickens in the yard, when she caught sight of the two youths approaching the grotto. On the appearance of Iohannes her eyes expanded, her limbs loosened, and the basket of chicken feed slipped through her left arm that was girthed around the basket. She wanted to run into Iohannes' arms, but her feet refused to move. In his absence, her heart had yearned for him, and forbidden thoughts had invaded her mind and her innocence lost the battle. It was a dream-like world she had created but now she could not move to make it real; her shyness still held her feet.

"Welcome, lads!" shouted the monk as he passed by the immobile Flavia and extended his sinewy arms to hug them. The two lads respectfully greeted the Father Nicholaos, who appearing more white-haired than last seen motioned them inside. "Come in." But Iohannes turned around and headed back toward Flavia. "Iacobus, I guess we are alone." He directed a welcoming smile for his returned orphan.

"Father, I have something for you. It belongs to Iohannes, but I thought it better to hand it to you first," said Iacobus, flashing back a bigger smile as he reached into the fold of his breeches for the spinel stone. Upon seeing the glinting stone, the monk muttered something about Alphaeus, thanked Iacobus, and then placed it in the fold of his garment as both made themselves comfortable inside. "

"You did right, Iacobus, giving it directly to Iohannes could lead to another scuffle between the two.

"I can say I just found it here rather at the scuffle," volunteered Iacobus.

Meanwhile, Iohannes approached the poor girl; he found her stiff as a stone statue, in a daze and mouth wide open. He picked up the fallen basket and returned it to those delicate little hands. "I believe this is yours." Only an 'eeeh' managed to escape from the statue's mouth. Then the young man outlined a warm smile and joined the other two in the hovel for the lessons.

Inside, Iacobus was proudly saying, "We brought supplies from Maria."

"Thank you, put the bags in the corner for later." The monk unrolled Cato's Disticha. "I don't suppose you would be interested in sitting in on the lesson?" he asked Iacobus, but before Iacobus responded, he jumped into the lesson, knowing the language was foreign to everyone but Iohannes. The monk was forced to pause when Flavia entered the hovel after her body had returned to flesh and bone. Iohannes, now focused on Flavia, and wished to postpone the lesson as did Iacobus, who was bored from the start.

She dragged her feet with caution as if in darkness and sat next to the more familiar Iacobus. Her residual shyness held her back from sitting next to Iohannes.

"Where are Leonellus and Iulia?" asked Father Nicholaos.

"They were right behind me but decided to wander off to the stable," said Flavia.

"They have become more self-assured and more engaging," offered the monk, who had noticed that after the cultivation Iulia was less clingy to Flavia. They are coming out of themselves as their childhood memories fade, he assured himself.

Flavia looked around inquisitively. "Isn't this a lesson, Father?"

"Yes indeed, a Latin reading. If boring you need not stay," he emphasized, as Iacobus slowly rose, propelled by the upcoming boredom.

"I think, Father, it is better that Iacobus, and I go and see what the children are doing," Flavia proposed.

"You took the words right out of my mouth, Flà," he said, turning to Iohannes, who began to suspect something other than the lesson was in the air.

"You are going to finish your story about your family, aren't you, Father?" Iohannes asked.

"I promised, didn't I? But for your ears only. Parts of it are to remain between us and the mountain behind us."

"Consider them buried under it," Iohannes promised.

"Fine." The monk continued his saga to his listener, who was enchanted by the external world which for him was as far as the stars above.

His wide eyes squinted now, and his eyebrows furrowed; the end had come too soon for Iohannes. Many questions remained. "Which part are we not to talk about, Father?" asked Iohannes, true to the promises between the two.

"All, my son. The children's ears are too sensitive." The monk rose from the table and inserted his hand into the folds of his garment. "Now, enough of this talk," he said, while extracting the sparkling gem which he placed in Iohannes' outstretched hand. "Don't lose it this time."

"Where did you find it?"

"Oh, Iacobus found it somewhere."

Iacobus and Flavia just then returned inside. Flavia now had an easygoing air about her carried over from the playful interaction with the little ones and heartfelt talks with Iacobus about Iohannes. This time she sat next to Iohannes, more relaxed but still slightly timid as before and observed Iohannes rolling the stone around in his fingers.

"What's going on? She asked. "Can I see that gem?" Iohannes handed it over and while she examined the stone both sensed its special meaning around which their hearts would unite. It seemed to speak of what was in their hearts, shinning and glittering almost on par with her eyes as she held it in the light.

The following week, Eugenius, Iohannes, and Alphaeus arrived at the grotto with the sheep as pre-planned for every season. Together, they herded the Florus flock into the higher greener elevation where Peter was pasturing the grotto's sheep acquired just before the cultivation. He and Alphaeus were to shepherd both flocks.

Eugenius' sympathy fell upon the unfortunate Peter, who might experience trouble from Alphaeus. Nevertheless, he hoped the misguided lad would come to his senses and mend his ways during the long season, a necessary condition for his daughter's marriage to the youth. If Alphaeus does not mend his ways, at least my son will be out of harm's way for a while, he reasoned.

Afterward, father and son returned to the grotto, where the monk and orphans were waiting. "Good morning, Master Eugenius! Everything went well?" shouted Father Nicholaos, mimicking the children's way of addressing elders, a game he often enjoyed.

"A pleasant day to you. The flock is all there grazing." Still panting from the trip, Eugenius pleasantly maintained a smile in the same game.

"Where's Flavia?" interrupted Iohannes.

"In the garden. She is....." Father Nicholaos could not help but smile contently that Iohannes was already on his way before he could finish.

Eugenius, smiled likewise and yelled at his son's back, "We don't have time. It is getting dark."

"And we are afraid of the dark, father!" screamed Iohannes, facetiously challenging his father and already at a distance too far for Eugenius to counter.

Both men stared at each other for a moment over the incident and shrugged in unison. Eugenius then dived into his worries, "About Alphaeus, Father, I remember when you rescued him. He wrestled and struggled against your helping hands."

"His father was killed by your scouting party from the garrison." The monk's eyebrows moved together in concern for his wayward orphan. "He still has scars that have not healed yet."

"But he was a child and so long ago."

"He had no mother. His father was all he had. I think she died in childbirth. No one knows if she was raped or simply a willing spouse," offered the monk in a further explanation to his orphan's character.

"You know, Father, if it were Saracens who were landed one of ours, they'd make him a slave."

"What has the lad to do with that? He is not responsible for the sins and follies of others." The Father's heart had room for even Alphaeus.

"Sorry, Father, but my daughter is in love with him. Even my wife supports her. This for me is madness."

"I admit, I have struggled with the devil denned in his soul. These wars are to blame, not the lad. I have not given up." The devil's favorite playground is the field of religious battles, thought Father Nicholaos.

"What should I do?" cried Eugenius in desperation over his daughter's welfare.

"Life is hard enough, but love, like water, flows on its own accord and always settles in a tranquil place. Like a river pool." But a tad of doubt still floated in the Father's mind left over from the bonfire discussion and the scuffle with Iohannes.

"I will yank the devil out of him with my bare hands, if need be," Eugenius burst out, fists in air.

"Let us not place more obstacles in this affair; too many are already there. You do not want to lose your daughter's confidence in you. Leave it to me."

"Father, I hope you are right," Eugenius shrugged as his concerns, battling in his brain, now settled into an uncomfortable peace.

Chapter VI: The Slaves
1037 A.D.

The merchant Berber, with eyes stuck on the eastern horizon of the bay of Panormos, stood motionless searching for something. But he could not pierce through the haze and glare of his cataracts, a veil that blocked the blue skies and fluffy clouds. His eyes had lost their crystalline sparkle of prior times and suggested the end of his days. He tried very much to maintain the dignity of his youth, but his former prowess and quickness of mind were fading and leaving behind frustration and cantankerousness.

His age was the least of his problems; the civil strife between the Berbers and the Arabs of the city had reduced his wealth to half, a patrimony granted by Allah himself. Things were changing too fast, and it was not due to the symptoms of his age. There was no real leadership in the city, and the Christians were getting bolder, some even ceased to bow before the Muslims.

He tried to stop time and contemplated on the graceful Hellenic beauty of Nicholaos' mother, who had passed away in incremental stages grieving for her son. At his stepson's hasty departure, he had promised, at a future time, to send Helena to her beloved betrothed, but the uncertainty and confusion of the city in rebellion prevented it.

Her final breath, which had arrived too soon, had made his promise a burning obligation of conscience, a conscience matured by a spark of her Christianity, which somehow gently grazed his heart. His beautiful Greek bride disappeared into the emptiness before him. Perhaps she is wandering about in the fuzzy horizon that will surely bring chaos and divine vengeance, he imagined. Every cloud assumed a semblance of her, ghosts seeking to torment him until he met his obligation.

Twenty-six years had passed since his stepson Nicholaos had left Sicily. Meanwhile the years were full of civil rebellions that cracked the political order with the force of an earthquake. The age-old friction between the Berbers and the Arabs, who politically ran Sicily for centuries, was now boiling hot beneath the daily life, ready to explode with the force of magna.

As if things were not bad enough, the participants of this belligerent chaos had raised the ante, beginning with the emir, Al-Akhal, who allied himself with the Romanoi for protection, two years ago. Consequently, his brother, Abu-Hafs, who led the Berber faction, appealed to the Khalif of Kairouan (Tunisia), who in turn sent his able son, Abdullah with about six thousand Zirid troops.

An astute man, Abdullah put in motion an effective and cunning strategy. He incited revolts everywhere, mostly on the northern coast, and forced the emir to squelch the uprisings with his unpopular mercenaries. The local governors, qaids of the various cities, quickly joined the revolt with the promise of independence.

The forces, now were engaged in battle in the nearby town of Termah (Termini), as the old man gazed into the empty horizon surrounded by a feverish merchant activity on the Palermitan piers. Men, including his oldest son, were unloading an Arabic ship and dividing the goods to be distributed to their respective local market, suq, where the anxious buyers would take possession and store them away for an anticipated shortage.

"Baba! Is it coming today? This fleet headed by Leo Opos?" asked his son, who had just approached his father after he finished his work.

"Today, tomorrow, who knows? Surely it will come. Our emir made himself a vassal of the Rum *Byzantines*. He needs help," the Berber answered nonchalantly.

"What do we do when the Rum come?"

"Without Abdullah here, there is nothing for us to do. He is rallying the locals in Termah against the emir, trying to draw him into a trap." No one in the Berber faction knew any more and both turned their attention toward the sea, one waiting for the Rum and the other waiting for a ghost.

Catepan Opos, in command of a fleet of galleys or dromons, had completed gathering local troops, called Italoi, and supplies along the Ionian coast of Calabria, and now was in Sicilian waters heading toward Panormos. His orders were to return Al-Akhal's son, collateral for the emir's fidelity to Byzantine hegemony and to pre-announce the empire's upcoming grand operation. Constantinople was intent on giving the rebellious population a sample of their military might allied with the emir, with an armada of dromons able to shoot fire, transport cavalry, archers, lancers (konteratoi) and various catapults. And this was a sample fleet. General Maniakes with one more formidable would follow. Proven in battle, he was given the rank of strategos autokrator, a rank just below the emperor.

News of the approaching naval activity by Opos traveled easily from one hilltop town to another that lined the coast in the direction of Panormos. In this manner, the news arrived at the town of Termah, where al-Akhal, the emir, was engaged in a losing battle with the local rebellious qaid. Proven as a successful warrior in prior battles with the Rum, the ever-increasing number of locals, joined with the revolt and allied with the Zirids, were too much for even his skills. The Rum's arrival trumped all activity, however, and the emir withdrew his forces and quickly headed to his new allies about to port in Panormos.

From one of these hotbeds of revolt, likewise skillful, his counterpart, Abdullah, also received the news and decided to intercept al-Akhal before he could merge his forces with the

Rum. When the two rival Muslim forces had reached the city piers from opposite sides, the glassy gaze of the old Berber was still trying to focus on the horizon of the bay. Each player, in adjacent areas to the bay, drew up its forces in battle formation as one would initialize chess pieces, and waited for the Rum to harbor.

The Berber's son tapped him on the shoulder. "Baba, look, the Rum have arrived, but so have the others." The old Berber said nothing. It is a waiting game; one party carefully awaits the other's move, and the most cunning yells checkmate, he thought.

With the emir's son, Catepan Opos felt confident as he docked his dromons. He sent a representative to the emir to draw up a plan to attack the rebel Zirids before returning the hostage, but the representative discovered the situation had changed. The ingenious Abdullah had reconciled with the emir, who now sat comfortably on his throne, uncontested. Betrayed, Opos realized making a full landing was now impossible, but he still held an important piece on the chessboard. In exchange for the hostage, he demanded a return of the agricultural slaves *mamluks* acquired in past raids by the Arabs, hoping to inflict economic harm on the island. Maniakes' invasion, the following year, would be easier, he reasoned.

This traffic of Greek messengers going back and forth between the ships and the emir piqued the old Berber's curiosity. He instructed his son to gather information on the matter. When his son returned with the news of the release of the field slaves, an idea suddenly flashed in the mind of the old Berber. If he could find a way to include Helena in the group of slaves, he would fulfill his obligation to his Greek wife. Surely her ghost hovering in the horizon would haunt him no more.

Helena was already in middle age and still waiting to hear from her beloved Nicholaos when his son found her. She came willingly and allowed to board a dromon through his father's connections.

The line of slaves arrived at the piers, some lacking shoes, and all in rags that barely covered their sunburnt, leathery skin. Their eyes, if one could see them, for they walked with head prostrate, were sunken in the sockets like the eyes of the dying. Spines curved by harsh labor announced a premature age and could hardly support the bundles of personal tatters for belongings. Among the old women thrown into the mix, who were no longer useful to the Saracens, walked Helena, veiled and wearing a black gown, indistinguishable from the others. Stationed next to the ships, the Romanoi sailors assigned each one to an appropriate vessel. This was an exodus deserving of its historical significance, fifteen thousand beings.

Lying low in the water, too low for an unexpected storm, the dromons slowly set out for the various ports—Rhegium, Bovi, Locri, Skylletion, and finally Bari. The military chess game was over. The Muslims had won the chess game, but the catepan had saved the day, or so he thought. His mandate was to set down a beachhead, a safe harbor for the troops of the second campaign. Failing to accomplish this weighed on his mind, but what was he to do? His successful military career had ended in ambiguity, neither a victory nor a defeat. Nevertheless, he believed it had weakened the enemy's resolve and helped with the second campaign.

His doubts began to vanish when he immersed himself into the complex humanitarian task of tending to the freed slaves and their distribution to their former lands. There were Calabrians, Lucans, and Apulians of Latin or Greek descent. All had been taken away in past raids by armies organized by Sicilian emirs or Saracen pirates. Only the gracious and beautiful Helena was not born on the mainland, but she would accompany the other women destined for Saint Giriaca and its surroundings, the homeland of her dear Nicholaos. Always veiled to protect herself from unwanted advances, she waited for the appropriate port at Locri where she would seek her other half.

✦

Early one fall morning, on the monk's usual walk to scan the countryside and make his morning prayer, he noticed smoke rise from the oratory on shore. Then, at a time when there was no prayer vigil, the hollow sounds from a semantron reverberated throughout the mountains of Isthmic Italy, with its low frequency able to travel long distances. The two events together told him something was in the air whose origin had to be Skylletion. He must check on his laity, he concluded, beginning with the Florus farm. Leaving Flavia in charge, he left.

Once there, and still panting, he hammered on the door with his fist and waited for his friend to answer. Eugenius immediately opened the door, anticipating his arrival. "Hello, please enter."

"Are you all right? Do you know the reason for the semantrons sounding like this?" the monk asked, in between his heavy breathing.

"We are fine and no, I don't know, Father, let us find out. I was waiting for you." Ready and eager to leave, Eugenius wanted to deal with the potential danger before it reached his family. They both rushed out the door.

They reached Saint Elias first, where a group of villagers, made curious by the event, gathered to speculate with heated discourse.

"The Saracens are back. The Saracens are back," some shouted in outright hysterics, anticipating incursions and renewed bloodshed.

"But the ships are Romanoi, I saw them in the horizon." Others swore they had seen ships resembling dromons.

Leaving the fray behind them, the two men headed for the original source of the commotion, Skylletion. Surely, they would find the truth there. But darkness fell before they reached the town and they took shelter in a squalid shack, whose inhabitant, an old man, had nothing other to offer but chestnuts and a roof.

Early the next morning they left for Skylletion. Since the semantrons had played for the normal prayer vigil the previous night, their apprehensions and concerns began to yield to a lighter mood. On the way, they met people of every type, mostly from the town, who had returned to their daily routine of tending to their gardens and orchards in the nearby areas.

"Good morning, Father," yelled their first encounter, a villager with a grin and eyes beaming with joy and an eager mouth full of good news. "The local soldiers have returned, all alive and healthy."

"You mean the ones with Catepan Opos?" asked Eugenius.

"Yes, yes."

"And even better, the kidnapped from prior years were liberated to return to their homes." Another villager happily joined the conversation. One story after another was expressed in the same triumphant mood.

The day before, on the shores near Skylletion, after disembarking, the conscripted local soldiers and former slaves had assembled to form a line that would make its way inland in search of loved ones. The first destination was obvious, Skylletion, with its fortress at its center. It was the closest and safest place to seek relatives.

As they made their way up the hill toward the village, every now and then one member would disappear into the arms of a relative, but rarely would a liberated slave be so lucky. Their absence had been too long; deaths and faded memories had severed their ties. Most wanted only to take refuge in the church or the fortress to heal their wounds. They wished to be human again before embarking on a new life filled with fear of the unknown, the irony of freedom.

When the two men arrived at Skylletion, they found the place crammed and in confusion. Prompted by the news, already diffused into every part of the county *turma*, people, whether simply curious or with real interest in lost relatives, merged there. The anxious friends and relatives seeking loved ones swarmed about the liberated sheltered in the church and under trees and porticos, wherever space allowed. They begged for information from the town's bishop or deacon or any volunteer who attended to the medical and nutritional essentials.

After being updated by the fort commander and the town bishop, Eugenius and the monk leaped into their respective duties without a second thought. For Father Nicholaos, the material needs, including medicinal ones, seemed straightforward. However, the spiritual emptiness and hopelessness of this multitude of human flesh was altogether a different matter.

Those faraway looks he had seen before in his beloved children. Incredulous as to their rescue, the former slaves withheld every spontaneous emotion for fear of waking up from their favorite dream. Father Nicholaos' real patients were their crippled spirits. His calling was to raise them to the glory of God from whence they came. The flesh although first in order was secondary in importance.

Father Nicholaos made all feel at ease. With the former slaves, captured in youth, who had forgotten the mother tongue and only understood their master's, he warmed their hearts with his soft-spoken Sicilian Arabic. A simple "Hi, there" while lightly feeling their foreheads for signs of fever would ignite scintillas of life.

Attracted to a group of weary elderly women by an unclear impulse, he slowly worked his way to this huddled mass of mutual support. He had witnessed such women in his youth, with their now-unveiled faces aged with countless wrinkles of domestic servitude and abuse. "Ladies!" he said. "Do you need anything?"

The youngest of them cried out in an infantile Greek. "Please help me, Father; where do I go? I do not remember my relatives."

"She does not speak Greek. She was kidnapped in youth," her companion said.

"I also speak Arabic and my name is Father Nicholaos."

"How's that, Father?" they asked in unison, glancing at each other as Nicholaos made himself more comfortable before the women.

"Well, I was born in Panormos," he replied in Arabic, suddenly realizing its use was opening his own wounds that time had stitched shut. But the women were made at ease by the man of God who spoke in a familiar language. They dived into the conversation, one after the other, asking questions or describing their lives in a language that was neither Latin nor Greek but always heavy with Arabic. All this lively discourse of the city he had left so long ago brought out the former Nicholaos in the Basilian monk. The stitches were losing their integrity.

"Tell us more about your life there, Father," one said, and after a moment of no response, she added, "Is there something you wish not to talk about?"

"I would like to ask....." He hesitated. "Forget it." He stopped himself abruptly. "Do you need anything?"

"We are fine; what we want is already given by God. The hole in our hearts is filled; we are in our homeland. But you, Father, being born there, have you not left your loved ones?" the oldest wisely observed. Nicholaos now felt unmasked. He had found God, yes, but he still tormented himself in having left behind Helena and his mother in a world so dangerous for Christians.

"Have you heard of a Christian family called…..? They live just outside the Saqalibah quarters."

"No, I cannot say that I have, Father," replied the eldest.

"Wait, I remember this Helena that spoke of living in that area. She went on the other ship," interjected the youngest, who conversed in the infantile Greek.

Stunned, the Father's face turned white. Incredulous, he failed to grasp the significance and wiped his forehead with the back of his hand. The women now reflected the same concern and empathy he had so naturally exercised upon them.

"Ship? What ship? My Helena here, in Calabria, where?" The words left his mouth on their own, barely audible, and he had to decide whether to breathe or talk.

When the others realized, he was gradually coming to grips with this news, the youngest proceeded but in the Sicilian Arabic this time. "When we were about to embark, she was at my side. She spoke a perfect Greek that I barely understood. Her face was fair, her demeanor graceful. She said she was a Greek Sicilian with a special friend in Saint Giriaca, and with God's help she would meet him there. At that moment, she was directed to the ship destined for Locri."

"Was there an elderly Greek woman with her?" he asked, worried also about his mother, but the woman shrugged. He had learned to live without Helena or his mother but now the gap in his heart had returned. It was necessary to go to Saint Giriaca to find her. Surely, she had made her way to his relatives.

He went to find Eugenius, who was on some detail with other militiamen and pulled him aside. "When we finish here, I have something to ask of you."

"Yes, Father, but these two lads have no next of kin." He gestured to the boys at his side. "Should we take them with us?" Eugenius' hands reached around their shoulders and welcomed them with a hearty rub.

"Why not?" They decided to take the children with them to become part of the grotto.

The following day they all left for Saint Elias.

During the trip, the monk's heart pulled him elsewhere, far away, in another ridge of mountains where Saint Giriaca lay. Compelled to get there as soon as possible, he turned to Eugenius, for help. "Genè, can you help me obtain a horse or mule for a long trip?"

"Perhaps in Saint Elias you can borrow one, but why do you ask?" said Eugenius, puzzled.

"I want to go to Saint Giriaca; it's urgent."

"Is that what you wanted from me back there? With the children on my mind, I have completely forgotten."

"Yes, that was it."

"You have walked there many times before; why not walk now?" Eugenius replied, curious over the monk's haste. And not receiving an answer right away, "Why there? So far away and right now?"

"I would like to see my relatives. I haven't seen them in a long time." The monk was vague.

The turn of the events had reopened the door to his past, and now opened, he needed to integrate that chapter of his life into his present life. Helena's arrival collapsed the wall that time had built. Those cherished moments with Helena, the awful feeling in his gut as he held that bloody dagger, and his mother's tears at his departure would now haunt him again.

"Genè, can you keep an eye on the children?"

"Of course. These lads will stay with me and on occasion I will check on the grotto."

"And this urgency, Father, it is more than a simple visit?" Eugenius asked, subtly prying the holy man.

"It involves my early youth. I knew one of the freed Greek women. She may be at my relatives'."

The dignified demeanor that usually accompanied the man who wore the holy garment began to wane in Eugenius' eyes. "Ah, a romance?" he said, with the freedom granted Eugenius from their long friendship.

"Her name is Helena, beautiful and warm as the rays of the sun, but how do you know?"

"You are a man, Father."

"I am also a man of the cloth. I need to find some reconciliation between her and me."

"If she is as beautiful as you say, if I were in your shoes, I would rid myself of the holy garment."

When they arrived at Saint Elias it was in jubilation, with a brand-new mettle. The propitious event had raised the black pall smothering the long-forgotten vigor of yesteryear. Everywhere, the villagers discussed the next military campaign led by general George Maniakes with the confidence that he would defeat the Saracens and usher in a true peace.

Every traveler coming from Skylletion was queried on the latest. Only Eugenius managed to respond. the monk, who was anxious to find an animal for transportation, had his own issues. He decided to leave immediately from Saint Elias to make time after he had procured the victuals and a mule with the support of Eugenius and some first citizens.

Chapter VII: Saint Giriaca

Castello Gerace

The monk gave his final greetings and vanished into the Le Serre's complexity of trails. His haste shoved the usual concerns to the back of his mind, robbers lurking in the thickets, murderers around the next bend and the night wind, all trivial as his past ghosts would haunt and pursue him along the way. In the three-day journey, perhaps four, he hoped that prayers and self-reflection would prepare him for encountering his ghosts.

Nicholaos, the man, had made peace with God over the death of that man in his past with self-imposed flagellation, prolonged isolation, and a monk's celibacy, but this emotional encounter could open a new direction in his life. Would I become a layman in Helena's arms, and would God permit it? he mused. At one time, there was no doubt; he would relish in her splendid loveliness, without hesitation. But now he was tormented by ambivalent sentiments.

His first lodging was a type of farm colony called a *stratiotikon ktema*, which dominated the coast of Subertum (Soverato) and Sant'Andrea. He had become sweaty and sticky under the stubborn sun, which lingered overhead and refused to bed down behind the mountains. He dismounted to stretch his cramped legs when far off into the distance, he noticed a figure waving his hand in a sign of greeting. It was the owner, or *proasteion*, of the holding; he had become a dear friend to the monk during prior sojourns and was now making his way toward him.

"Father Nicholaos, what a surprise. Pleasure seeing you again; it's been a long time." His friend greeted him, extending his hand, which led quickly to a heartwarming and firm embrace. Then his friend grasped the reins of the animal and handed them to his farmhand, who quickly took it to water and then into the stall.

"I am dead tired. Can you shelter a friendly Christian wayfarer?" His voice struggled to exit his dry mouth as he walked alongside his friend toward the farmhouse.

"Of course; let's go inside." The host placed before him a towel and a small basin of fresh water from which Father Nicholaos splashed the cool liquid on his face. He then grabbed the towel and spoke through it as he dried his face. "This heat is my ordeal before God." Then he meticulously wiped his hands.

"Not you, your conscience is transparent and cleansed." The friend offered him a ladle of precious water and began preparing the table with wine, cheese, and bread.

"Georgios, my dear friend! We are all born with sin, even a monk." The monk rubbed his lower back, pushed to straighten it, and cringed in the stretching pain. Then sat down slowly musing over the surroundings and his friend's status.

Georgios Kamateros was well established in the provincial hierarchy as owner of a vast estate that occupied the biggest valley in this corner of the county. Lying below the northern stretch of the Serre, it gently sloped toward Subertum and its gulf. Its size made it ideal for the numerous tenant farmers *paroikas*, whom he treated well. Like Eugenius, owning land obligated him to military service whenever needed, but in the capacity of a higher officer, a captain, *komes*, and he had just completed his duty in the Opos campaign.

"Tell me, how was Panormos?" Father Nicholaos noticed his military equipment and attire thrown against one wall, not yet stored away.

"We found the city in disorder with most of its daily activity suspended, but the two opposing factions had come to terms, cutting us out of the treaty. If you were to ask me, the Zirid faction has swindled us out of a victory."

Perplexed with the answer, the monk stole a moment of reflection by taking a sip of the wine and then said: "I'm sure General Maniakes will make a victory out of it. When does that campaign start?"

"The operation is being planned as we speak. It should take place the spring of next year." Kamateros had his own questions. "But you, Father, you surely haven't come here to interrogate me on what you already know."

"I'm heading for Saint Giriaca to see my relatives, you know, the town once called Gerax by the Romans."

Kamateros spoke slowly, displaying disbelief. "Oh, my dear friend, we are still in trivial talk, our friendship merits more. You owe me the true reason."

"Those women that returned with the operation, those that landed in Locri, did you notice a Sicilian woman near my age?"

"The mariners took care of the liberated slaves. They registered them, and the documents went to Bari with the catepan. I could make an inquiry." Georgios was sincere in his offer.

"It is not necessary; her name is Helena, and I am assured that she landed in Locri intent on looking for me in Saint Giriaca."

"By Jove! Does she mean more than the garment you wear?" Curious, he demanded, "Tell me all."

"I had a life before my vows. Besides, it's a long story. I will tell it on my return." Father Nicholaos yawned. "Now I'm too tired."

The sun had now laid down to rest.

Kamateros, accompanied by the farmhand, woke Father Nicholaos early the next morning to a hearty breakfast prepared by the farmhand's wife. Outside, the farmhand had tied the mule to a nearby tree, packed and ready for departure. When finished with breakfast Father Nicholaos proceeded to the animal accompanied by Kamateros.

"I don't know how to return your hospitality. God bless you."

"Your blessing is sufficient, Father," and projecting supplicating eyes, "Please stop by on your way back."

"How could I not!"

The monk scanned the hills in their autumn attire with the yellows, browns, and oranges overwhelming any remaining green. The scattered beech had shed their leaves first and shot up like white-gray swords in the array of colors. A man and his mule would blend in with them.

He mounted the mule and resumed his journey into this mountainous range. The monastery near Mount Cucco was the next stop that housed monks working the land. In prior pilgrimages on this path, he was making his peace with his God, and now he may be dismantling it. He felt he was going backward in time, into his youth, and the monastic rock he stood on was yielding to a dizzying mix of sentiments.

After covering the rugged terrain for most of the daylight hours, he spotted a young lady along the road, supporting a basket of figs on her head. In his exhausted state, he took her for Helena. The warm desires he left back in Sicily wrung his heart. He was back, leisurely walking with Helena at his side. The young lady's fair face and gentle manner in walking were on par with the Helena of his youth. Her slender, graceful form swayed with the tempo of her walk and projected a suggestive image for the former youthful Nicholaos. His heart yelled out, "Helena!" but his voice simply asked, "Lady, the monastery?"

"Up there, after the pines and maples and just below the beech thicket lies its tower." Her words took on the pleasant rhythm of her walk.

The monastery, like most in the remote areas, was a simple structure of stone serving as a farmhouse and place for prayer and meditation, furnished with small rooms for sleeping. Father Michael, a bald centenarian with a pointed beard, who dragged his feet, met the visitor in the street and led him in.

"Make yourself at home," said the old monk, showing a reluctance for words and using gestures under the umbrella of sworn silence. His delicate smile and curious eyes sought his guest's destination.

"I'm headed for Saint Giriaca," Father Nicholaos answered to the curious eyes.

"It is far, my son." He kept his words to a minimum.

"I plan to make stops. Monte Pecoraro, Malea (Mammola), even at Canolo. I regret, I cannot pay homage to Saint Nicodemus. So many miracles are credited to his tomb."

"Yes, his monastery of Kellerana is out of your way. From Malea, take the mule trails to Saint Giriaca. The locals always use the shortcuts," the old monk volunteered.

Father Nicholaos wondered if the monk had exceeded his quota of words, for he motioned him to retire to a nearby room.

Three days had passed after the stay at Mount Cucco. He arrived at Malea on the evening of the third where he slept in a shepherd shack that clung to the feet of Mount Palazzi. The villagers of Malea waved him on the next day with a full belly and proper directions in his head.

The long journey had bonded man and beast, and the animal quickened his pace to the beating urgency in the monk's heart as they approached Saint Giriaca. They stopped at the Church of Our Lady of Prestarone, where he could see winding trails far away leading to the other half of his heart. The mule trails went east, then west, up and down, but more often in the direction of the village.

At the last descent, animal and beast waded a shallow section of the Torrent Novito, where the two refreshed and restored their spirits. Before them appeared the village of his quest, the town of many churches, which consequently served as the seat of the area dioceses. Its signature landmark, however, was the fort originally built by the Romans, which now needed repair.

"My dear friend, thanks for your service. Now I too will walk, for you seem so tired," he said, pitying his companion. Then the monk took the reins and led the animal up the steep, winding ascent toward the town, entering by way of the Varvara Gate.

After passing the little church of Saint Giovannello, he ended up in the Tribune Square before what used to be the Church of Saint Haghia Kyriake. He was struck by the organized bustle and yelling of the work crew, dedicated to replacing Saint Haghia. On his initial stay here, he recalled there was talk of rebuilding the church. After all, it had given its name to the city, but the opposing faction had won.

His memory of the place served him well and he headed to the administrative palace, where the civil administrator *praesopus* referred him to Saint Parasceve, the female monastery organized the prior year. The order had kindly received Helena for a few days, then sent her off to his uncle, who assumed responsibility for her care. Located near the fort on the north end, he found himself at his door.

Those joyful moments in Panormos returned. He was at Helena's door waiting for her or her mother to answer. There was a knot in his throat, and his hand for some reason did not respond to commands to knock, but fortunately, his uncle sensed someone outside and opened the door.

When Nicholaos crossed the threshold, the moment of the encounter seemed to expand into eternity before he embraced his uncle, his aunt, and the three cousins. They had gathered at their parents' home to witness the mysterious lady in black. Excitement and incomplete questions flew about with little opportunity for a response, each being eager for the other's tidings.

Contrasted with all the commotion, in the center of the room, an enigmatic middle-aged woman sat silently, wrapped in a modest demeanor. Hesitating at first, she rose from her seat; the commotion settled into whispers; the two long-separated souls then inched carefully toward each other, but the uncertainties that time instilled in their relationship stopped them short before they embraced.

Time had transformed the two figures; they were almost unrecognizable. Their memories clashed with the present as each attempted to discern familiar characteristics in the other.

What stood before Helena was a thin, untidy monk, neglected in attire, with a bristly beard and wild hair, while Nicholaos encountered a stranger with traces of encroaching facial wrinkles, dressed in a habit-like dress. Those shapely curves which I yearned for so long ago must be hidden under the habit, he told himself. But those qualities, personal and unique to each in youth, gradually began to emerge before each other's eyes, rekindling past, sweet moments.

The remainder of the household was now not only motionless, but also speechless, suspending all together their queries and sentiments in midair once over the wonder of seeing the two rediscover themselves, a fairy tale come true. Surely their eyes were lying.

"Helena, is it you?" The four words took more energy than the long monologues with his scholar.

"Nico," she answered with an elongated, soft whisper as they reached for each other to fall into an ever-tightening embrace. His aunt, caught in some cathartic moment, sighed with relief while her two sons smiled at what they deemed to be their mother's mushy reaction.

The smiles quickly vanished, however, when Helena released herself from his arms and began cascading fists on his chest, repeating, "Why? Why did you leave me?"

The accumulated fury of twenty-six years of his absence without news now controlled the relentless motion of her hands as she released her pain. No one had the courage to attempt to stop her, above all Nicholaos, who felt responsible for all that sorrow.

His aunt, who completely sympathized with Helena, yelled, "Oh my!" Hearing these consoling remarks from the aunt, Helena halted her innocuous pounding to hurl verbal blows instead.

"Why? Why?" Her voice became harsh and raspy from the strain.

"They were going to decapitate or hang me," he said, feeling somewhat vindicated as he adjusted his garment stretched out of place from the upheaval.

"No, no, I mean to say, in the first place, why did you go after them?" Nicholaos had no answer. Perhaps she was right. He had succumbed to his youthful pride. "None of this would have happened if you did what I had told you." Now she scowled at her Nicholaos who extended his arms in sympathy, and she relaxed for a while before continuing, "I learned of your imprisonment and your sudden flight out of the city from your Berber stepfather," she said.

"And my mother, is she alright?" Nicholaos narrowed his eyes in a strong curiosity.

"Your mother wanted me to come here to meet you. It was her wish she had pleaded before the Berber with her last breath." A tear furrowed down Nicholaos' left cheek. His aunt teared as well although she had been hit by the news prior to his arrival through Helena.

"How did she die?" Nicholaos inquired, while gradually recouping his spirits.

"She died of the heartache caused by your absence," Helena sympathetically answered as tears now fell copiously down the aunt's cheeks and she mopped them with her handkerchief.

"My sister Clara was a saint," emphasized the uncle. "We insisted she stay here within the walls, but she wanted to be with her beloved husband who was working on their land. Unfortunately, the Saracens controlled the countryside at that time. They killed Cyrus and whisked her away as a slave." His uncle felt compelled to repeat what everyone knew.

"Clara was pregnant with Nicholaos at the time. I will never forget that. God bless her soul," ruefully added the aunt as the tears were joined with sniffles and sympathy from her daughter.

"Let's not forget Cyrus, that brave goat managed to cut down two Saracens before falling to them." The uncle retorted.

"My mother will always be in my heart, my dreams, everywhere. Her angelic spirit abides in the absolute presence," Nicholaos spoke as a monk. Helena quietly observed the man before her. She struggled to see the cocky Nicholaos of yesteryear.

"My dear nephew, in what sense is she present, save, in memory only?" the uncle challenged, being a practical man. He, with the assistance of his sons, was the head builder (arkhi tekton) in the town and was responsible for the new church.

"In the sense that we are more than flesh and blood, my dear." The words slipped out naturally from his wife and mother and daughter gave each other glances of satisfaction.

"My dear, you are quipping at my expense. Every thing is comprised of earthly materials which time eventually crumbles into dust. Our bodies will succumb to the same fate." The verbal jibing became an amusement for the sons, but the others were curious and waited for an equally insightful retort from the wife.

"My dear husband! Certainly, you are not saying we are merely earthly objects subjected to the forces of time. You are a builder. Does this not mean you are more than the material you work with? If we are simply things, how can one thing be aware of another thing? Awareness, I'm sure, is the domain of the soul, and the soul has no expiration. Father Nicholaos can testify to that." Testy, she turned to her nephew for help.

"Awareness of the other is the essence of the soul, and the soul shares in the everlasting communion with God."

"This communion is enigmatic and only vaguely understood." The uncle was becoming a stubborn devil's advocate.

"Yes, but…." Nicholaos was interrupted by one of his uncle's workers, who thrust the door wide open. Panting and excited, he related that he had just learned of his cousin's death. The unfortunate hermit had been killed by isolated Saracens-turned-bandits roaming in the mountains, and the worker needed time off to attend the funeral rites, which the uncle immediately granted.

"The barbarity never ceases. Not even the hermits' grottos are sacred to these pillagers." The aunt grimaced as she offered the worker something to drink.

"The county militia are cleaning the countryside of this danger." The elder son comforted his mother.

After his worker left, the uncle quickly turned his attention to the family and company.

"I don't know when we will finish the cathedral. With all these delays, it will not be ready for the consecration." He received no comments as mother and daughter were preparing the table.

After dinner, the sons and daughter left for their homes, while the uncle and aunt disappeared into their rooms, leaving Helena and Nicholaos alone. For a while, their starving eyes met off and on, both seeking to merge their past stories smoothly into a possible single future. Nicholaos leaned toward Helena, extended his hand, and delicately grasped hers. Helena's frustration returned; she withdrew her hand and said, "What am I to do now? We were so much in love, a love embellished in the presence of the Saintly Virgin."

"True, she blessed us then, shone a warm light upon us." He did not know what else to say.

"Two times you have betrayed me; you left me and then you put on that garment," she cried. "Does the garment cover your sins? Are its vows your penance?" she admonished him, not fully knowing why, other than her heart pained. Their future, stripped away, demanded a sensible reason, and without one, frustration turned to anger.

Nicholaos insisted on caressing her delicate hand. "God has entered my heart in your absence; he filled the void. My love for you, God's hand has transformed and elevated onto a more profound plane. If it were, otherwise, I would have given up, and my remains would have been found in some ravine in these mountains, a victim of the anguish."

Helena began to relax again, her hand softened in his, and her stern look yielded to her former graceful beauty. "I have never stopped loving you. I have always felt that a true, earthly love has also a spiritual foundation; as a monk, you know this."

"Yes, we all can rest in Christ's arms." Nicholaos knew where she was going.

"A lay life can also be in God's graces?" Her voice was graceful, and he listened pensively.

"How can I shed this garment that has rescued me from destruction and won't allow me to marry?"

"And me?" cried Helena.

"I still love you. I always have. But I was graced with a new life. My responsibilities are now to God as a monk," he pleaded.

"A Greek priest can marry. You can become one and still do God's work, but of a different nature." Deep down Helena knew that the maverick in her Nicholaos could never accept the rigidity of the church.

"I cannot be myself as a priest let alone a lay person. In that prison the veil of egoism fell to the glory of God. I had an epiphany there. Man shares in God's divine sovereignty. That is true freedom, and it can't be separated from responsibility and a sense of good and evil. It is then that the world acquires a spiritual hue. I cannot abandon my vows as a monk," he said sincerely.

Helena understood more than she desired. Her issue with Nico was really with fate. Her Nicholaos had crossed over into the land of values, values with a concrete existence, and the human experience is divine. Man, here, is the author of his own destiny. This was his salvation and maybe hers also, her heart told her.

Her handsome Nico was truly transformed into a monk; he could shed his holy garment, but the lover was no longer there. She remembered tugging, cajoling him toward Christ; now he would gently lead her deeper into that pious domain, to a place she had never imagined.

It was now up to her to choose. She could remain here and join the female monastery, but she would be too far away from him. She loved him too much to start a new life without him. There was only one choice left.

"Come with me to Saint Elias," Nicholaos softly asked.

"Yes, I will." Nothing else was spoken that night, nor was there a need. The two destinies would converge beginning the next morning. The dawn would announce the new relationship.

PART TWO

Chapter VIII: Return

As the returning travelers entered the little valley, they heard the barking of a dog echo and megaphone off the surrounding mountains. And since they had avoided Saint Elias to take a short-cut, the trail could only finish at the Florus farm, where they were first greeted by the now full-grown dog and then by Iohannes yelling after him, "Argè! Argè!"

Iohannes accompanied them to the house, where Laetitia, who regularly sat outside in the afternoon sun, stood up to see better the cause of the commotion, and in her drifting mind of old age saw the Holy Virgin and Saint Joseph seeking shelter. When the travelers reached the house, those images faded into the background of her mind and she uttered, "Enter, please," keeping her eyes on the Virgin Mary.

Meanwhile Iohannes led the tired mule to the stall and went to notify the rest of the family scattered about in the nearby fields. "Are you going to introduce me to this elegant woman?" Laetitia directed her question at Father Nicholaos as she prepared the table for the guests.

"Helena from Panormos." He leaned back a bit in his chair and glanced at Helena also seated.

"Ah, of course, the mystery woman my son was talking about," Laetitia said, proud her memory still functioned at the appropriate times. The rest of the family strolled in after they had washed their hands in the little washbasin outside. Feeling presentable, they introduced themselves to Helena, Eugenius first.

"We are happy you escaped from Sicily, safe and sound. We have two lads here with us who have suffered the same fate." Then Eugenius turned to Iohannes. "Iohan, go fetch the lads; they are still out there. They are so dependable."

"Yes, I want to see the new members of my flock, and the work that awaits me. How deep are their wounds and what measures should be taken?" commented the monk.

"Father, young wounds heal easily; besides, your hands work miracles," Laetitia earnestly interjected.

"It is really the hand of God and his mercy," responded the monk, whose words barely made their way through everybody's intense interest in Helena. She was the mystery in the room who caught everyone's eyes.

Maria was the first to redirect the conversation to fulfill the other's curiosity, "Helena, please tell us all about yourself, and the life in that Palermitan world?"

"Honestly, as a Christian it was difficult, but we managed." Helena hoped the subject would be otherwise, but the hosts insisted, and, with the help of Father Nicholaos, the two reciprocated the hospitality by entertaining their hosts with stories of the city and its people.

But the attention grew ever more on the charming Helena. Reserved and complementary to the now Father Nicholaos as she was once to her Nico of prior years.

What was this couple's fate? Would the community lose a monk or gain a nun? Prohibited by politeness, these questions hovered about the table and finally were verbalized when the spirited Laetitia asked, "Father, are you going to keep your vows as a monk?"

Everyone turned to the monk and waited for him to choose his words. "I will always be a monk; my orphans are always in need of spiritual guidance."

"But what of Helena? Yes, Helena?" others shouted, after Laetitia had broken the ice.

"First, she is coming to the grotto where I need help with the children." He glanced over to Helena who was blushing. "Then maybe we will talk of the convent in Skylletion." The blushing turned to signs of graceful disapproval making him change the conversation altogether. "And how are things here?"

Laetitia felt responsible for the sensitivities of the guests and, nudging her son to answer, she tapped him on the shoulder, cleared her throat, and interjected a fake cough as an added measure.

"Everything has been normal, except for some mysterious thefts nearby, a sheep taken away or items stolen from the homes. Fortunately, for us we have Argus to alert us."

"In my opinion, there is a gang in the mountains and Alphaeus is involved," Laetitia blurted out, unable to contain herself.

"Mother, we are not sure," protested Eugenius.

"When we get back to the grotto, I will send Iacobus to check on the lads. As for the thefts, it could be anybody," said the monk finishing with a suppressed yawn that contaminated the rest of the table.

The next day, the monk slept through the normal breakfast time. Maria and Saverina had prepared the table, and all, including Helena, were patiently waiting for him. He slowly made his way to the table when he finally woke up groaning from the aches of the long journey.

"Good morning, Father," they all said as they sat eagerly waiting for him like the faithful await a mass. Being host to a monk accompanied by a nun was a privilege; in their eyes she was already a nun. They waited anxiously for his benediction before turning the morning meal into a homecoming celebration cut short for the orphanage needed tending.

A woman in black garment with a black head shawl riding on a mule, a monk and two former raggedy slaves, later left for the mountains. The two lads who were once treated as beasts of burden would become seeds replanted in solid ground and fertilized with science and above all the conscious of a Christian God.

Once at the grotto, the children rushed toward the home comers shouting with joy and blocking the hovel entrance. Stuck within its compressed mass, Father Nicholaos embraced as many as he could, beginning with the littlest.

The orphans welcomed the two neophytes into their social circle displaying a vibrant curiosity for their life's experiences while Helena and Flavia, after being introduced personally by the monk, began conversing as if they had known each other in some other time and place.

The monk had the sensation that all was well, at least at the grotto. In his absence, the orphans appeared to have behaved well. They had carried out the boring chores as adults, and the bickering was minimized and kept in check by Flavia's good judgment.

There remained only one serious thorn in his side, Alphaeus. The rumors of the thefts that buzzed about in the community did not trouble him that much, for in this corner of the world they fall like rain. What emerged from the depth of his mind were suspicions of the lad's involvement, something he could not tolerate, and when he saw Iacobus he gave him his instructions. "You must go to the high pasture as soon as possible. I want to know what is going on up there. Go! Go now! Before dark." Then he turned his attention to Helena. "What do you think of our little nest up here?"

"I am truly fascinated by your passion," she answered thoughtfully while absorbing the sight around her in its dim light cast by the partial orange sun whose lower part lay hidden by the western mountains.

That night, Helena found herself unable to sleep. The speed in which her new life unfolded before her preyed on her. She wandered back in time when she was intensely in love. Those sweet moments once closely shared with Nico, gently re-surfaced, and for the Helena who had once yielded to their bliss, her heart still could not let them go. Tears gently furrowed their way down her graceful cheeks before she finally fell asleep. She dreamt of a life that could have been with her Nico.

She was awakened by the morning light. The night's sweet memories were vaporized by reality, and she returned to the elderly Helena. Is this my fate with Nico, so scruffy and unkempt? she mused. She wondered if she could share his passion, in that hovel? The place needed her; she was educated and still possessed her youthful vigor; a vigor still laced with desires for Nico. Can this vigor be consumed as tutor, mother, and loving healer to the orphans at the side of Nicholaos?

The decision, she realized, would come naturally in bits and pieces as her sadness would be nibbled away by the children's joyful appreciation. This revelation came to her from the contented eyes of Nicholaos in his dealings with his precious children.

At noon that day, Iacobus returned from his mission with news that sent Father Nicholaos into a rage for the first time since he left Sicily.

"Peter told me, that Alphaeus often departed for the higher ground and would leave Peter alone," began Jacobus. The monk's eyes opened wide in a scowl. "Alphaeus never gave a reason, and Peter would discover some sheep missing the next day."

"That scoundrel!" screamed the monk. "And Peter, what did he do?"

"Peter prodded Alphaeus to notify Eugenius. Alphaeus always refused and Peter could not abandon the sheep," Jacobus meekly responded.

Poor Iacobus, struck unjustifiably by the flames ejected from the monk's eyes, withdrew frightened and confused for what should have been directed at the absent rascal.

"This fool has not listened to a word of mine; he has become a villain." At this, Iulia began bleating like a lamb away from her mother. Flavia gently whisked her away. "If he were here, I'd take a willow branch to him, that devil!"

Helena, who had seen this face before, jumped before him. "Be calm; you are a man of the cloth, a monk no less," she said, out of pity for Iacobus.

"To hell with it! How can I calm down?" he growled. Her sweet and supplicating eyes were, however, drawing him back to himself. His face slowly acquired that welcoming glow so appealing to the children. "Oh, wretched me!" he moaned as he became playful and witty again before the children. Iulia returned to his lap.

Father Nicholaos then turned to Helena. "On Monday I will tell Iohannes to relay the news to his father."

The day after, on Sunday, Father Nicholaos, as usual, performed the Liturgy to the group and the laity nearby who had constantly beseeched him for the sacrament although he was not ordained. The locals understood little on such matters. They hungered for that special communion with the Lord, and for them the distinction between priest and monk was bureaucratic.

He prepared the premises for the mass. The cave section became the altar, and the adjoining hovel became a nave for the faithful. The holy vessels, altar cloths, and vestments that were once inside the large wooden case were now displayed on top, and, with the schema on the Father's back, the make-believe church became real. As Father Nicholaos passed the chunks of bread dipped in the wine from the Patina to his flock, in the high forest, Alphaeus was laying a malicious trap.

A Devil's Pact

When Alphaeus had learned of the monk's return, he knew the lessons would resume, and on Monday Iohannes would pass by that ominous overhanging cliff. He proceeded to scheme his nemesis' permanent disappearance from his life.

Reasoning that he had already established an initial rapport with the local bandits, he felt it would not be difficult to present them with a proposal of mutual benefit. Three mujahidin who had escaped after their group was defeated by the militia of the county, and now survived as bandits in the hills, fit into his plans.

Alphaeus made a pact with those three. They sneered at every word of his proposal while intimidating and challenging him until they were sure of his loyalty. If he would spy for them, they swore to shove the lad over the cliff to his death. It would be an accord sealed with Christian blood, and for Alphaeus, there would be no turning back since the devil always gets his due.

The greedy rabble felt, however, that the lad was worth more alive than dead. In Alphaeus' absence, they consorted among themselves and decided on a kidnapping instead. They would deal with Iohannes' fate after the consignment of the ransom.

The day after the lesson, Eugenius hurried toward the grotto, retracing his son's footsteps to his lessons. Early that morning, he left his wife wailing and screaming nonsensible phrases concerning the disappearance of her Apollinus, which had lasted the entire night. He stopped, initially, at the home of Matthaeus, where the family insisted that they did not have any news of Iohannes' whereabouts.

Before he reached the grotto, however, he stopped at the rugged cliff that dominated the rocky ravine hosting the torrent. Down below, all seemed normal, just the usual scattered livestock bones and partially decomposed animal carcasses. They had been disemboweled by the wild animals and the inner flesh had been hastily ripped away. Only their skeletons still attired in their hide remained. There were no signs of human remains, no foul play, just shepherd negligence when they guide their animals through the narrow, craggy paths, he comforted himself.

Eugenius arrived at the grotto at about noon with sword at his side, dripping with sweat and panting like an exhausted hunting dog.

"Father is Iohan here?" the anxious knight blurted out to the monk in between his gasps.

"My dear friend, come in." The monk was alone.

"I have searched everywhere, in the gorges, in the thickets; he has vanished into thin air."

"Slow down; what are you exactly saying? Are you telling me Iohannes has not returned home from yesterday's lesson?" Eugenius gave him an affirmative nod. "Is he with friends?" then asked Father Nicholaos.

"He always tells us where he goes."

"I hope it is not serious," said the monk, struck with an awful presentiment of Alphaeus' involvement.

"Oh my God, those thefts, do you think the pirates have returned?" The paternal concerns were winning over the seasoned knight as the panic grew.

"Come on now, Genè. Let us take it one step at a time."

"So, what are we to do?"

"First, we must find out what happened. We can start by questioning the lads at the high pasture." Alphaeus flashed into the monk's mind.

"Why?"

"Well, they are all of the same age. Perhaps Alphaeus and your son have made amends and they are all together." Father Nicholaos dared not mention the lad's mysterious treks to the high forest.

"You don't think he is there?" asked Eugenius, somewhat relaxed.

"You haven't looked there yet, have you?" Eugenius accepted Father Nicholaos' logic and the monk continued still holding back his suspicions. "Besides, while there, we can bring back the sheep."

The two left for the higher pasture at a frantic pace and found the two shepherds sitting under a beech tree near the flock. Iohannes was nowhere in sight. Alphaeus was nonchalantly picking his teeth with a grass stalk while Peter was absorbed in sketching figures on the soft earth with his sheep herding stick. The remaining sheep appeared healthy and well fattened, thanks to Peter's diligence.

At the sight of the adults, Peter looked relieved. "He leaves me here, alone. He disappears into the night and the next day sheep are missing," the trustworthy lad explained. But the sheep were the last thing that worried the adults.

Eugenius fixed his eyes on Alphaeus. "Have you seen my son?"

Alphaeus blushed and bit down hard on the grass stalk. "No," he said with a suspicious tone.

"Do you know anything about the missing sheep?" The monk demanded.

Alphaeus hesitated, became irritable. "How should I know. They just wandered off." He deflected the question stupidly in his guilt.

"Peter says you go off into the night. Where do you go?" demanded Eugenius, his eyes still piercing the now cowering Alphaeus.

"A place to think, make sense of my life." Alphaeus slyly wished to win over the monk's sympathy.

"Where's that?" shot back Eugenius.

"The clearing overlooking the Wolf's Pass." Inadvertently, the lad had revealed the hideout of his accomplices.

"Come off this! You take me for a fool. What do you really do there?" Eugenius reached for the lad's throat, squeezed with a fatal force that only the monk's hand and imploring words loosened. Liberated and breathless, the boy fled in the direction of the yet higher ground above the Wolf's Pass. Eugenius wanted to pursue the rascal, but Father Nicholaos stopped him.

"The lad is too fast. Let us take the sheep to the grotto and then think this through," said Father Nicholaos, studying his friend.

"Damn the sheep. My son! The delinquent has done something," insisted Eugenius but reluctantly obeyed the monk's advice.

They gathered the sheep to take back on that Tuesday.

The three arrived at the grotto at night and herded the sheep into the fold to be divided later. They encountered apprehension in the grotto; most of it weighed on Flavia. It had become obvious to Flavia that the story of the stolen sheep was only part of the ugly news. One word thrown here, and another thrown there by the children, who happened to be in earshot of prior conversations, added up to something awful. Furthermore, there was Alphaeus' puzzling treks reported by Iacobus and the unexpected appearance of Eugenius, in arms. These all funneled her worries into a suspicion of some dreadful incident.

Flavia wondered if she had seen him during the Monday lesson for the last time, as she carried on with a glassy look that focused nowhere. "Are you all, right?" Helena asked, trying to console her. Flavia remained silent and Mother Helena just held her hand.

The two men, nevertheless, managed to withhold their deepest fears from the group—a kidnapping or worse, murder. They strolled outside, away from the children's ears. Although they had not found any traces of Iohannes, they still clung to some hope. "We must reconnoiter that forest area where Alphaeus headed," Eugenius suggested.

"I will go. I speak their tongue," offered Father Nicholaos.

"But you are a monk in a monk's garment," protested Eugenius. "They will recognize you as a Christian."

"Let me deal with that," Father Nicholaos said. They returned inside, where he headed straight to his large chest. He rummaged through its contents and extracted his forgotten Arab tunic and turban buried under his precious religious items.

"I will put these on in case I am spotted during the scouting. I will leave early tomorrow," said Father Nicholaos, glancing at Helena as if to seek approval. She was following his every move; her eyes seemed to softly say, "If you must go, go!" as she still held Flavia's hand.

The monk turned to Eugenius, "In the meantime, you will stay with the children. Let us hope he is still alive."

The following morning, Father Nicholaos slipped into the Berber cloths as Eugenius looked on. then exited the hovel.

"Be careful, Father," warned Eugenius.

Late afternoon of that Wednesday, the monk, in disguise, finally arrived at the high forest where he noticed the smoke of the campfire located in the center of a small field. He inched his way toward it while trying to remain under the cover of the nearby foliage. Hiding safely in the forest's perimeter bordering the camp, he observed the dreaded figures of the marauders, with their weapons lying at their side, each enjoying the warm campfire while eating hunks of freshly roasted mutton.

Partially armored, they must be wayward Saracen soldiers, he thought. One was muscular, with an aquiline nose, the obvious owner of a mail shirt and sword lying by his side; another was a smaller wiry man with buck teeth and eyes too close together; and a third had the appearance of a simpleton who wore an oversized metal helmet. All wore their leather greaves, now serving only as protection from the underbrush, as well as sheathed daggers at their sides.

In their jubilation, they boasted about the treasure they thought forthcoming and stopped their chuckling only when biting savagely into the stolen meat. "We are going to get a sack of riches," one was saying.

Iohannes could not be seen anywhere, likewise for the devious Alphaeus, so the monk moved closer when he accidently stepped on a dry branch that emitted a snapping sound. The three heads jerked in his direction. He froze in place, but when the simpleton and the smaller one rose and edged in his direction, he carefully backed up, retraced his steps. In the process he lost sight of the third, who had quietly circled the field.

The man's location became known as a sharp, digging pain in his lower back, and the man's piercing sword prevented any further retreat. "I have him!" the man yelled in Arabic. Meanwhile, the others rushed toward the scene, wielding their daggers in a jabbing motion.

"Let's take him to the camp," demanded Buck Teeth.

"Move," grunted the man to his rear while pressing his sword into his back. No sooner had they arrived in the open camp when they began the interrogation.

"Who are you? What's your name? What do you want? Say something." He felt the sharp blade dig in deeper, and he had a sense of reliving the nightmare in Panormos, only now he was unarmed.

"I am from Sicily." The words came out in fluent Arabic with the proper Palermitan accent.

Dumbfounded by his skills to speak their language better than they did, the bandits relaxed to the point that the smaller Saracen, doing the inquiry, re-sheathed his dagger. The other with the aquiline nose withdrew his sword. Meanwhile the simpleton danced around Father Nicholaos, repeating, "We have a Palermitan. We have a Palermitan."

Of course, Father Nicholaos had to tell some story and since his vows did not allow lies, he simply said the truth. "I am seeking a new life. I come from Panormos, for reasons of avoiding prison and want to join others like me." Thus, the false Berber continued his story.

"You came from Panormos, hmm? Landed on the Tyrrhenian coast, hmm? Now you wander through these hills. Lies! Lies!" said the smallest of the three, now materializing as the kingpin. The simpleton reinforced his role by repeating his last words: "Lies! Lies!"

"Be quiet, you fool, and get that spy; bring him here!" barked the leader.

The simpleton quickly vanished into the forest for Alphaeus, who stood guard over Iohannes. When the two returned, the gang thrust the bewildered Alphaeus before the monk, and the leader demanded from their spy some accounting of this wanderer from Panormos. "Do you know this Sicilian?"

A silent pause ensued as the monk and his pupil eyed each other; one was speculating on his pupil's repentance while the other pondered his response. Whether it was due to true misgivings or simply a lapse in determination under the fixed eyes of his former mentor, the lad finally uttered a flat "No." Then he turned around and headed to his post in the thickets.

"Go, my illustrious Berber; go on your way," commanded the leader.

"Go away, go away!" repeated the simpleton, skipping about with his helmet bobbing like a cork in water above his head.

Father Nicholaos withdrew slowly, noting the direction of his former wayward orphan.

The three bandits were left to themselves and their conspiracies. "Why not ask the stranger to join us?" inquired the muscular bandit to the leader.

"And have one more to share with."

"What about the spy and the hostage?"

"We will rid ourselves of them at the proper time."

"Let's bring them with us and sell them to the nearest pirate ship."

"Let's see what happens," concluded the leader.

With the camp at his back, and the bluish light of the moon overhead, Father Nicholaos utilized the dangerous shortcuts taken only in daylight. They quickly brought him to the grotto towards midnight. All had fallen asleep except Eugenius and Helena, who waited anxiously for him as they nursed themselves by the fireplace.

He was hit with wide-opened eyes when he entered, their lips shut, holding back a flood of questions. Their eyes followed him until he disappeared momentarily to shed the Berber attire. Dressed in his normal garment, he then approached the fireplace and flung into the burning flames the Saracen clothes of his painful past, the fire consuming them forever. Helena looked on her Nico and let out a sigh of relief while Eugenius began peppering him with inquiries.

"I am sure Iohannes is there, for I caught them talking of a ransom. I saw Alphaeus, and it appeared he had been standing guard over your son."

"Where? Where? You must know something," demanded Eugenius.

"To the right of the marauders' camp, in the beech trees, that's where Alphaeus went."

"I will use the dog to find him," shot back Eugenius, overly excited over the crumbs of information he had received.

"Genè! He is guarded and those are Saracen cutthroats," commented Father Nicholaos.

"That poor child, alone and frightened." Helena cringed at her own words.

The men looked at each other, internalizing the situation, and finally, the monk said, "Let us wait for the notice of the ransom."

"You are right, Father." Eugenius settled down a bit.

"Can we help with that," offered Helena in the same tone.

"Let's see what happens first, Helena," said Eugenius.

"Should we tell Flavia of the kidnapping?" asked Father Nicholaos.

"I will talk to Flavia," Helena volunteered.

Chapter IX: The Plan

After the monk's return, Eugenius felt less helpless; he was slipping into his former military self. He would remain at the grotto until the ransom was determined and the procedure of his son's release was negotiated; that was priority number one, he told himself. However, he foresaw obstacles and deceptions, and needed a plan to account for these, some advantage of his own. Putting himself in the bandits' shoes, he determined their greatest concern would be a retaliatory manhunt by the locals after the ransom was paid and Iohannes released.

To avoid this, they could quickly slip away and leave his son to die of exposure while he patiently waited for his return. Or they could bring his son with them to ensure their escape and as a bonus sell him into slavery. For now, Eugenius was sure his son was alive, and he would stay alive until the ransom was paid. As for Alphaeus, his value to the gang rested only on his function as a messenger and an interpreter. "He deserves what he gets," he grunted to himself.

The next morning, on Thursday, the two men were awakened from a well-deserved sleep by a sudden frenetic clucking from the chickens in the yard, announcing a visitor. They both darted for the door and no sooner had they opened it when before them stood the figure of Alphaeus, wearing a turban and carrying a leather sack. They dealt with him outside away from the ears of the children and Flavia.

"Who are you? Their lackey?" Eugenius angrily demanded of the knave.

"Let him speak!" Father Nicholaos intervened.

Alphaeus related the message of the ransom with a hasty impertinence "Fill this sack with coins, gold, jewelry, and anything else of value. Bring it to the shepherd's shack and place it under the solitary pine, then leave.

My son? Demanded Eugenius, full of anger.

We will free Iohannes after we get the sack."

"Where?" Eugenius reached for Alphaeus, but the monk held him back.

"On the path between the shack and the high forest. If we see any militia, we will slice the hostage's throat." Alphaeus dropped the sack and cowardly fled, avoiding any questions.

"Wait! Traitor! I swear; you are not going to get away with this," Eugenius shouted at the new marauder now too far to hear.

Eugenius settled down, returned to himself. Iohannes is still alive, he reminded himself. He would do everything the kidnappers wanted, follow the demands to the letter, and turn over the sack full of precious belongings, even knowing their word meant nothing, they were simply cutthroats. Do not anger the kidnappers before my son is returned safely. It was the order of the day.

He turned to the monk, "I will leave right away, Father," and once on the path, he shouted back, "I will be back with the ransom."

All the way he reflected on that needed edge in case things went afoul. When he had barely entered his home, Maria, after she realized her Apollinus was not at his side, jumped up and screamed hysterically, fearing the worst of all possible news. Saverina rushed to her side and slowly calmed her down returning to her to a light sobbing.

"Iohannes is safe," he insisted. "He has been kidnapped and a ransom must be paid."

The family began searching throughout the house. The matrimonial jewelry box was emptied, necklaces were taken off, expensive memoirs located, and all the gold coins of that household were piled up on the kitchen table. They, Maria included, channeled their energies to a single task and gladly stuffed that sack, for the activity itself seemed to alleviate the helplessness and frustration. Once filled, the sack comprised a tantalizing fortune. Its value was sufficient to buy a small farm complete with oxen, still a small price for the son's life.

On Friday morning, before he left, he put on a positive face before the family. "Let's keep our hopes alive. After all, we are paying the ransom," he assured them. He flung the bulging sack over his shoulders, sheathed his sword at his side, summoned Argus, and left the family hanging on that hope.

When he arrived at the trail leading to the grotto, he turned right and took the road to Saint Elias in search of his advantage—former military compatriots. Out of deep-rooted friendship and civil obligation, the two available eagerly volunteered. They quickly armed themselves. One grabbed his Norman crossbow acquired in the battle of Cannae, the other a lance, and each strapped on a scabbard with sword.

By afternoon, they had set foot on the rising trail to the grotto, with faithful Argus at their side displaying his puppy-like energy. He would sniff the terrain on one side of the path, then on the other, and when falling behind, he would make a wild dash to catch up. Sometimes, certain smells drew him into the thickets, but when called by Eugenius, he would circle widely around the men to end up unexpectedly in front with all his vigor intact.

Eugenius began to feel optimistic about his son's rescue with his two friends, who now shared the ordeal. He was doing something; his plan was taking form and it appeared more sensible every time he recycled it in his mind.

"How in the world did all this happen?" asked the huge comrade, who happened to have an oxen-like strength and was nicknamed Ox.

"One of Father Nicholaos' orphans, a Berber by birth, is mixed up with a Saracen gang and is a spy for them. He has betrayed us." Eugenius barely held his tongue from cursing the knave.

"And where were you told to place this sack?" asked the other comrade, whose stature resembled the monk, with ruffled hair and a sinewy body, conducive to his accuracy on the use of the crossbow.

"At the shepherd's shack. There, I will go alone so I will not alarm the bandits during the exchange. You will head to their hideout, encircling it, always under cover."

"Where is this hideout?" Ox asked.

"At the end of the higher part of the mountain ridge overlooking the Wolf's Pass. Father Nicholaos knows where; he will accompany you."

"What do we do there?" asked the bowman.

"You will remain there for the night, keeping an eye on the bandits until I get word to you. Meanwhile, make sure they don't escape without releasing my son."

They arrived at the grotto Friday evening. As soon as they entered the farmyard, the children greeted them screaming and yelling for the Father's presence, but Leonellus had already gone to fetch him, pulling him outside by his garment. Eugenius introduced him to the new arrivals. Everyone then entered the hovel and Father Nicholaos introduced the two strangers to Helena and Flavia.

"Let's go outside," said the monk, wishing to discuss openly their upcoming actions without preoccupying Flavia or frightening the children. The monk spoke first. "Gene! They said they will kill Iohannes if we bring the militia."

"I don't believe that. Even if they discover our backup, they will need Iohannes alive as a shield to ensure their escape," responded Eugenius, and, turning to Ox and the bowman, "If they try to flee without freeing my son before or after the ransom is paid, feel free to do whatever is required to detain them. In the meantime, Father Nicholaos will search for Iohannes."

"And this dog?" the bowman asked.

"The dog will help Father Nicholaos in the search should they not release him."

"And if they release Iohannes safely to you," inquired the monk.

"Father, you and I will tend to my son on the return home while the others pull back and follow us for protection. I have no interest in retaliation."

"Later, we can handle these Muslim boors as a community affair," commented Ox.

"Let's just focus on my son," ordered Eugenius.

Everyone had their assignment.

Eugenius stayed behind to pay the ransom the next day. The others arrived at the camp under the cover of darkness. The weather was agreeable and under the starry light they found their appropriate places undiscovered. Father Nicholaos found his place on the far side of the camp where he felt they had imprisoned Iohannes, while the others stationed themselves in the opposite thickets but nearer to the camp and its makeshift shelter.

"Only the kidnappers will sleep well this chilly night," the bowman noted crossing his arms for warmth.

"We certainly won't. I will take the first watch," volunteered Ox.

On the other side Father Nicholaos prayed for his pupil's release without any bloodshed.

The next morning there was movement in the camp beginning with the simpleton, who held his loose helmet from falling over his eyes as he rekindled the fire while the others filed out from the makeshift cover. Then the buck-toothed boss gave his orders to the simpleton, who disappeared in the direction of the shepherd's shack.

Now, the militiamen waited quietly for the simpleton's return. He finally showed up with the sack over his shoulder and handed it over to his boss, anticipating adulations that did not materialize. After the gang inspected the contents, they took no apparent measures to free Iohannes, but instead scurried about for their belongings.

The two militiamen became suspicious. The bandits were packing and Iohannes was not released. "Hey, Ox! You don't think these cutthroats are fleeing?" whispered the bowman as they instinctively prepared for battle.

The bowman stood up, loaded the crossbow, and took aim at one gang member while Ox inserted his left arm in the leather strap behind his shield before raising it to his chest, then unsheathed his sword with his other hand.

"Should we attack now?" asked Ox.

"For now, let's make sure they don't leave or harm the lad in any way until Eugenius gets here," replied the bowman.

At the same time, on the other side of the kidnappers' camp, the passing time only increased the monk's apprehension. The payment should have occurred by now and someone should be fetching Iohannes, he told himself. Did they plan to slip away and possibly leave Iohannes to die of starvation? His mind now raced through all possibilities. He wrestled with each succeeding thought. They could bring the lads with them, using one as an interpreter and the other as shield against a pursuit by the locals and then sell them both. Father Nicholaos began to pray.

Suddenly he heard a dog sniffing behind him. He turned around to see the disillusioned face of his dear friend.

"I waited and waited but they did not release him to me. Is my son with them?" whispered Eugenius, agitated.

"No, I don't think so. I saw nothing. He must still be kept hidden somewhere nearby."

"Things are not right. I don't know what they have in mind."

"What do we do next?" asked the monk.

"I will check on the others. Meanwhile, you search for Iohannes." Eugenius reached into his pocket. "If you don't find him, we will force them to tell us." He extracted a rag once belonging to Iohannes' attire and rubbed Argus's muzzle with it. "Use the dog to find my son; then stay with him."

"And the rest of you?"

"Um, I don't really know. If necessary, we will do everything possible to deny them an escape until my son is free and unharmed." Eugenius passed the rag to the monk and quickly left to join the others, moving as silently as possible.

"What's going on?" Eugenius asked when he arrived.

"They are preparing to leave, and your son is not in sight," said the bowman. "Was he let go?"

"Oh God, no, but the dog will find him." They overheard the pirate leader grunt for the simpleton to fetch Alphaeus and the hostage.

"Are we taking the two with us?" Asked the simpleton, dropping the gear he was preparing for their leave.

"Yes, you idiot," replied the leader. "Go!"

"They are not going to release Iohannes," uttered the bowman who understood a little Arabic.

"You are telling me? My son should have been released a long time ago when I was on the road." Eugenius feared the worst.

"We must stop them now," insisted Ox.

Eugenius turned to the bowman, "On my signal shoot the idiot down before he is out of range. Ox and I will surprise the other two; hopefully, they will tell us the location of my son." Then turning to Ox, "Take the big one; I will handle the one growling out orders. Go! Now!"

The bowman took his shot, and the arrow with the power of the crossbow pierced through the lout's helmet and lodged itself in his temple. Then Eugenius and Ox unsheathed their swords and rushed toward the other two who managed to recover their swords in time. It was now a battle, for the bandits were once Saracen fighters, unwilling to surrender. Ox managed to slice through the stomach of the muscular man, who had failed to wear his mail shirt. He, however, received a minor cut on his arm before his foe fell dead under his sword.

Eugenius insisted the leader surrender in between the exchange of blows, but he kept fighting fiercely and Eugenius fatally struck him in the chest with his sword. Wounded, he still refused to divulge Iohannes' exact location and only gasped, "He is somewhere in the woods."

On the other side, Argus sniffed the ground, zigzagging through the forest with the centuries-old enthusiasm of canine loyalty, maintaining a general direction that confirmed the monk's prior suspicions. When Argus ceased his forward motion and began to circle just in one small rocky area where recently cut branches were scattered, he began desperately pawing through the foliage but was unable to penetrate the planks below, which covered a cavern.

At the same time, Father Nicholaos glimpsed Alphaeus running away like a wild rabbit. Ignoring Alphaeus for now, he threw himself to the ground and began to scrape as well. He pushed the branches and soil aside, while calling for his pupil and the dog yelping for his master.

After they had lifted the planks, Father Nicholaos lowered his head inside but saw only darkness through his dilated eyes. A musty odor attacked his nostrils, he felt a rush of dank air upon his face, and he heard a faint voice struggling through a parched throat. Gradually, he made out the shape of a hand stretching out for help. He grasped the soiled hand with bloodstained fingertips and sure enough, it belonged to his pupil, weakened, and malnourished. He pulled him out and gently dragged him next to a tree where the lad sat and recouped his senses. Argus jumped on his lap and licked his master's face as he wagged his tail energetically.

"Are you all right?" Father Nicholaos inquired as he diligently made use of the rag to wipe the lad's face and the various scrapes and bruises found elsewhere.

"Father, I am fine," Iohannes stressed, breathing in the fresh afternoon breeze as his eyes squinted against daylight. Then he shifted himself into a more comfortable position. "I apologize for missing Thursday's lesson; there was an unexpected delay." He outlined a smile of irony in his revived spirits.

Contented and not surprised by his pupil's wit, the monk replied, "Remain here awhile, with the dog. I will notify your father." He quietly made his way toward the camp. From afar, he caught sight of Eugenius just entering the thicket of beech, darting toward him, clutching his bloody sword, and calling for Father Nicholaos. "Where is my son? Is he alive?" he yelled, his pulse still racing with the madness of the fight when they met.

"Back there, leaning against a tree; he is fine," the monk assured him.

"Thank God," blurted Eugenius, slightly bent and resting the left hand on one knee as his lungs refilled.

"What in the world happened back there? Are our men, okay?"

"Yes, but you may still be needed, hurry!" Eugenius pushed the words through his heavy breathing, slowly rose, and headed for his son.

The monk internalized his friend's desperation for a moment, then headed toward the camp.

"How's the wound?" inquired the monk when he arrived at the scene and saw the bowman applying a tourniquet on his comrade's arm.

"He's fine, strong as an ox," hammered back the bowman, inadvertently catching himself in a pun.

"And Iohannes?" demanded Ox, who never flinched over his wound.

"The dog found him. He is fine."

Father Nicholaos looked around and saw the dead lying frozen in the pose of their last moment, their faces petrified with eternal agony. Both lay in pools of fresh blood that had oozed out of the gut of one and the head of the other, whose ridiculous helmet was now pinned to his skull with the bowman's arrow.

Next to the dead also lay the buck-toothed boss, with scrapes, cuts, and gashes throughout his body, but the left lung had endured the serious wound and put him on the verge of shock. The blood oozing from his mouth impeded any normal breathing. The body trembled as if suffering from cold despite the hot afternoon. His sunken eyes within the pallid face sought desperately to hang on to the world that was vanishing into a fog.

Father Nicholaos noticed an earie stillness in the air. Nature's normal activity had mysteriously ceased. The occasional scurrying of a dormouse ceased to be, and the chirping of birds was heard no more. A pair of vultures flew in and watched hungrily as their presence attracted more of their kind to the area. The monk wondered if Nature herself was making her complaints, showing displeasure over the bloodshed. Later she would send in her envoys, more vultures, flies, and maggots, to clean up any trace of man's folly, he mused.

"What a mess man makes," said the bowman, reading Father Nicholaos' pensive face.

"Man has stolen Nature's prowess, in his birth, but rejected her gifts of humility and responsibility. You are right, my son, what a mess." Father Nicholaos knelt before the dying man, covered his deadly wound, and carefully propped up his head with his bundled belongings no longer serving for his escape. He then prayed for a spirit about to exit a body that no doubt had once slaughtered Christians with the blessing of his God.

"Aeeh! Sicilian! I knew you were the local monk," the moribund Berber gargled due to the blood in his throat.

"What can I do for you?" asked the monk, using the same Arabic dialect.

"Tell me, Christian, where have we erred?" The gargle grew stronger, and the words grew weaker.

"Clothed in a religious fervor, your vanity has overshadowed your sense of truth and goodness."

The Berber appeared momentarily to reflect on the Greek monk's words and then said, "I am sure you know the ritual obligations to the dead, *wajib*, to assist me in my death?" Then he slowly began to gargle his declaration of faith, *shahadah* but passed away after a few incomprehensible words.

The Father gently closed his eyelids. In the meantime, Ox's arm had stopped bleeding, and with no more medical emergencies to tend to, each sank into a quiet self-absorption, trying to understand the gravity of it all, questioning himself whether things could have been otherwise.

The lull broke when they spotted father and son emerging from the thickets with Argus at their heels; one was limping as the other offered support. When they arrived, Eugenius quietly looked around to update himself, and then sat his son next to the fire pit.

The two militiamen focused on Iohannes, and the bowman spoke first with a banality. "Genè, they are all dead."

"We have Iohannes, and he is fine. We did what we had to do," Eugenius replied then ordered, "Let's gather all the arms and anything of value." And turning to the monk, "What happened to Alphaeus?"

"I got a glimpse of him running away when I found Iohannes," said Father Nicholaos as he scanned Eugenius for signs of sympathy for the lad, which he did not receive. "He must have been overwhelmed with shame."

"Who cares about him? He will probably join another gang," grunted Eugenius, who noticed the monk's attention still focused on the dead.

"First, we must bury the Muslims. Remember to lay them on the right side and turn the heads toward *qiblah*," insisted Father Nicholaos, who knew something about the ritual of the Islamic burial.

"This is foolishness; they would not do this for us Christians. Let's leave them to the vultures that they are." Ox was resolute in his stance.

Eugenius sided with the monk, however, and encouraged the bowman to help in the burial, disregarding the reluctant Ox.

They made three shallow graves perpendicular to Mecca's direction. Afterward they stripped kidnappers of arms, placed the bodies in the ground on their right side, and covered them with rocks to prevent wild animals from scavenging the bodies. This display of respect for the dead seemed to relieve the uneasy feelings of the bloody day, at least for Father Nicholaos.

"The wild animals destroy and desecrate the graves. This is useless work," growled Ox.

Eugenius gave the order to gather all the arms and whatever of value including the family gold and jewelry, a part of which he later donated to the grotto in appreciation.

After a night's lodging at the shepherd shack, the exhausted rescuers showed up at the grotto just before noon the next day, on Sunday. With Iohannes in their midst, they entered proudly, and were greeted by the gawking children who jostled for a better look. The two ladies instinctively began to boil clean rags to clean the wounds. Helena tended to Ox's arm, first washing the gash, then sewing two sutures into the flesh, which did not faze Ox but horrified the garrulous children. Afterward, she carefully wrapped the arm for its protection.

A fair maiden has tended to my wounds, mused Ox, and thanked Helena, who had maintained her grace throughout. "Thank you very much."

Meanwhile, Flavia took her cues from Helena. She scooped each needed rag out of the cauldron with her ladle, strolled to Iohannes now seated, and gently washed the many scrapes and bruises. His limbs were inflamed and sore, but since he felt no serious pain, the young man's imagination drifted elsewhere as he fixed his eyes on those small feminine hands washing his wounds.

The din of the conversations grew louder and so did their hearts as they beat in unison, reaching their ears only. Iohannes felt warm now; the chilling exposure was being sucked away with Flavia's attention. The blonde hair gathered at the back by the skillful hands of Helena now debuted a woman. It changed colors from yellow to light brown depending on the flickering light from the fireplace. An ancient Latinity radiated from that hair.

The modesty between the newly enamored couple moved to the background. And, although it had released their voices, their hungry eyes and her delicate touch said all that was in their hearts. Having washed and wiped all that was needed, her distracted hands would wipe where no wounds were to be found, and at times they trembled a bit in her new delight.

Iohannes' imagination now wandered outside of the usual territory. It transgressed the limits of his younger days and stepped onto adult territory. His eyes fell on the décolletage of the once loose-fitting dress. Two melons, measured to her delicacy, now seemed to want to exit where once dangled two apples not quite ripe. They had grown to fit the dress teasing him, and the warmth he felt before now concentrated in his breeches.

What occurred afterward was natural, as dusk gave cover to the countryside with its enchanted secrets. In the din and bravado of the guests, they came to a silent understanding of intentions, and they slipped away into the dusky surroundings.

They found themselves alone, in the farmyard, behind the animal shack, looking at each other in wonder, touching and exploring a corporeal world. It was a new world for them, earthly and wonderful. All the while they were serenaded by a cosmic melody, an aria written just for them.

Chapter X: The Felling
Late Dec 1037

A common phenomenon in the theme of Apulia, where a constant resentment boiled in the Latin-speaking locals toward the Romanoi, were tax revolts, which led the empire to forced recruitment and confiscation of required supplies. In the Greek Calabrian province, this general friction toward the empire did not exist. Frequent abuses by the Romanoi officials, however, created a disgruntlement not easily set aside when the tax collector showed up on their premises for lodging. They often sought to enrich themselves in an unscrupulous fashion by seeking side gifts.

Fortunately, at the Florus farm, the official had brought only his wife one afternoon with just enough baggage for a single night. After he made, what appeared to be his insincere greetings to the apprehensive family, he unrolled that parchment containing figures and scribbles that only he seemed to understand. He began to transform them into sensible words audible throughout the house in the fashion of an emperor in the flesh, rarely glancing at his hosts.

The cruel list appeared to have no end for the family, who did not know what to say or do, and a lull permeated the residence after the reading for fear the unwanted guest would vocalize additions to the list. Maria made use of the time to prepare something to eat. Filling the guest's stomach should shorten that odious list, she hoped.

"This village is small; there aren't more than five or six lads available to muster for this expedition, nor is there enough grain and fodder to turn over," Eugenius protested.

"I have the names here: your son, Matthaeus' son, that Alphaeus at the grotto...." The official flashed back demands, never lifting his eyes from the list.

"Alphaeus has disappeared; he is dead or has become a brigand," said Eugenius as he offered the guest wine from a ceramic cup.

The official smirked. "His absence will cost Father Nicholaos twelve numismata." He gulped down the wine and slammed the empty cup before Eugenius.

Eugenius quickly refilled the cup, servant-like, an attentiveness he felt the petty man did not deserve. Others besides his family were involved, for the village paid the taxes as a unit, a community affair. He then turned the subject for a moment to relieve the growing tension. "Is there any news on the civil war in Panormos?" he asked. digging his eyes into the man.

"We do not know any more than you already know by way of mouth from the Christians in Messina or Rhegium. It is said that al-Akhal was strangled in his own palace and Abdullah, the Zirid, is in some way in charge."

"So, the reconciliation between the two factions was apparently a ruse," interjected Eugenius, wondering if he should have more wine as well to tame the scowl written on his own face.

"Yes, yes. All this makes the upcoming expedition more complicated, hence the extra tax levy." The official now mumbled from the wine.

Noticing a weakness in the man, "May I?" Eugenius said and reached for the parchment. "I would like to look over the special assessment due to the war."

The buzzing from the wine in the official's head took up the space where discretion lay, and he motioned his acceptance. Eugenius took the parchment and handed it to Iohannes, the only one in the family who could read. The levy was for the entire village of six families.

Iohannes read it slowly for all to absorb the full weight of the levy and was stopped when Eugenius repeated out loud the troublesome items. "Two pack animals and barley? We have no pack animals and enough feed only for our sheep and oxen. The flour is for our winters. And the money?" Eugenius had reached the pinnacle of his protest. "Each family barely earns ten numismata a year."

The official said nothing. Eugenius continued, "If we double the wood, can we halve the flour and feed?" The drunk accepted or seemed to accept, thought Eugenius.

Irrespective of the lighthearted spirit produced by the wine on their guest, uncomfortable feelings still lingered in the family. They felt they had endured some judicial hearing. After his departure, he still was a detestable man, they concluded, and the villagers felt the same when they learned of the meeting's details. A general meeting was scheduled at the Florus' farm to hammer out their predicament.

The town's folk arrived at the established date. More than two dozen anxious people showed up, whose discontent had peaked by the prior gossip whirled in the neighborhood. Even women with their small children showed up in the mix of the family heads and older sons. They swore and condemned all, Constantinople, the taxes, the Arabs, the upcoming fleet to be billeted, and even God.

"What tribulations has the Almighty brought upon us?" screamed one attendee.

Questions that did not allow time for a response were intermixed with the general curses, creating an uncontrollable situation for Eugenius and the monk. Some complained of Eugenius' legal status, for they felt he was exempt from some taxes, and that he had come into possession of his land from war booty or grants.

Father Nicholaos finally took control, waving his spiritual hands over the bedlam and imploring a toning down of the noise. "I have known Eugenius for a long time as all of you have. You know he pays his share and sometimes the share of one who cannot. As for his land, it was handed down to him before the Romanoi set foot on this land." Father Nicholaos eyed individuals as he talked. "He has taken arms against the Saracens, who devastate our crops and hunt down our children like wild game. If there is anyone here who does not owe him a favor of some sort, come forward."

Then he approached various individuals. "You, Metrios, when you carried your little one, suffering with malaria, to the Floruses, did not his mother tend to his healing?" He then walked over to another, "Stephanos, who paid your taxes last year?" and pausing for the audience to digest his words, "Our survival is owed to the Floruses; let him speak."

The assembled settled down and Eugenius once again stepped forward to answer questions that now streamed in an orderly manner and selected by the monk's intervening hand. "Why so much wood?"

"To substitute for some of the grain and fodder."

"How come so much money taxes?"

"The expedition is mostly professional soldiers, the tagmata, and they have to be paid."

One wife who had two young daughters wanted to know where the troops would be quartered. "In Skylletion" came the answer. She gave a huge sigh of relief.

Another, while sobbing and wiping her tears, expressed her desire to withhold her son from the muster but had not the money to pay for an exemption.

Another yelled. "At least we can substitute wood for grain?"

"I believe so."

Even the monk had a question. "Where do we get these pack animals?"

"Our friend Georgios Kamateros, the officer who is to accompany the catepan on the expedition. As you know, he has a large holding exempt from taxes, and since we were in war together, I am sure he will help us," Eugenius answered proudly. "Two animals from him are not much to give up."

Eugenius now addressed the issue of the wood and began to explain the need to fell the trees before the onslaught of full winter. He immediately formed a felling party from the family heads and their older sons to extract the logs from the high ground not far from the shepherd's shack.

"Individual supplies and necessities are your own responsibility and should last at least a week," Eugenius stated. "My son and I will bring the wagon and oxen for hauling the logs back to my farm for storage. We will supply the tackle, rope, axes, and other tools."

All agreed to leave as soon as possible the next morning and meet at the shack.

The wagon arrived after the other villagers, who had already felled one tree. The serious work began at first light the next day, organized meticulously by Eugenius, who divided the men into four crews, each with its own task. Two crews would be assigned to the time-consuming felling of the trees and their debranching, working at a prudent distance from each other. A third crew would drag the logs out of the thickets with the oxen and the last crew would hoist them on the wagon using rope and pulley.

Mishaps and accidents occurred frequently. The rudimentary equipment was no match for the woodland, which was thick with both trees and bushes that hindered movement. The falling trees at times would jam or entangle themselves with the nearby trees, creating a very precarious situation to free them.

When a tree fell, so did the felling crew. They dropped to the ground in exhaustion as the de-branching crew took over. Only the crews utilizing the oxen worked continuously, since the oxen did the work. The crews produced four or five logs a day before dusk arrived, when they made their way to the camp where food and wine were waiting to help them forget their aches and sores.

The morning, in which they were to return the first load, arrived too quickly, even for Eugenius, who was always the first to greet the dawn. As was his normal regimen, he threw open the rickety door that allowed the invasive rays to enter and irritate the eyes that dared to open. "Get up, up; a beautiful day awaits you," he said mocking their reluctance to another day of work.

The slumbering limbs of the lads stirred under the authoritative weight of the former knight. As soldiers being given orders, however, each readied himself for the day's respective task. Iohannes and Peter shoved down a piece of cheese and stale bread, then fetched the oxen and headed for the field, the rest following silently behind.

When they arrived at the site the two lads had already hitched the oxen to the wagon. The oxen pulled, but the wheels kept sinking into the soft earth under the enormous weight. Just before the wagon reached the solid bed of the road edge, the front axle began scraping the ground. The load was excessive, and the wagon was weak and old. "I hope this isn't the first of things to come," Eugenius grunted. "Maybe we should have lightened the load."

The men pried the front wheels with levers as the lads pushed from behind and the animals were whipped. The front axle and wheels were now on the road. "Sir, we've made it!" came an enthusiastic shout from within the crew.

"Yes, I see," shot back Eugenius, bringing his eyebrows together in serious thought, "but we are still not completely on the road." They all pushed even harder and all four wheels began their creaking rhythm as they rolled along the more compacted road picking up their pace downhill and slowing down on the ascents.

They stopped at the grotto for a short rest and to drop off the monk and Peter just as a gentle wind approached. There, Iohannes unhitched the tired oxen and slowly led them to the water trough while anxiously glancing about for the object of his desire. He contemplated an accidental and spontaneous encounter in the manner of a novice suitor when suddenly at his back he heard a "Boo!" He turned around and was confronted by the figure of Flavia.

"When are you coming back?" asked Flavia.

"I believe tomorrow; there will be more log trips." He said trying to ignore her dress, fluttering suggestively in the wind.

"Kiss me," she said. Her round blue eyes flirted with his. He had never seen her like this. Her lips were soft and moist, an inviting suppleness that permeated through the rest of her body. She took his hand. "Follow me." She led him in the same place as before, behind the stalls and away from the open area, but then they heard a shout coming from the yard.

"Iohan! We are already eating." It was his father.

After lunch, they found themselves alone again and Flavia asked, "Are you really going to war in Sicily? Why?" A mumbled "Yes" reached her ears. Flavia's heart jumped. She had seen him saved from the jaws of death. Was that pain not enough? she asked herself and ran to a mother's understanding, Helena.

Iohannes yoked the oxen, and they re-entered the road, which now waited with new and devastating surprises while Father Nicholaos and Peter stayed behind to be picked up for the second trip.

With the bending and twisting, rising and descending, the road appeared not knowing where to go or what to do. Worse yet, its bed, once level when originally cut from the mountain, often sloped dangerously toward a precipice. Countless mountain rains had worn its outside edge. Often, the road turned completely in the opposite direction just where a cliff lay waiting. The wagon staggered with the rugged road like a drunk, and when it approached a precipice, they had to set up block and tackle to a nearby tree to stabilize the load.

In these tense moments, the knight volleyed his commands in true military fashion. He worried most of all, as did the others, not necessarily for the loss of the wood, but rather the loss of the oxen, which were badly, needed for the cultivation and harvest. Even man was expendable to the oxen.

But there were moments of calm when the road was civilized, and father and son would walk together up front where Iohannes guided the animals. "Your mother wants nothing to do with this military thing. I don't know what to say to her," commented Eugenius.

"Neither do I, but I am ready; you trained me," insisted Iohannes, excited by the thought of glory.

"And I, like your mother, want you to come back safe and sound." Eugenius noticed a sparkle of youthful indiscretion in his son's eyes.

"Papa, will I own land, have rank in the chorion, upon my return?"

"Yes. This is true. However, I was reckless in my youth, often saved by luck. Don't go in the same way, dependent only on luck."

Iohannes prodded the oxen to the center of the road, then gave his father a puzzled look.

"As a well-trained and well-armored cavalryman your chances improve. But most of all you must be focused." The wagon jarred a bit. Eugenius did not notice.

"This Maniakes, is he as great as they say?" Iohannes had a youthful fascination of the hero's deeds whetted by the rumors.

"He is supreme commander *autokrator*, his men have complete faith in him. The first phase of the expedition at Messina should be easy." Eugenius raised his voice to override the screeching of the wheels. "They say Messina is mostly Christian, and the Arabic control is at a minimum."

Eugenius relived his youth in his son. He had been daring, adventurous, but prudence came late for him. I will find a way to instill it in Iohannes before he leaves, he decided.

Distracted in his thoughts, he failed to see another temper tantrum of the road.

At the base of the road's descent, the outside ox began to struggle. Its hoofs sank deep into the mud formed by a small underground spring oozing from the outside edge of the road. The ox managed to move on, but when the wagon's rear wheel arrived, it suffered the same fate, and the load leaned perilously toward the cliff below. The oxen ceased to move the load regardless of Iohannes' prodding or the crew tugging on the wagon rails in the direction away from the cliff's edge; nothing worked. The awful creaking continued with the leaning, and the ground sucked in more of the wheel. It slid as well inch by inch toward the cliff. "What luck! What damn luck!" Michael cursed.

Meanwhile, Matthaeus, who was walking along the edge of the cliff, slipped and fell on the narrow disintegrating ledge, under the threat of the tilting cart. Tiny furrows leading to the cliff edge showed where his bleeding fingernails had clawed the ground to stop his slide. Before being devoured by the abyss below, his feet found a protruding slate-like rock on which to plant themselves, and with his hands he latched on to a scrub sufficiently rooted for support. But the friendly rock was fragile and suddenly abandoned him, tumbling noisily below, leaving the scrub as the only life support.

Shouts came from everywhere.

"What's going on?"

"Grab his arm!"

The shouts drowned out the feeble cries for help. A crew member extended his hand in an attempted rescue, but the dangling victim was too fearful to let go of the precious branch and made no attempt to reach the helping hand. His grip was weakening, and the wagon was right behind him.

Horrible choices pummeled Eugenius. He thought of detaching the steering hitch from the yoke and save the valuable oxen that were bread and butter for the community, but the man, the man was his friend. A cold calculation demanded only this alternative, for if he tried to secure the load to a nearby tree and failed, they would lose all, including the man. With a troubled heart he began to unhitch the oxen in order to save them.

"Help me, help me," the cries repeated with a pitch that shattered his heart into fine glass.

"Tie the load to that tree, now! It's leaning even more!" Michael screamed.

"Mattè! Hang on!" Eugenius now jumped into the moment, assailed by second thoughts now coming from the heart. To hell with the oxen, he is my friend, he reminded himself.

Dropping what he was doing, he grabbed the extra rope in the wagon, and with the time miraculously granted them, he tied one end to the wagon frame and wrapped the other end around a nearby tree. The load stopped its creaking and backward movement long enough to rescue Matthaeus.

They formed a human chain, one holding the hand of the other. The first leaned over the cliff's edge, seized the helpless man's belt, and all pulled until all of Matthaeus' limbs touched solid ground again. Terrified, Matthaeus crawled away from the edge, lurid and riddled with bloody scrapes and hands frozen in their grasping state.

"Are you well?" asked Theodorus, who added more words to the few he had spoken up to now.

"Yes, yes, I am fine; I think?" rasped Matthaeus, slowly coming to life with the help of his son, who offered him water.

The crew stepped back, regrouped, and stared at their predicament with a hopeless stupor. Then, suddenly struck by the same fear of losing the animals as well, they unhitched the oxen from the tilting wagon.

"Now what?" one demanded.

"Let the wagon go," another added. "Hell, with the tax collector. We have our oxen," he insisted.

Michael, however, suggested a more optimistic approach. "Let's save the load with block and tackle on the tree and with one ox at the other end of the pulley."

They now heard, anew, the creaks and sounds of snapping wood. Eugenius' prior hasty rigging was not holding. The logs were shifting, and the wagon sides were no longer sitting square with its frame. The irritating sounds now came from all over its structure.

They quickly fastened the first block and tackle to the same tree, hitched one ox to the rope, then connected the other end to the load, and had the animal pull. Slowly, the rickety wagon and its load acquired its prior square form, one creak at a time.

Now they set up the second pulley, identical to the first but situated up ahead, on the rise of the road. Iohannes immediately hitched the second ox to the pulley's rope as in the first team. The object was for the forward team to pull the wagon out of the rut while the rear team kept the tension on the rope, maintaining the stability of the load.

Eugenius coordinated all the movements, and the familiar creaking accompanied by the pushers' grunts in the rear began anew. The wagon moved forward a bit but also leaned over if the rear team released the rope too quickly.

"Myrtilus, slacken the rope. Iohannes, pull. The others, push." The commands seemed contradictory, but every slight move required a concentrated calculation. When the creaking and orders stopped, the teams found themselves on the road's rise, the load intact and all safe.

The group arrived at the turnoff for the Florus farm under a carbon-black darkness. A silent exhaustion now reined tyrannically throughout the crew as they crossed the little bridge except for the talkative Georgios, who not only asked the questions, but also at times had to answer them himself. The others, eager to put something in their stomachs within the vicinity of a warm fire, only returned grunts.

The darkness hid the origins of these grunts, and the crew simply followed the screeching noises of the wagon pulled by the tired animals, who headed to the barn on their own. They passed the house first; then at the barn they unloaded the wagon, stacking the logs under a makeshift overhang adjacent to the barn. The animals, they led to their stalls for feeding and shelter. Above the stalls was the loft storing the fodder and various farm equipment, which would also function as lodging for the crew.

As soon as they were done, Saverina arrived, Argus at her side, wagging his tail as he sniffed around looking for Iohannes. She shivered under a hempen shawl, which she held tightly around her shoulders, and greeted them pleasantly and announced dinner. The villagers in turn gave their greetings as she threw an inquisitive stare at her father and brother, wondering when all would come in.

"Go, go, we will be there in a minute," said Eugenius, closing the barn door as the crew waited for some signal from him to head for the house.

Chapter XI: The Old Woman

The crew filed in, almost in single file, and each greeted Maria with a warm welcome who responded with dignified smiles. When Eugenius approached his wife, however, he sensed an unusual stiffness about her; something was on her mind. Maria avoided any eye contact with him, she focused only on the guests, and when they found themselves in the same conversation with the guests, she would turn her shoulders away from him. Even his daughter, still wearing that shoulder cape, seemed to do likewise. The women have been talking during our absence, he thought, issues that waited for our return.

Iohannes also sensed the tension in the family and tried, during the hectic, merrymaking gossip after dinner, to pull his sister out of her ill mood. He teased her as he often did as the little annoying brother. Jokingly he whispered in her ear, "Some of the men wish for you to take off that shawl; they are betting on the abundance underneath." His satisfaction in himself was struck with sheer disgust and he stuttered as he tried to make amends. "It isn't true; it is just a joke," he sputtered.

"You are a pig, just like the other dirty old men, damn you!" she screamed and scurried to a closet-like room off the kitchen, which she shared with the grandmother as their bedroom. Iohannes, perplexed, followed her, wanting to remind her of all the pranks and quips displayed at the cultivation in which she enjoyed them all and even instigated many herself.

Meanwhile, in the crowded kitchen, the boisterous conversations echoed throughout the house, even infiltrated to the bedroom.

"My dear host," Georgios was saying to Maria, "it seems some family member is missing." He was referring to Laetitia, who was known in the village as a witch, but the guest in him refrained from using the pejorative word. Eugenius, however, sensed the usual, hidden mockery in the man and gave him a look of disapproval.

"Who do you mean?" Maria asked. She had become less sullen and feistier in the conversations.

"I mean Eugenius' mother, the old seer," he said, avoiding the witch reference again when belted with disapproving faces. "I had a dream I need help interpreting."

Eugenius played along, "My mother hasn't felt well these days. She spends more time in her room. What kind of dream is it?"

"I dreamt of serpents shedding their skins, but their new skin was of another color. They were everywhere. They invaded the whole countryside." Suddenly the air was filled with bits of snickering bursting toward Georgios.

"Really now, Georgios?" said Eugenius, wondering if the family should be offended.

Laetitia, listening behind her door, took Georgios to be sincere. She loved to interpret dreams, a passion and talent she possessed and turning to her nephew, whispered slowly every syllable of her assessment with a strange certainty. Then sent him to the kitchen to relate her message.

"My grandmother apologizes for her absence, and said that new masters will arrive, but nothing will change."

The guests began mumbling and bickering with each other over its meaning.

"That is a strange thing to say," said Michael. "Maybe the Saracens will be back." The suppositions flew about the room in an ever-increasing loudness.

Iohannes returned to Saverina, who was still in a somber mood.

"I did not know you would take my joke badly," he said, hoping for an explanation.

"Forget it. It's not you; it's Alphaeus," Saverina exclaimed, drawing sympathy.

"Why this attitude? Your brother was the unfortunate one who was kidnapped. He lived in a tomb as if dead, for a week. Come on now! Your problem is not so bad," pleaded her grandmother, whose second passion was the family.

"I feel at fault. You were right, Alphaeus is bad. What do I do now? I will be a spinster forever, withering with time and not wanted."

Iohannes mused on his big sister's sniveling. She strayed little outside of herself, but her fears almost made the grandmother cry, and after a wordless moment, he reminded her of the furtive ogles she received at the cultivation from the other lads.

"Peter and Myrtillus like you. They are the most promising and sincere youths in the village." He extracted a subtle smile. "They would die at the chance to see the abundance underneath your shawl."

"You are teasing me." She forced a giggle against the stubbornness of her heart. It refused to let Alphaeus go regardless of the kidnapping that had cemented in her mind his incorrigibility. She glanced at her grandmother, for support, who outlined a compassionate smile that seemed to say, "Time heals all."

One after the other, the guests finally left for the barn loft to pass the night. Saverina and Iohannes retired to their respective rooms. But Laetitia was feeling better with the rowdy villagers gone. She strolled to the kitchen guided by a curiosity to gather the morsels of the night's discussions left behind by the neighbors, her curiosity still lively in her old age.

There she surprised Eugenius and Maria, who were in an awkward silence; neither could find words to speak. Laetitia broke the silence first. "I have also had similar dreams," she said, sitting down before them. "In my dream, I saw the powerful kastron of Skylletion squirting blood from within as its walls crumbled. Foxes and weasels came to establish their lairs in the ruins."

"Oh, my dear Apollinè, you saw him bleeding?" Maria wailed as her heart jumped to her throat.

"No, no, not Iohannes. He will be fine. I mean the empire will bleed profusely, my dear."

Eugenius intervened, "Mother, this is foolishness, old wives' tales. It has Maria upset and frightened."

"My presentiments are not about Iohannes; they concern the powers to be. The empire is bleeding from the inside and soon these lands will be taken over by others." Laetitia now regretted that she shared her passion with her daughter-in-law. "I do not wish to put fear into Maria."

To Maria, Laetitia's dream meant war, and war would take her son away. Laetitia's words fluttered in Maria's head, and she unveiled a distant stare. She was superstitious as many were in her world. The fiendish dark powers, the mysterious, the good, all incomprehensible to her, were everywhere and hiding under the layer of daily life that few could penetrate. Laetitia was one of the few who unfolded the secrets of the future for others like her.

Eugenius, on the other hand, did not believe in such sorcery-like interpretations, especially ones so pessimistic. He saw the empire regaining its strength. Bulgaria was conquered; Maniakes had taken Edessa and now was moving toward Sicily. His mother's dream meant little to him for he had survived on wit and practicality.

"Let's go to bed; I am tired," he croaked, and remained behind as the two women went first. Maria headed to the other cubbyhole-like bedroom and slipped into bed but could not fall asleep.

Eugenius paced up and down near the fireplace, contemplating the family situation. He accepted life for what it was; it did not change for one's wishes. If his son did not go on this expedition, sooner or later they would take him on one riskier, he reasoned. There are dangerous expeditions and there are well-planned ones with capable leaders; this one is the latter, he told himself. And the question of his daughter was one of obstinacy and female sentiments that escape male understanding but should resolve with time.

He walked slowly to their bedroom, yawning along the way, where an unpleasant discourse awaited, which started immediately with pleadings and relentless questions.

"Even your mother has doubts; why don't you pay to nullify his conscription?" She scorned as if he were at fault for her torment.

"We don't have the money. The tax levy is too much, and it may not be in his best interest," he replied pushing his irritation and fatigue aside.

"You don't know how much I suffered when you left, soon after we were married. I can't go through it again," cried Maria, with the anger she had withheld in the company of the villagers. Her world was the family, Saverina, Apollinus, mother-in-law, and the farm, and it was collapsing before her eyes. She generally had confidence in her husband, but this involved her precious child. It was more than she could bear.

"If he does not go now, they will snatch him for a worse war." Eugenius crawled into bed.

"Let's hide him." Her unsettled nerves compromised her judgment.

"And make him the coward of the county? Maria! It is his life to choose. Is it not?" Press gangs trampling on his farm searching for his son flashed through his mind.

"These Saracens will slit his throat like a pig."

"My mother has made no such predictions; they seem rather favorable," he stoutly emphasized, using his mother to win his wife over. "You shall see, everything will be all right. His commander will be Kamateros, a man of good character."

Maria did not respond. Doubts and frustration lurked in her mind, and they couldn't find a voice.

Eugenius wrapped a comforting arm around Maria's waist, and exhausted, he soon fell into a sound sleep. Maria, however, was awake most of the night. She recalled the period of her husband's absence in the war when she counted every long day, without end; the succeeding day was longer than its former. In the little sleep she had, she was troubled by an absurd dream where she cried hysterically.

She usually woke up in darkness to begin her chores, but this morning the autumn daylight was already streaming into her room. Her husband was not by her side; he had since departed with the crew to fetch the second load. It is all for the better, she surmised, for she was anxious to consult with her mother-in-law before confronting him again. Since the mysterious dream would not let her go, she dressed quickly and ran into the kitchen.

She saw her daughter, who had put aside the usual sunken mood and showed a new spirit as she washed the tableware diligently in a little basin. The mother-in-law was hanging the pots and pans from a grating suspended from the rafters of the ceiling next to the fireplace. Her bony hands twitched with old age but with time and concentration, however, they found the hook that held the washed kitchen ware. Breakfast *ariston* was over and the wood crew had since gone.

On the table lay a leftover section of salted pork, which Maria did not eat. She was observing the Christmas fasting started in mid-November. Nevertheless, she washed down a piece of barley bread with a cup of goat's milk.

Then, contented to see her daughter in better spirits, she approached her and delicately regathered her smooth reddish hair into the original chignon, which had fallen apart in the vigorous washing. Afterwards, she helped dry the tableware, made of rudimentary terra cotta, which she placed on racks fastened to the wall, one shelf below the finer ceramic tableware, sgrafitto.

The everyday activities improved her mood and now she sensed the tender eyes of Mother Laetitia at her back, eyes that always sparkled with the family's interests. Maria felt obliged to speak and began the discourse with a banality. "When did the men leave?"

"A while ago, but you slept too much, my dear," Laetitia replied as she hung another pot.

Maria watched her mother-in-law and said, "What do you have to say about Iohannes leaving?"

"Why not? He is of age." The old woman noticed her daughter-in-law put on a grim stare. "Look, last night; I dreamt Iohannes was eating an eel." Maria's face now showed an intense curiosity. Saverina also listened closely.

"Tell me it is good news," returned Maria.

"Your precious son will come to a certain wealth."

"What form of wealth?"

"I don't know," said Laetitia.

Maria now jumped on her chores with renewed energy.

No sooner had the crew stored away the remaining log loads for the winter than the Christmas holidays were upon them. They introduced a type of winter isolation that would last all the way to the Feast of the Annunciation in late March. The villagers rarely made guest visits in the winter except for specific holy days or some unforeseen emergencies, which did not occur this winter. This idle period dragged on more than usual for Eugenius, who wanted to put the matter of the tax levy at his back. There would be too much to do, the procurement of the pack animals and the warhorse for Iohannes, the training and preparations of the recruits, and of course the upcoming cultivation in the spring.

Finally, the proper time arrived, just prior to April. He gathered the villagers at his home to assemble all items owed to the state which required wagon trips for delivery to the garrison at Skylletion.

When they reached the garrison and the final tally was registered, the assistant tax collector, whose memory of the verbal agreement was conveniently lacking, became extremely dissatisfied with the missing fine flour, wine, and pack animals. He threatened to dispatch a small contingent to confiscate the rest whereupon, they voiced their intention of seeking assistance from Captain Georgios Kamateros, and the tax agent became sensible.

Next, Eugenius and Father Nicholaos readied to make a trip to see Kamateros, for they were close friends with the captain. They arrived there at noon, found him in the field instructing the tenant farmers of their duties during his upcoming military absence. He had become white-haired and plump since the war days with Eugenius, but his voice still betrayed him, especially to a comrade such as Eugenius, now in the flesh.

The old comrade listened patiently to their request. He offered to sell a mule and donated a horse for Iohannes, whom he would take under his protection for he felt it was an honor to receive a new knight in the theme.

Furthermore, on the issues of the fodder and the wood, he decided to write to 'this annoying little man', as he phrased it, that he as captain in the theme will consider the village offer adequate for the state.

The two solicitors exchanged gestures of approval and satisfaction at what unbelievably had just reached their ears.

Chapter XII: The Muster

It was somewhere at the end of May or the beginning of June 1038—history is vague—when at dawn three ships broke off from Michael Spondyles' main fleet as it approached the Gulf of Skylletion. One was a commandeered sailing ship used for supplies, another was a dromon for the ordinary infantry, and the last was a modified dromon equipped with larger hull and sturdier structure to handle the cavalry's horses. Their squadron commander *dougarokomes*, Alexios Kamos, led the squadron toward the promontory and its nearby river, a suitable location for the horse transport to beach, which beached on the south side of the river with the starboard aft resting on shore.

The other two ships anchored offshore, and their crews were kept on board for fear of desertion on the part of the Apulian marines. Apart from the horse transport, which required a tedious beaching procedure of many men, Kamos' landing team was comprised of the other ship captains and the required oarsmen for the two rowed tenders called *sandalia*.

Originally, from Opsikion and assigned to the Thematic force at Bari, Kamos boasted his role in an unrivaled navy of the Mediterranean world which he displayed obsessively in action and in dress. An ambitious man, his main interests lay in pleasing his superiors which often were primary to the welfare of his men. He was an intractable man with little cohesion in his ranks.

Outside of war zones, his officers dressed just in their quilted full-length coats with their swords hung from their sides. He, however, donned his lamellar cuirass over his coat with its countless metal plates, which sparkled in unison with his shiny helmet. He stood on the fore of the lead tender as the men rowed in shore and looking taller than normal, he fancied himself a fleet commander, a rank he coveted dearly.

After the two tenders landed, Kamos waited for the horses to be led out of the transport's hull for their exercises and grazing. He took possession of one for himself while the rest of the contingent would walk at his rear on the trek up the hill to the Skylletion garrison. Before leaving, he gave orders to the remaining men to pitch tent and prepare for the upcoming loading of supplies while keeping guard for any Apulian oarsmen attempting to escape from the ships.

Along the way, the local farmers and shepherds marveled at the small Romanoi contingent with its well-polished leader on the semi-armored horse. Although their arrival was expected, they were accustomed to receiving larger, more numerous troops to lodge at their expense and some wondered if the illustrious soldier on horseback might be the great General Maniakes himself, foreboding a larger unit.

When the contingent entered the town, the local leader of the garrison, Commander Ouramos, received them in his headquarters where the local tax representative anxiously waited to update Kamos on the supplies and recruits. The eager tax collector hoped to impress his superior, and suggested they dine at the local tavern to conduct business.

"I hope your trip was without difficulties," the tax official said, submissively, as they passed through the threshold of the tavern with the lower rank men behind them.

"Let's get down to business; I can only stay one night here. I expect you have done your part in every detail," Kamos impatiently demanded of the tax official.

"Of course! Of course!" replied the official, repeatedly bowing his head as they sat at the elongated table.

Unrolling the parchment, the man tried to jump into his supply list, but Commander Kamos turned to Commander Ouramos. "How many men can you spare for the expedition?"

"I have roughly forty veteran lance throwers, twenty bowmen, and two horsemen. In the countryside there are about twenty untrained lancers, plus one new horseman from the Florus farm," confidently replied Ouramos, who was his equal in rank.

Finally, Commander Kamos asked a reading of the compiled list of supplies from the tax collector, who had been fiddling anxiously for the opportunity. He read them nervously and Kamos gave him his orders. "Tomorrow, take two horses from the fort stables and one of my men and notify the area recruits to assemble at the beach, fully armed. On the next day, I will be there to supervise the affair."

"What if they don't show up?" asked the tax collector, fearful he would be held responsible.

"My men will form a press gang to hunt them down," Kamos snapped, without reservation then winked at Ouramos for support.

"No need for that. They are Greeks like us and willing volunteers. The Latin Lombards are the difficult ones," protested Commander Ouramos. Kamos now winced at Ouramos.

"The fleet you came with, is it not led by Maniakes?" Ouramos asked straightening himself in his seat in defense.

"No, it is led by the new catepan of Longobardia, a certain Patrikios Spondyles, also Duke of Anatolia. We are to meet up with him in Rhegium after he picks up additional supplies on his way." Kamos slouched back a bit.

"And General Maniakes?"

Kamos Kamos turned his eyes around the place. "Maniakes is picking up more men and supplies in Bari. He too will end up in Rhegium with his professional army, *tagma*."

The next day, when the Florus farm learned of the muster location and date from the tax collector, Iohannes quickly bridled the horse and headed out to the grotto to get Peter. He found the two women engrossed in their chores and the Father reading with little Iulia at his side.

"The ships are here; where's Peter? They want us at the beach tomorrow," Iohannes yelled as he gazed at Flavia while addressing the monk. She returned a glance that was interrupted by Father Nicholaos' reply.

"Is it really Maniakes? A passing shepherd said he saw him riding on an armored horse."

"No, the tax man said it was just a ship commander and Maniakes is still in Bari." Iohannes' eyes darted between the Father Nicholaos and Flavia.

The monk read into his pupil's eyes the longing for privacy with Flavia. "I will get Peter from the field." Then gently nudged Iulia toward Helena, who welcomed the child with a small task in which to occupy herself.

Flavia and Iohannes' followed the monk outside; the monk went one way, and they, hand in hand, slowly made their way to that spot of privacy, once sweet but now turned insipid by the war. However, time had made our young couple more mature and ready for life's disappointments.

"This is it; this is our good-bye," Flavia said softly, accepting his inevitable departure. The tears escaped against her will and flowed majestically down her cheeks as her heart encountered another of life's tests. She shivered silently in the new clothing of a woman waiting for comforting words from her man.

He tugged on her hand until their bodies met. "You needn't worry. I will be back."

"I am afraid like when you were captured by the bandits." She pressed herself against his sturdy frame.

He felt her pain. "I came back, didn't I?" he said and wrapped his arms tightly around her waist as if to ease that pain.

"But this is different. Even Father Nicholaos cannot hide his doubts," she protested, resting her head on his chest. "And Mother Helena, she says women touch the raw realities of life more directly and completely. We hurt more."

"What else has she said?" Mother Helena must have ended with the usual comforting words, he reckoned.

"She said we will endure with prayers, our daily chores, and the spiritual guidance from Father Nicholaos." Flavia raised her head to catch his eyes. "What about you, away from family and me?"

"I'll miss everyone, you most of all. But my duties in the war will eat the time away for me." He said while she laid her head back on his chest anticipating a mundane life that offered few distractions from his absence.

He thought for a moment, squeezed Flavia tighter, then gently lifted her chin back and gazed into her sobbing eyes. "I have something for you." The other hand reached into his pocket for the spinel stone. "Keep this; it is yours. I swear on this stone, blessed by Father Nicholaos, that I will come back for you."

Flavia locked it in one hand and together, hand in hand, they strolled silently into the grotto where Peter and the monk were now waiting patiently.

"Let's get Peter ready," said Father Nicholaos as he gathered Peter's armor.

Peter put on his homemade quilted coat and turban-like helmet for head protection. Since he was missing a sword, a lance, and a shield, the monk promised to buy them from the garrison depot at Skylletion the next day just before muster.

The two lads, both on horseback, departed for the Florus farm in a boyish false bravado that clashed with the grotto's general melancholy. They would spend the night there while the monk would catch up the next day.

Under the general apprehension over their future, the lads lapsed quietly into themselves but Peter, sitting behind Iohannes on the horse's rump, finally broke the silence. "Is Saverina over Alphaeus?"

"Of course. She doesn't mope around the house anymore. Anyway, he is a scoundrel and a marauder."

"But do you think she can like me?"

"My grandmother says you are handsome."

"The witch?" blurted Peter.

Iohannes shrugged. "She is not a witch; she simply has a gift."

When they entered the Florus dwelling, they encountered a household of mixed feelings. After Eugenius had carefully gathered the military equipment for their muster, he anxiously waited to offer his advice on their use. Nervous, Maria tried hard not to fret about her Apollinus, and her mother-in-law, now calm, had long ago accepted the situation. Saverina was stuck somewhere between sulking and being just indifferent.

Peter was struck by her lack of spontaneity and that flirtatious smile, contrary to how he had remembered her from prior encounters. Occasionally straying in her direction for answers, his eyes questioned his chances with her, that would shine a mitigating light on the anxiety wrapped around his recruitment in the war.

"By Jove! This makeshift padding alone won't work." Eugenius laid the recovered armor from the bandits on the table: a sleeveless mail shirt, a mail coif, and the helmet with the arrow hole.

This fussing over Peter's incomplete military attire, stole his gaze away from Saverina to the shirt of mail which he slipped over his head. Then Eugenius covered Peter's turban-like skull cap with the coif of mail, which tangled down his nape and chin with its countless intertwined little rings. "Walk around; let's get a better look." Eugenius boasted over his handiwork, hoping to dazzle his daughter with a viable substitute for Alphaeus.

Saverina lifted her eyes toward the young man for the first time since he had entered. She had tried to shed her sulkiness and be polite, and now she began to regret having not succeeded. Alphaeus was wild, unpredictable, and exciting, and this excitement she glimpsed in Peter with every article of war he put on. Plain Peter did not seem ordinary now, she mused. There was something intriguing in the square jaws protruding from his hood of mail. His brown, round eyes were inviting her to a safer adventure than the mischievous one with Alphaeus.

Her interest in him grew more intense when her father fastened over the youth's shoulder the scabbard strap for the sword that hung at his side. And then the leather greaves that wrapped around his shins, coupled with the teardrop shield, hinted that even Peter could be a hero in her life.

Peter now felt free to glance at Saverina and capture her half-coquettish gaze and he sensed that his feelings toward her may be reciprocated.

"I have a sling and helmet for you, but Father Nicholaos must procure the lance tomorrow at Skylletion," Eugenius said, showing satisfaction for his accomplishment.

In the cool and motionless air of the next morning, just outside the farmhouse, began the frantic and final preparation for the youths' military debut. A pensive air overshadowed the family as Eugenius fitted each piece of protective clothing and gear onto the novice militiamen, one a head taller than the other. "Peter, remember the triangular shield and the bowl helmet taken from the Berber bandit?" Eugenius held them up before Peter.

"Of course," acknowledged Peter as Eugenius helped him slip his arm through the rear loops of the shield.

"Your shield, keep it always between your body and the enemy," Eugenius whispered, fearful of stimulating apprehension in the women onlookers.

Iohannes had a round shield typical of the cavalry and a pointed oval Romanos helmet and was left pretty much to himself but still paid attention to his father's experienced advice. "The sword stays firmly in your scabbard; use it if you should lose your lance or are ordered to do so in some special formation." Each item donned became an extension of the man and required some helpful advice from Eugenius as to its use.

Maria stood in the doorway of the house, indecisive on whether to completely cross the threshold or turn back inside. Her anxiety over her dear Apollinus' departure was once again creeping in her heart regardless of her mother-in-law's previous reassurances. I will not participate in war's bogus garb, she decided, the flickering mail, the shiny helmet, and the bravado that follows. These are not the true realities of war. She whispered to herself.

"Mama, don't they look glorious?" Saverina, who was caught in the moment snapped her mother's thoughts to the spectacle she was trying to avoid.

"There is nothing glorious about war." She grimaced and was taken by that same desire to withdraw into the house, but the need for a final farewell, no matter how unbearable, won over.

Eugenius' attention was glued on the youths. He knew the armor was only one facet of their survival; the other was their emotional state in the chaos of battle. The medley of swords clashing, the cries of agony, the grunts and the bloody mangled bodies everywhere can make one freeze in place. "Keep calm; remain focused on your task at hand, at all times. Cast your indecisiveness to the devil. Don't hesitate; keep moving." He hammered his consoling on the novice soldiers.

Then Eugenius went to the stable to fetch the steed and mule as the monk made his way to the farm emerging from the bend in the road near the olive grove from where the group could be seen waiting anxiously.

"Father Nicholaos is here," cried Maria to Eugenius, who now was bridling the horse before the others. The monk had traveled in the darkness of early morning, as he often did to fulfil his spiritual obligations, and arrived at their doorstep just in time. Maria sighed with relief.

"By Jove! I see the lads are all prepared, except Peter's spear. God bless you. We can stop at the garrison for one," observed the monk, directing his comment at the lads with a cheerful grin.

"Almost ready," said Eugenius, loading the mule.

"The prayer and blessing?" Maria cried, desperately.

Father Nicholaos gave the prayer to the two about to do battle as he had done many times before. He began, "Oh Lord our God," and in the middle of the prayer, while referencing David and Goliath, his words magically invoked the still air to a subtle motion that caressed the pudgy leaves of the nearby olive trees.

Maria was convinced the Spirit had followed him, and when the Father Nicholaos made his final amen, the pleasant breeze mysteriously dissipated like a soft dream in daylight.

Her faith was strengthened, and it calmed her heart. In the final good-byes, she embraced her son so firmly that his mail coat left chain-like imprints on her arms and it took a gentle and patient prying by her husband to free Iohannes. Then she ran inside, too embarrassed to show her sobbing.

The road from Saint Elias to Skylletion together with the river Alessi function as the southern boundary of an elevated lush basin. It meanders along with its partner Alessi, sometimes kissing its banks of cane, other times playfully avoiding it before finally parting company altogether as it heads directly to the fort with the surrounding village stone structures. At the point of separation this part-time river veers to the right, encircling Skylletion on the south side. In a similar fashion, the Karknios river encircles Skylletion on the north side. The Ghetterello, which begins at the east base of the town, swallows the two rivers, then quickly drops to sea level to be swallowed, itself, by the Gulf of Skylletion, the muster location.

The men trudged behind the lads and sweated profusely when the road beneath their feet broke company with the Alessi, bringing into view the old man's shack and then the town.

"We must stop at that shack and water the animals; the heat is too much," Eugenius bellowed at length while wiping his forehead. The monk did not respond.

Eugenius then puzzled over Peter riding on the horse's rump. The two lads had drifted outside of hearing range. "I am troubled for Peter; he is a good farm hand, dependable, but shows no emotion. I don't think he has the stamina for war," Eugenius commented.

"He is quiet and reserved but a hard worker, always focused. He will be a good militiaman and make someone a good solid husband, one who knows right from wrong," added Father Nicholaos.

"After the spontaneous and wild Alphaeus, Saverina's heart is slow to accept him," Eugenius concluded.

They reached the old man's shack. This time they received no enthusiastic greeting outside and wondered if he was home. Eugenius tended to the animals as the rest went inside.

"We thought you were not home, mind if we spend the night?" asked the monk.

"I've been a little under lately, Father. Make yourself at home." His voice crackled out of a mouth with missing teeth as he gazed at the lads, expecting an introduction.

"Peter and Iohannes. They are to join up with Maniakes," boasted Eugenius, who caught the question in the old man's look as he entered the shack where upon he laid a quilt for his bed next to the monk. Exhausted, the two men left the youths to their youthful, nervous energy, who now introduced to the host, wanted to know him better.

They observed his cloudy eyes and leathery, suntanned skin that reflected a life of toil and wondered if his advanced age had the stamina to stay awake. However, a talkative glint came to life in the old man's eyes. He began to draw on tales that the location of his humble domicile had offered over the years. Each furrow on his forehead, each scar, was a vestige of some worldly event taken place here.

"Has Father Nicholaos told you of the freed slaves passing by here, last fall?" the host began with an aging, raspy tone.

"Yes!" the youths replied in unison, struck by his protruding cheeks crisscrossed by blood-filled vessels.

"I remember when I was a child, I witnessed our people going in the other direction into slavery. Like cattle, they were prodded along by the Saracens, whose heartless arrogance deluded them to feel more human than their captives. Those bay hands with the African sand still embedded under their filthy nails had roped the necks of their victims into a single file of misery. There were daughters, sons, cousins, wives, and husbands, and their wailing still lingers in my ears." The old man cleared his throat and a tear dripped on his cheek. "Behind them the fort burned like a funeral pyre. The air had an awful stench of burnt flesh." The young soldiers were appalled.

"You, young men, are the last hope against this scourge," he dolefully insisted before winding down. Iohannes then dozed off, believing he saw death in that decrepit body.

The next day, the group left their host for the garrison and then to the muster at the beach. Meanwhile, behind them, the old man closed his teary eyes to see the angel of death emerge from the glow of a pain-relieving light.

The group was carefully descending the winding path leading to the delta, which was the source of the Ghetterello. A galloping horseman, armed, came to an abrupt stop just before them. "Have you seen any strangers in your travel?" the rider demanded.

"We haven't seen anyone, but there are so many places to hide," Eugenius said humbly, guessing that he was on a patrol hastily organized to return deserters.

"Do you know that Commander Kamos has ordered a flogging for anyone who harbors them?" the horseman threatened.

Father Nicholaos quickly interjected with his own higher authority. "Let us poor Christians be on our way. We must report before dusk to this commander of yours. Are we going the right way to the camp?"

"After the marsh, just follow the river and keep the escarpment on your right."

Finally, they reached the delta below, where they followed the Ghetterello River toward the shore leaving behind that wild growth of mostly cane and ferns. A proliferous area with lots of water and sunshine, it should have been the most productive in the area. But the location that graced it had also cursed it as well. Too easily accessible by sea, the periodic Saracen incursions forced the inhabitants to settle in the higher terrain.

The group labored its way through the swamp on an elevated snake-like path in single file. Occasionally the horse would snort and nicker when one paw would slip into the softer ground and Iohannes would have to dismount and lead the animal by his leash.

When safe on the other side, Eugenius picked up the conversation, "Father, what do you think about the old man? Peter and Iohannes were impressed."

"Yes, indeed. But I think he hasn't told us all."

"What's that, Father?"

"The neighbors told me once that while he was working in his field, pirates kidnapped his wife, two lovely daughters, and son."

"It is a wonder he has not gone mad or why he survived so long," Eugenius offered.

"He was deranged for almost a year. They say he burned his home down to erase all memories and shut himself in that hovel, refusing to tend to the farm."

"What brought him out of it?"

"I don't really know; perhaps no man knows, only God."

"What about you, Father? Where does your strength to live come from? I know you have likewise suffered as much."

"I have cleansed my heart of its anger and its desire for vindication with Christian prayers and my vows."

"My sword is my strength, Father!"

"That is why you will not live as long as the old man."

"Maybe you're right. I saw a faint spark in his eyes that wished a final peace," concluded Eugenius.

When approaching the temporary camp on shore near the promontory, the youths experienced an organized hustle and bustle for the first time, a military operation in full display. Its wonderment and apparent confusion crowded out their apprehension, as they observed before them the pavilion or cone-shaped tent for the ship captains, sides opened exposing cots and a table to transact business. A disorganized line of recruits waited before it for their turn at their fate. Farther down were three smaller ridge tents for the assistant captains *bandophori* and crew tents facing a hitching post for the horses.

Supplies were piled up near one tender, which was to ferry the items to the supply ship where a crane with block and tackle would hoist them on deck. The other two tenders served to ferry the men to the assigned ships determined by the officers. All decisions of the operation were made within the cone tent by the officers, including the fort commander and the tax collector. Names were checked off the tax official's damned list, supplies verified, men directed to their proper muster area, and officers running back and forth allocated each man to the proper ships.

The placid, expressionless faces of the youths in line gripped tightly the monk's heart. Which ones will not return? he asked himself. The villager before Peter and Iohannes, poorly armed and poorly supplied, was surely a candidate.

"Please don't take my son, he is my last," pleaded his poverty-afflicted mother, who had brought the youth.

"Madam, if you don't have the money, he must go." A heartless voice erupted from the tent.

"But the war has already taken my husband and older son!" She began wailing and refused to unclench her hand that held her son's arm like a vise.

"Madam, let go." One officer tugged on the poor lad, but the mother did not yield.

"Who will work the little land we have?" she battered back, screaming with hysteria.

Father Nicholaos placed his hand on the officer's arm. "I have in my hand a letter from Captain Kamateros, a dear friend of ours who has some recommendations concerning our lot. Please hold the lad aside until our matter is resolved."

"Let the lad be, for now," ordered Commander Ouramos sympathetically stepping forward. He was now in charge, for Kamos had gone to tend to another matter.

The Florus group reported next, and the letter cleared the whole matter of the logs and the shortfall in the taxes. The mule was whisked away, Iohannes and horse were led to the hitching post area where the other horsemen were tending to their horses, and Peter joined the other recruits.

Next the unfortunate lad and wailing mother presented themselves before that fateful station. However, with the magic force of the letter and Commander Ouramos looming over the tax collector's shoulder, the lad before them was erased from the record, and mother and son slipped quietly away. And so, did Eugenius and the monk who joined them.

Iohannes was directed to a squad leader *dekarchos* Leo Astolfi, who introduced him to the others of the cavalry. From the capital of Bari and in permanent service to the empire, this section of the Thematic cavalry would take to Iohannes like lads to a frisky puppy.

Among themselves, it wasn't the Latin he had learned from the monk that they spoke; the strange words carried just enough of the classical meaning to be understood but produced a comical interchange between Iohannes and the group. The Greek tongue tied the squadron to the main unit, and their dialect cemented the personal bonds. From these special connections, Iohannes became Ioan. His family name, now, Floro, was rarely used.

Full initiation into the military routine for Iohannes would begin the next day at reveille; meantime they tended to the horses, some exercising them, others grooming them. Iohannes brushed his as his eyes rolled around at the frantic activity. The carpenter crew was cleaning the familiar logs, which would repair some of the horse holds in the horse transport's hull. The other ships were being loaded with men and supplies. The archers and lancers were put on tenders and rowed to the appropriate ship. After settling in, the men would hang their shields over the ship's side for protection. They must also function as oarsmen when on board, and he wondered what ship would bear Peter's shield, whom he last saw with the lancers.

By dusk the area was almost cleared, the carpenter work completed, and a sleepy silence took over. The commander's pavilion was gone, and only the three small tents remained to house the horsemen. With their lateen sails stowed on deck along with the yards, the two ships offshore, now fully loaded, waited patiently for the horse transport to unbeach the next day.

Iohannes slept rather comfortably that first night. His fears were mitigated by thoughts of the friendly reception of the squad. The next day, he was abruptly awakened by the yelling of the squad leader throwing half-hearted insults, an effective tool for reveille. When Iohannes emerged from the tent, the sun had not peeped over the dark waters yet with their wave crusts sparkling in the moon light. He mulled on the fact of being greeted by darkness every morning of his military life.

They dressed and ate.

Finally, when daylight debuted in its full glory, they were mustered for the day. They stood before their squad leader, whose cheerfulness and unflappability mitigated the gloomy overcast of war. Astolfi's pep talk preceded his orders for the day, and it cut through their encroaching fear with his magic. He spoke in Greek when dealing in matters of his duty, but the magic was laced in a personal dialect.

At first, he wore a serious tone. "Gentlemen, before I give your orders since we have some new recruits, I will explain our mission. We will make one or maybe two stops to refresh the horses; then all the ships will meet in Rhegium." Now he cleared his throat "Enjoy the stops; they are a diversion from the hell waiting for us."

But then he lightened up to meet his squad's desire for his humor. "We will get there despite our able and gallant commander." He rolled his eyes in mockery.

The veterans laughed and chuckled; they knew Commander Kamos' real talents or rather lack of talents. "There, we will meet up with the rest of the light cavalry to be assigned to a regular cavalry captain. I am sure some of you will miss our present one." More snickers and laughter now joined by the recruits as well. "Now, halter your horses for the boarding." Confidence spewed from his mouth and the tension of war bowed before the man.

The horse transport was a modified dromon, wider to accommodate the stalls, and a section of the gunwales at starboard aft could swing open to receive a ramp *climax*. It was anchored in the shallows with the ship's bow slightly in deeper waters.

The horses and mule became jittery and balked when approaching the ramp. But the men were excellent horse handlers, and once on deck, man and horse descended into the hull by way of a huge open hatch with a gangway that led to the stalls. The stalls were lined fore and aft, and as the first animal reached its spot, it was sectioned off from the other animals coming in after it. This went on until all the animals were in their place. With each animal boarded, the draft would increase, and the keel moved closer to the sea floor, so the marines rowed the ship a little farther out to compensate.

Chapter XIII: The Patrol

Rhegium was three days away, requiring two stops where not only would they exercise the horses but also perform some basic military maneuvers to familiarize the recruits with the essentials. Caulonia was the first stop, and when they arrived the next day at daybreak, they landed only the horse transport, but the crew on the commander's two other dromons tendered to shore to engage in the military training appropriate to their individual function. On shore, they set up camp as quickly as possible before training.

The horsemen walked the animals for a while, but Iohannes was given orders to scout for water and fodder. At his back the clumsy new lancers tried to assemble into different formations, pushed and shoved into place by the baying senior men. A stern hand was needed to knock out those idiosyncrasies and habits, not conducive to military life. The squared formations then withstood make-believe enemy charges while the better armed pike men formed a human wedge and marched into an imaginary cavalry, cutting through and scattering them to be picked off by imaginary bowmen and horsemen's lances.

After the horses' walk, the surly officers growled out orders for the horsemen to ride them up and down the beach with lances pointed forward on the first run. On their return they were to fix their lances to their backs, take out the bow, and feign shooting arrows to their sides, rear, and front. When they reached the other end, they would quickly revert to the lance in the flash of an eye. The process cycled under the critical eyes of the demanding Astolfi, who wanted to find out the recruits' weakness before the enemy did.

Astolfi's concern did not exclude Iohannes, and upon his return Astolfi made sure Ioan did not miss his exercises. "Grab the mace and swing it like you are fighting the devil," he shouted and slapped his horse into a gallop. The hoofs pounded up puffs of sand, up and down the shore, until Iohannes saw the signal to stop.

Reveille came too soon for the newly initiated. They dragged their tired bodies into formation in the darkness under the relentless barking of the superiors. Finally, they broke camp to head for the next port or beach, which was rumored to be Bruzzano Zeffirio or Cape Zephyr. (3)

To the delight of the oarsmen, the gentle spring wind, the zephyr, befriended the ships as they headed for Cape Zephyr, the same wind god who brought the ancient Greeks here before the Romans. With sympathetic breaths, he bellowed their sails until they lowered the yards to beach the horse transport which as usual, was first. The ship captain and the squad leader had pre-arranged a new drill for the cavalry. As the marines struggled with the landing procedure, they ordered the horsemen to fully arm themselves and mount the horses in their stalls.

The smell of urine, manure, and human perspiration assailed Iohannes' nostrils, but none of this registered in his mind. His legs barely cleared the sides of the stall; his horse nickered and pawed, anticipating his grazing. Others, restless and confused, snorted and jerked their heads. When the order was given, they filed out of the hold, up the first ramp or gangway to deck, and down the final ramp to shore and charged once again into a phantom enemy waiting on shore. Then, while some were put on watch, others set up camp under the medley of ghostly enemy fire. This was the last stop before Rhegium; from then on everything would be as real as flesh and blood.

They broke camp in darkness and by the time all had boarded, the sea had shed its nightly silver and wore a shiny aqua blue. When in the deeper waters, the wind grew in strength and the triangular sails gorged on it, giving relief to the deck oarsmen. As the triangle pennant on top of the main mast fluttered proudly, they shipped their oars and strolled about on deck.

A new tempo of confidence filled the air now, for everyone knew what was expected of them, and they carried out their duties routinely. It was the first time the squad was entirely left to itself without the usual barking of orders or the monotonous drills. Astolfi had decided to give the men free time.

Iohannes had just tended to his horse, and since there was no need to relieve an exhausted oarsman, another of his duties, he went on deck and leaned over the port gunwale gazing at the marvelous expanse of the open sea. His thoughts scurried home to Flavia, his mentor, and his father. He missed dearly the fresh smell of the earth of a recently cultivated field as opposed to the putrid odor of the body sweat in close quarters.

However, the clean, biting sea breeze that cleansed his nostrils and filled the lungs, was a great substitute. He also mused about his Lombard comrades who were so different yet the same. They had adopted the Latin culture eons ago. Their blood had fertilized the land in its defense, and their sweat had furrowed it for their subsistence. They had their rights, but so did the Greeks.

A tap on his back yanked him into the now. "I was wondering where you were." Iohannes turned around to face his squad leader but did not answer. "How come you are not playing at knucklebones?" Astolfi attempted to understand better his learned squad member.

"I don't gamble." Iohannes wondered if he should have come to attention.

"Ah, a good Orthodox Christian. Some pray, mostly just gamble, and womanize, all distractions to the labors of war. They take his mind off what he's done in battle or what he will have to do."

"What happens when he gets home, away from war and with his loved ones?" asked Iohannes.

"The wounds of the conscience sometimes heal on their own in the bosom of the family; other times they open up and fester with nightmares of guilt and never heal. Either way the man does not remain the same."

Iohannes pulled out a small wooden amulet he was wearing around his neck. Saint Georgios, the patron saint of soldiers, was faded and barely visible on its surface as he speared the dragon. "My father has given it to me. Saint Georgios will protect me, for it has protected him. What about you, sir?"

"My dear Ioan! My wit is my protection." Astolfi was never shy.

Iohannes' attention turned to the Lombards of Apulia. "These Apulians, why do they resist the Romanoi?"

"We resist everybody. That is why the Greeks call us barbarians." He gave a hearty laugh of irony. "The truth is we are just protecting our land from petty dukes and princes as well as Muslims. You have your mountains for protection; we don't."

"So, your race is always on guard?"

A commotion had erupted at the game, and Astolfi left suddenly to straighten the matter. Iohannes, still holding on to the amulet, heard his father's voice through the saint: "Remain focused on your mission and come home." Suddenly, the saint's voice was overpowered by an officer screaming at his crew to properly trim the sails.

Now that they were circling the toe of Calabria, the wind became moody and fickle. The marines kept busy adjusting the yard. At times, they would lose the wind and the sails would flutter, requiring a greater reliance on the oarsmen. Other times the lateen sails would come to life and drag the ship relentlessly forward toward its destination.

The Rhegium coastline came to view at starboard. On the port side, Mount Etna and the Peloritan Mountains occasionally made themselves known through the clouds, dressed in a blueish white haze, almost indistinguishable from the sky. The ship captain now ordered archers placed on the ship tower and others to man the ballista to guard the port side facing enemy territory.

Nothing came of the precautionary maneuver and the gambling resumed where upon Astolfi returned to continue the conversation. He was an excellent trainer and squad leader and had an eye on Iohannes. Iohannes was different from the other recruits; he was ready although not yet tested and Astolfi saw himself in him. "Your father has taught you well; my father taught me also," Astolfi said to Iohannes as he overshadowed him with his tall Lombard body inherited from his father.

"Yes, sir," said Iohannes, flattered.

"Who do you think has rights to this land?" Astolfi asked with the look of one who already knows the answer.

"I think we do, sir."

"You know what my father used to say, Ioan?" Astolfi pressed on. "It is our land, because we are from this land and the deeper the roots, the more solid are the rights."

"That's curious; Father Nicholaos used to say the same back home but in different words, sir." Iohannes threw a glance at his eyes, as a recruit careful not to fix his gaze. The eyes were black like a Greek's.

"Anyway, my father was a Lombard, and my mother came from a well-known Greek family. The two families were tied together in a common interest over land and commerce." Astolfi fell into a pensive moment but finally found his voice. "The damn Normans burned our crop and offered to put it out only if we paid a tribute. It was then that my father joined Catepan Basil Boioannes to battle those scoundrels at Cannae where the Normans were allied with the Lombards. Now they have joined the Greeks. They lack loyalty and shift sides as easily as these treacherous waters of the strait change directions."

Iohannes relaxed in Astolfi's informal and personal tone. "They must be as bad as the Saracens," he concurred, his kidnapping ordeal flashing through his mind.

"They are only glorified bandits that take credit as we build their forts and churches."

"What's their mother tongue?" the student in Iohannes asked.

"A Frankish dialect spoken through the nose. You, who are learned, think we speak like peasants? I should introduce you to them. To me your family name is Floro, but to them it would be Fleur." Astolfi cleared his throat and proudly continued. "I also joined the cause when the new catepan arrived with the Strategos Leo in 1032. He brought with him some of Maniakes' battle-tested men who had fought in Edessa. We rode all over to destroy the brigands and their lairs, from Apulia to northern Calabria, not far from where you came from. Some were Lombards, some Franchoi, and the rest were mujahidin."

Rhegium (4) *Reggio* rests on a shoreline plane and gently genuflects to the majestic Aspromonte, whose west slope looms over it from a height of 6,414 feet. In return for this devotion the mountain nurtures the town with water, natural resources, and sanctuary.

It wasn't until the end of summer that the Spondyles' fleet was fully assembled in its harbor facing Messina, object of the first invasion. The patrician immediately gathered information for the invasion of Messina from the local merchants who claimed, its harbor had only merchant ships, save for one roaming warship manned by Slavic mercenaries. The fort itself was run by Arab officials and protected by a skeleton crew, which was outnumbered by the Christians who managed the daily affairs. The towers, overlooking the harbor, were empty with no garrison assigned, and the main gates facing the harbor were left open during the day. The Christians inside were eager for help and ready to fight.

To make sure there were no possible enemy reinforcements in the countryside, Spondyles then ordered a landing of two squads of horsemen, one to land on the north section of the city and the other on the south. They would reconnoiter the area and inquire from the locals the local enemy strength. One of the squads would be led by Leo Astolfi. They would circle around the fortification, meet in the center, exchange information, and then turn back to re-board and make their report in Rhegium.

Astolfi's squad of about eight horsemen landed, in darkness, on the north side of Messina beyond the reach of possible archers stationed in the wall towers. The city was fortified completely by protective walls, and lookout towers jutted out here and there for the guards. A shallow trench at the foot of the walls obstructed siege engines or frustrated attackers trying to scale the walls. Beyond the southwest trenches and their adjacent fields of wheat loomed two hills which hosted some sort of fortification each. One was a simple tower while the other was a little more extensive.

They rode in a walk and in single file, keeping their distance from the wall with careful vigilance. Astolfi was in the lead and Iohannes right behind him. The rear horseman along with Astolfi was fully armed in the tradition of the Avars. The lance slung over the shoulder, bow in case, and sword at their side; the rest were with lance and sword but no bow.

As daylight began slowly to reveal the surroundings, the north wall appeared to have no guards, unnerving the men of the patrol, who worried that cunning plots and traps may be hatching behind them. Astolfi kept his men away from the walls, but he himself would gallop toward the towers and out again trying to draw fire. There was no sign of life.

When they turned the corner, Astolfi motioned Iohannes to rush the first tower as he had done. Iohannes' heart skipped a beat, for up to now all had been a drill, a practice in which there was no real enemy. He froze for a moment but suddenly his father's words unlocked his muscles. 'Be focused on the mission at hand. Think of nothing else.' He raised his shield and galloped toward the wall, but before he could ride away, he heard a thump from the shield. An arrow had penetrated the hardened leather layer and remained fixed to the wood underneath. Nevertheless, he returned safe.

"You are a knight, now," said Astolfi, bursting into a guffaw as he watched Iohannes struggle with the stuck arrow for a moment before ordering the patrol to resume the mission.

They came across an open field located below the two fortified hills where they encountered a field slave of Greek origin coming the other way, hoe in hand, preparing to work. Stunned by the vision before him, the poor man soon realized that the rumors of the incoming invasion had materialized, and his face lit up with eyes glinting.

"My good man, how many armed Saracens are behind the walls," inquired Astolfi. Suddenly, the Greek lost his radiance, and for some unknown reason not apparent to the squad, he did not answer and stared past Astolfi, over his head and toward the wooded boundary to the field.

A rustling was heard and out charged a Saracen on horseback, wielding a sword, and heading straight for the patrol. The horseman in the rear, who was equipped with bow, could not maneuver his horse in time for a clear shot. Astolfi, however, turned his horse to confront the enemy on his right side, then gripped his sword but did not completely unsheathe it. Emboldened by Astolfi's apparent indecisiveness, the enemy increased the gallop.

Iohannes was baffled by his leader's hesitations. At the proper moment, however, Astolfi sheathed his sword, quickly grasped his lance strapped to his back, and leveled it at the enemy, who had no shield. Since the lance was longer than the enemy's sword, it dug into the Saracen's exposed chest before the slashing sword could come down on Astolfi with its deadly slice. The quick and resourceful response to the moment stamped Astolfi as a true leader in Iohannes' mind. For Astolfi, such improvising was necessary to stay alive, learned in the years fighting brigands who often employed such guerrilla-type ambushes.

With the Saracen moaning in his death throes, Astolfi seized the man's dagger and sword, then attempted to interrogate him but soon discovered that his condition made it impossible to extract any information. The seasoned soldier who formed the rear of the patrol, with his sword, ended the Saracen's ordeal with a gesture of mercy. "We also have an extra horse," he boasted.

Shocked at first at the emotionless act of mercy, Iohannes then experienced a general numbness that would last intermittently throughout the war. The desensitization would serve as a protective shield to the horrible realities of war just like his shield had halted the arrow aimed at him. He learned to set aside these unpleasant events and remain focused in his mission. But the realities return and must be assimilated. During his quiet moments, he would hold onto the wooden symbol of Saint Georgios. Clarity would then begin to displace the numbness as Flavia's spirit filled his heart and the wisdom of the monk filled his mind.

Attention now turned to the frightened Greek, who now had calmed down and resumed with his account. "There is only a skeleton crew for defense, and the nearby towns are well protected by fierce Saracens on horseback, more worried of losing their own towns."

"What about help form Panormos?" asked Astolfi.

"There is no one in charge in Panormos to send troops to the problem areas," the man said with an air of certainty.

Marveling with satisfaction at the well-informed man, Astolfi outlined a smile of approval and gave his thanks. "The Christians are aware of what is happening in the empire?"

"Of course, in this area, we are almost part of the mainland," the man replied emphatically.

"Hail! Valdemone, the Christian spirit still lives on," rallied a member of the patrol.

The field slave had his own questions as well. "Is Maniakes here and when will he attack?"

"He is not here yet, although the patrician Spondyles is. We are carrying out his mission and we have not been told anything about the actual attack," answered Astolfi, wishing he had more comforting news for the Christian.

It was now midday; the sun beat down on their metal helmets and mail armor, making them unbearable to the touch. Astolfi led the patrol into a small thicket, an arrow shot away from the southwest corner of the wall, for its shade and cover, below the lesser fortified hill. He then set up a guard for any possible surprise attacks and sent Iohannes up ahead to meet the other patrol, which was long overdue.

Iohannes headed east along the south wall toward the Ionian, walking the horse with a loose rein to concentrate on the surroundings rather than the horse. A heightened awareness gripped all his senses simultaneously. This was new to him, but he did not reflect on this state; he did not have the luxury. No sounds escaped his ears, and there were no motions, natural or otherwise, that his glancing darting eyes did not instantly capture. His senses bypassed reflection and seemed to be connected directly to a single purpose drilled in him in training. His right hand, always ready for the sword or lance, took orders not from his mind but from his senses.

He heard some merchants wheeling their wares toward the south gate. Remaining hidden, he let them pass and turned his attention toward the east. The other patrol suddenly appeared in the distance, grudgingly making ground toward him.

They had not fared well and Iohannes sensed a dejection about them, a lack of spirits that contrasted with his group. They rode their horses as he did, loose on the reins, but he wasn't sure if they did so out of sound judgment or simply exhaustion. Their downcast eyes rarely took in the wider surroundings as they followed their squad leader, Dekarchos Pastilas, in single file.

Just before the straggling rear guard, he detected a bundle of some sort straddled and tied down over the back of one of the horses whose reins were being pulled by the man riding before it. Iohannes, kicked his horse into a trot and then into a short gallop. As he got closer, he discerned two arms dangling out of one end of the bundle as well as two legs protruding from the other end. He halted his horse before the squad leader.

"Dekarchos! Astolfi has sent me; we have found a safe spot to regroup," he yelled.

"Where, soldier?" demanded Pastilas.

"Toward the end of the wall, below the southern hill, sir."

Iohannes rode next to the leader to indicate the route. The men followed behind them sunk in a malaise, and when a horse attempted to graze on some convenient grassy growth, the weary rider struggled on the reins.

Iohannes glanced behind him, noticed another horseman with a bandaged arm turned red with blood. It was not his place to ask, but it was clear one man was wounded, and another was killed in some scrimmage. He sensed an uneasiness in Pastilas' men. A lack of confidence, he thought, unlike Astolfi, who set an example of personal courage that permeated throughout his men's spirits.

After a while, the regrouping area suddenly popped up into sight, promising safety. Before dismounting, Pastilas bellowed out the order to dismount and tend to the horses, an order which everyone took to be redundant and only boosted his vanity.

Pastilas removed his helmet and headed toward Astolfi to plan the return to the ships while the men intermingled. Astolfi was a head taller with rugged square jaws and piercing black eyes while the other had a boyish look about him with Middle Eastern features. One appeared natural to military life while the other seemed out of place, gawky, and avoided eye contact. Astolfi had met this kind many times before; with their connection high up the political chain their experience often did not match their easily begotten rank.

After the two units exchanged their reports, they were faced with two alternatives. Return now or return in the cover of darkness, both equally laden with uncertainty. Although the gathered intelligence depicted favorable conditions for a full-scale takeover of Messina, it said nothing of the lone fighters lurking in the countryside or the loosely garrisoned walls that threatened the patrols in their return.

"We should remain here until dark; we will not be easy targets in the dark," volunteered Pastilas, showing pride in his assessment.

Astolfi's quick mind had already passed beyond that initial assessment. He was focused on the fortified hills behind them and the quickness that news of one's presence can surreptitiously fly about in unfamiliar enemy territory. "They are aware of our presence; they could be gathering for a possible ambush, right now," disagreed Astolfi, taken by a hunch honed by experience. He felt the piercing eyes of the enemy all about them, a sensation he often felt routing out the bandits of Lucania.

"The men need rest; we can move faster at night under its cover." Pastilas became testy and was hit by the questioning eyes of his own men.

"This is their territory; they know it well. What if there is a cloudless night, and we are visible. Then, we would gain nothing," countered Astolfi.

"But we are more visible in daylight," Pastilas snapped back, staying firm under increasingly doubting eyes.

"We need to leave as soon as possible," Astolfi demanded. The men began drifting toward him in a gesture of support while Pastilas became aloof in his pride.

Astolfi had decided on instinct to leave with his men prior to any discourse with his colleague. Pastilas would incur further casualties by staying, he thought. He had to think fast to also save Pastilas' men. "Let's ask the men what they think."

Pastilas detested the informal rapport Astolfi had with his men who complied so willingly to his orders. He looked around for support.

"Who prefers to leave now?" yelled Astolfi.

A resounding bellow echoed back, "Hell yeah! What in Hades are we doing here, anyway?" Pastilas' rear guard shouted, and everyone hastened to gather their gear to leave.

Perplexed and wroth for losing control, Pastilas reluctantly accepted the common verdict and the teams separated. They headed back following the specific orders of the mission, which were to exchange the intelligence and return the same way each had come. It was a hedge against one team not making it back with the intelligence.

Astolfi, mechanically and without hesitation, ordered Iohannes to ride point first, a dangerous role reserved for the new recruits under the cold calculations of war. He rotated them to spread the risk while sparing the veterans, who were needed for the heavy fighting. Later, as Iohannes became seasoned under his skillful hands, the situation would change.

For now, Astolfi was still pounding and forging the youth into a proficient soldier in his own image like a blacksmith shaping iron.

Iohannes made his way forward about one hundred paces ahead, shield up and right hand ready for the sword or the lance, strapped to his back. Every now and then he would double back to report anything unusual or just to make it known he was all right. He set a path for the team that hugged the tree line whenever possible; not doing so was the reason for the other team's casualties. When he arrived at the northwest corner of the fortification wall, he paused and waited for the others in a suitable place for cover to switch the point.

It was late evening when they crossed the channel for the Rhegium port. The water was now black in the darkness except for the wave crests, which shimmered in the moon's silver light. Countless silhouettes of ships filled the southern horizon of the strait; they seemed to bridge the two land masses. General Maniakes, a monster of a man in size and boldness, was making his way into the channel with the main invasion force transported by Admiral Stephen Kalaphates.

The two patrols landed safely, and the two squad leaders made their report to their superiors, who in turn reported to Spondyles. The patrician decided to invade Messina as soon as possible before the enemy could properly reinforce it. Maniakes would then have a port to land the tagma with its siege engines and other offensive heavy equipment.

Chapter XIV: The War

Georgios Maniakes

Strateges Autokrater

The Sicilian campaign had been two years in the making with its careful planning and complicated logistics. The plans finally bore fruit with the arrival of Maniakes' tagma, transported from Dyrrhachium to Bari, then to the coasts of Rhegium. Its presence, along with the general's reputation, triggered an ecstatic enthusiasm that spread throughout Spondyles' Italic forces, *Italoi Stratiotoi*. In the two small cavalry squads, led by Astolfi and Pastilas, morale and camaraderie were at their zenith further whetted by their initial contact with the enemy.

After their patrol, the two squads merged into Georgios Kamateros' bandon of about 300 cavalry men, which on the day of the invasion split into two units and encircled Messina. Their tactics this time, however, were offensive: rout out lone fighters, attack assembled fighters wherever encountered, and finally set up camp below the west wall under the fortified enemy hills.

All this took place as Spondyles's infantry was ferried into port for the actual invasion, which met little resistance. Shortly afterward, General Maniakes landed on Messina's south shoreline to assist and later merge the two forces completely under his command. His admiral, with the fleet, was given the task of patrolling the northern coastline to prevent enemy forces from escaping to Panormos and obstruct reinforcements coming from that city.

With Messina (5) taken, Spondyles took the horse transports to Salerno to procure whatever military assistance possible from Prince Guaimar, (6) who had at his disposal the growing number of Normans entering Italy. General Maniakes was ambivalent as to their reliability but felt more comfortable with them under his wing rather than have them roam mischievously throughout the Italian province. The prince offered 500 mercenaries consisting of 300 Normans, commanded by William of Hauteville, and 200 Lombards led by Arduin.

As this was taking place, Maniakes organized his army to take the rest of Sicily. He would leave behind the able Katakalon Kekaumenos in Messina, in charge of 500 Armenian cavalry men and 300 infantry men to garrison the fortress. His Varangian guard of 1,000 men would monitor the eastern coastline in small ships to prevent possible enemy reinforcements from reaching inland to the scene of battle.

Foreign and domestic forces would be kept separate and under their own command, for the foreign mercenaries could disrupt the troop cohesion. The quick shift in field tactics that often was required on the fly, he could perform more easily with the professional army alone (tagma).

Panormos, the capital, was his objective, but to reach it with his army from where he was presently, he would have to go through Erymata (Rometta), a fortress that stood at the crossroads to the main highway leading to the capital. Erymata was garrisoned with Saracen troops who could exit the fort to harass his movements as he marched his troops toward it through enemy territory consisting of cliffs, gorges, and defiles ideal for ambushes. The initial phase of the march would take him through the Neptune mountains, today known as Monti Peloritani, whose narrow, arduous passages can funnel an ideally protected formation on the march into a single defenseless line struggling to make its way forward. Each man, horse, or wagon would become an easy target under the enemy lying in hiding in the surrounding countryside.

Since the fortress was well manned and the countryside infested with the enemy, the bulk of his army would be annihilated before reaching its walls. He needed to turn the table on the Saracens to gain the advantage before moving the bulk of his forces in place. He sent the scouting patrol reinforced with the better armed infantry of the tagma miles ahead to flush out the enemy, hidden in the thickets. Following behind them would be the thematic infantry, who would replace the enemy in the environs and thereby secure the route for the full army. Few horsemen were initially used since the cavalry was almost useless in such terrain and could be easily ambushed. Those few used would scurry back and forth relaying information to the commanders in the main body.

Among the first squad *bandon* of light spear carriers to participate in the advance maneuvers was Peter, who with two veteran archers of his unit was ordered to take a perch from the enemy. They inched their way up the rugged Monte Antennamare slope, taking cover behind rocks and the abundant cytisus shrubbery.

"Stay here. Distract them while I circle around," demanded the senior archer in charge. Before his comrades knew what happened, he had shot his arrows into the Saracen lookouts, killing both. "I got them," he yelled triumphally, pushing the dying bodies over the perch barrier and into Peter's path who barely dodged one while climbing to the perch.

"Aye! Watch out!" shouted the other archer.

"How long do we have to stay here?" asked Peter, aghast at his first enemy encounter as they settled in.

"Lad, you have a lot to learn. If they come to get us, it will be only after the siege of Erymata. If we are lucky, we'll sit out the war." The first archer chuckled.

"Do you have someone back home waiting for you?" The senior tried to distract Peter, now staring at the bodies below entangled in the shrubbery.

"Yes." Peter wasn't sure, but he had an answer.

"Our mission is to routinely comb the area to prevent enemy regroups in the main unit's rear. Are you up to it, Peter?" The senior archer drew Peter's focus to the mission.

"Yes." Peter had always been reliable and steady in his duties, and this was no exception.

Below them the endless marching column of men, horses, and wagons slowly made their way down the rocky path that wrapped Mount Antennamare like a decorative brown ribbon. Behind them, at 3,698 feet, loomed its rocky mountain peak, where Maniakes had placed another watch to survey the area for ships and enemy forces on the march since it allowed one to see both the Ionian coastline area as well as the area on the Tyrrhenian side.

The gully through which the men marched widened into a colluvium as it approached the citadel and then partially circled it and headed for the shores of Spadaforo. Peter imagined that the gully, beneath him, was hacked into the vegetation and shale by some huge supernatural ax. It waited ominously to engulf anyone or anything that tumbled in.

At its bottom, the forces in single file, seemed to take forever to make their way past their perch. Its length was in miles, and during the constant stops ordered by Maniakes, nothing moved until he received clearance from the scouts. All cavalry units were dismounted, and each unit was separated by infantry. The baggage train was in the center, protected by pikemen and the heavy cavalry called *kataphracts*, which are used to punch holes into a stubborn enemy.

The wagons carried not only supplies and provisions but also the artillery, some wagon mounted and ready to fire, others to be assembled in place. They could fire stones and arrows and combustible material, a Byzantine hallmark. Bow ballistae, catapults, battering rams, all sorts of torsion and tension equipment requiring an operating crew filled the many wagons. Digging equipment and plenty of wall-scaling ladders consumed two other wagons. Engineers, craftsmen, and operators walked alongside the wagons who were needed for their maintenance as well as to fabricate makeshift equipment for the siege.

Erymata sits majestically on top of a massive mound 1,837 feet high and is fully protected by walls that hug the cliff edge and overlook the roads below that surround it in the form of a wheel. With a diameter of approximately one mile, the wheel has three roads branching off it. Although the fortress has two entrance gates, only one path into the fortress is used by normal traffic. It snakes up the southern slope and reaches the main gate, situated next to the Byzantine church, and is called Porta Terra or Porta Milazzo.

Toward the east are the foothills of Monte Antennamare from which now emerged Maniakes' men heading for the town, then called Rimtah by the Saracens. As determined fighters set on stopping Maniakes, they decided to make sorties from the fortress and harass the Romanoi making their way to the open areas before the Romanoi could assemble.

As the Greeks approached Erymata, the Saracens stormed out of the citadel like bees buzzing out of their hive, swinging swords, and shooting arrows on horseback, taking advantage of the ill-prepared Romanoi. They cut down with ease any Greek infantry or horseman who had just made his way to the open area. Initially, Maniakes did not have access to his pikemen, but as they trickled their way up front, he put them into a wedge formation to break up the Saracen drive. He then ordered the tagmata cavalry to pick off the scattering enemy from regrouping or returning to the safety of the citadel. When the thematic forces, which had been in the rear and in which Iohannes participated, also became available, he assigned them to the tasks of reinforcing the tagma and retrieving the wounded.

The bees slowly diminished in number, mostly were killed, and a few returned to their hive. However, the Romanoi suffered a huge loss as well. In the battle's wake, the wagon train finally entered the field with its medical supplies and the wounded were treated. The Sicilian Muslims were valiant fighters, making the Greeks pay dearly for the victory.

From here on the war becomes harsher, overwhelming, and grueling, regardless of the well-equipped army led by the genius of Maniakes and the addition of the Normans and Lombards who finally had made their way to the main force. Every effort by the Romanoi to make their way west toward the capital had been thwarted by the enemy in unpredictable ambushes. The whole western terrain of the Neptune ridge was infested by the enemy. Maniakes' raiding parties were not enough to soften the resistance and prevent the determined foe from regrouping and making effective strikes. The more time elapsed the more troops the enemy could scrape together for more formidable assaults.

All four seasons came and went, and the Romanoi could account for only thirteen additional towns under their control. At this point, the general decided to pitch camp in the Neptune mountains to consolidate the troops and assess the situation. The trumpet was sounded, and the camp was set up in the standard layout reinforced with a ditch at its perimeter and where they could not dig, they piled rocks. The commanders' tents, baggage train, and animals were placed in the center of a large circle of the cavalry and infantry.

It was now spring again and the mountains revived, water flowed everywhere, and new smells filled the air. Likewise, Iohannes was transformed anew. with the boyish look vanishing behind a mask of manly scars and even a few wrinkles. The civilian threads in his life had been completely woven into the military cloth. His philosophical journeys into himself were rarer, displaced by more interaction with the unit. He clung only to images of Flavia for escape. His focus was on the present and the diversions of gambling and drinking were becoming more amendable to him.

Astolfi had introduced him to Arduin, the leader of the recently added Lombards whose mastery of Greek and Latin dialects overshadowed Iohannes' knowledge. The man was polished, learned, gregarious, and completely at ease with the Greeks as well as the Normans or Lombards. There was, however, something devious in his smile that contradicted his forthcoming nature. Next to him stood the Hauteville brothers, William and Drogo, along with another Norman, Hervè Frangopoulos. They appeared more as huge bodyguards rather than as leaders of the Norman contingent.

Both Normans and Lombards complained Maniakes used only the thematic cavalry or the professional cavalry to raid, harass, and procure supplies instead of them. Their interest seemed more in pillage and personal gain even if it was at the expense of the local Christians. Their camp quarter was the loudest and unruliest, often fighting among themselves; Maniakes was justified in keeping them at bay.

On one occasion, Iohannes had asked permission to wonder about in the thematic area of the lancers to look for his friend Peter. Peter was nowhere to be found. He was last seen heading for the higher ground around Mount Antennamare near Erymata. Someone suggested he may be part of a garrison team to hold a conquered fortress somewhere. Iohannes also checked the infirmary—nothing. This saddened him, for that bond with Peter was a source of strength and hope, another reason to keep going and stay alive. He also imagined Peter as a future brother-in-law, a sort of gift to his wailing sister.

One morning, after reveille, Iohannes heard the trumpet signal to break camp and fall into their unit for the march eastward toward the Ionian coastline. The general decided to make his way down the eastern coastline to lay siege on Syracuse, which had been the beloved Byzantine capital of Sicily prior to Arab rule. Capturing it would be a psychological blow to the enemy and a boost for the Romanoi. Since local qaids of various surrounding towns did not hesitate to organize guerrilla-type tactics and harass the Romanoi in their tracks, Astolfi's squadron was ordered to protect the rear. They drew the hostile locals away from the main unit and surprised those fighters heading to Syracuse.

When the Romanos army arrived, most of the Arabs had retreated into the heavily fortified island quarter, Ortygia, where they could retaliate with equal firepower of stones, combustibles, and volleys of arrows. The Greek ships surrounded the impenetrable walls while inland, Maniakes marshaled his forces into battle formation occupying the north shore of the Great Harbor, close to the city gate, Porta Urbica. The concentration of his forces was directed at the castle guarding the main entrance to the island. Various roaming cavalry squadrons were left behind to monitor the higher northern countryside of the city to prevent enemy regroupings that could threaten the main body. Again, Astolfi's squadron was called, disappointing Iohannes, who wished to see the city so eloquently described by Father Nicholaos.

There was daily coordination between the field patrols and the high command of the operation. Messengers travelled back and forth, relaying orders, updating the field squadrons on the siege, and gathering intelligence to take back. News changed little from day to day. The enemy garrison had provisions to last a long time. The walls of the main fortification, the Ortygia section, were too thick and could not be breached by tunneling, and siege towers were too cumbersome to construct, for it was surrounded by water. The huge torsion catapults hurling boulders had negligible effect on the thick walls.

Only once did a messenger bring news of a different nature to Astolfi's squadron. The qaid of the city himself, frustrated by the stalemate, made a dash outside the gate with some of the garrison troops, and on horseback they personally challenged the invading Romanoi. With the excuse that his Lombard comrades were being killed, the burly Norman leader, William Hauteville, rushed into the fray, heading straight for the qaid. The warrior of fortune from Normandy got the best of the Arab commander with a single blow. "Finally, a victory!" A unified shout was heard in the squadron.

Astolfi had listened patiently, something did not set well. Individual heroic acts such as this one can rally the troops to victory, but often they overturn well-laid plans to foil the enemy and gain an advantage.

"What do you think?" he asked Iohannes.

"Maybe we need more of these impulse warriors," and bringing his brows together in curiosity, "but why do you ask?"

"First, I have another question. What happened after the qaid's death?"

"The qaid's men fell back inside, more determined than ever," Iohannes shot back.

"Do you see my point now? What have we been doing when we draw the enemy out of his stronghold?" Adolfi was at his best.

"We keep on luring him into a vulnerable situation that is to our advantage."

Contented, Astolfi went to tend to other matters and Iohannes pondered the difference between bravery and rashness. Perhaps William had foiled Maniakes' plan to do what Astolfi was doing so well with the squadron in the countryside.

Later, in the history of southern Italy and within the lifetime of Iohannes' children, the incident grew into a story with a striking resemblance to Achilles slaying Hector in Homer's Iliad. William was henceforth known as William Iron Arm.

The battle raged on; the debilitating tension grew by the day, and their spirits rested on a fulcrum of uncertainty. Astolfi's unit was now ordered to move in to patrol the area, which stretched north-south from the Great Harbor on the south and the Little Harbor *Trogylus* on the north, then ran east just past the Epipolae Plateau's edge.

As they moved in closer to the fort, they saw ancient remains (7) everywhere. They brought the monk's narratives to real life in the moments of self-reflection for the pensive Iohannes, but Astolfi had been mulling over some serious concerns of his own. At the end of one patrol, he approached Iohannes like many times before. "This city has many layers, doesn't it?"

"Are my thoughts always visible to you?" Iohannes was a little testy.

"I've put the soldier in you, but I can't take out the monk."

"I don't want you to. Because of him, I know more than what most men know. We are standing in Neapolis; to the shore lies Acradina and north sits Tycha. I have even found where the Church of Saint Lucia once stood in defiance of the destructive Arabs. And the Temple of Apollo, now a mosque. I can name the layers."

"You have borrowed your monk's eyes."

"Yes, indeed. I see spirituality, hate, and destruction here, all vying for the city's soul. But you have come on another business?"

His squadron was thinning out, mostly from incapacitating injuries rather than deaths. Lucky and unlucky, they left behind legs, arms, or whatever limbs the enemy or the surgeon severed. Pastilas had lost even more men, and there was talk of combining the two squadrons. Astolfi worried the incompetent Pastilas would take command if he were taken down by the enemy. "I've recommended you take my place, in case....."

"In case what?" broke in Iohannes.

"In case the bastards kill me. Your prudence and quick thinking save lives," Astolfi said, but Iohannes did not want to hear it.

"I'm tired and wish only to go home. Are we no different than the Arabs when we burn their crops and kill the ones resisting?"

"Look at what they have done to our people, enslaving them, raping them, stealing their land, and defiling the churches. I ask you do we not have the right to defend ourselves?" demanded Astolfi.

"We also hate," retorted Iohannes.

"A Christian does not treasure his hate or wear it as a badge of distinction. We, as soldiers, summon it to reinforce our will to survive with the blessing of the priest. Our soldiers do not go to heaven because of their deeds in battle, heroic or otherwise, but rather their love shown to others. Is this not what your monk would say?"

"You are right, I will think it over."

While the Romanos' siege of Syracuse lingered for the rest of 1039, back at the Sicilian capital of Panormos, control of Sicily fell into the hands of Abdullah after the Berber faction executed the emir, al-Akhal. Abdullah then requested more troops from his father, but the caliph had his own problems. The thousands of men he managed to muster were ill-trained and ill-equipped, probably of peasant stock, and all foot soldiers. When they arrived, Abdullah set out toward eastern Sicily, to surprise the Romanos general on his rear.

Along the way, local fighters joined his ranks and even before he got to the fortification of Troina at the edge of the Nibrodi mountains not far from the foot of Mount Etna, he had amassed a considerable army. By having in the past outfoxed Constantinople, Abdullah was imbued with optimism, and was determined to either annihilate the Romanoi or push them back into the sea with the sheer size of his forces.

When he reached Troina, he picked up the garrisoned troops and headed east, following a narrow valley that widened on the northwest foot of Mount Etna, a plain where three torrents meet the Simeto river and ideal for a camp. He chose this spot because it would allow him to follow the Alcantara valley to Taormina on the north side of Etna or if he decided he could follow the Simeto river, on the south side to Catania and Syracuse itself. Either way he felt he could attack the Romanoi unawares.

Valdemone, however, was heavily populated by Christians due to their proximity to the mainland, and as such Maniakes was constantly informed on matters important to his campaign. (8) Abdullah's march to hit the Romanoi on the rear was no exception. Maniakes regrouped his men and headed north to encounter his enemy, leaving behind a skeleton force to mimic a continuation of the siege at Syracuse.

As usual, the scouting fell on small units of the thematic cavalry, which in this case happened to be Astolfi's reliable squadron. After being briefed thoroughly by the locals regarding the best passage, they carefully made their way up the Simeto river valley with the main unit trailing behind. They surveyed the terrain and other conditions that were vital for the safe passage of the main body, and on occasion, one horseman would relay vital information back to the general.

When they passed the small hamlet of Adranos, two huge red boulders on their left verified the description of the halfway point given by the locals. Farther up the winding river, a hill on their far right, which once was a small volcano, had the appearance of a boat due to its sunken crater and indicated their next turn was not far away. From then on, the river on their left changed its decor from the normal wider riverbed of multicolored pebbles to fast-moving waters squeezed within a tight gorge. Formed eons ago by lava flows and further eroded by water, the gorge walls of basalt rock, at least forty-five feet high and at some places fractured vertically, formed natural columns. They supported a smooth plateau, very accommodating for their travel.

When they reached the junction where the Troina river meets the Simeto, the next marker, the décor of the riverbed retuned to its more leisure state. They continued upstream, knowing the Arabs were marching toward them, following the Troina river valley and when they heard the rumble of men on the march, they climbed to even higher ground to estimate their number and equipment.

Philip

As both forces were on the march toward their historical destiny, a young Christian shepherd of about seventeen years was tending to the family's cattle in the area, a precious Christian holding despite the Muslim rule. What the shepherd saw that day, and the consequent events that ensued, would be written into the pages of history.

From the small dell above, which overlooks the Troina river and the Saracena torrent to the left, he saw an endless horde of men making their way toward him, a few on horseback and the rest on foot.

The vision of the disorderedly column appeared in the sun as moving water stretching into the horizon, mimicking the river beside it. Each member of the column carried a weapon of some sort, and the lucky ones had shields; they were prodded and goaded into a makeshift marching order by better armed horsemen.

This was not good news for the faithful of the area, their garb indicated Arabs. Careful not to be detected, the shepherd followed them with awe and the fear that deer experience in the presence of man.

Farther up the Simeto, far but still in the young shepherd's view, a plain cut into the Nebrodi mountains and followed the Saracena torrent to the Simeto. The column was so long that although the van began to funnel into the plane and begin setting up camp, its rear still was nowhere to be seen.

Suddenly, to his rear in the thickets he heard a snapping of twigs and snorting of horses. His heart jumped; it was Astolfi's squadron. After assuring the lad that they were with the Romanos campaign, Astolfi questioned the frightened youth. "Where are you from?"

"From Troina. My family has a farm near there." The shepherd fiddled with his walking stick.

"What is your name?" Astolfi softened his tone.

"Philip." The youth had settled down to the realization the men were Greeks.

"Do you know if there are more coming from there?" Iohannes jumped in, now second to Astolfi in command.

Philip answered "no" in the straightforward, respectful manner that Peter might have made. In fact, the more Iohannes looked at the lad, the more he saw Peter, courteous, truthful, and reserved. Then the squadron left, and Philip returned to his cattle.

The next day Philip woke up to see that a small city had emerged during the night at the scrubby feet of the Nebrodi mountains, facing the green vegetation nourished by the Torrent Saracena. The entire column was now a mass of newly settled inhabitants barricaded behind an improvised palisade with the mountains at its back. The colorful vegetation, there the day before, had yielded to the dull, dusty rags of the inhabitants who began to stir in the early morning light.

A few days afterward there appeared an additional smaller army, more equipped and better armed. It was scattered in strategic formations throughout the gradual, sloping mountain facing the enemy on the other side of the Torrent Saracena. On the Simeto side of the same mountain, out of view of the enemy but easily seen by Philip, were horsemen—man and horse heavily armed and surrounded by men with pikes for their defense. The horsemen were the famous kataphracts, and next to them was the baggage train protected by the thematic infantry or lancers.

On the slope facing the Arab camp, a line of artillery extended east to west. There were wagon-mounted tension weapons that could handle both stones and arrows, hand-bow ballistae, and crew-operated ballistae. A formation of professional lancers from Constantinople stood their ground before the artillery in case the equipment should be attacked. Their cavalry counterparts with bows in hand flanked the lancers, waiting on a moment's notice to shock the enemy before it reached the lancers or the artillery. On the highest level of the mountain were the colorful tents of the commanders who had a clear view of the impending battle.

The night before, the Arabs had stealthily placed here and there pointed metal objects called caltrops used to cripple the horses in their charge, for the qaid Abdullah knew of the special armored horsemen that the Romanoi had, although he did not know where they were or from where they would attack. Of these kataphracts, Maniakes had about 100 at his disposal along with the 300 foreign units who were not as impressive in their armor but almost as effective as a complement to the kataphract unit.

Knowing what he was up against, Abdullah planned to attack before the volleys of missiles would begin to rain down on his men and thin out his numerical superiority. Within the camp, there was frenetic activity and shouts as the Arab leaders began to assemble the mass of human bodies into some semblance of an attack formation. The object was to push as many men as possible through the storm of missiles and arrows and get at Maniakes' better organized formations, who stood on hilly, rugged ground not suitable for horses.

Philip watched the first swarm of Saracens exit the perimeter, pushed by horsemen who made sure they kept moving forward and in formation. When they were in range, just before the river, the Greek artillery salvos fell upon them like a hailstorm. Many of the enemy fell on the far side of the river, others, in equal number, fell in the marshy riverbanks or the rocky riverbed as they scrambled to ford the waters.

Their blood oozed from their wounds in little floating streaks that quickly defused in the cold spring water. Downstream, the water had lost its green translucent color and acquired the pink tone of the oleander flowers on the banks. The ones who made it across were taken down by the tagma's cavalry of archers who swooped down on them. The few who made it all the way to the artillery line were too exhausted to fight effectively and were easily picked off by the lancers, close by.

Meanwhile, Abdullah's cavalry immediately pushed out another horde at the wake of the first and then another at the wake of that one and so on until they bottle-necked before the Romanos line. Maniakes' cavalry archers and front-line lancers were now overwhelmed. The Arabs' numerical advantage was beginning to have an effect, regardless of their weakness in discipline and inconsistency in their formations.

Maniakes ordered more lancers up front to replace the fallen and give relief to the exhausted. The cavalry had to use its relief section to carry back the wounded and supply remounts. The number of enemy fighters grew with each one killed, and the mass had to be broken up into smaller more manageable sections that could be picked off by the cavalry and infantry archers.

Maniakes gave the order to send in the kataphracts, who moved into the field in their usual wedge formation. After the front line opened to let them through, they cut into the enemy mass, splitting it in two and pushing them to the sides. At the same time, mounted archers behind the wedge who shot over the kataphracts killed and scattered the Saracens further.

Their forward thrust was assisted by a mysterious and unforeseen wind at the kataphracts' back which gathered dust and debris and hurled it at the enemy. Nor did the steel spikes sown throughout the battlefield stop the horses, for they wore steel plates on their hoofs.

The carnage intensified until most of Abdullah's men were dead or scattered beyond the scrubland and into the thicker vegetation of the higher ground. Astolfi's squad was ordered to chase them and prevent them from regrouping. Only the qaid's cavalry was left and would protect the qaid in his retreat to the Tyrrhenian coastline.

Still watching, the lad vomited at the horror of the bloody bodies; he covered his ears to not hear the yells and moans of the wounded, but deep within he was elated at the outcome. In his Christian heart, Philip felt a divine intervention, a feeling later to become a calling when he rendered his account to history.

He decided he had enough; it was time to head back to the farm and inform his parents of what he had seen. From there the news of the Christian victory traveled like the wind back to the fortress of Troina and the rest of Valdemone. This and Maniakes' future successes reverberated throughout the Christian enclaves like a bell. The Christians displayed the cross everywhere along with the slogan "Christ Wins." Solemn thanks for the liberation were given in the churches, including the churches of nearby Calabria. The people felt vindicated for having endured this scourge for so long. There was hope that the migrations into Calabria would finally cease, for the true Sicilians could now reclaim their lost lands.

But the winds of change were also blowing in an adverse direction for the campaign. During the Sicilian operation events elsewhere came to bear on its tenuous success. The local Lombards in Apulia, who had been resisting the levies for both man and materials for the war, erupted into a full-scale revolt. In the early part of 1040, the new catepan Nikephorus Dokeianos, who was attempting to muster up new troops in Apulia, was assassinated in the town of Ascoli. Other dignitaries suffered a similar fate in nearby Matera, Lucania, and Mottola. The news had finally made its way to Maniakes' men as they headed to Syracuse to resume the siege.

To the foreign contingents, this wind was a soft breeze that bore the sweet scent of opportunities. It whispered alluring ideas into the receptive ears of the respective foreign commanders. There arose a giddy-like restlessness in the Normans, Lombards, and the Varangian troops that grew as they approached Syracuse. During the encampments, there was talk of winning kingdoms in Southern Italy or acquiring vast riches from the locals and the Romanoi authorities.

Their greed peaked when the news arrived that the emperor who was defeated in Thessaloniki had to flee to Constantinople and had left behind a huge amount of treasure to the Bulgarian rebels. Their ancestral Viking spirit was whetted and fine-tuned to its former rapacious character as they secretly colluded and began to put their own interests above the Sicilian operation.

Arduin, clever as he was, inserted himself into these rudimentary machinations as their representative, the news of which bubbled up to Maniakes, gnawing at his mind with doubts on the viability of the operation. They would push the brilliant leader to make decisions that fate either blesses as a stroke of genius or curses as complete failure. Either way, the outcome is rendered over for History to judge.

Chapter XV: The Spoils

When the victorious men reached Syracuse, Astolfi's squadron was rotated out of scouting duty and placed within the protective perimeter of the camp to rest the horses as well as the men. The siege continued but since the Arab resistance had waned from the loses at Troina, news of which had arrived earlier, the city quickly surrendered to Maniakes. Jubilation broke out among the men and temporarily cloaked the underling schism between the Romanoi and the foreign contingent, which relished at the prospect of laying their hands on all that wealth. It was owed to them, they demanded. It was part of the agreement, but the Christian general felt otherwise.

Like Messina, the inhabitants were mostly Christians under the Arab yoke, and had kept the city prosperous with commerce and arduous work, no less than the past when controlled by Constantinople. Consequently, a just and rigid Christian, Maniakes forbade plundering or looting, causing murmurs and grumblings in the foreign groups.

At the center of the impromptu gatherings of malcontents always seemed to be Arduin with his linguistic and social skills. They appointed him bearer of their complaints to the general himself, who, renowned for his quick temper, ordered him stripped. Then he himself flogged the opportunist with his trademark battle-flail, a short whip with metal-tipped leather straps, carried everywhere. Done before the eyes of anyone who cared to look, the angry general set a cruel example.

Iohannes watched in amazement and turned to Astolfi. "What has he done? So, he is greedy?"

And still molding his prodigy, Astolfi spelled it out as both men paused and cringed at each slash of the whip, "The man's behavior threatens the overall discipline and morale required for the success of the campaign. He is undermining the general's orders and therefore the mission."

For the onlookers, time stopped. The thrashings were endless; most remained immobile except the foreign mercenaries who walked away disappointed. They had their answer from the general, and it was verified at the first strike of the whip. He had choked the subtle coup fomenting in their mist.

Due to the humiliation, Arduin demanded a pass to leave the campaign and go to the mainland. The other foreign mercenaries deemed the disciplinary act to their informal leader to be an affront to their integrity as independent fighters, so they too followed suit. Astolfi and Iohannes reasoned it was all for the best. "We could win without the foreigners, wait until the admiral returns," Astolfi told Iohannes.

The admiral's task of patrolling the coastal routes on the Tyrrhenian side during the battle of Troina was especially critical and shortly there after, the admiral's flagship pulled into the harbor. All hopes skyrocketed, anticipating news that Admiral Kalaphates had captured or killed the fleeing qaid, a sure sign that the Arab resistance would soon end. "We can enter Panormos, victorious, with Abdullah's head as a trophy," boasted Astolfi to Iohannes as they watched the admiral enter Maniakes' headquarters. But the little man, head prostrate, walked out slowly, accompanied by a guard detail and Maniakes following behind, who had the whip folded behind on its handle waiving it in the air and scowling with fiery eyes.

The general's harsh mood worked its way through the whip, turning the poor man to a groveling wimp, begging for mercy. It was clear to the onlookers that the admiral had failed in his mission, their spirits cracking with every stroke. "He comes from a family of simple ship caulkers," sighed Astolfi. "What could we have expected from the man?"

To the detriment of the general, however, the admiral's brother-in-law was John Orphantrophos, the minister and advisor to the emperor. The admiral notified his brother-in-law of his treatment and accused Maniakes of treason.

As these measures taken by Admiral Kalaphates trickled down through the ranks in the ensuing weeks, everyone's mood swung between the elation of the victories and the uncertainty of Constantinople's reaction to the affair. "If we lose our beloved general from a political maneuvering, it would be disastrous to the men and campaign," Astolfi warned his men.

But Iohannes put those thoughts aside and began worrying over Peter's whereabouts and safety. As an experienced soldier basking in Astolfi's respect, he was able to converse informally with leaders of other units. He discovered Peter's whereabouts from one captain in charge of whatever was left of the thematic group of lancers.

Most were scattered in the various conquered towns doing garrison duty, and Peter's squadron had been left behind in a small fort near Erymata. His friend was still alive but frozen in his stationary duties, cut off from the main unit and vulnerable to a resurgence of enemy forces.

The general now moved more of the main unit within the Syracuse walls and this included Iohannes who took the opportunity to study the city from one of the towers near the Great Harbor. Around him refortification crews labored at various corners of the city as they had done in every town. The Christians scurried about resurrecting their Christian symbols and celebrating their new lives without masters. Outside the walls, now that the admiral's fleet had returned, both harbors were brimming with dromons.

The docks close by, however, were left vacant for dignitaries and communication boats. Iohannes noticed one vacant dock now held a flagship, and next to it were its escort dromons. The standard indicated another general or patrician, and as it turned out he was the new catepan, Michael Dokeianos, who was given the task of quelling the rebellion in

Apulia. But why was he here, wondered Iohannes? Was it the emperor's response to the scathing message sent by Kalaphates? Iohannes returned to his unit hoping for answers.

Iohannes walked into the fray of a heated debate over the news. "Dokeianos has sealed orders by the emperor to recall Maniakes," one man said. "And who is going to take over, that bulbous Kalaphates and the eunuch Basil Pediatita?" asked another.

"These two men have shown only their incompetence up to now," offered Iohannes.

"What makes the situation worse," jumped in Astolfi, "is that any advice from Maniakes or from his field command *drungars* would be set aside by an inexperienced comand."

Matters went from bad to worse. Dokeianos had his orders, and when the field command warned him of the treachery and deceit of the Normans, especially Arduin, the advice fell on deaf ears. He reasoned that Maniakes had erred in not allowing the Normans to sack the city. "Treaties should be kept," he barked.

Dokeianos then shackled Maniakes in the hull of his dromon intent on eventually handing him over to Constantinople. In the meantime, he returned to the mainland first to gather more troops, for his campaign in Southern Italy. There he encountered Arduin and his Lombards making their way back to Salerno. Dokeinos made a pact with Arduin which allowed the northern conspirator to rule Melfi in consideration for his support in the uprisings in Apulia.

Meantime in Sicily, Abdullah, beaten and disgraced, had escaped to his father in Tunisia, but now, Maniakes' fate emboldened the enemy and refreshed the war drumbeat. The new rhythm fed the local qaids' ambitions. They saw opportunities, formed their own armies, some made alliances, and others resisted in small groups. Towns previously lost to the Rum were regained.

One day, Iohannes found Astolfi beside himself after receiving new orders from the captain. Astolfi had just learned that Pastilas was killed in some ambush and his men were integrated into Astolfi's squadron, increasing its size.

"What's going on?" asked Iohannes, noting wrinkles on his brow.

"Pastilas is dead," Astolfi sighed, as if taken by regret.

"Better him than his men," Iohannes said dryly, perplexed by Astolfi's mood.

"That's not the problem." Astolfi grimaced.

"Then, what?"

"We have wasted too much time here because of the political turmoil and indecision caused by this smug Kalaphates. Damn that idiot!" Astolfi's muscles tightened with every word.

"What do you mean?"

"If Kalaphates had done his job, we could now be marching into Panormos. Instead, we are putting out fires while the enemy regroups," blurted out Astolfi, with ever increasing anger. But Iohannes' eyes reflected that mutual support both relied on, and Astolfi relaxed.

The new commander had no strategy nor was he sufficiently capable to improvise to the rapidly changing circumstances. His troubles or rather the campaign's problems streamed into his command center like a flood and shattering his nerves, which he masked with an artificial composure. Never hardened in experience, the man was a poor substitute for Maniakes with his reliable instincts.

The local qaid forces were like rivulets slowly merging into large rivers, attacking the Rum, and befuddling the new command. They attacked smaller fortifications around Syracuse first, not so much to take them as to lure the Greeks out of their heavier fortifications.

One day, a group of local Christians burst into the command headquarters demanding to see the commander. Muslim warriors were battling to control their small fortress in the higher ground. "We need help. Our women and children are in there," their spokesman said before Kalaphates, who cringed at the situation presented to him. He thought of dismissing them, insisting that he had not the men to help. He looked around at his officers who from experience now withheld their advice for fear of his constant rashness. He turned around and sat slowly in his chair to steal a few moments.

"Send a kentarch," ordered Kalaphates to his staff, boasting his prowess before the civilians.

"But, sir, shouldn't a scouting party be sent first?" A brave officer spoke against the commander's false confidence that seemed to always contradict everyone's advice.

"Arrange two squads of cavalry archers, one with that dekarch Astolfi." Kalaphates stood and held chest out trying to compensate for his small body. "Send his unit as one of the two. NOW!" he shouted.

When the hastily assembled contingent arrived at the fortress, the attacking Muslim force was scanty in number and was having limited success. The jubilant Greek garrison was easily picking off the enemy from the defensive walls of the fortress who appeared to lack breaching equipment.

Astolfi, however, felt uncomfortable; it all seemed too easy and the thickets and bushes nearby displayed an eerie stillness. He let his reservations be known to the kentarch, chosen for the mission. The kentarch ordered the charge anyway for fear of retribution from Kalaphates. Astolfi held his squadron back as much as he could without showing any signs of disobeying orders.

Those hunches, nurtured in experience, proved true. The surrounding thickets came to life with waylaying Muslims, tenacious and wild. They slashed and struck the backs of the kentarch's men before they were able to neutralize the attacking Muslims before them. Now, the squadron surrounded by the enemy was easily struck down.

Astolfi, gave the orders to move in and protect the other squadron but his squadron was attacked at its side hindering the maneuverability of his men who seemed barely able to protect themselves. The battle raged on, the sanguine bodies littered the ground, and the horses, sensitive to the human mass at their hoofs neighed in protest as they stepped on the soft flesh that squirted additional blood. The blood was disproportionately shed to the disadvantage of the horrified Greeks, and more precise, to the first squadron which was almost annihilated.

There was nothing left to do. The survivors hastily rode away, leaving the dead and wounded behind. Shortly thereafter the fortress fell, and the inhabitants were taken captive, another blow to the already shattered morale in the Romanoi forces.

Thereafter, the conscripted Lombards from Apulia mysteriously vanished from the ranks in the dead of night. Only the tagma and the Calabrians maintained their allegiance to the cause.

Matters deteriorated; every encounter with the enemy ended in some defeat. Kalaphates would let the enemy choose the place of battle, call up the wrong unit to battle or at the wrong time. Discipline and cohesion in the troops waned to a dangerous and unrecoverable low. Physical and emotional exhaustion prevailed, and the force was shrinking to an ineffectual size. There appeared more wounded than able men.

The gains under Maniakes fell, one town after another. They had since lost Syracuse, and began making their way north toward Messina, losing ever more towns. Each battle, each encounter, led to more deaths, more wounded, and more captives for the enemy as well as more desertions. Even the full-time thematic troops from Apulia started to leave, hoping to find a friendly ship to bring them to the mainland.

At this dire stage of the campaign, Astolfi received an arrow in his belly during one of the ill-planned missions. The field medics whisked him away from the battle and brought him to the surgeon's tent, who first made him drink some concoction of poppy juice and henbane for his pain before removing the arrowhead. But the medic encountered a foul smell as he cut into the soft flesh. An infection had set in, and like a lot of the wounded Astolfi was destined to die of collateral causes. He now was lying still on the hospital cot, recuperating from the hallucinations and the semi-conscious state induced by the concoction.

Meanwhile, Iohannes was on his way to see his friend after being informed of his promotion replacing Astolfi. Astolfi's eyes were glazed and focused on something far away when Iohannes approached him. Staring at the vanishing life before him, Iohannes reached for words that refused to come. Finally, Astolfi spoke first. "You know, Ioan, what man fears most about death?" he coughed making his face redder than it already was.

"What!" said Iohannes, glad the silence was broken.

"Regrets! Frightening death comes fully clothed in our regrets." He paused to let a spasm of pain pass by. "Your heart pleads that it is not ready. It needs time to correct its former sins, which could be as trivial as harsh words spoken to a loved one. But death has none of that. I'm lucky, I have none—regrets, that is."

Iohannes rested his compassionate eyes on his friend's eyes who had taught him to stay alive in hell.

"Yes, I've been a philanderer, a gambler, a brawler, and a ready soldier but never the slayer of innocents. Earthly riches were not my calling, and although I've never been inside of a church, I've paid homage to the Patriarch." Astolfi started to breathe heavier, his eyes disappearing into their sockets.

"Rest awhile, you don't have to talk," begged Iohannes.

Shortly thereafter Astolfi regained his strength. "Were you given the rank of dekarch?"

"Yes."

"Don't take it. This is not for you. Flee like the bloody Normans or the Lombards." Astolfi paused and outlined a difficult smile as he fought his pain. "Have you heard? Dokeianos has lost three towns in Longobardia to Arduin and the Normans. We tried to warn the catepan those scoundrels cannot be trusted. Oh God, we are losing Italy too."

Another spasm took the moribund; his body became rigid in response. Iohannes laid his hand on the man's shoulder, hoping it would siphon the pain away. The words returned as the body relaxed.

"I was born in Venosa. That town was one of the many fallen to the Normans."

"The birthplace of Horatio the Roman poet," added Iohannes.

"The monk again....," Astolfi forced a smile at the remark.

"Yes, he still lives in me.

"Flee, there is nothing of which to be ashamed. We have done our duty. It is Constantinople that has failed us, not the other way around. We have fought these power-seeking hordes from Europe as well as the ones from Africa for the emperor; look at how we are rewarded."

Iohannes watched his friend drift in and out of consciousness. When he came to again, he uttered his last words. "Our beloved general," he paused to take a breath, "was paraded around the Hippodrome," paused again, "sitting on a donkey," Astolfi stopped breathing all together.

"Before the clueless people by the orders of a corrupt court," Iohannes whispered to himself.

A monk nearby must have felt the chill of death and strolled over to the departing soul for the blessing.

Eastern Sicily began to vanish in pieces from the control of the new leadership. Drifting groups of detached soldiers who happened to survive the previous battle inched their way north to the next un-fallen garrison. And when that garrison fell as well, the group moved on to the next fortification and finally to Messina or the sea.

Iohannes' squadron, which had been reduced to half its size, found itself in the same predicament. Completely cut off from the main unit and the enemy always at their backs, they could only move northward into safer territory. All action was defensive without new provisions and proper leadership from Constantinople. At each fortress, he desperately searched for Peter, but no one had seen or heard of him.

Iohannes led his squad by way of the higher ground, where there was more cover, in sight of the mainland. Family memories reached over from across the strait and bade them home; they healed their broken spirits from afar as they rode slumped on the saddle. The men fought their exhaustion, their fears, their longing for home by quarreling over the identification of shoreline villages on the mainland, which Iohannes had to mediate.

For Iohannes, Saint Elias' heart-breaking distance at the other end of Calabria just made him more homesick. He envisioned Mount Elias and its hovel with his precious Flavia inside, dutifully doing her chores as usual in her torn dress that enveloped her natural beauty, a celestial jewel in earthly garb. She was a gift for his eyes only and, most of all, a gift to sate the manly hunger accumulated in these years.

Then, there was the Father Nicholaos, who kept the law and order in that unwieldy bunch with which God had blessed him. He had so many things to say to Father Nicholaos on his return. And his grandmother surely would put into perspective for him the world where the word corruption seemed to explain everything. It indeed explained this mission. She had an eerie talent to see things others did not, he mused.

If she were right, he would return with a new rank in the county, allowing him new fiscal and legal privileges as his father and Father Nicholaos, perhaps even some largesse, his own land separate from the family. The fear of not returning gripped him. "God, help me, let her be right," he mumbled to himself.

She had been mysteriously silent about Peter, and he hoped it was a lapse of memory and not done to spare feelings after consulting with her dark gift. Finally, his parents' welcoming smile and embrace seemed to reach over from the other side of the strait. And he unwittingly speeded up the squadron's march to a world they left behind. But things do not always remain the same.

At the Grotto

At this very moment that Iohannes was on his way home, Alphaeus was resurfacing in the mountains of Saint Elias. The Normans were in control of sections of Apulia and Lucania and were setting their sights on Calabria, whose constant conscriptions of men weakened the local resistance. The insufficiently garrisoned forts lured the voracious Normans to new opportunities. Chaos was becoming the norm, and Alphaeus' band of lawless followers were filling the void in the prior authority.

The band freely roamed the hills and forests, unimpeded, taking what they wanted at will. Alphaeus still longed for that flower called Flavia; his plan was to pluck the flower from the protected garden where she was rooted. He knew that one day the organized Greeks would leave, exposing the peasants to wolves like himself.

The marauding life had left its mark on him; signs of constant internal brawls for leadership were imprinted on his leathery skin. With age, his father's Arab genes displayed their dominance over his mother's finer ones. He had become rugged but handsome in his own right, an attractiveness with proportional features. Bold, more than ever, he made frequent unwanted visits to the hovel when Father Nicholaos was away, unnerving Flavia with his crude advances.

If Helena were present, he would put on a gentleman's face but quickly returned to his crassness when they were alone. His favorite tool for wearing down Flavia's resistance was to lie about Iohannes' fate. He planted a seed of doubt in her delicate mind. "Fla! The Normans that passed by on their way to Salerno from the Sicilian campaign. They told me that the cavalry from this area was annihilated at Erymata, the year before."

"You're lying. How do you know this?" She burst into tears.

"They mentioned that the unit had a man they called Fleur. I took that to be Florus in their Frankish tongue." He cleverly weaved his story into a misleading cloth of probability.

"Then I will remain a spinster and take my vows," she answered with frayed nerves, and shouted angrily, "Go away, leave me alone before Father Nicholaos comes."

The man was insolent; he did not move, "We joined up with them for a while to show them the way through the mountains. This is how I learned all this." The cloth of deceit was now hemmed in quasi-truths that nibbled on her hopes.

"Get out of here, you scoundrel," screamed Helena, angrily chasing the mocking bandit away with her broom when she accidently dropped in on them. But Alphaeus was relentless; there were no militias in the area to come to the rescue. Like the wolf, he stalked his prey and returned when the monk and Helena were away.

Once, realizing his verbal concoctions led nowhere, he laid hands on the delicate flower, squeezing her waist into his.

"You're mine," he whispered harshly into her ear. She twisted, pushed, turned her head away in disgust and fear, but he tightened even more.

"You have the fires of hell in your soul, Alphè," she scowled. He let loose and returned to his preying post, somewhere in the hills.

All this stayed within the confidence of the women, reasoning if they resorted to Father Nicholaos and then the community, it may further escalate to something worse. The gossip warned of reprisals from these malicious bands, in which Alphaeus was a participant. A parallel justice now ruled the countryside.

The days passed grudgingly slow for Flavia, one apprehensive day following another more tense than the previous. The chores became just that, chores, as she waited for more concrete news. She yearned to hear from anyone, a passerby, a returning soldier, anyone but the devious Alphaeus, but no one broke the apprehension until Saverina showed up. She brought the usual supplies from her mother as an excuse to spend a couple of nights with her closest friend. There were things on her mind that can only be aired in the company of another young woman—men, the shortage of which worried all the women of the village.

"He was here the other day." Flavia broke the news of Alphaeus.

"I get angry every time I think of him. I cannot let go. Where does he go?" asked Saverina.

"Around; he pops up whenever the Father is not around. I am angry too, but Father Nicholaos says we should forgive."

"Forgive? Look what he did to Iohannes," pleaded Saverina. "He ruined everything."

"Is your anger over that or is it over an un-returned love?" asked Flavia, reading Saverina's mind.

"It's easy for you to say. Things just fall in place for you." Her jealousy escaped from her better judgment.

"You cut yourself short, Saverina. Peter loves you, and how am I more fortunate than you?"

"You're prettier."

"Nonsense! Saverina, look at your pretty, round face, your fine reddish hair cascading softly over your shoulders. And your body, it is your weapon."

"You are right. I love Peter. I must love Peter if he returns." Saverina yielded, trying to convince herself and feeling less mature than her younger friend.

That evening, Saverina felt a need to escape, to be alone. Something was stirring in her female body. She was unusually warm, restless, and paced before Flavia, who knew what it was, for she too had felt it in the presence of Iohannes. Saverina strolled outside, in the fresh air for a walk and imagined being called by a feral call from the natural surroundings.

Behind her, the hovel diminished to a small shadow, a shadow of a civility that lost its grip on her new sense of freedom, at least for the moment. Her heart beat faster, and she was warm and moist where no manliness had yet explored. The soft, cool wind of conscience bellowed her dress; it soothed and tried to tame the fires underneath to no avail. She experienced no fear, just an uncontrolled curiosity of what may lie ahead.

Suddenly, she heard a rustling and the flamboyant Alphaeus jumped out on the road, but she was not surprised nor afraid; she had unconsciously longed for the moment born of suppressed dreams.

"I've spotted you from a distance," he said nonchalantly, disguising his hunger and lack of scruples.

Saverina did have scruples. But I love him, she reminded herself, casting away her hesitation, and then released herself to him. They walked into the thickets, his lair, where he plunged into her femininity and ravished her warm passion without remorse.

It was an angry, ecstatic affair that left her empty and morally rudderless, made worse after the feral man jumped up and left without the courtesy of a word, maybe looking for another victim. Her wild feelings for him disappeared and turned to anger.

She went home the next day, loathing herself, and waited for Peter's return. A wise decision, for Alphaeus now teamed up with the Normans in his quest for fortune and power. His plan was to return later, wealthy, and influential under the growing Norman power. Then Flavia's resistance to him would be useless.

One day, Father Nicholaos, when he had just returned from Skylletion, claimed he was told that some of the local troops were crossing the strait into the mainland. Alphaeus may be lying, Iohannes could be with this group, Flavia imagined. Her heart acquired new life. She ceased to drag her feet from one chore to the other; instead, she floated everywhere. Visions of her knight on a ship sailing to Calabria for her floated daily in her head.

At Messina

When the squadron finally arrived at Messina, it found Messina well-fortified, thanks to the genius of Commander Katakalon Kekaumenos and his group of 800 battle-seasoned Armenians. Prior to their arrival, the fortified city had overcome a siege that choked the inhabitants of life-sustaining supplies. The 500 infantrymen and 300 cavalry soldiers successfully broke the hellish ring of overconfident and jeering Arabs sometime before or during the Pentecost of that year. After haranguing his troops in its church, Katakalon led a charge out of its walls to surprise an enemy that had let its guard down.

Entering its walls from the south, Iohannes began searching for higher-ranking officials and found the old Captain Kamateros, his sponsor. The captain himself was forced to work his way north with his men and now was desperately organizing the men into manageable groups for boarding the scarce ships available. The logistics were not centrally planned and hence chaotic. It would take days before Iohannes could cross the waters into the mainland.

This repatriation of the men was not officially sanctioned; but remaining and fighting was pointless without any real effort on the part of the empire to resupply the campaign. Michael IV, the emperor, had put most of his resources toward pacifying the Bulgarians at Ostrovo, Greece. And although he substituted Kalaphates with Michael Dokeianos in the campaign, his military prowess was not that much better.

"Sir!" Iohannes saluted Kamateros.

"Oh, my, it's Florus Junior," his sponsor said.

"What's going on?" asked Iohannes, who already had a sense of what was happening.

"My son, we are going home. By the way, I see you were issued a remount."

"Yes, the horse you gave me was worn down. I set him free in the pastures near Syracuse; he was a good horse." Iohannes deflected his trivial question with grace before coming back more seriously. "Will there be a ship for my squadron?"

"Have patience! We are in good hands with Katakalon and his Armenians. The rumors around here say that he turned the battle around just as Julius Caesar did in Gaul a thousand years ago when he personally took control of a last-ditch effort to save the day." Then his sponsor indicated the area for the squadron to camp and concluded, "make yourself and your men at home."

On the third day, a horse transport was available, and the captain decided to board Iohannes' squadron on it.

"I've registered you in the thematic roster as Astolfi requested. You should do well when you get home if the Romanoi remain in control. And give my greetings to your father and Father Nicholaos."

"Yes sir, I will."

"Be careful of the Normans; they are getting too close to home."

This was the last time Iohannes would ever see the old captain again.

Spring was around the corner when they boarded for home. They left behind the Sicilian landmass draped with stringy clouds, but the Neptune Mountains peeked through, spotty with evergreens and young pastures. The majesty at his back inspired Iohannes to write a poem in honor of Astolfi during the free times on his return trip.

> *"To Astolfi, who kept us alive.*
> *His sins, many, the man did contrive.*
> *A womanizer, indeed,*
> *and gambling was his creed.*
> *He loved the land dearly,*
> *fought for it sincerely.*
> *His sins, as Hercules, he shed*
> *when he cleansed his soul as he bled."*

Chapter XVI: Home

Along the way home, Iohannes could not help but notice unoccupied houses, some with crumbling walls, their fields neglected and overwhelmed by wild shrubbery and weeds. Worried that a similar fate had taken his family, he quickened the horse's pace and when he had crossed the bridge leading to his home, he could hear Argus' bark echoing throughout the valley. Each bark as he approached the farmhouse tightened his homesick heart further and when he saw the dog running toward him, he dismounted. In recognizing his master, Argus whimpered and wagged his tail like a tadpole swimming upstream. He leaped toward his master who caught him in midair; and both fell over and rolled on the soft ground. In the moment, the veteran forgot he was an adult, carefree and secure as in his youth.

When they arrived at the door of his precious home, Iohannes opened it ever so silently, and stood at the threshold as the dog brushed pass him, while he eagerly waited the family's reaction to his impromptu presence. The faces turned toward the door, jaws dropped, and eyeballs widened in their sockets. There before them loomed a reincarnated ghost, a ghost that was alive to the touch.

Maria was frozen in place for a moment then raced to correlate the image of her Apollinus engraved in her dreams with what now stood before her. The two matched; he had left with helmet in hand, mail shirt over a quilted coat, and sword at his side. Now he was back in the same attire with which he had left, but the lad inside was now a man.

She pushed toward him, unable to talk, and embraced him until completely reassured her senses had not deceived her. Then Maria stepped back to allow Saverina to follow suit, and cried, "Oh dear lord," inhaling slowly in awe as she cupped her hands over her mouth and stared once again at the apparition.

Both women created a mawkish scene that in any other circumstance would make Iohannes blush with embarrassment. Meantime, his father looked on with his enigmatic smile of approval waiting for his turn.

"Where's Grandmother?" Iohannes asked looking around when he had freed himself from the female embraces.

"She is in her room. She hasn't been feeling well lately," said Saverina, wanting to be recognized by Iohannes.

"What do you mean?" he asked while discarding his military gear.

"She stays in her room a lot, kneeling before the wooden cross fixed on her wall. We've encouraged her to come outside, but she says she is at peace alone," elaborated his mother after finding her natural voice.

The hungry veteran sat down and began gorging on the food being placed before him.

"How are things at the grotto?" Iohannes squeezed out a question between bites.

"As far as we know, everything is fine. The group is doing well and Father Nicholaos as usual is on constant errands between Saint Elias and Skylletion. But I am sure you're anxious to see Flavia?" His father sensed the burning in his heart.

"Oh, of course he misses Flavia, she is the one, you know." Maria could not help herself; his prospect of marriage was always on her mind.

"Mom, I've barely taken my coat off, please." Iohannes protested just a little to much to be sincere.

"You're right, you have come back so thin." She brought out wine, more cheese, more barley bread, and dried figs.

"Did you plant the winter wheat, Papa?" Iohannes took a huge bite of the bread and gulped down some wine.

"No, son, we are missing field hands. Maybe with you here we can plant the summer wheat if these Normans don't come around."

"After they left Sicily, I was told they took up arms against us. They established themselves behind the walls of Melfi, using it as a base to attack the towns to the south and east, maybe even Bari."

"We were told the same thing by the garrison at Skylletion. At least they are not in Calabria."

"Not yet!" Iohannes emphasized.

"Iohannes, you must be tired; there will be plenty of time to talk on another day," his mother insisted for the subject matter made her uncomfortable.

"Before I retire, I would like to see Grandmother." He went into her room with Saverina following close behind. He found her sitting on the edge of the bed, deep within herself. Her back had acquired a deeper curvature, and her additional wrinkles presaged what was obvious to her time of life. But her eyes, with that grey haziness, were still in tune to the world around her.

"Oh my, Iohannes, come here," the old woman said, while extending her arms for her grandson. He knelt before her; she laid her hand on his head. "You see, Saverina, I was right that he would come home safe and sound," she said proudly.

Saverina acknowledged the blessing the family had received, but after the recent fiasco in the thickets of the mountain, she had her own concerns. Mother Nature did not visit last month, and Peter had not returned. "What about Peter? Where is he?" She panicked. The eyes of the other two met as if both knew something she did not. She screamed again, "Where is Peter?"

Iohannes hesitated and looked at his grandmother, seeking subtle signs of support for what he was about to say. "He was performing garrison duty in some town after Erymata. Captain

Kamateros will bring him back as he has done for me," he said, slowly and affectionately. The old seer sitting on the bed nodded, hoping to reassure her anxious grandchild, but her mysterious gift of insight had no voice on the matter. Saverina ran to her mother.

Since his internal clock had been reset to the natural rise and setting of the sun, the next day, Iohannes woke up early, before the others. He felt a need to re-immerse himself in the peace and quiet of yesteryear. The fresh air, the chirping of birds, and the rest of the familiar surroundings pleaded for his company. He bypassed Argus curled up next to the fireplace; the dog cracked one eye open while giving him a sleepy snivel, and before Iohannes could close the door behind him, Argus was at his master's side.

His stiff military stance kept him upright and self-assured as he focused on the important matters in his life. He was a man now, and it was time to forge his own destiny. There were plans to be made; first, he would ask for Flavia's hand in marriage; then the parental agreement was in order, followed by a marriage agreement legally sanctioned by the church, an orthodox mandate prior to the betrothal and marriage. Father Nicholaos, the legal guardian of Flavia and member of the local orthodox hierarchy, was the man to see.

When he returned to the house, the family was eager to discover and share in their hero's plans. "Finally," shouted his mother, "where have you been?"

"I've been thinking, I have decided to propose to Flavia." He touched what he knew was already on their minds, but he did not know his father had already talked with the monk.

"You know, son, Father Nicholaos and I have agreed to the particulars of the dowry as well as our contribution. You can have the extra field and half of the orchard, while Father Nicholaos will donate a small plot below the grotto. The rest of his property is to go to Peter when he returns," Eugenius proudly volunteered.

"Those orphans are so poor. I'll have to make the wedding dress for her, and your father can purchase both wedding bands," his mother offered.

"I can help make a list of the invitations with Flavia." Even Saverina was caught up in the excitement.

"Why must it be so complicated to get married?" complained Iohannes.

"It's all very important," his sister emphasized. "In the betrothal the priest must make sure the couple is committed to each other in body and spirit, hence the exchanging of the rings. Then in the marriage ceremony or crowning, the new couple enters the kingdom of Christ, and this is symbolized by the wearing of a crown, usually a garland."

It was obvious that his sister had dwelled a lot on the matter as most young unmarried women, probably too much since Peter still had not come home, Iohannes pondered. "Sis, you're always sentimental."

"But that is how it is," happily interjected his mother.

The community had its own spirit, manifested in religious holidays, masses, cultivations, and harvests, which strengthened the people's resolve. But weddings and baptisms were the most precious since the collective spirit regenerated itself in the offspring.

In the shadow of this preeminent status of the marriage ceremony, Saverina's enthusiasm to assist in her best friend's wedding arrangements appeared to have no bounds. She had awakened from her slumber and insisted on going to the grotto with Iohannes the next day.

Along the way his sister pestered him with questions and suggestions that took away from his own excitement. So many things to tell his former mentor and equally that many to Flavia, his head and heart were about to explode.

When they arrived, they were attacked by the children, who promptly followed them inside. After the initial greetings, followed by Iohannes' sincere but insufficient explanation of Peter's absence, Saverina edged toward Flavia and Helena, leaving Iohannes to the monk and the children.

"Father, Syracuse was all you said it was, and so were Messina and Erymata."

"The churches, the ancient sites…..," inquired his mentor, who felt a piece of his soul had returned.

"We never made Panormos, but I saw parts of the Basilica of Saint Lucia and Archimedes' tomb in Syracuse." Iohannes glanced at Flavia momentarily. "But Father we are in great peril. We lost Sicily and the Normans will eventually arrive here."

"I know, my son."

The monk, who never lost contact with other monks, was well informed and had things of his own to relate as well. The network of monasteries and hermitages scattered throughout the Calabro territory provided a rapid flow of information from Sicily as well as from the north, a hot bed of Norman activity. The never-ending flow of people who had escaped those war-torn areas related their firsthand experiences to the network.

"When the Normans arrive, they will latinize our monasteries." Iohannes was voicing the monk's fears. "They have already threatened the local Greek monastic autonomy and legal authority in some northern towns."

"You are telling me what I know, my son."

"They now are aligned with Rome," emphatically stated Iohannes.

All this was happening too fast for the monk. Any legal or ecclesiastical activity would have to be done now, and this included his pupil's marriage.

"Again, I know, my son," the monk repeated. And noticing that hungry sparkle in the veteran's eyes again directed at his fiancè, made fierce by the passing years, the monk softly coughed for the attention of those eyes and motioned his head toward Flavia and then simply said, "Go!"

The discipline that served Iohannes so well in the military now abandoned him. His legs were willowy; the ground moved. If Astolfi were here, he would be laughing, Iohannes mused. But Astolfi was a philanderer.

Iohannes could not talk, but then there was no need to talk. He reached for her hand, and when she offered it, the ground ceased to move. They walked outside to their favorite spot for what was obvious to everyone; it was destined. How would he propose? The question repeated itself a million times before they reached their spot despite the short walk. When there, he finally uttered the magic words, "Will you marry me?"

"Yes! Yes!" she shouted, jumping to her toes and locking her arms around his shoulders. He grabbed her waist, pulled her tight against him, and then his hands wandered unimpeded and helped his mind recreate the sensuous curves. To Flavia, her dreams had come true. He had come back for her, in the flesh, and she was embracing that sturdy, sinewy, and lovely form.

He would sweep her away to a heavenly and carnal place more secret and private than this spot. It all felt natural, so natural that to be happy; all she had to do was be herself. Once Father Nicholaos had told her that an ancient philosopher named Aristotle had written that happiness is doing what is natural. Oh! How wise that man was, she thought.

Their privacy was suddenly broken by giggles and playful heckling. Becoming suspicious of the lengthy proposal, the monk had sent his little envoys to fetch the couple.

The betrothed joyfully followed the children back where the rest were waiting for the announcement of what was plainly obvious. Iohannes made the announcement in the manner of a proud peacock. Everyone cheered loudly. The women jumped up and down screaming and hugging each other. Most affected was Saverina, who began to immerse herself in Flavia's happiness as if it were happening to her. The onlooking monk, however, was silent and displayed a fierce objection that shot from his eyes and frightened all.

"Stop!" he yelled, summoning the wrath of God. Everyone stopped breathing. The crackling cinders of the fireplace could now be heard. He spoke with the firmness of an ecclesiastical authority, focusing on Iohannes. "Have you not forgotten something? This union must be sanctioned first with parental permission!"

Unfazed by Father Nicholaos' Moses-like stare, which had gripped everyone, Iohannes stood his ground. He knew his mentor well and that included his exaggerations and wit. Iohannes waited for his mentor to crack a smile and for the usual twinkle to return to his Greek eyes. "May I have Flavia's hand in marriage?" he asked.

The monk burst into a got-you guffaw, and struggling through the laughter, he said, "Of course, son!" The cheers and excitement reached a new height, and the event was celebrated with wine.

The marriage plans quickly took root. They set their sights for the betrothal and the actual wedding shortly after the cultivation and planting in nearby Saint Elias. A small monastery run by a priestmonk *hieromonachos* in the town center was an ideal place for the anxious couple. In the meantime, Eugenius, Father Nicholaos, and the couple trekked down to Skylletion to procure a prenuptial agreement *theoretron* mandated by the orthodox church.

The document would stipulate what provisions would be made for Flavia in case of Iohannes' death after the marriage. The monk had made the appointment with Bishop Mesimeros, also the prefect or civil authority of the area authorized to draw up and seal the agreement.

After the completed document was consigned to Eugenius for safekeeping, they went looking for the wedding bands. Two bronze rings with plates on top, one oval with the cross imprinted and the other round with the image of the Christ etched into the soft metal, testified to their proud humbleness.

When they returned to the Florus farm, they were surprised by a stranger who resembled someone from a distant past. He sat there at the kitchen table holding a makeshift cane, a simple stick with round nob. His leathery skin was marked by labors, and his right leg was permanently crippled by a broken bone that had healed in its mangled state. His facial features, however, had retained that ambiguous combination of plainness and attractiveness experienced only by Saverina.

Saverina had been the first to recognize him when she answered to the mysterious knock on the door. Her mother and grandmother, who was feeling a little better, stared at each other with blank faces as he introduced himself at the threshold before an incredulous Saverina frozen in place with mouth and eyes wide open. Finally, she let him in, and led him to a chair followed by the four scrutinizing eyes of the other two.

Argus, who had barked at the knock now wagged his tail and licked the stranger's hand evaporating the suspension in the household. Saverina, still unable to speak now tried to imagine her life with this man, who was so different yet the same.

When the men and Flavia entered, the two women had convinced themselves of his identity and waited to see the returning group's reaction to the stranger. Like his sister, Iohannes recognized him immediately. The ravages of war could not disguise his dear friend and fellow soldier, Peter.

"Look who's here," shouted Maria to the men as Peter rose with difficulty to face the newcomers.

Iohannes lunged toward his long-lost friend. "I looked all over for you. Thank God, you made it back."

"How are you, my son?" The monk followed after Iohannes, hugging and patting his lost orphan on the back. "God has blessed us." The monk stepped back. "Let's look at you." Thank God, he is safe, he sighed to himself.

Eugenius marveled at the veteran. "Give me a hug, son." His training had returned the man home and maybe into his daughter's arms, he hoped.

"I would have come home sooner but was captured," said Peter, leaning hard on the cane, hand trembling with joy.

"How did you escape?" Iohannes asked that which all wanted to know.

"They released me. I was useless to them, my leg, you see?" Peter carefully settled into his seat.

Everyone gathered around him to listen to his tale. The monk looked on with contented eyes, and Laetitia realized her dream of Iohannes had included Peter. Content, she watched Flavia and Saverina slip away to their own corner of the feminine world to share in Saverina's hidden joy.

⸎

The current and hectic nuptial preparations were unfortunately interrupted one day. It began one morning as Saverina was dressing when her grandmother motioned her to come by her bedside.

The inevitable prospect of her grandmother's passing away, which the family had brushed aside as they wrapped themselves in the pleasant wedding preparations, suddenly was a reality. The old woman's coughs, wheezing, and nightly sweats had become more frequent. She had become bedridden, and contrary to the family's naïve hope of recovery, Laetitia sensed an overwhelming certainty of her death.

Laetitia's visions of crumbling Romanoi fortifications that were being repopulated by foxes and weasels were revisiting her.

The visions repeated themselves every night, but each day as her consumption progressed, they began to fade away to be replaced by another dream of bat-like demons fluttering about her bed.

Her uncanny gift was her curse; she had delved in the dark forces, and she needed absolution. But before her confession, she wanted to tell Iohannes what the first visions portended since her mind was still lucid.

"Please, call Iohannes here, and tell your father to get Father Nicholaos," she told Saverina between attempts to draw air into her deteriorating lungs.

Saverina was taken by fear and confusion but did as she was told. Iohannes ran into the bedroom with his mother behind him carrying a wash basin of cool water and rags. Eugenius headed for the grotto.

Saverina stayed in the kitchen and sank into her own thoughts after the initial shock. The approaching death had put everything wonderful on hold and the world around her stopped, still as a portrait, she was angry. Didn't God know that her brother was getting married, and it would be her turn next?

And all this was happening just when Mother Nature had also turned against her by refusing to visit her as in the past. She was afraid of her father's reaction, especially if he knew it was due to Alphaeus' fire growing in her stomach. And grandmother Laetitia would have been the only one to successfully intercede on her behalf and make "papa" understand. She was hurt, angry, and had no one to confide in. Fortunately, her ample, healthy figure still disguised the initial signs.

Then her vexation started to disappear, under the lugubrious weight of the moment. She was taken by bits and pieces from her adolescence when a precious little bundle of maleness that her mother had brought into the world seemed to do nothing other than cry and cry. Then one day it was silent and motionless like her doll. All this was accompanied by her grandmother's incomprehensible Latin chanting and magic to chase the evil spirits away.

Later, when her age offered a better understanding of the incident, her father explained all to her for her mother was too mournful to relive the loss. He was he said, a little boy, an exemplar of the Florus progeny born before Iohannes and called Iohannes, after his father's father.

They wrapped him in a white sheet and inserted him into a clay jar, then placed it in a deep hole that belonged to his grandfather's pit grave near the monastery. Of all this she could only remember her mother's sadness and the many similar jars scattered everywhere. Then a new bundle arrived, all was forgotten. Life no longer was a still portrait; it had depth and motion again. Life does go on, she thought and so would hers.

Maria sat on one side of the bed gently wiping the percolating sweat from her mother-in-law's forehead, still hoping for the illness to go away. Iohannes positioned himself on the other side, leaning over to capture every syllable escaping from his dying grandmother. All those omens and visions, which his grandmother had assembled into a neat coherent picture of the family's future, had to be released.

"Iohannes, it is you who will have to negotiate our family's survival; the bandits are coming," she uttered softly.

"Yes, Grandmother. I know the Norman's tongue and their ways. But you must save your strength," he reassured her.

"When the Greeks came, they brought law and order. Now it is decaying into anarchy," she paused to catch her breath, "because power is in the hands of the incompetent." Iohannes and his mother simply listened. "You know what's worse than incompetence itself? When that power uses corruption as a shield of defense." Her voice crackled.

At this moment, Eugenius and Father Nicholaos entered the bedroom, and Laetitia asked to be left alone with Father Nicholaos.

"What can I do for you, old woman?" He maintained his usual air of familiarity with the family.

"Why do you ask such a foolish question, Father?" He did not respond. "My dark beliefs and practices do not square with the church." She took a precious breath. "Reading omens, doing magic, and summoning demons for their secrets have been a part of my life, Father."

"But you have used them for the good," he shot back.

"Yes, but they're demons nonetheless, and I have consorted with them, Father." She gained new strength in her conviction.

"If they speak to you, that does not make you sinful."

"If you say so, Father, but I would still prefer your blessings." Her eyes fell back as if looking at something afar, and unable to carry on, she slipped deeper into that eternal sleep. Father Nicholaos began to read the Canon of Supplication, and when she had given her last breath, he closed her eyelids.

The wailing promptly began, first by Maria; then as the other women who had accompanied the monk entered the bedroom, it grew into a real dirge. Father Nicholaos insisted on silence since he had not yet said the prayer of absolution.

When he finished, the women began to prepare the body. They washed her with water and wine, clothed her in her normal attire, and finally laid a white shroud on her which attested to her purity before her maker. Then, still discouraged by the monk, the lament began anew. Maria cut off some of her hair and laid it on the body during the wailing, which ceased at times to give way to prayers and the singing of Psalms. Saverina was instructed to place lit candles everywhere and set the table with food for the guests. This was the beginning of a two-night vigil where the living come to terms with death.

The Florus family was wealthy in friends who felt obligated to pay their respects. This little farm in the darkness of the two nights was lit up by eerie, flickering lights emanating from the candles and the fireplace. The slightest motion of air upon the candle wicks cast skirting shadows of evil spirits hunting for departing souls. And so, they lamented and prayed for Christ to receive their dearly departed into his everlasting arms before the shadows snatched them away.

On the final morning of the vigil, the shroud was tightly wrapped around the body, which was gently placed in the wagon with a wreath of flowers next to her head. The procession began toward Saint Elias' monastery with the priest at its head, his deacon at his side carrying the cross and the mourners trailing behind with first the wailing women, then the villagers with the youths waving palms in the air. After the Mass, Iohannes and other able youths carefully laid the body in its final resting place.

"You are of the earth, to the earth you shall return," concluded the priest.

Saverina dropped a small wooden cross down into the grave and began to cry. Its purpose was to guard the soul from the malevolent spirits while on its journey to everlasting life. Then Maria dropped the old woman's mixing bowl which once held her herbs and potions and together with her medicinal knowledge had chased away diseases and countless demons.

Iohannes sensed a part of his life vanishing forever into that burial pit. He had seen death in the battlefield but had not the leisure to delve into its meaning. Now, he had time. If we are of the earth, both in life and in death, then death loses its finality and becomes a transition, a mystery without explanation, he reasoned.

Then the party gathered nearby for the funeral meal while some men sealed the grave with heavy slabs, one of which simply chiseled with the sign of the cross and the name Laetitia

Florus below it. The meal shifted the solemn focus of the ritual toward lighter matters, pertinent to the living.

The women formed their little gossip groups, discussing all and everything from births to marriages and other people who were not present. Initially Father Nicholaos and Iohannes debated philosophical questions, but soon politics and the military were in order.

"Have you heard anything on the war?" Iohannes asked his comrade from the garrison.

"Not much since I saw you last. The Normans have taken more towns in Lucania and Apulia. Maniakes was freed from prison and has landed in Taranto."

"I hope this time Constantinople keeps the general in charge," volunteered Eugenius.

⁓

Not surprisingly, the nuptial preparations nibbled away at the gloom from the death. Its pain was soon engulfed by the ocean of everyday life. Helena, being true to her motherhood status, prepared the bride in matters of advice and fittings of the wedding dress. Maria did her best for the betrothed by sewing and washing Iohannes' best attire and assisting Helena with Flavia's gown. The men went to the monastery to reset the timetable for the wonderful event which was made for the first week of June.

It so happened that the humble ceremony coincided with the empress' royal third wedding, a juxtaposition in time but obviously not in place. On one hand, Flavia, pure as spring mountain water, was being fitted in a humble white gown by equally humble women of the earth. Whereas, the aging empress, still well preserved with exotic cosmetics and oils, across the sea in her palace was surrounded by a retinue of servants fussing over her every whim. The pleats and folds of her garment or chiton were all in their proper place and draped royally to the empress' chamber floor.

Augusta

Zoe

*mosaic in
Hagia
Sophia*

Illustration by Alice Wright

Saverina made Flavia's wreath with myrtle leaves speckled with white flowers that in the ceremony would garland her silky hair. The empress was fitted with her lavish crown of precious metals and gems, whose powers granted her the freedom of scheming with impunity. Happily, immersed in court intrigue, she was shielded from the repercussions of her manipulative ways and indiscretions in her other imperial bed. The crown functioned in the way of the magic ring of Gyges, giving invisibility to her moral transgressions.

There were no elaborate outer vestments for our bribe, just a veil covering her natural beauty, which she would first lift for her knightly groom. The empress, on the other hand, would wear an outer garment, sparkling with expensive stones, and woven with threads of gold and silver.

Zoe was the empress' name. Her union with the new emperor, chosen by her, would be immortalized in mosaic on a gallery wall of the famous Basilica, Saint Sophia. Flavia's and Iohannes' union would also be immortalized, in the bosom of their God and his everlasting kingdom.

Formal invitations were sent out by the empress' personal guard, written in a scroll properly sealed and delivered to important players in the court and other dignitaries. Whereas Saverina made the rounds with Peter at her side, notifying the neighbors of the time and place of the wedding.

The exchanging of the rings, the first part of the Florus ceremony, was held outside, a sort of make-believe narthex or vestibule. The priest blessed their rings, which were placed on the fourth finger of their right hand and were exchanged three times, symbolizing their pledge to share their lives, both earthly and spiritual.

At the very same moment, the royal couple stood in the inner lavish narthex of Saint Sophia just before the imperial door. Their priest was a representative of the Patriarch who presided over the illegal third marriage, for the Patriarch of Constantinople had refused. Afterward, the imperial retinue followed the priest through the nave and to the apse, where the political marriage was completed but never actually consummated, for she had her lovers, and the emperor had his mistresses.

Our earthly couple and their peasant retinue filed into the little apse of the monastery before a willing priest, who crowned the two with the simple wreaths. For these faithful people of the earth, the marriage ritual itself was an actual participation in the kingdom of our Lord, symbolized by the crowning. The chanting, the litany, and the prayers, all made God's presence real as they were captured by the eternal moment of the ritual.

The joyous guests sang and played music as they marched back to the groom's house for the festivities as they followed the couple with Flavia still wearing the veil, which she removed only after entering the house. A new family unit was added to the community, in defiance of life's challenges, and the people relished in the small victory.

When the royal couple and their guests at this stage of the wedding were entertained by dancers and professional singers as they feasted on their extravagance, our couple and their community experienced real joy which emanated naturally from their hearts.

It fell upon Peter to toast the newlywed; mustering all his skills in reciting pastoral verse, he put together the following rustic ode to the happy couple.

A toast with wine to the princess and her knight.
A new branch has the Florus tree.
As they cuddle in the privacy of the night
New buds, I am sure we will see.
Everyone listened attentively, eager for more.
Our chorion shares their destiny.
All our hearts beat in unison.
They play a sweet, marvelous melody.
Thank God, Flavia did not become a nun.
All laughed.
This ritual has most sincerely inspired
Saverina and me within its blessing.
And since our love has never wavered and tired
We seek the same of our future wedding.

Another couple was waiting in the wedding queue, no less in importance. Those maternal signs had become obvious to the immediate family who knew Saverina's normal, rustic cut. Plans were hatched in the Florus bedroom, where Maria filed the sharp corners of Eugenius' wrath over Alphaeus' fire in his daughter.

The crippled groom also knew of the fire, but the union was an orphan's dream to be invited into a real family. When the child popped out too soon, he was passed as premature, and everyone said he looked like Peter with his round brown eyes and hair color, dark as the raven. Baptized Little Peter Savium, he preceded and survived Flavia's first, named Little Eugenius.

PART THREE

Chapter XVII: Northern Wave

To the Italic people, the people closest to the earth, the Hautevilles were the brothers from hell who relentlessly sought their place among the powers of the world. They eventually carved out a kingdom by their fierce tenacity, astuteness, and deception, so history tells us. But these lofty qualifiers of the family do not quench the serious onlooker's skepticism. How in the world can an obscure family conquer half of Italy beginning with only a hundred knights? Credit is surely due elsewhere! Other players invisible to history, such as their nobles back home who trained them, or their hosts who welcomed them to Italy must have had a role.

Underneath the gilded veneer of their deeds, the family, more like a wolf pack, relished in their bloody greed and viciousness. When one wolf died, another would descend from their lair in Normandy. When William died in 1046 and Drogo took over, their younger brother Robert arrived to join the pack. Drogo, who died in 1051, handed over his domain to Humphrey. Then Humphrey died in 1057 and Robert inherited his title of Count of Apulia, at which time his younger brother Roger appeared on the scene ready and eager to seek his fortune at the feet of Robert.

All were a scourge upon the innocent land; Robert may have been the worst. Upon his arrival in Calabria, the older brother Drogo received him in apprenticeship, granting him the small fort of Stridula for his central venue of operations. The standard or banner under which he fought was of his own making, for his deeds were unsanctioned by higher authority. He was simply a bandit who recruited other bandits and adventurers.

They stole from the defenseless population to build their leader's war chest and when confronted with resistance, they held hostage the people's crops and livestock until the gold and jewels were relinquished. Thus, the band evolved into an army fit for conquest, ravishing the rich basin of Constantia, but. if overwhelmed by Greek authority and its local allies, the cunning Norman would slip into the nearby Sila mountains.

As his reign expanded, famine and excessive tributes led to revolts, which Robert crushed revengefully with ever more blood. (9) Finally, the church could bear no more and was drawn into a battle which it lost. Latter, however, a form of peace occurred when Pope Nicholaos II reversed the church's policy against the Normans. In the Melfi Synod of 1059, he granted Robert the title "Duke of Calabria and Sicily," an investiture which was still not completely under Robert's control.

But under this legitimate standard, further conquests were sanctified. Towns in the Calabrian landscape which still had stood firm, finally succumbed against the inevitable. But Reghium, Saint Giriaca, Skylletion, and its nearby villagers of Saint Elias, were still going about their daily lives trying to cope with the unfortunate events elsewhere.

They at first directed their attention on the greatest prize of all, Rhegium, the city most faithful to the empire apart from Bari. Robert would sweep down from the Sila mountains, where he had access to the Ionian coastline as well as the Tyrrhenian on the other side. His other brother, Roger, was denned in Mileto Vecchio just behind the mountains of Saint Elias that surrounded the Florus' little valley. From there he would head for Rhegium and set up his siege apparatus at its walls and wait for Robert and his army.

After three attempts, the rich city finally surrendered without resistance, yielding its precious wealth to Robert as if prior victories had not yielded enough in tribute. Other towns like Saint Giriaca, the birthplace of the monk's mother, also had paid dearly for his bloody tyranny. They were pearls incidental to the wealthy Rhegium of which one was left, Skylletion, this endeavor was headed by Roger.

In the meantime, the villagers of Saint Elias cultivated, planted, harvested, gave birth, and prayed under the spiritual fervor of Father Nicholaos. Alphaeus' name occasionally came up in conversations with no one ever having any news. His story faded away for now along with the hate and pity surrounding it.

Saverina brought six others into the world after Peter Junior: two of whom died, one stillborn, and the other died of pneumonia at the age of two. Flavia gave birth to five; the first died shortly after birth due to a difficult labor. The male newborn never had the chance to carry his chosen name of Eugenius. Three girls followed baby Eugenius, after which another healthy Eugenius popped into the world to carry on the family name.

Naturally, the two families were accommodated on the Florus' holding, each with its own little plot of land and house. Together with Grandmother Maria and Grandfather Eugenius, they formed a closely-knit unit that benefited the children's upbringing, beginning with birth.

Grandmother Maria had inherited the midwifery skills and other medical and nursing knowledge from her mother-in-law, which she utilized when needed. Each newborn had passed through her gentle hands first. Cousins, uncles, aunts, and grandparents were sheltered here on the Florus' holding, a generation skipped over by the Norman fires of destruction raging elsewhere. Even the imperial human levies and taxations failed to reach them.

A frequent visitor to this generation was Grandmother Helena as the children called her given that the grotto's orphans had dwindled to a few. They found his or her future elsewhere throughout the countryside, expanding Helena's precious time with Flavia and her children. The grandchildren, who now ranged from two to nineteen, were always first to greet her, alerted by a new frisky Argus as they played in the yard.

The monk's still boundless energy was concentrated elsewhere, his general laity, and friends in other monasteries. He had just returned from the Valley of Salt, where he befriended Philip of Troina. Tonsured in the Basilian tradition with the title of Father Philaretes, he refreshed and enriched the monk's memories of their beloved Sicily. The discussions also centered on the Norman attacks on Rhegium and the possible siege of Skylletion, a revelation that compelled the monk to return home. And on his rush back home he gathered more somber tidings revealing its imminence.

Once home the monk decided to accompany Helena to the Floruses.

"I'm coming too, Helena!" he said as Helena was preparing to leave, thinking she and the Florus group should be told.

"You are sixty-six. Slow down. These trips will have the best of you. You have just returned from the Tyrrhenian." Helena fussed over her Nicholaos.

"My rickety old body is least of my concern," he boasted.

"You have always been a stubborn man. Stay home and relax." She waited as he darted out the door.

"The war is at our doorstep. When I passed by Mileto, Roger was not there. I was told he was laying siege on Rhegium, and Robert was on the march from Sila to join his brother."

"But that is Rhegium, not us." Helena fought the unwelcomed news.

"Worse than that. On my way here, someone approached me from Skylletion. He said Rhegium's contingent has already surrendered, and the officials are exiled in Skylletion. The town is preparing for a siege. We must prepare too." With this, they jumped into a brisk walk.

When Helena and the monk entered the home of Iohannes, they found all three families there. A malaise was written on their faces but not explained to the children. The seriousness of the matter before them travelled silently from the eyes of one to the eyes of the other skipping the little ones.

Iohannes had been notified to appear at the fortress of Skylletion for the impending assault and was gathering his military gear. Peter, although exempt, was also getting ready. Eugenius, in his sixties and incrementally yielding to the rising role of his son, still fashioned himself as the main authority.

"I've seen this scenario before and so have Peter and Iohannes. The attackers stop at nothing. Even the women and children are in danger; we must think of them first." Eugenius broke through the pretentious air, after the older children took possession of the smaller ones to the next room.

"Skylletion is too far for our families, and its fort will fill with the town's people first. There must be another way," questioned Iohannes.

"They could take shelter at the grotto along with others of the nearby area. It's happened before when the Saracens came," volunteered Father Nicholaos.

"Why don't we just surrender? Let them have what they want; perhaps they will leave us alone. After all, they are Christians too." Helena knew well the atrocities of the Arabs but had no familiarity with regards to the Normans.

"They are Normans first and Christians by convenience and opportunity." The monk offered a sober assessment learned in his travels.

"Mother Helena, they are treacherous and only understand the sword. One day they are on your side and on the next day, they are against you," Iohannes confirmed the monk recalling their behavior at Syracuse.

"Oh, my God, what are we to do?" wailed Maria as Eugenius nudged her toward her grandchildren for distraction.

"We must resist and then negotiate the safety of the women and children," Eugenius said. Then turning to his son, "Son, you're familiar with their tactics; what are we to expect?"

"They will surround the Skylletion fort and set up towers at its walls. If they can not break through or we refuse to surrender, they will raid the countryside, kill the innocent, and destroy God knows what."

"We need another team of fighters to hide in various spots to hinder their plundering while the garrison holds firm. We did this under Maniakes. I can form the team," Peter contributed.

"Papa, I'm with you," volunteered Peter Junior, now nineteen.

"Sorry, son, you will protect your mother and the children at the grotto." His son read the correctness of the words in his father's eyes.

"If only Maniakes were still alive," Eugenius looked at the monk.

"Betrayed for the second time, he tried to overthrow the emperor and his corrupt court but was accidently killed in a battle that he had already won. But that was seventeen years ago shortly after your son's wedding. We have been on our own since," said the monk.

"It seems to me that we must find a way to surrender with the least amount of bloodshed and damage to our property," Iohannes repeated his father's suggestion. "I am sure our garrison commander will do just that."

"From what I understand the Romanoi have not returned since Maniakes left and local rebellions have failed," Father Nicholaos said.

"We are the Romanoi now," concluded Iohannes with old memories of the war coming to life.

The discussion now leaned elsewhere, for it was not only the physical threat at hand that frightened them but the uncertainty of their future life in its aftermath. The scanty and conflicting news that filtered out from the towns already under the Norman chokehold only confused and terrified them, and they naturally turned to Father Nicholaos.

"What happens after they take over? Will we still own our lands, or will we become slaves?" wondered Peter.

"I must be honest, my son. Some will be serfs, not slaves, but if you ask me the difference, I would be hard pressed to explain it. I can only say that all lands will belong to them which they may grant to lesser nobles, mostly allies who will pay rent and homage to them. This is the Frankish way." Father Nicholaos wondered if he had been too honest.

"But what of the small farmers and tenant farmers who have freely worked their land and paid taxes to Constantinople," inquired Iohannes.

"My understanding is that they will be bonded to the land and obligated to work it in accordance with the nobles' wishes. Our blessed rights under the orthodox tradition will be lost."

"What does that mean?" Flavia had edged her way toward the men, drawn by the topic of the conversation.

"I believe, but I'd have to check on it, one cannot marry or change occupation without the master's permission," The monk said bluntly. Flavia's spirits dampened; her children would not have the same rights as her, and noticing her sadness, the monk focused on the Normans' reluctance to enforce the new order.

"My child, for now, they are interested only in confiscating wealth to subsidize further conquests," his comforting eyes fell on her. "Most towns under them are still behaving as if still under Greek rule. The Basilian monks still have their special place in the community. We will be here for you, a long time."

"Long enough for our children?" retorted Flavia.

"Of course, my child," he answered with sincere sympathy. This was the monk at his best, fulfilling his calling as the good shepherd.

"Some at the garrison have heard that the Normans already have set their eyes on the Saracens in Sicily. They have acquired an interest in amassing a fleet for the mission." Iohannes felt the need to second Father Nicholaos' optimistic statement. "If they encounter the same problems we had in Sicily, we will be left alone for a long time."

That night, the frigid, winter wind howled the words of war into the bedroom of Flavia and Iohannes making their bed unusually cold; it weakened the spirits and pumped the heart. The room was where within the bed's sheets, their two bodies would conjoin, intertwine into one that lit the fiery furnace within. The carnal senses would displace the cold, but this chill refused to go away. The furnace only whispered against the unbearable chill of war. Nevertheless, their worries did give way to fatigue and then sleep.

Chapter XVIII: The Kastron

Wars, wars, and more wars. So many wars that no man was exempted from military service except those already dead in its clutches. It was an unwanted guest who ferociously pounded on their door demanding their participation. Answering its call again was Iohannes, now forty, and still possessing the stamina and resolve of his prior active duty in Sicily. Then he had fought for liberation; now it was for preservation; once for unknown Christian brothers, now for the closest of kin; once for gain, now for survival.

Met before in Sicily when they were comrades, this enemy worshiped the same Christian God, one or two had even been in his squad. Friend had become foe and another war was resurrected at the Florus doorstep.

Iohannes had made his way to Skylletion, where the Rhegium contingent and the local makeshift garrison prepared for the assault, both headed by the old Commander Ouramos. Within the walls of the Byzantine fortress, the haphazardly assembled aging soldiers and whatever available male youths of fighting age wait for a war, a war ordered by Robert Hauteville still looting Rhegium, and carried out by his brother Roger.

Outside of the Skylletion walls were Lombards, Normans, wayward Saracens, bandits, and even Greeks, who cast their lot at the possibility of a fiefdom from the new order.

Roger set the camp on whatever level ground found near and about the town walls, and early, on the second day before the frozen dew of winter melted, sawing and hammering noises echoed in the stillness of dawn. Conscripted craftsmen from coastal towns, where shipbuilding was a necessity, were busy as ants, constructing a wooden tower to scale the walls while the surrounding Norman camp readied for the actual assault. Units not part of the siege were dispatched into the nearby country devasting the landscape to soften the resolve of the poor souls under siege.

The tension within the walls grew into an unbearable intensity, compounded by the audible prayers from the women hugging their children. Commander Ouramos tried to ignore it as he stood on the highest point of the fortress and swept the countryside with his aging, glassy eyes made tearful by the nippy wind. He watched attentively the returning raiding parties of the enemy, who appeared haggard and demoralized. They came back wounded or did not return at all. His men in the fields were successfully ambushing the enemy at every turn and minimizing the damage threatened by them.

He had set up two teams in this guerilla operation, suggested by Iohannes, one around the enemy camp and the other near Saint Elias headed by Peter. But he lacked reinforcements from Constantinople, and the small Greek contingent from Rhegium did not add much to his own garrison. A defeat was still inevitable, his experienced mind surmised. He hoped to gain as much leverage as possible from the ambushes to negotiate a palatable surrender. Although he encouraged his men with true passion like any good commander, he knew they would have to ultimately rely on the tenuous Christian mercy of the attackers for some peace.

The wooden tower kept rising; each additional log or board fastened to it inched it higher. Soon it would overshadow the wall and usher in a horde of sword-wielding madmen. Although the garrison archers shot flaming arrows at its structure, the freshly harvested wood was not compromised and the workers, being shielded, worked unfazed.

What made matters worse, the besiegers had rounded up locals to function as human shields by forcing them to stand between the rising tower and the wall. Some ran, not in fear but to give the archers inside the walls a clear shot at the structure. They were quickly killed and replaced by other innocent souls.

Others stood frozen in place with a fear that denied the reality of their predicament. Others, still, prayed in the manner of a martyr content to meet his God. All this revolted those inside. Some vomited at the horror; others forced their focus elsewhere.

Iohannes had enough and besieged the commander to let him take a party outside the gate in the dead of night to rain havoc on the camp. But the commander requited with a flat "no" and gave a commander's explanation: The camp was too well guarded, and he was needed inside.

There was nothing left to do but suffer through the agonizing wait prior to the actual attack. The wait, that eternal wait, consumes the spirit in never-ending nibbles. The knees feel weak when walking and the mind is flooded with thoughts of mortality. You feel death's chilling breath down your spine and grow weaker, but then the battle starts, and the thinking stops. This is what Iohannes had felt in his debut to war when it was only himself to worry about.

But now it was worse for images of Flavia and the children, caught up in the same stupid war, feasted on his mind. They had been reduced to defenseless animals burrowed in the bowels of the earth. His own safety became insignificant; his muscles tightened, as never in his life, to the temper of the steel lamellar corset that he wore and the lance he clutched. Fear turned to anger, and anger turned to fear, and fear turned back to anger, and so on and so on within that damn, eternal wait.

He could almost see the Norman raiders in the fields, invulnerable, armored and sitting on an equally armored horse. Even the lightly armored bandits who rode along in the mission of plunder displayed a similar cocky countenance. Their hired chronicles of the same race have portrayed them as courageous, gallant knights, but what valor, what probity could they possess when they maliciously hunt down their fellow Christians as prey?

Iohannes was very aware of that savageness that their ancient Viking blood carried in their veins. It would overflow and blend with the wild stubbornness of their horses as they tugged the rein from side to side, scouring the countryside for prey. He anticipated them to set ablaze their homes with torches that seemed lit by the fire exhaled from the snorting horses and then cut down the fleeing souls—the primitive hunted the civilized. The world was upside down and being taken over by barbarism.

The road between Skylletion and Saint Elias gave the enemy access to a vast hunting ground where Peter's squad was scattered about, under cover of thickets and scrubland not far from the trafficked roadway. Father Nicholaos, feeling no religious remorse in his participation, had taken a smaller group up the road leading to the grotto, but since he was a monk, the only human the Normans hesitated to kill, he wandered up and down the road misleading the enemy or acquiring information to relay to Peter.

Peter like Iohannes had learned his soldiery well. His squad had set up roadblocks, forcing the Norman knights to dismount or go around into the rugged ground where they would be more vulnerable to surprise attacks. His spirits were no different than Iohannes', energized by visions of Saverina, wimpled as a nun and surrounded by his precious children. His blood boiled with the needed hate, man's greatest strength in the moment of attack.

The crippled leg did not hold him back when he and his men would rush insanely toward the enemy as willing sacrifices to save their loved ones. Then there were the archers who released deadly arrows from unsuspecting places. None of the barbarians who ventured deep into the territory escaped his cunning tactics and returned safely to their camp.

The covey of local villagers labored tediously up the slippery path to the grotto for shelter where they would join Helena and the families from the Florus farm hosting them. With their humble homes at their backs, they struggled against the increasing colder air of the higher country and moved no quicker than the toddlers and the elders could bear.

Sneezing and coughing broke into the silent air of dejection in the middle of their journey but a young, expecting mother walked with head held high, holding tightly her belly as if to protect her baby from the evil outside before it reached them all. It attracted the others' attention and help, the only diversion on the journey.

They brought with them whatever belongings they could carry, for they had no idea how long they would be away or if they could ever return. When they arrived, Helena and Flavia welcomed the weary group into the hovel with a warm fire, blankets, and hot soup. Gradually the coughing stopped.

The younger ones did not know the journey's true purpose; if told by their older playmates, the quick and loving denial from the elders only greased their joints for more frolicking. Each mother, hair covered due to the solemnity of the place or just by custom and often holding a crying toddler in her arms, scolded her others halfheartedly.

Daily needs had to be met, infants needed nursing, mouths had to be fed, scrapes and wounds needed care, and rampant fear and uncertainty needed a rational counterbalance from a steady hand. The oldest of Flavia's girls, Little Helena or Helè, now seventeen, was the spitting image of her sweet mother. She, along with Peter Junior were called often to assist their parents.

Most of all, the regenerative essence of life moved forward when the young pregnant woman began experiencing for the first time those dreadful contractions. The veteran mothers surrounded her with comfort and advice, and when that telltale sign of a ready birth (amniotic fluid) arrived, Maria was at hand with her birthing paraphernalia. Shortly after the maternal groans and moans, a screaming, healthy male child announced his passage into the world, attracting curiosity and excitement.

However, this bubble of euphoria vanished quickly for Helena. She appeared to be everywhere attending to every one's needs and became so fatigued that Flavia had to help her to her bed, where she was overwhelmed by congestion and a severe headache.

At the fortress, the Normans were having trouble completing the wooden siege towers. The work lingered for they were frustrated by the constant volleys of arrows and stones hurled from the walls, days had passed, and supplies were running low. The Norman scouts, sent out to harass the local population and procure foodstuff and other supplies, often returned with little or nothing due to the defensive guerilla tactics of the fort commander.

The enemy summoned an additional contingent of archers to return a heavier volley of their own to pin down the fighters inside, so they could resume the building. With the structures finally completed, Roger gave the order for a small unit of lancers and swordsmen to scale the walls with the purpose of opening the gate for the rest of the invading army.

They were an expendable group of local traitors and brigands and began climbing onto the tower like ants crawling up a pile of logs. When at the top, they pushed their way onto the battlement. There, swords and lances clashed with other swords and lances, creating visible sparks in the early morning. In the fray, the lucky fighters parried off the blows with their shields while the unlucky fell under the wielding weapons that cut through to the bone.

When the clashes shifted to the courtyard below, the Norman commander unexpectedly cut off the supply of ants. The seasoned Greeks, recently returned from the Sicilian

Campaign, were now frustrating the enemy, which was now inside but could not reach their goal of opening the gate.

Nevertheless, one enemy fighter seemed to defy the success of the Greeks. Stubborn and haughty, he slashed and jabbed while slowly moving toward the gate. He stood out among the attackers and Iohannes caught him through the corner of his eyes. He took note that the fighter had the facial tone of the Berbers in Sicily, his curly black hair sprinkled white, and he was wild and flamboyant in his fighting. Something was familiar in the man and Iohannes fought his way toward him.

"Alphè! Why are you fighting us?" he demanded.

The man fixed his hellish eyes upon his caller, and in his frenzy he lunged toward him, cutting the air with his sword. Iohannes sidestepped, deflecting the blow with his lance.

"The monk always favored you," Alphaeus yelled as Iohannes purposely missed his opportunity to shove his lance into Father Nicholaos' former orphan. Each stepped back for an instant to read the other's determination.

"We all were equal in his orphanage!" Iohannes dropped his lance and unsheathed his sword to bring equity into the sparring, a compassionate obligation only for Father Nicholaos.

"That meaningless Greek orphanage! I gave up on them. There is wealth and power in the new order." Another slash arrived and Iohannes parried and locked it in place only to be momentarily transfixed by those devilish eyes in the closeness of the fight.

"How could you betray us?" Iohannes pushed his nemesis away and instinctively initiated his own defense.

"I wanted Flavia, but you got her," Alphaeus complained, blocking Iohannes' blows.

Flavia's cherished name, the name that gave meaning to Iohannes' life, was too much to bear coming from that spiteful mouth. It was uttered by a traitor, a bandit, and his heart filled with pure hate. His powerful blows quickened and landed harder on his opponent's sword, forcing him to inch backward.

Alpheus resorted to a continuous mindless, downward slashing and jabbing which Iohannes continuously blocked, but the final one he deflected and simultaneously thrust his sword into the bandit's chest, all done in one smooth motion with his battle-hardened hand. Alphaeus fell slowly on his knees with sword in his chest and Iohannes still holding onto the handle. The dying man's eyes were still challenging the eyes of Iohannes when he finally rolled on his back and Iohannes yanked out the sword. Iohannes then leaned over his dying nemesis and could not find a word to say. He wrote his own fate, he concluded in his mind and walked away.

The initial wave was stopped, but Ouramos realized more would come later, for this was a test battle by which the Normans measured the resistance. If only he could hammer out an agreement that excluded hostages, raids, and outrageous tributes of their harvest or livestock, he pondered.

His men, however, wanted to keep on fighting and so did most of his officers, including Iohannes and the imperial contingent from Rhegium. Its bishop and its prefect were even more steadfast than his men. They were resolute and often interfered with his commands and it was difficult to ignore their suggestions due to the contribution of their well-trained men to the fight.

"They stopped the attack. They must be running out of supplies," said the adamant prefect. "We must keep fighting."

"I only have two guerrilla units out there, if they are still alive; besides, the Norman home base is just over the mountains, at Mileto. They can easily send for more supplies," the commander snapped back at the heedless suggestion.

"Sir, I believe our field fighters are doing their job. Roger's knights are returning wounded and empty handed. We can hold out," replied the prefect.

"We can send for help from Constantinople," the Rhegium bishop naively added.

"Constantinople didn't come to help your Rhegium. Why should they come here?" impatiently responded the commander, now irate.

The bishop fixed his eyes on Ouramos. "We are prepared to die for dignity and freedom, a noble and honorable end."

"But how can this be noble when we know that afterwards they will rape our women and starve or enslave our children?" Ouramos yelled for Iohannes. "Iohannes. We need you to talk to the Franchoi. We must find out why they stopped the fight and see if they are willing to negotiate. I have a feeling the first round was to test our defenses."

"Yes sir, now?" said Iohannes, snapping to a rigid stance.

"Go to the wall facing the siege engine and get their attention. I will meet you there."

When Ouramos reached Iohannes, he had already gotten someone's attention. The man was a Lombard and former member of his unit, who now had a unit of lancers of his own. Recognizing his former dekarch, he yelled back, "Ioanfleur, it is I," in his muddled Latin. Iohannes was in no mood to be cordial and refused to soften his exterior shell toward his former comrade in arms, who appeared pretentious and haughty.

"Our commander wants to talk to Roger, your commander," bellowed Iohannes.

The Lombard showed a simile of respect for his former friend; perhaps the fleeting memories of their former comradery brought an inkling of shame. "I will get him," he replied dryly as he turned his horse around.

Shortly thereafter, Roger appeared before the wall, along with his personal guards and interpreter, a Norman monk fluent in Latin equal to Iohannes. Roger was fully armed, mail coat glinting in the sunlight, a shield embellished with the family coat-of arms, a sword sheathed at his side but no lance. He had an uncanny eye to read the true nature of his circumstances; the lance was not needed.

His physical features were far removed from the barbarity of his elder brothers. Handsome and refined, soft spoken, amenable to the present realities, and pleasant but all the while his mind raced through calculations for his next move. Strong but not rugged or tyrannical in demeanor as Robert and although there was a family resemblance in body features such as straw-colored hair and rosy complexion, he lacked the intractability of Robert. The man was twenty-nine with a formidable future before him.

A bit of silence fell upon the scene, interrupted only by the occasional pawing and neighing of the horses as the two commanders eyed each other, squaring up the other for hints on how to proceed. Neither of the two blinked nor deviated their pensive stares. One, whitehaired and experienced, and the other was an upstart but cunning and had learned quickly to perform well in battles, which, ironically, included the many against his own older brother Robert.

Roger leaned over to his interpreter in a subtle effort either to seek advice or relay what was to be translated. Quickly changing his mind, he looked up once again to the old Greek commander and confidently yelled in his limited Latin, "Quid velis, Praefecte?" (What do you want, Commander?)

Ouramos, still focused on the Norman, said to Iohannes, "Tell him we seek peace terms."

Promptly and assertively Iohannes shouted, "Salve, condiciones pacis ferre cupimus."

Roger whispered into the Norman monk's ear something that prompted the monk to shout toward the walls, "Se mihi imperio subicere velitis, vobis auscultabo." (If you submit to my rule, I will listen.) Both commanders displayed dignity and diplomatic grace, sometimes speaking through the translators;

other times one or the other on his own would jump into the haggling insisting on some passionate point.

Roger persisted for a while on a complete surrender, but since he had his men tied up here for so many days, laden with past spoils from other towns, and the food was running out, he reluctantly became receptive to succeeding demands.

Ouramos, bluffing, insisted that they could hold out until word could filter through to Constantinople for help, a possibility made real since the two high officials from Rhegium were important enough for the Romanoi to return. On the other hand, Roger was smart enough to know, all this posturing on the part of the old commander could be a ruse, but what had he to gain by risking it?

Roger offered a gesture of goodwill by allowing the two Rhegium officials along with their contingent to leave for Constantinople. The Normans would cease their raiding and devastation provided the town accept Norman domination.

Not a bad deal considering the town's precarious predicament, pondered Iohannes, after he delivered the translation to the commander who agreed.

Roger then gathered all his men, took whatever wealth lay in the town along with other supplies that were needed for the trek to his permanent fortification at Mileto, and prepared to leave by way of the Catacen Isthmus. The nightmare was finally over with limited casualties. Calabria was now fully under the control of the Normans and would slowly drift away from the Greek Orthodox culture.

The Norman field raiders began to withdraw from the countryside and headed toward Skylletion, leaving the resistance lying in their concealed positions in a state of confused relief. Peter's men, which were scattered around Saint Elias, slowly, one by one appeared onto the main road at the enemy's rear, keeping a cautious distance from the retreating plunderers. A few of his brave men even shadowed the hastily moving force by pursuing them along the road's bank, hoping to overhear their conversations.

Father Nicholaos, who was up ahead on the main road had approached one of the Normans and was now tugging on the horse's reins, in hope of extracting information on the enemy's activity. He demanded, in the name of God, to know what was happening. From a distance, Peter could hear disrespectful shouts directed at Father Nicholaos.

"Get out of the way, old man! You cowards have already surrendered." When the monk had his fill of insults, he simply watched as the Normans disappeared into the horizon. It was then that Peter caught up to him.

"Did they tell you what is going on?"

"No, Peter, I suspect there are more riches in Skylletion for them to steal," the monk said, unfazed by the wrangling and insults.

Meanwhile, the men who were shadowing the enemy, in which Myrtilus participated, returned to report to Peter. Myrtilus, still panting from his run back to the main group, approached Peter and said, "We overheard them say that some agreement was concluded between Roger and the garrison commander under which the women and children would be left alone."

"We also heard them say that after taking what they want, they will return to Mileto by way of the Catacen Isthmus," someone else added.

"That is a good sign; that means that they will not use the shorter way through the mountains where our people are hiding," interjected another.

"Laden with so much loot and supplies, I don't think they will make it through the mountains, especially on the mule trails. I remember the difficulty with the logs," confirmed Peter.

"I suggest going to the grotto; we can also check on people along the way," interposed the monk. Peter agreed.

Along the way, they encountered further devastation, areas where the opposition forces such as Peter's were unable to rescue. They were dumbfounded and depressed. Their precious food source, the fields of recently germinated winter wheat, was all too easily trampled by the relentless enemy horsemen who now had vanished like a bad dream. In their wake, a tomb-like silence hovered over the countryside, and occasionally they witnessed smoke in the distance emanating from where once stood a shack or farmhouse.

Not a word was spoken until they reached the path that led to the Florus', where they found the wooden bridge spanning the stream had been dismantled. Only the stone abutments were left intact, and most of the logs comprising its bed had since floated away, creating the appearance of abandonment. They waded the stream at its most shallow spot and headed to the farm, where they knew Eugenius was held up to protect his livestock.

They skipped the usual greetings with Eugenius, and all headed back toward the broken bridge.

"Are all your animals safe, Genè?" questioned the monk, letting down his garment which was held up as they crossed the river and now were on its bank.

"Of course," grunted Eugenius and then asked, "The battle?"

Peter took it upon himself to answer. "We really don't know much. There is a truce and Roger is returning to Mileto."

The others, who lived in Saint Elias, split from the group after everyone had reached the crossroad to the town, a little way beyond the stream. The rest undertook the mule path to the grotto.

"Has there been any news from Saint Elias?" inquired Eugenius, while glancing at the departing inhabitants of the town.

Peter felt compelled once again to answer. "We blocked the two roads to the town; it should be all right. It is the fields we had difficulty protecting."

"We will find out soon enough when we reach my father's farm up on the ridge. There is a full view of the town from there," added Myrtilus, who was working his way up front, anxious to meet his father, who had stayed home in its protection.

When the others met up with him, they found him in a state of shock, white as if someone had drained his blood and staring into space. The little shack he called home was reduced to a pile of stones with a partially burned roof situated where once lay the floor and his father was nowhere to be found. The only signs of life came from whimpering pups licking the teats of their dead mother, whose wound hinted of a violent death by a lance.

Peter and Eugenius scouted the surrounding area for possible dangers lurking in the vicinity, and the rest rummaged through the debris for signs of life. One found a burlap bag in which to place the pups to carry them to the grotto.

"Saint Elias looks calm to me," noted Eugenius, gazing down below. "There appears to be no destruction, but I see little movement."

"Must be the people are hiding in their homes. Wait till they get the news," said Peter.

By this time, Myrtilus was feeling better, and everyone had gathered around him.

"Are you all right?" Eugenius asked.

"I'm really fine; I'm staying to look for my father and straighten things around here," Myrtilus blurted after catching his breath. "Convey my loving greetings to my mother and younger brother at the grotto."

"Are you sure you are fine?" repeated Eugenius.

"He's been through worse," Peter reassured everyone.

"The grotto! Let's go!" cried Father Nicholaos. They returned to conquer the steep, tortuous path up the mountain, occasionally glancing back at their companion, who was now clearing the debris.

"What do you think happened to his father?" inquired the companion, who was carrying the sack of whimpering puppies.

"I think Matthaeus escaped into the countryside," responded Peter, who was struggling to maintain the pace due to his distorted leg.

"The dog's barking must have warned him in time to flee," said Eugenius.

They arrived at the hovel safely tucked away in the mountainside. The skies propagated an orange glow about the mountains and kept the area still peacefully visible. Everything was in its proper place. The monk gently pushed the door open while announcing their arrival.

Chapter XIX: Helena

The men made their way inside, and their smallest children rushed into their arms to be picked up and lovingly thrown in midair as they giggled and laughed. And when the puppies were let loose, the children in their blissful ignorance scrambled to get hold of them, quickly neglecting their fathers, who were cornered by their wives for news. The air was full of inquiries, and Father Nicholaos and Peter were compelled to cut through it loudly with the good news.

"There is good news. The Normans are leaving," yelled Father Nicholaos.

"We believe there is a truce of some sort," said Peter.

"How can you be sure?" demanded an elderly man.

"We saw the Normans withdraw from the fields," affirmed the monk, hoping not to be the target of more inquiries.

"Where is Matthaeus?"

"Have you seen such and such?"

"Oh, my son, is he still at the fortress?"

The questions were mostly unanswerable, a volley the authors shot relentlessly.

Finally, when they managed to extricate themselves, Father Nicholaos and Peter scurried over to Maria, Saverina and Eugenius, who was already there.

"How's my son; is he safe?" Maria, whose face showed signs of worry and fatigue, ruefully inquired of Father Nicholaos.

"We don't know, we were on the patrol," the monk said warmly. His eyes searched for Helena.

"I'm sure he is fine. He has returned before," Eugenius reassured his wife.

"Where's Helena?" the monk desperately inquired. "And Flavia?" He knitted his brows into a puzzled look.

Saverina and her mother eyed each other, each hoping the other would answer. "Father, she is in the next room with Flavia at her side. It's nothing; she must have the flu," Maria finally said.

When the monk entered, Flavia was helping Helena drink a cup of warm milk since Helena had developed a stiff neck. Flavia acknowledged him with a nod, ceased trying to feed Helena, and moved aside for him. "How is she?" He knelt before the bed and gently grasped Helena's hand.

"Maria thinks it's the flu, but I'm afraid other things are going on." Flavia looked frightened. "Look at her; she is sweating profusely and can hardly move on her own," she cried, hoping Father Nicholaos could shed some light on the matter in his usual worldly way. He did not answer, just leaned over the bed to get a better look at his lifetime spiritual companion.

"How are you doing?" he softly asked.

With her head fixed to the ceiling, Helena shifted only her tired eyes toward him. "I'm fine but my muscles ache all over and sometimes they twitch."

"You know what I think? It is the flu and old age. My muscles ache all the time as well." The monk forced a lighthearted tone, and Helena cracked a semblance of a smile, then fell asleep. "Let her rest." Flavia and the monk quietly left the room.

That night, after retiring to her childhood bed in the grotto, Flavia found that her downy pillow that once hastened sleep had lost its prior magic. It felt lumpy, uncomfortable. She pondered nervously on the events that circled their lives. Regardless of the truce hammered out after the battle, she still had not heard from Iohannes. Saverina's husband had returned safe and sound. If only Iohannes would do likewise as soon as possible.

And there was Helena's condition. Her adoptive mother, over the years, had helped to fit together the ugly puzzle of life where marriage and children formed the final complementary pieces. Now, crushed, she felt as an orphan again.

When she finally fell asleep, a faint and distorted image of Helena assailed her, wavering and undulating as if reflected off a restless pond. It grew larger then faded away, only to come back again with a warm celestial smile. The image floated toward the peak of the grotto's mountain with a glow that burned into Flavia's dream.

Flavia tried to follow but the road was treacherous, and her children tugged on her dress while Father Nicholaos motioned her to return. She pleaded to the phantom, "I'm sorry, my family needs me." Her voice broke out of her dream and into reality, but the sleepy guests did not hear. She had awakened herself and then went back to a sweaty sleep.

The next day, Helena's symptoms were worse. The times when she did not lose consciousness, she appeared confused, incoherent, and forgetting at times where she was. The monk prayed at her bedside while Flavia, in silent tears, wiped her forehead with a cool, damp cloth. Other times when Helena appeared lucid, she rasped through the ever-increasing wheezing to her holy companion, "If I don't make it, promise me you will not give up your holy garment."

"Don't talk like that. With Maria's help, God is not going to take you away from me."

On the fourth day, the blackouts came more frequently, and her legs were acquiring a bluish color. Maria kept saying that she had never seen nor heard of such a thing. It reminded her of the evil air that hovers over swamps and attacks the innocent within its vicinity, but even when the illness reaches this level, often they recover.

But everyone knew that the evil air comes only in spring and summer; now it was winter. Nevertheless, they clung naively to this false hope. Meanwhile, Helena in her lucid moments kept begging her Nicholaos not to withdraw into his anger as he had done in his youth.

"My death is God's wish; he has a purpose even if unbeknown to us. Please give me the Holy Communion," she pleaded as every effort to communicate snatched a piece of her precious strength. The ancient torment of his youth suddenly returned to Father Nicholaos, and he struggled to fulfill her wishes. He had a real physical enemy back then; it had taken away his mother and separated him from his love, but now it was God himself taking her away.

On the fifth day, Helena spoke her last words. "Don't grieve for me, I'm in God's hands. I am leaving you in body but not in spirit." Her sweet lips froze on the last syllable for eternity; her dark Greek eyes froze open, and all swore they saw a sparkle of light emanate from them and then vanish.

For the monk she had been the physical cornerstone of his faith. He became disillusioned; his faith began to crack, and the spirituality that inured him to so many hardships seemed elusive now. Nevertheless, he kept his face and gave the last rites and then slowly backed away from whom was the center of his world just before Flavia broke into a hysterical wailing joined by the other women in an all-out keening outburst.

Nicholaos then went outside, hoping the cold mountain air would cool the wrath festering within and perhaps allow him to settle down into that holy garment that now was uncomfortable. He had always felt that life and death are intermingled into a single, cosmic process. Death is as much of life as life is of death, he told himself.

The common thread that ties the two together is a mysterious vitalism that religiously translates into the eternal presence of Christ, and the dead are victorious in His resurrection. These were the sagacious words shared with his celestial Helena and spoken to the laity. He tightened his fists as if to hold those eternal truths from escaping.

The two shared a communion with God and it was rooted in the eternal now. But the hurt overwhelmed him, and he squirmed and fidgeted inside that wool garment. Death is final, the hurt was saying. It prevails as life's opposite, shadowing it, always close by. It is what life is not. Helena was gone forever. His heart needed mending.

It was on this day that Iohannes ended his mission at the fortress and headed for the grotto, making a short stop at the Florus farm to first check on his father. He found the farm untouched by the enemy and the animals well and his worst of fears vanished. His hunches told him he must be with the rest of the family.

When he arrived that afternoon, he encountered Father Nicholaos outside the hovel in a state of self-absorption. "Hello, Father. Is everything all right?

"I just need a little fresh air. Go inside son, they are waiting for you." The monk replied halfheartedly.

No sooner had he made his way across the threshold little Eugenius, who was clinging to his grandfather, screamed "Papa!" and ran into his arms, followed by the equally enthusiastic youngest of the sisters. Helè, the eldest, patiently waited her turn in the background.

While lovingly wrestling with his children, Iohannes sensed something amiss. The wailing in the next room which had died down to a whispering chant cut into his joyful mood, and he shot an inquisitive look at his father for an explanation.

"It is Helena. She fell ill awhile back and passed away this morning," Eugenius said dolefully.

"And Flavia?"

"She is with her. She is taking it badly. She needs you."

Iohannes walked to the origin of the mourning, encountering a church-like solemnity, which forced him to make his greetings in whispers or with a simple nod of the head. He gently took Flavia's hand and led her outside the room where she hugged him tightly. "Thank God, you're fine," she cried with her head buried in his chest and began to sob. "Mother Helena is dead."

"She is in heaven now," he comforted her. "I will stay here with you and the women. The children can go back home with my father and Peter until the funeral mass.

The next day, after the body was washed and properly dressed by the women, the reality of Helena's death began to settle in the reluctant consciousness of the mourners, especially Flavia and the monk, the two closest to Helena. Iohannes' worried mainly over Flavia for his understanding of his former mentor was second only to Helena's, and the student knew God would return to the Father's heart, for it had never left his soul.

The monk now began to assess his future without her and accept a new chapter in his life shared by other Basilian monks in Calabria. The Skylletion surrender, the final blow to Calabria, announced their replacement by Catholic monks. In the meantime, there was need to comfort and educate his laity to the new order about to come. The Greek community is waiting for me to fulfill my last and most important calling, he reasoned. He pushed the pain away and revived his vows with a new vigor.

Iohannes sensed this and resolved to let the grieving monk sort things out on his own, leaving him time to focus solely on his wife. He hoped that her active involvement in the wake would soften the crushing blow to her heart. He prompted Flavia to deliver the eulogy, an idea that attracted the attention of the silent Father Nicholaos.

That evening, as the three sat by the crackling warmth of the hearth, the couple worked on the words for the eulogy. How natural it was for two loving hearts to heal each other in the face of a heart-shattering loss, mused Father Nicholaos.

"What do you think, so far, Father?" asked Flavia, now comfortably absorbed in her task. The monk merely outlined an approving smile. He marveled at the two as their project grew incrementally into a refined poem of Helena's last wishes as seen with Flavia's eyes. This is the divine presence working, he reminded himself, the one I shared with Helena and hastily discarded in anger. 'Helena is still here, firmly and forever,' he whispered to himself as he left to retire.

"Good night, Father," the couple said in unison. After completing the eulogy, both retired and before falling asleep, Flavia repeated the eulogy, line by line, again and again, stamping it into memory. She wanted to deliver it melodiously in a manner that would make her adopted mother proud.

Helena's body was transported to the Florus', where it was more convenient to hold the wake *pannychia* for it was easily reachable by the village priest. There the priest would perform the *trisagion*, a singing of hymns coupled with homilies in the presence of the neighbors, paying their respect to the magnanimous Helena, mother of the orphans and teacher to the village children.

On the first night of the vigil, the compassionate priest, stepped aside for Flavia who timidly inched herself forward, her pretty eyes firmly glued to Iohannes and Father Nicholaos for encouragement. Although she was barely literate their faces were animated by her natural and earthy wisdom.

Flavia began with a slight crackle in her voice that quickly smoothed itself into a pleasant rhythmic pitch and tenderly touched everyone. She genuinely felt as the ambassadress to Helena, a special legate representing her angelic mother to the souls still incarnated. Everyone's eyes supported her feelings, they sparkled in their yearning to feel Helena's presence in their hearts.

"Helena was the only mother I knew. She also was a mother to us all. She believed in us. She often said we are all precious in the eyes of the Lord. But most of all she believed in Christ and his promise of everlasting life. With the help of my husband, Iohannes, who inherited some of Father Nicholaos' literary talent, I would like to pass on her last wishes." The silence was deafening; she was the focal point of everyone's attention. She gazed at Iohannes; then her lilting voice sang.

Please do not weep for me,
I am still somewhere within your hearts.
When the gentle wind caresses you,
It is my tender hand.
When the pregnant hearth warms your body,
It is my soul's embers.
When the pillow soothes your troubled mind,
At day's end,
It's my beckoning lap.
When evil is called out from your hearts,
It's my expelling cry.
Where queen faith dominates,
And the inner struggle fades away,
You shall find me nearby.
Look not far, do not search with your eyes,
Close them and you shall see where I am.

The vigil lasted three days. Helena's popularity in her adopted homeland attracted villagers from all over. They drifted in sporadically, at all hours, for their farms that fed them needed tending. Some stayed for the nightly vigil, and everyone requested to hear Flavia recite her tribute to the deceased which she delivered before each vigil.

The funeral mass was equally crowded with mourners. Only the immediate family fit in the nave; the remaining worshipers patiently stood outside and simply waited for the final burial after which the men slowly slid the heavy stone slabs over Helena's remains. One contained the chiseled inscription, "Helena the Angel died in 1061," and was headed with the cross.

Greek resistance to the Normans occasionally would flare up but, the uprisings were more like death throes of a culture meeting an uncertain future. The Normans would scour the countryside from Apulia to Calabria to make sure their victim was fully dead. The little Saint Elias community found itself neither near nor far from all this. There was hope in the air but also apprehension. The feudal lords were still at bay.

But life had its own pulse, and the sorrowful gaps that Helena's death cut into life's continuous march were pushed further and further into memory. At first, the mundane daily life weakened the sadness by its toil, but then pleasant events replaced it altogether. Births, baptisms, marriages, and celebrations of patron saints united and invigorated the community. In this manner, five years passed, and young Peter Savius tied the knot with someone from Saint Elias.

And Helè Florus, who had inherited her mother's honey blond hair, found her true love through her mother's artful dealings with other mothers of the village who constantly offered their prospective sons. The monk resumed his spiritual and charitable rounds, responding to the needs of his laity within his reach, but always returned to his bosom flock, the Floruses and the Saviuses, whenever possible.

He lived alone at the grotto since the orphans had taken to their own lives, and it was used only seasonally by the two families to pasture the sheep and make cheese during the summer months. The monk made sure he was there during these events, which were a collective experience like the cultivations and harvests but mostly performed by the women and older children. The elders such as Iohannes, Eugenius, and

Peter tended the main farms. All others including the recently married couples went to help as much as possible.

The cheese-making expertise had been handed down through Maria's family to Maria, then Saverina and Flavia. However, Maria's supervision was never lacking, and her orders worked their way through the women, down to the children and older lads who tended the ewes and goats.

After milking the animals, the older girls returned to the grotto to dump their jars of milk into larger vats where Maria would stir in her secret formula to bring about the curdling. Saverina and Flavia then strained the whey from the curds and separated them into other jars and then into molds.

Flavia while working the cheese cloth to separate the curds from the whey in the vat turned her attention to Father Nicholaos, seated nearby. She was forty-two now, and fussed over the aging monk, compensating for Helena's absence. "Father, you aren't really going to Nicoptera, are you?"

"My dear, it's my duty. The Greeks in Paleocastro have suffered too much. The duke (Robert Hauteville) has punished them for their rebellion by giving their town to the Franchoi and making them settle in Nicoptera. They are treated as slaves, rebuilding the town for him as well as the ships needed for his conquests." Already general news, he still felt it needed repeating.

Father Nicholaos. had been the shield before all those horrible things in her youth. I can not bear losing him, she reminded herself. "It is dangerous there. Don't go!" she pleaded.

"They need my help. They are Greeks." Images of the barbarians billeting in their homes flashed through his mind. He knew they often felt entitled to the women's services beyond normal.

"You're not young anymore, Father! You are approaching seventy; the mountain trails are dangerous." Maria eagerly reinforced Flavia's sentiments.

"My legs still have life in them. I must go before they crack altogether," he protested.

Another Journey

There was no changing the monk's mind, not even the pleading from Flavia, nor did the beckoning and alluring faces of the adorable children overcome his resolve. Early one foggy morning, before the children were up, he said his farewells to the cheese-making group and headed for the trails that snaked through the Elias mountains. He arrived at the higher pasture as the morning fog cleared, giving him a view of that dreadful camp of Iohannes' kidnappers.

From there the rapid descent brought him to the Wolf's Pass, which was the portal to the western side of the Elias ridge and guarded by Monte Serralta overlooking the pass. Exhausted, he spent the night in a wooded area sheltered by an overhanging rock away from the ever-present bandits. Early next morning, awakened by a biting fall breeze penetrating his joints, he scurried back to the road.

He climbed once again to an elevated valley that reached Rocca Capana, (Monterosso Calabro), nestled at the feet of Monte Copari. The road zigzagged and twisted such that he often lost faith in its general direction. Fortunately, the many hamlets along the way unharmed by war offered direction and rest to the traveling monk. He spent the night at a small village just outside of Rocca Capana. The next morning, he made a rapid descent into a marshy valley fed by the River Angitola as Rocca Capana wished him well in the dawn's reddish light.

Before him, high above his head, Rocca Nikephoros, razed to the ground eons ago by Saracens, greeted him and egged him on as he turned south where the valley opened into a plateau leading to the Tyrrhenian. Nicoptera clings to the plateau's cliff, overlooking the sea, and lay waiting for him.

After a good day's walk, however, he stopped at a monastery called Sanctus Onuphrius, or Sant'Onofrio, just outside Vibona (Vibo Valentia). It looked abandoned but the hamlet surrounding it boasted of life with smoke rising from the hearths attesting to the evening meal. The Father was fatigued and breathing heavily, and his tired legs barely carried him to its door.

He carefully pushed open the heavy wooden door, making sure it would not detach from its hinges. Beams of light fought their way through the cracks and open windows revealing no benches for the faithful nor any holy vessels at the altar, just cobwebs proving the monastery's disuse. He walked into the apse and was greeted by a faded Christ, painted onto the vault ceiling, barely recognizable but still reigning sovereign over his deteriorating kingdom. He crossed over the threshold from the apse into a small chapel that sat adjacent to the monk's cells. Choosing one cell, he threw his belongings on the ground, extracted a blanket, and lay down to fall soundly asleep.

The next day, he felt a gentle poke, he resisted, then came a gentle shake. He turned away and was struck by a beam of late morning light entering the window opening, a lighthouse type of beam that penetrated his closed eyelids. Finally, opening his eyes and adjusting to the light, he saw the figure of a peasant lad in rags and bare feet looming over him. He struggled to get up but the pain from the arthritis in his aging joints held him back so the peasant lad grabbed his arm, wrapped it around his little shoulders, and supported him the best he could until he found his equilibrium.

"God, bless you, my child; where are your parents?" moaned Father Nicholaos, fighting his morning crustiness.

"A little down the hill toward Vibona, Father," responded the fair-skinned lad with charcoal-black hair.

"Hold my arm for a while, son, until we come across a good branch for a cane." Still unsteady in his walk he managed to carry his satchel of belongings in his other arm. "What is this monastery called?"

"Saint Onuphrius, same as the village, Father," dutifully retorted his human crutch, who had his own questions on his tongue.

"Have you come to service mass for us, Father? There are children here not baptized; my younger sister is one."

"We shall see, my son, we shall see." No sooner had they caught sight of the humble dwelling when the lad ran toward the entrance, leaving Father Nicholaos to hobble on his own with the support of the recently improvised cane found in their walk.

"Mother! Mother! A monk has finally come," the lad cried as Father Nicholaos tried to keep pace.

"Oh! Father, please do come in," said the mother. She had undulating black hair, a face bubbling with joy, and eyes secretly tearing from the joy of his presence. She sat him down at the table, ordered her son outside to summon his father from the field, and began a continuous chatter interspersed with questions that Father Nicholaos was at odds to answer. All the while, she fussed over her daughter at her side and prepared warm milk and bread for her guest as she continued in her excitement.

"The monks rarely come since this new duke has taken Calabria. They used to make their way from the Valley of Salt. Where are you from? My daughter is three and still not baptized."

When Father Nicholaos sensed a fortuitous gap to interject, he was stymied by the abrupt entrance of her husband and the lad.

"This is Father Nicholaos, dear." The woman was happy to turn some of the hospitality duties over to her husband, who gave his greetings with the utmost respect.

"I don't know how much my wife has told you, but around here, we still pray in Greek. If we are lucky so will our children."

"Bless your family," said the monk.

"We are always happy when a Greek monk passes by. You will stay to perform mass and baptize my little one?" asked the woman.

"I'm sorry, I am not a priest," the monk protested.

"But our monasteries have been taken over by the Benedictines of Saint Eufemia. You have seen our monastery, falling apart from disuse. The Latin Order's domain stretches all the way to the Valley of Salt." The man's face was tense with desperation and anxiety. "Help us please!" The monk listened with sympathy to a familiar lament.

Roger had even made a fortified base of Mileto, a day's walk from this humble home. The Father was their only hope. He had to yield at some point as he had done in Saint Elias.

The next day the villagers cleaned and prepared the monastery, and he performed the Eucharist for the villagers and christened the little girl 'Agatha.'

The villagers pleaded for Father Nicholaos to stay, but he slipped away early the next day, in darkness, to avoid any gatherings that might try to impede him. Hardly a half hour into his walk, he came across old Hipponion, or rather what was left of it, built by the ancient Greeks, and now known as Vibona for those who had a memory of the Romans. Others did not refer to it at all or simply called the area the place of the ruins since encroaching nature had disguised most of the human presence.

The gently sloping area had become a pasture sprinkled with partial columns lying on their sides. The remains of a few, barely standing, pretended to support a phantom roof. And barely discernable were stone footings under the overgrown shrubbery and grass. They told of neat squares of ancient living spaces, bedrooms, *androns*, where the men gathered, and *gynaeceums*, where fair maidens conducted their daily household activities.

To the southeast, but not far, once stood the majestic Temple of Proserpina with its granite and alabaster columns. Its precious ruins, scattered in the darkness of time, were gathered by Roger, and sacrificed to build the church of Saint Michael in Mileto. Myth and reality have intermingled here.

The wind whistled the ancient myth of the Rape of Proserpina as it worked its way around and through the telltale ruins and reached the monk's learned ears. The fair maiden had been whisked away by Hades, who took her to his infernal den on a flying chariot, like the inhabitants who were despoiled and taken into slavery by the Saracens. Ceres, her mother, supplicated Jove for help in her release; Jove, in turn, had partial success irrespective of his power.

The monk wondered if he possessed the persuasive power of Ceres to free his laity from the duke. A Basilian monk, however, had no such divine gift, just determination and prayer. Father Nicholaos, almost quixotic by his vows, would push on anyway.

Before him continued the expanse of the plateau that gracefully undulated until it met the sea with a two-step drop. As he walked in the direction of the Gulf of Gioia, the sea appeared and reappeared from sight, depending on the elevation of the terrain. The little villages sparsely sown on the fertile land also teased him in the same way, appearing and disappearing.

On the last leg of his journey the monk questioned once again his motive before the famed Norman duke who was at Nicoptera with his soldiers and probably a Benedictine monk or two, intent on furthering their agenda of Latinization. Would he be like Moses and demand the liberation of his people from the recalcitrant pharaoh with fiery, angry eyes? If only he were graced by God's miracles, he would cast his humble but divine cane at his feet, see it transform into the biblical serpent hissing as it crumbled the vain pedestal the pharaoh stood on.

The sun which had followed him now sat resting just behind the Aeolian Islands and outshine Strongyle's (Stromboli) fiery breath, which could only be seen through the bellowing smoke once the sun retired completely. The duke's Nicoptera, which hugged the cliff and overlooked the bay, the islands, and Sicily, emerged as a shadow through the evening golden haze. The monk's destination was but a stone's throw away.

Nearby, he noticed a lonely structure, and as he knocked for the inhabitant's warm hospitality, the sun slipped under the cover of the Tyrrhenian waters to sleep. The spewing, red embers of Strongyle now could be seen against the night sky.

Chapter XX: A New World

A gentle but bustling wind struck the monk the following morning, as he made his way to the town. It bore all the acoustical hodgepodge that emanated from the construction. The monk could distinguish the ping and clatter of hammers striking chisels, stone cracking under their sharp 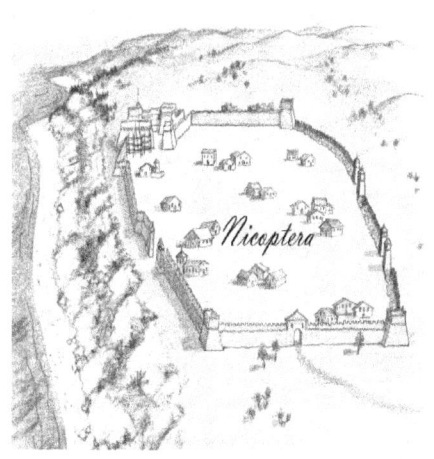 edges, the rhythm of busy hand saws, and the hollow snapping of wood yielding to the ax.

The occasional barking of orders, some in recognizable Greek, others in the Frankish tongue and barely understandable, comingled with the noises. A remote Greek village was being resurrected and reinforced on the cliff above the shoreline of ancient Medma (a town abandoned by the Romans).

Approaching from the east where the stone wall was partially erected, he first encountered the digging crew desperately excavating away the soil to reach bedrock. Their shovels were guided by a surveying rope laid out by the master mason. Closely behind the diggers were workers who leveled the uneven bedrock with gravel and small pebbles from shore which would function as a footing. The surveying rope connected four already completed pyramid-like structures, whose sides in talus mode functioned as towers.

A guard on the nearby tower yelled to the crew overseer below, "There is a monk coming." A lull displaced the grunts and choppy conversations of the working men and began to spread throughout the complex.

"It's a Greek monk!" an excited woman screamed, carrying a jar of water on her head.

"Return to your work," their overseer, a Lombard and minor mason, shouted angrily.

"My name is Father Nicholaos; I came from Saint Elias, just over the mountains," he cordially said.

"What do you want?" growled the massive Lombard.

"These are my people; they need the services of a Greek monk."

"Go, Monk, tend to the women but leave the workers alone."

The center of the fortress where he now found himself consisted of the original settlement expanded to accommodate the recent arrivals from the defeated town on the other side of the Catacen isthmus. From here he had a more extensive view of the works. The main tower, situated in the northwest corner, was itself made of four smaller towers conjoined with curtain walls to form a donjon, headquarters for the duke. The towers, like the others, were equipped with crenellations that cut into the clear blue sky like a saw.

Since the outside walls of the donjon were complete, the workers were dismantling the scaffolding made from rough logs fastened together with rope. The west fortress wall was also complete and was anchored on the edge of the cliff whose scenic elevation of 660 feet dominated a vast shoreline.

Coming through the west gate were pack animals, mostly mules, some laden with sacks of small stones, others with blocks of squared granite or calcareous rock. (10) The monk exited the gate to get a better look at the animals that trotted slowly up the steep slope on the winding path. Dozens of animals and men were little moving dots in the distance on a path cut into the cliff face ages ago and no wider than a man's feet.

To the south, the waterfront below, where once proudly stood the ancient city of Medma, now entertained the duke's docks that moored his warships used on prior Sicilian campaigns and would serve in future ones as well.

Someone tucked at his garment. He turned around to face a skeletal figure of a woman with pale face, strings of brown hair slipping out of her head scarf, and deep-set eyes that spoke of a life of exhaustion. "Would you please give me your blessing, Father." She spoke in perfect Greek reminiscent of some prior social standing.

"Where are you from, child?" Anyone younger, he addressed as child.

"My name is Hyacintha, from the feet of the Sila mountains. We were force-marched here by the duke," she said in a tone of acquiescence to her fate.

Father Nicholaos outlined a smile of understanding and gave the proper Orthodox blessing.

"We are here as punishment for our uprising to his yoke," she continued after the monk was done.

"I've heard," he replied sympathetically.

"Most of the men were killed in the battle; my husband was one. The survivors are workers to this fortress." Doubting the utility of narrating her sad story, she tacked to a more pressing matter. "Enough of me. We are hungry for Greek blessings and the Greek Eucharist."

A small group had slowly gathered around the two and began begging for the Father's blessings, which irritated the guards and crew supervisors. "Get back to work," scowled a stocky guard, wearing a mail hood and who held higher authority over the others. As the spontaneous gathering timidly dissipated to their waiting work, the guard addressed Father Nicholaos. "You, monk! I don't know where you are from but move along."

"Can I speak to anyone in charge? These people need me," the monk politely asked.

The Norman burst into a sarcastic laugh and roared, "The duke is inside the main tower; ask the guard at the entrance." Then he headed to his station still laughing at the dubious prospect of the monk getting an audience with the duke.

"Where is this tower?" Father Nicholaos asked Hyacintha, who had remained as a self-appointed guide. Her worn fingers, once graced with a healthy smoothness, pointed to the donjon and the two strolled in its direction. For a moment, the monk felt Helena at his side.

"What are you going to say to the duke?"

"To release us from his...." He quickly realized the demand was preposterous.

"We have nowhere to go." Hyacintha was beginning to think of herself as a companion rather than a guide.

"Do you think he will allow Greek masses and maybe Greek civil rights?" returned the monk.

"It would be a more reasonable request." Her remark reminded Nicholaos of the supporting words often given by Helena.

Byzantine Nicoptera was vised between two encroaching Latin ecclesiastical orders. They were the recently formed Benedictine Abbey of Saint Eufemia, whose jurisdiction stretched all the way to Seminara to the south, and the Latinized archdiocese of Rhegium, which had been transformed from Greek to Latin in 1060. However, the duke used subtle tactics in his obligations to the Pope regarding the Latinization of his conquests. On one hand, he made sure the vise-jaws moved unsuspectingly slow, and on the other he rapidly clamped down if the resistance to his rule was too fierce. It was the latter that worried Father Nicholaos, for the duke's temper was well-known.

He needed to tread lightly. "Is the duke easily taken by anger?"

"Yes," she said dryly as they made their way.

Suddenly, they heard a cry coming from the external wall at its junction with one of the donjon's towers not far from the guarded entrance to the donjon itself. "Maria, water, I'm thirsty." (Most women were called Maria.) The young, handsome, and curly-headed worker, Alexios, was dismantling the last of the scaffolding and made his way to his spouse, who was carrying water for her beloved.

Maria had a beauty that broke through her humble simplicity, she wore a rustic hemp dress tied at the waist with a rope, which highlighted her femininity. She walked ever so timidly toward her husband under the ogling eyes of the Norman guarding that crew.

Alexios' first swallow was deep; the others were slow and stole a moment of intimate gestures and whispers, a moment extended further against the Norman's gaze. His fiery and animal yearnings shot out of his eyes, singeing her wifely devotion, and silently igniting her husband's ire.

"Return to work," the guard finally grunted to neutralize the challenging eyes of Alexios, who then reluctantly returned to work.

At his back, the aroused guard with a fiendish smile grabbed the hapless girl's arm. She spurned against the vise-like grip, tugging and jerking her arm away, uselessly, as he drew her nearer. Only her unshakable eyes were left to fight the fierceness in his as the animal whispered a demand of Maria that was contrary to her innocence. Her resistance temporarily waned from a silent fear, a fear of consequences to her husband if she were to yell and he come to the rescue.

Father Nicholaos and Hyacintha hurried over to the impending calamity, and so did Alexios. Alarmed and insulted by the scene, he jumped down off the scaffolding to attack the

Norman with a stick he had at his disposal. "Let her be," he yelled.

The Norman shoved the woman aside and unsheathed his sword against Alexios and the monk jumped before the wieldy, long sword, relying on the holy power of his garment as a shield. Two swipes were made by the huge Norman sword. The first shattered Alexios' stick and the other put a gash into the monk's right side.

Meanwhile, a second guard rushed to the scene and checked Alexios in place with his sword tip against his throat as the monk knelt in pain, holding his bloody side with his right hand.

"Leave the Father alone. Haven't you done enough?" Hyacintha's agony was hurled at the brute as she leaned over to prevent her Father Nicholaos from falling completely.

"Move out of the way, woman!" The first Norman wanted to bury his sword into the holy man's chest.

"Stop!" screamed his comrade, reminding him of their knightly homage to the Pope. The warning miraculously transformed the deadly thrust into a single sparring blow, a feigned jab that still managed to pierce Father Nicholaos' outstretched left hand held in a frantic motion of defense.

The Norman sheathed his sword and then seized the girl's arm again, pulling her closer to him. His eyes drilled into the sweet eyes of his innocent victim and worked their way downward toward her bosom.

"Leave her alone," yelled Alexios as the sword tip dug deeper into his throat.

Hyacintha, still supporting Father Nicholaos, pleaded for the release of Alexios and Father Nicholaos did likewise when he burst through his excruciating pain to summon God himself this time. "In the name of our Christian God, let them both go."

The Norman brute now was focused elsewhere. It was a shiny coin-shaped emblem, gold, engraved with a Christogram and tied around her slim neck with a leather strap. His huge chubby hand clasped the emblem, yanked it from her precious, delicate neck, and he shoved her aside.

Suddenly, from the entrance to the donjon emerged three figures alarmed and curious by the commotion. One, the shortest, was corpulent and would appear to be a jolly insignificant character if it were not for the religious tunic that he wore, ample at its waist and typically Benedictine. Another armored with a full coat of mail *hauberk* was without question the personal guard of the third, who towered over them in size and authority.

The towering leader wore only the normal wool undergarment, over which he would have worn the hauberk and hood in time of battle. Strapped to his side was the usual Norman long sword, which on an average-sized man would drag on the ground. Its dark leather scabbard or sheath was laced with lighter leather. The exposed hilt was comprised of a delicate gold inlaid cross-guard, leather laced handle, and rounded pommel embossed in unrecognizable symbols.

He had straggly blond hair dispersed with the telltale whiteness of age and the harried life of glory seeking. His piercing eyes could intimidate any man. Always in control, he spewed out anger or compassion as dictated by the circumstances.

The Norman had earned his realm beginning as a cunning bandit leader operating near Costantia, stealing and killing his way to nobility; hence his nickname, Robert the Guiscard, French for weasel, which in their culture stood for cunning and astuteness.

"What is the meaning of this?" roared the duke.

The guards implicated in the ruckus began in unison with their tale that started to twist and turn with deviations further and further from the truth. But the cunning duke, wise to his men, cut them off. "Let's hear from the Greek monk if he is able to talk," he bellowed.

Feeling a little better with some renewed strength, since Hyacintha had delicately wrapped the wounds and managed to stop the bleeding, Father Nicholaos began the truthful version of the incident. Stopped frequently from the pangs of pain and the gasping, he removed the layers of lies piled on the incident by the untrustworthy guards.

"My lord, it is true what our monk has said," Hyacintha seconded; her pale face now acquired color in the controlled situation.

Turning his attention in the direction of the paunchy Benedictine monk for reassurance, Father Nicholaos insisted, "He should turn over the necklace and leave the girl and husband alone."

"Monk, we are the victors. This is my land now; the necklace and the girl belong to me." The biting words of the duke held everyone in suspense.

In a gesture of religious comradery, the paunchy monk, Brother John, whose jowl danced with his voice, felt compelled to speak. "In the name of Abbot Grantmesnil, whom you have granted authority over this land, grant these Greek souls their rightful wishes."

The duke's fiery eyes momentarily softened, then lit up again to their former intensity. "Let the man and the girl go. Return the necklace and man your posts," he ordered as he turned around and headed toward the donjon with his retinue.

Cane in one hand and the other arm around Hyacintha, the monk limped to her simple dwelling not yet scavenged for the new fortress. Hyacintha's face took on a permanent rosy ebullience from the sheer presence of the Greek monk and the honor it brought to her humble abode.

That evening brought anxious visitors, all curious, firstly about his health and then about the length of his stay. Some were jealous he was lodging at her home, but all pleaded for his blessings only to be discouraged by his host, who pointed to his need to heal. Maria and Alexios were the first to visit, bearing their most sincere gratitude for his holy intervention.

After chasing all visitors away, the host, now blooming with pride, tired the spiritual patient to sleep with her garrulousness and over attentive nature.

A whispering chatter in the next room woke Father Nicholaos the next day, and when he rose the wound at his side split open, he let out a groan. The whispering stopped, and Hyacintha rushed in followed by Brother John. "You should have called me; it started to bleed again," she panicked. Then she proceeded to remove the bandage, cleaned the wound, and helped Father Nicholaos into bed.

"I will get the garrison surgeon." Brother John slid his draping gray hood at his back, over his head, and fled out the door.

The monk lost consciousness from the pain. When he opened his eyes again, the surgeon had left. Hyacintha was preparing to spoon-feed him with a nurturing broth, and the corpulent monk from the other side of the religious schism was studiously observing his colleague as he lay in bed, barely able to swallow let alone talk. We are two pawns caught up in the clash of their respective world order and its Titans, pondered Brother John, hoping to verbalize it as a question. But the monk closed his eyes again and went to sleep before finishing the broth.

The next day, Father Nicholaos felt much better and made his way to the kitchen table alone, where Hyacintha and Brother John enthusiastically waited for his presence. Both greeted him," and Hyacintha, content on his state, moved about preparing the breakfast.

"Have you come to tame the excesses of the barbarians?" Brother John gave a friendly jab and Father Nicholaos greeted him with a silent nod and sat down. "You are looking well this morning; we must thank the lady of the house." Father Nicholaos said nothing. "I have travelled up and down this coast, meeting many Basilian monks. Surely we must have mutual acquaintances somewhere?"

"Father Philaretes, in the monastery of Saint Elias from Enna, do you know him? We are both from Sicily." Still weak, Father Nicholaos managed to push the words out as he took the slice of bread being handed to him by the host. "Thank you," he said and turned once again to face Brother John.

"Yes, indeed I do; he is now assiduously tending to its garden. You say that you are from Sicily?"

"From Panormos."

"Amazing! I am from Normandy. I came here with Abbot Grantmesnil."

"You don't look Norman," Father Nicholaos puzzled out loud.

"Their Viking blood has long been diffused into the local more numerous, population of Gaul. Enough of small talk. Why are you here, Greek monk?"

"As you say, I came to tame the excesses of serfdom and uphold the Greek tradition so dear to my people." Father Nicholaos made a bold smile.

"Can you be more specific for my message to the duke?"

"Provide Greek services and be a spokesman for my laity. At least for a month or two." Father Nicholaos' eyes searched for favorable signs from the Benedictine.

"The duke is uncouth at times but also generous. I can not see it being refused. After all, the Norman archbishop in Rhegium allows Greek rites in the city churches, and this does not offend the duke." An acquiescent smile stretched across Brother John before he continued. "Where have we parted, my dear Greek friend? I mean, God has given us one church and we ungratefully split it in two."

"What your Norman warriors have done here to the Greeks certainly does not help. Even your former Pope has admonished their greedy and bloody behavior," asserted the monk.

"The seeds of division were sown again and again in the obscurity of time, first starting, ages ago, when Constantine moved the capital to Byzantium," insisted the other.

Sensing his interlocutor's knowledge on the matter, Father Nicholaos pondered a bit, weighing his counter. His exhaustion would not allow an exchange of esoteric facts. "Eight hundred years of reasons and excuses," he added philosophically.

"Many good men have tried to sow the theological wounds and have failed. We cannot ignore that." Brother John wavered between a question and remark and paused for a moment. "The adoption of the Greek language where once rightfully Latin reigned, to me, is most important."

"I think that the common thread tying those eight hundred reasons together is arrogance and sanctimony as our leaders argue over God's nature." Father Nicholaos headed for a summation.

"Go on."

"Well, each claim to possess the truth of God's nature, but the Truth of God cannot be possessed. This is sheer intellectual hubris." He paused to regain his breath. "Truth comes from the grace of God. It shines through the clouds of ignorance in the form of a gift to the humble and receptive soul."

"Do you mean the patriarchs of God's church should be flexible in their theological skirmishes?"

"There is only one spiritual communion with God, a mystery that defies earthly explanations. The words to describe it are nothing more than morsels of its reality. Morsels that once applied to the wholeness of the mystery self-destruct in contradictions and semantics."

"You mean we are divided over words?" Brother John felt foolish in his simple response.

"The Living Communion is the Truth; words fail before its mystery. Once in the Holy Bond, questions on His nature are meaningless." Father Nicholaos was winding down.

"I see you need rest, my friend. I will ask your wishes to be granted," said Brother John, still bemused by his colleague's words as he prepared for his return to the donjon.

The cold evening air bit into the bemusement of Brother John and he chewed on Nicholaos' lingering words. The Greek was talking about the limits of reason, he told himself. It brings man at the Mystery's feet, but Faith envelops it, and it ceases to be a mystery. It is a living truth.

When Brother John approached the duke, he had just dismissed his master mason and was barking out orders to prepare his troops for the march to Apulia, where he would form a fleet to sail to the port of Dyrrachium.

"My Lord, on this matter of the Greek monk....." Brother John was immediately interrupted.

"Do as you wish with the Greek." The duke gazed into the Brother's eyes to make sure he was understood. "My own relatives are plotting against me," he complained. "I must go." Disgruntled local barons, some of whom were his nephews, had joined the efforts of Perenos, the duke across the Adriatic.

Brother John slightly raised his eyebrows and thought: If you had not stolen their proper inheritance, maybe your relatives would not oppose you now, but his words were different. "You are most generous, Duke. Father Nicholaos will help me with the Greek rites and his people."

"He is your responsibility," growled Duke Robert.

Left in charge by Robert, Brother John kept the Greek rite and culture in Nicoptera through the person of Father

Nicholaos. But Father Nicholaos was aging and had promised himself to retire to his initial vows as a hermit. After a while, Father Nicholaos left, and Brother John was gracious enough to replace him with another Greek monk.

Chapter XXI: Bishopric

Spring arrived with its budding greens pushing through the wet, partially snowy ground, and the winter wheat made its initial greetings. Plans were made for the community cultivation for the feudal system, although still on the horizon, had not made its appearance to this world, and the Greek chorion structure near Saint Elias was still intact.

The Florus farm had grown into a *casale*, a group of stone buildings that had not yet evolved into a hamlet. Grandparents, children, grandchildren were all within touching distance of each other. Only Saverina's son Peter Junior lived elsewhere. He had built the family home on the lower section of the grotto's property granted to him through his father, who had received it from Father Nicholaos just before he left.

With the death of Helena, the well-being of the monk had fallen on Flavia's delicate little shoulders. She fussed over him as any loving daughter would do and more so as Helena's memory gently dissipated into her daily life. The aging Father Nicholaos was overdue to return, and she blamed herself for not protesting enough before his leave. He at the helm of her young life had magically healed her orphan wounds and now was gone, possibly forever. Her heart was tied in knots of guilt.

Yet, there were moments of distraction. Her daughter, Helè, who visited often with her newborn baby and the attention he required, drew Flavia to the grateful moments of her family's affairs. And there were her other two finicky girls, protected and spoiled, who in their marriageable age were indecisive in any prospects the parents suggested.

Mother Maria, still springy in her middle sixties, would hustle toward Flavia's home across from hers, after tending to her husband, who, being marginalized by old age, seemed to always be in her way. His constant attention, a trait she once cherished in her youth, had slowly turned into an annoyance.

Her escape was other people's lives, and she never announced her arrival, just barged in.

"Hello, I've brought a fresh loaf of bread." She placed it on the table, caressed the baby on the cheek, which was held by Helè, mumbled sweet words, and plumped down in a nearby chair.

"Grandmother, grandfather impossible again?" asked Helè, snickering to her mother.

"I can't get anything done with him around," Maria complained, for the millionth time.

"Mother Maria, in his old age he feels neglected," said Flavia, bored by the usual complaint and yet thankful for the distraction from Father Nicholaos' absence.

"You're right. Since the children have taken over most of the farm duties, he sulks. By the way, where is my son?" Maria gently took the baby and began making silly sounds and faces.

"Iohannes and Peter are on some business at Skylletion. I hope they return with some news on Father Nicholaos." Flavia reverted to her frown she bore prior to the arrival of her guests.

"Something will materialize, somewhere," uttered Maria in between her silly entertainment of the baby which began to cry.

"Now, this too could be brothering grandfather. After all, Father Nicholaos was his best friend." Helè reached for the baby and began rocking her in her arms.

"You are wiser than your twenty-three years," Maria complimented.

"Why can't my little brother, Genè, ask around in his travels?" continued Helè. "He is fifteen and gets around a lot." Helè threw a teasing smile at her brother, who made constant visits to his girlfriend near Saint Elias.

"I'll go, now" came a reply in the background from Genè, who extended his tongue to counter his sister's tease. They were enjoyable errands for the lad, sturdy as a bull and whose height challenged his father's. It gave him an excuse to visit his girlfriend, Iris, a cripple from Saint Elias who had stolen his heart from when they were children.

"Yes, that is a clever idea." Flavia questioned herself for not having thought of it herself and reacquired her levity on her face.

Skylletion-Autumn

Throughout the spring and summer of that year, Flavia's fears concerning Father Nicholaos grew. But in autumn, news of an unusual event in Skylletion would find its way to her home and give some hope for her apprehensive heart to chew on.

The old commander Ouramos, in Skylletion, had little left of his former garrison. The few loyalists who remained under his command functioned only in civil matters, which fortunately were still under the aegis of the Greek diocese. The church, located in its center, ruled over the land from Stylon to Taberna in the lower Sila mountains.

It would be another generation before a Latin bishop would take over; in the meantime, the bridge construction between the two worlds was gradual and forgiving. The religious, legal, and civic formalities were still in the Greek tradition, thanks to Mesimeros, the Orthodox episcopal vicar, otherwise known as the bishop.

Nevertheless, these important citizens of Skylletion yearned for signs of reversal to the rumblings of change. Together, they often gazed at the eastern horizon from the fortress tower, wishing that somewhere out there lay Constantinople with its fleet of Greek warships coming to the rescue. But they never arrived at Skylletion, those ships of salvation. Only scattered local fishing boats cutting into the sky were seen, manned by brave men daring to venture into the Saracen-infested waters, goaded by their need to feed their families.

Constantinople did make some appearances, but not here, in Apulia where it gained back Brindisi, Taranto, and some neighboring port cities in Apulia. Nevertheless, the duke was invincible, and the very word Constantinople faded into memory.

On one of their watches at the tower, which were faithfully regular, there appeared in the bishop's line of sight a ragged figure of a man approaching the east entrance to the town. Limping and making full use of his cane with his good hand, he twitched in its control. His garment and hood were of ancient Basilian tradition, tattered, it barely concealed the skeleton-like body.

A hermit monk, probably from the south, in Stylon, thought the bishop, a location of many cave-dwelling hermits still under Mesimeros' jurisdiction. Crowded around him, he witnessed the normal area travelers going in the same direction, and one old woman engaged in conversation with the monk. When they passed through the gate, the crowd dispersed into their separate ways as the strange figure in the ancient robe and cowl headed toward the church.

"It must be about Father Nicholaos. Iohannes will be glad to hear. Let's go and meet the monk at the church," the bishop yelled, excited.

"My eyes must be getting old. I see only the local farmers," replied the commander, squinting.

The two climbed down the steep steps of the tower onto a stepped path, equally precarious, leading to the church courtyard and the adjacent building housing the bishop. They quickly climbed the few steps to the huge doors of the church narthex, which also served as a baptistry. Pausing and assuming the usual solemn demeanor required, they entered the narthex.

On their right stood the baptismal font, a huge bowl whose circular side revealed figures baptizing a child. Next to it, hanging on the wall, a similar bowl comprised the holy font, which was overshadowed by a mosaic of the icon Christ Pantokrator. They greeted the icon with the sign of the cross and slowly proceeded down the nave toward the apse. At first glance, they saw no one resembling a tattered figure save a young widow, all in black, wimpled and praying to her Savior at the uppermost pew.

They questioned the widow, who said she saw no one. Bishop Mesimeros knelt on the steps before the apse and its altar, *ambon*, got up, and then circled around the sanctuary, checking the sacristy *diaconicon*, a smaller altar on the right and a chapel on the left.

Commander Ouramos walked up and down the two side naves that flanked the center, larger nave. Each column running down the two naves, which were engraved with the Greek cross, obscured niches that housed sepulchral monuments—*cenotaphs* of former bishops or saints and one actual burial of a long-ago bishop. He saw nothing unusual.

Both went outside and strolled around the perimeter of the church, inquiring of whomever they encountered about the tattered monk. Everyone within the vicinity of the church simply shrugged and the crowd who had lingered awhile with the phantom was nowhere to be seen.

The bishop and the commander, bewildered, stood before the church, staring at each other. They began to question their senses. Was it a vision, a ghost of some sort portending some message of the town's fate? After all, the bishop's suffering laity deserved some divine intervention.

The sun was now low in the sky and the church's shadow began to invade the courtyard with its social and business activity. It was time to end their search and retire to their evening meals, the commander to his garrison quarters and the bishop to his residence *episcopium* a modest structure conveniently positioned next to the church.

When the bishop entered his residence, the deacon was setting the table. An aroma of boiling soup captured his nostrils and whetted his appetite. The faithful maid, whose bearing on the household seemed to have no bounds, was preparing it over the hearth. Knowing that he had just returned from the tower, which he did often, the deacon greeted the bishop. "Your Grace, what news does the tower bring today?"

"A strange thing happened. My eyes may have deceived me." Bishop Mesimeros, still excited and puzzled over the incident sat slowly down at the table.

"No Greek ships today?" asked the deacon light heartedly in contrast to the bishop's pensive face when he often hesitated to respond.

"Your Grace, your surveillance on that tower makes you tardier and tardier for your meal," interjected his spunky, petite maid, whose chronological age and dedication allowed ample participation in the bishop's affairs. She fancied herself the matron of the house. Her rosy cheeks protruded from her graceful, wrinkled face, and the salt-and-pepper strands of hair slipping out of the black kerchief gave her a motherly rank. She poured the soup, attentively and happily, then sat at the table.

"These wayfarers who sojourn to our town bring valuable tidings. It is essential that we keep a lookout for them," said Bishop Mesimeros and began the blessing.

"What is so strange, Your Grace?" inquired the deacon, when the table blessing ended.

"I saw a monk clothed in robe and cowl of an ancient time, ragged and eaten, entering the east gate, and heading for the church. My feelings tell me he is Father Nicholaos or one who brings news of him. When we went to greet him, he was nowhere to be found. Nor had anyone seen him."

"In my opinion, it is an apparition," jumped in the maid, proudly. "There was a report of the Virgin Mary appearing before a young bride who lost her husband in the siege. The vision appeared on the spot where he was buried."

"Oh Irena, you can't believe everything you hear. These shocking times spawn supernatural claims that circulate rapidly among old women. There must be some natural explanation," insisted the bishop. "This man is somewhere in our town, in flesh as well as in spirit."

"If it is Father Nicholaos, he can be helpful to us. He knows Latin and together with his student Iohannes Florus, who also speaks Latin and has friends in the Norman army, they can be great intermediaries between us and our new lords," emphasized the deacon while the bishop returned silent nods of agreement.

"The man is a saint and so was indefatigable and faithful Helena. He took over our orphanage and moved it out of harm's way. He scoured the countryside for the other frightened little souls," Irena said, never feeling out of place in the conversation.

"He saved so many of our most vulnerable from the clutches of the Saracens and pirates, our young women and children, our future." The bishop's assenting nods turned to words.

Daytime, with its normal bustle of activities, alleviated and distracted the people from their innermost worries, but night-time summoned them back and gave them reign over their sleep. The bishop was no exception. When in his bed, many things rolled around in his head in addition to the mysterious man at the gate. The constant dripping of news, originating from the battlefields and keeping the town in suspense, troubled him.

It seemed that their fate was dangerously fickle, good news commingled with bad news. The Romanoi still held Bari and took Taranto, yet the Norman duke took nearby Otranto and

Vieste after his loss at Dyrrachium. Count Roger was defeating the Arabs in Sicily and was close to its capital, Panormos. But the Greek Christians there indirectly suffered in the wake of the battles. Good and bad embraced each other, he thought, both seemed equally powerful.

When he finally fell asleep, the image of the old monk in tatters, passing through the gate, invaded his restless mind. He was withered to a starving state and kept pointing in the direction of Stylon with his perforated blood-crusted hand. His tattered garment barely covered the bleeding gash at his side. Then the image faded away with daylight and the bishop got up.

"Is Your Grace going to search for that wayfarer today?" inquired the deacon the next morning.

The bishop pondered the question for a while as he assembled the pieces of his dream into a day-time logical coherence. "I believe so; I have an errand for you. I have a strong feeling that Father Nicholaos is ill." He then instructed his deacon to set out for the Florus' holding to notify Iohannes that their dear Father Nicholaos was somewhere in Stylon.

The deacon promptly dressed accordingly for the long walk west toward Saint Elias, but prior to crossing the threshold, he was stopped by the bishop. "I caution you, please make no mention of this ghost-like figure of a man. I prefer this incident to remain within these walls. We have enough real problems without adding supposed miracles or incidents that arouse superstition," insisted the bishop.

"What am I to say?"

"Just say Father Nicholaos is quietly resting and meditating in the comfort of his peers on the Mount Consolinum slope." Both stepped outside into the church courtyard, which was coming alive in the morning light. The deacon headed toward the west gate, and the bishop searched in town for a ghost he knew he would not find.

Iohannes and his son Eugenius Junior were in the olive orchard picking the first appearing ripe fruit which every October was cured to constitute the green batch. Excluding Flavia and the toddlers whom she was watching in the house, the women and older girls were in the shed preparing the picked olives for curing.

With a knife, their nimble hands masterfully sliced each olive before tossing it into a vat of fresh water with a swift mechanical motion perfected from prior countless harvests. The tedious work did not interrupt the lively conversations normal to all harvests nor the scolding of the unruly children in their midst. There were different batches in the olive harvest, some picked green, others picked later when more mature.

First to spot the deacon grappling with the autumn heat as he emerged from the road and headed to the main farmhouse was Eugenius Junior. He yelled the news to his father, who shouted back, "Go and see what he wants. I will join you in a minute when I am done here." The sixteen-year-old ran enthusiastically toward the visitor.

"I'm looking for Iohannes and his wife," said the deacon as Eugenius Junior approached him.

"My father is in the orchard and my mother is inside. I will lead you to our house."

Flavia was surrounded by grandchildren. Her hair was neatly tied into a pleasant chignon that day and fully exposed her face, highlighted by barely detectible wrinkles below the eyes. When the deacon walked in behind her son, she froze, transfixed by the deacon from Skylletion, for she knew instantly the purpose of his visit.

It had to be about Father Nicholaos, whose absence had held her in an emotional limbo for too long. Her heart had been suspended between hope and nagging doubts. Some real tidings, she thought, and did not know whether to be euphoric or prepare for the worst. At this moment Iohannes strolled in, gave his warm greetings, which Flavia had absentmindedly neglected, and both proceeded to accommodate their guest.

"I never knew October could be so hot," said the deacon, wiping his large forehead with a handkerchief which ruffled his thick black eyebrows in the process.

"What do we owe this visit to, Father?" inquired Iohannes anxiously.

"Bishop Mesimeros has sent me here with news of one he feels is dear to your hearts." The deacon scratched his head, looking for a way to present the bishop's premonitions and hunches. "The bishop believes that Father Nicholaos is in Stylon."

"How does he know this?" inquired Iohannes.

"There seems to have arrived in Skylletion a monk from the south, near Stylon."

Flavia's heart skipped a beat. "And he has said that he has seen Father Nicholaos?"

"Bishop Mesimeros thinks so," said the deacon, skirting the fact that no one had spoken to the traveler as far as he knew.

"Is he all right? How far is Stylon?" Flavia strung her anxious inquiries. She had been brooding over them too long.

"Dear Flavia, we believe he is fine. The bishop assured me that he is resting and meditating in some hermitage on the slopes of Mount Consolinum." The deacon began sweating profusely again and asked for water. "These were the bishop's very words." He wiped his forehead again, then gulped down the water.

Iohannes remained silent while Flavia continued her questions at the visitor. He began to contemplate the journey to Stylon. It was a day's journey on horseback if one pushes the horse. The route, commonly referred to as Via Apulia, was well trotted and stretched along the Ionian coastline from Rhegium to Apulia with Skylletion and Stylon in between. Two days would make a comfortable trip.

Flavia kept peppering the deacon. "Is he hurt or sick? Where has he been so long?"

The deacon returned the salvo always in the same way. "We are not sure. We simply don't know very much."

"Flavia, I'm sure he is all right. It seems to me that Father Nicholaos has stopped at Stylon because from there the trek home is easiest." Iohannes' optimistic considerations availed the deacon to wander into generalities.

The deacon glanced at the window and said, "I see the Florus family has grown into many generations here. Soon there will be a little hamlet here, a chorion legalized by the bishop."

"When that happens, we probably will be completely under the Latin jurisdiction and our Greek bishop will lose his authority," Iohannes commented.

"True indeed, and our children will be baptized with Latin names and pronounced in a Frankish tongue. Your military acquaintances on the other side already refer to you as Ioan Fleur. Iohannes and Flavia did not respond, and the deacon realized there was nothing more to say. "It is late. I would like to return before dark. But before I take my leave, maybe your handsome lad can be so kind as to introduce me to the rest of the family members, especially the crew working in the shed."

"I see you noticed them. Genè! Walk the deacon to the shed and don't forget Grandmother and Grandfather; they too would like to meet our guest."

The emotional pendulum began to settle down for Flavia after the deacon's visit. What remained now, she reasoned, was for someone to go and get Father Nicholaos and bring him home where he belonged. He would live, close to her perhaps even in her home. Mother Helena would have wanted that.

Chapter XXII: Skylletion

Flavia helped Iohannes gather the necessities for the journey for Stylon, and then waited outside until he returned from the stable with the horse.

"Bring him back, Iohan," Flavia entreated as he bridled the animal.

"Flà, you know I'll do my best," he said, knowing Father Nicholaos began as a hermit and may have wished a similar retirement.

She handed him the bundle of provisions after he jumped unto the saddle. He kicked the horse into a walk and turned his head to see her waving good-bye.

He arrived at Skylletion first and stabled the horse there in the familiar garrison as he had done many times before while on active duty. Before he could head for the commander's quarters and see what he had to say concerning the monk, the commander appeared before him. However, Ouramos wished to engage in small talk concerning the Skylletion battle, but Iohannes courteously cut him short. "Sir, do you know anything about Father Nicholaos' location?

"Sorry, I have no news on Father Nicholaos, son. The bishop may have," replied the commander whose grey eyes sparkled in the joy of a visit from some one from yesteryear.

"Then, I must see the bishop. If you don't mind?"

"You are spending the night at my quarters? We have a lot of memories to run through." His aging eyes begged for a sign of affirmation. "Who knows, an enjoyable conversation can jar an old man's memory." He baited Iohannes.

"How could I not stay a while?" Iohannes offered a crisp reply and left in haste wondering if he had been rude.

Iohannes knocked on the bishop's thick wooden door. For a while, there seemed to be no life on the other side, so he mused over the frolicking and shouting of children playing in the church courtyard opposite the bishop's residence. Finally, the door partially squeaked open, just enough to allow the rosy face of the busy maid to fit through. He introduced himself and requested an audience with the bishop.

"And the reason for the visit?" demanded Irena.

"About Father Nicholaos," he replied, and she quickly closed the door without explanation.

He wondered if the maid had shunned him or indeed went to notify the bishop and turned his attention again to the church courtyard, where the children still played, noisily. The door squeaked again but this time she opened it wide, enough to fully see the rest of the figure on the other side.

"Follow me, please," she said, with a kindly air about her, yet firm and authoritative. He trailed behind, struck by the elderly woman's feisty and confident nature.

The bishop sat in his study writing with his feather quill pen on some parchment and looked up as the two entered.

"Your Grace, this is Iohannes. It's about Father Nicholaos."

"Thank you, Irena," replied the bishop, and the maid disappeared to tackle her household tasks.

The study was small. Opposite the entrance was the bishop's chair, a crude wooden replica of the church episcopal chair, *kathedra*, but which presently was not utilized, and behind it were shelves containing a multitude of scrolls of legal and church records. To the left, writing paraphernalia and an upright wooden cross adorned a bench-like table with a stool. The stool's normal occupant, the deacon, who also acted as a scribe, was absent. And in his place sat the bishop himself wearing only his inner garment with sleeves rolled up, and carefully writing with his feather pen.

Dumbfounded by the unusual informality and casualness of the bishop, Iohannes did not know whether to kneel before His Grace or not, so his eyes kept scanning the place in awe.

Everything appeared to have a commonplace practicality and lacked the luxury and pomp of his rank, save for a decorative bronze inkstand, probably a gift by a passing dignitary, thought Iohannes.

Next to it sat a small worn chestnut coffer. Its four upright corners were delicately carved into miniature columns, and true to the architectural requirements, the columns possessed a base, a shaft, a capital, and cornice. Its recessed sides were plain surfaced with countless cracks and the finish was worn off by the seriousness of the bishop's work. The hinged cover was open and revealed instruments for sealing documents commensurate to his holy office and its responsibilities.

"Come in, come in. Sit down." The bishop grabbed Iohannes' wandering attention by pointing to a bench up against the wall, with his pen. Then, he returned to his writing. "As you can see, the deacon is not here." When finished, he anchored the pen in the quill stand, a simple, circular wooden block, and set the parchment aside to let the ink dry.

"How's Flavia?" the bishop snapped to his guest.

"Your Grace remembers my wife? She is fine." Iohannes was pleasantly surprised.

"Of course, I remember certifying the marriage contract. Furthermore, Father Nicholaos has often spoken of your family, and so has the commander." The bishop's familiarity with his family gave Iohannes the impression that His Grace had a good handle on the visit's purpose.

"Those two have been very supportive of Flavia and me. Especially Father Nicholaos," Iohannes commented.

"Father Nicholaos is a saint and so are all the Basilian monks, earthly angels, I say." The bishop leaned back a bit to better assess his visitor and grant himself a thoughtful moment before continuing. "Have you ever heard of the Eucharist Miracle in Anxanon?"

"No, Your Grace," responded Iohannes, patiently hoping for relevancy.

"Well, in the town, about three hundred years ago, stood a Basilian monastery and its Church of Longinus. Its priest seriously doubted the transubstantiation that occurs during the ceremony of the Eucharist. When he was uttering the solemn words of the Consecration during the usual mass to his faithful, the host turned into a piece of bloody flesh in his hands and the wine in the chalice turned to blood. Amazed and shedding tears of bliss, he quickly called his congregation to witness what had transpired before him."

The bishop withdrew his eyes from Iohannes and took a breather, for the ink had dried on the parchment. He tightly rolled it, reached into the opened coffer, pulled out a string, and with it wrapped the document at its center. Iohannes watched closely, waiting for the bishop to continue.

"Meanwhile, the liquid blood coagulated into five pellets of unequal size. Was it truly the flesh and blood of Christ? Still skeptical, the priest had the pellets weighed with the bishop's scale. To their astonishment, the total weighed as much as each, and each one was of a different weight."

"What happened to the relics?" Iohannes became fully absorbed.

"They placed both holy relics in an ivory reliquary which remains in the town to this day. What is more amazing is that this town, called Anxanon by the Romans and situated just above Apulia's northern border, was the home of the centurion who thrust his spear through Christ at his crucifixion. The church was named after the centurion, who was declared a saint a long time ago."

"Your Grace, this is very interesting," "but has the maid told you of the purpose of me coming here?"

Before answering, Bishop Mesimeros extracted a candle, lit it, and watched the wax drip over the wrapped string and parchment. "I have been receiving news of the monk in bits and pieces from wayfarers and monks from Stylon. One hinted of a new monk arriving in the Stylon area. Another heard that he used to tend an orphanage. Finally, when all the bits amounted to something reliable, I sent the deacon to inform your family."

The drops of wax were now a nicely built-up blob and ready to be imprinted with the cone seal, which the bishop inserted into the molten wax and held in place until the wax hardened. Iohannes kept his patience during all this activity including his story telling. It must have a purpose, he mused.

"You see this parchment? The church has a favor to ask of you. Since you will be heading for Stylon, be so kind as to deliver this message to the priest." He returned the candle and cone seal to the coffer and pulled out two coin-sized objects of lead and the *boulloterion*, a plier-like instrument holding two dies.

"Yes, Your Grace, and its purpose?" Pride lit Iohannes face reasoning that the assignment would add authority to his own mission.

"I have been asked to authenticate an unusual incident which occurred in that town. I have not the time to go there myself, so I have instructed the local priest to document it himself."

Bishop Mesimeros took the two loose ends of the string, placed them between the two lead discs, pinched the discs with the boulloterion, and holding the handle with his left hand, he hammered the top die with a mallet. Both discs became one with the string ends sandwiched in between. When he unclasped the dies from the discs, an image of the Virgin Mary and Child *Theodokos* was imprinted on one side and a shortened inscription on the other side read, Theodokos help Theodorus Mesimeros Bishop of Skylletion. He then raised his eyes to Iohannes. "When the priest has finished the inquiry, return his findings to me when you return."

"What kind of miracle is it?" Iohannes' whetted curiosity temporarily had suspended his concern for Father Nicholaos.

"A leper from the leprosarium nearby had made a pilgrimage to the grave site of a Basilian monk and seems to be healed." He returned the boulloterion, picked up the feather pen, and started writing on the outside of the parchment. On one side he wrote the priest's name in the dative and on the other side he wrote his own in the genitive, then returned the quilt pen and continued, "Also, when you see Father Nicholaos, for I am sure he is there, tell him he is needed here."

"His orphans also want him home. They are his family, and Flavia misses him the most," Iohannes emphatically interjected, then paused to ask, "Has Your Grace received any news on his health? Perhaps that's the reason for his long absence."

"I'm sorry I have no concrete news on that, my son, but he is better off here among his close friends." Handing the scroll to Iohannes, he called for the maid, who with her usual deftness was doing her chores purposely nearby, anticipating the bishop's needs.

Iohannes had barely secured the scroll when she stood before the bishop. "As you can see, Irena is more than a maid; she is my personal assistant, if you will, a deaconess when the deacon is away."

"I will lead our guest out," said Irena, "and in the meantime, Your Grace must prepare for the confessional sacraments at the church. Some people are already strolling in."

"You see what I mean, Iohannes? What would I do without her?" joked the bishop while patting him on the shoulder. "May God be with you and may both of you return safely."

Iohannes shrugged off any doubts over his safety, "Thank you, Your Grace," and followed the maid outside where he headed to Commander Ouramos.

Her sturdy legs carried her everywhere in her duties to the bishop, household or otherwise. The steep winding paths throughout the town did not hinder the maid at all. Her favorite chore was trekking to the other side of the town to the marketplace to procure food items. It was the center of the latest gossip followed only by the community fountain.

Being so close to the town's main authority figure made the maid somewhat of a celebrity amongst the women frequently gathered there. She was both a source as well as a receiver of news. The burning question on Irena's mind that day regarded the identity of the strange, hooded wayfarer and report back to the bishop, relaying local news was one of her unofficial duties she relished.

When she arrived at the market, she headed to the farmer selling dried figs and eggs bypassing the chickens in wicker cages. She examined the eggs for freshness, took a bite of a fig under the consenting eyes of the seller who knew the purchase was for the bishop. But her real attention was elsewhere, beyond the usual haggling over prices and the quality of the merchandise. To her disappointment, she did not see those ad hoc groups that appear just about anywhere to share their gossip, most often meaningless.

Irena made her purchase without the small talk leaving the seller lacking in the courtesy that was normal to her character and when she turned around, she found herself face to face with an old woman. It was Cornelia, the one who had told her about the apparition of the Virgin Mary.

"Good morning, Irena. I have something for the bishop," said Cornelia as she pulled her aside away form other ears.

"Oh, Cornelia! What a surprise.?" Irena's face shone with a hopeful smile.

Cornelia began to whisper so that Irena had to bend down: "A hooded monk appeared before me at the east gate. I have never seen a monk in that condition. His robe and cowl were torn and deteriorating. His face was worn and burnt like those who live in the African heat. But strangest of all, there was a translucent and barely detectible glow about it, ghost-like."

"Did he say who he is and his purpose here?" Irena was astounded.

"He said he was bringing tidings of a sick brethren in Stylon but would seek rest in the church first. His words had a hollow tone as if coming, not from his lungs, but from a cavern."

"What happened afterwards?"

"I don't know. I went on my way and when I turned back, he was gone."

Extremely eager to relate the latest to her bishop, Irena hurried back to the bishop residence. Not finding him there and not having left a message, she reasoned he was nearby, probably doing something at the church, so she jumped into her next chore. The vestments which she had washed the day before were now dry and ready to be folded and brought to the sacristy.

When there, she encountered the bishop seated in one of the pews, which he often did to gather his thoughts for the homily of the next mass. Connecting current events with the scriptures was a task that his fertile mind found easiest when alone in the spiritual surroundings. Holding the neatly folded vestments against her chest, she greeted the bishop and related the old woman's experience at the south gate.

"I feel vindicated; the ghost was of flesh and blood," said the bishop. But when Irena continued, he realized the wayfarer's message was eerily like what he gleaned from his dream, and his face turned pale.

"Is something wrong, Your Grace?"

"No, no, I'm fine. Is there more?" the bishop asked acquiring back his color.

"No," she said, and the maid headed for the sacristy to place the clean vestments in the usual old chest. The chest cover, distorted by age and constant use, was not hinged, just sat on top, and she laid it aside, carefully inserting the priestly clothes in its depth.

When she replaced the cover, she was required to pull back the chest from the wall to fit the cover back properly, and she noticed a dusty, faded garment cramped between it and the wall, moth-eaten and infested with brown sand, the likes of which is not found in Italy. It barely held together as she picked it up. Holding it with extended arms to avoid breathing the dust, she scurried over to the bishop.

"Your Grace, what is this?" She coughed.

He took it delicately from the maid. "It looks like a robe the desert fathers wore; it must be hundreds of years old." He spread it carefully on the floor and it began to take on the form and condition of the wayfarer's attire as seen by the bishop. A ghostly shiver traveled down the bishop's back. "This must be nothing more than a series of coincidences," he whispered out loud.

"Did you say something, Your Grace?" Irena was puzzled.

"The robe! It is like the one the passing monk wore. I'll explain later." Bishop Mesimeros now knelt in prayer before the alter, a gesture Irena took as a wish to be left alone and gently walked away.

A passing monk in a dirty robe concerned about a fellow monk, leaving a message, then hastening on his way. The discovery of a deteriorating robe like the one worn by the passing monk; all could be explained by chance. Nothing is unusual here, he argued against his heart which told him otherwise.

Chapter XXIII: Stylon

Commander Ouramos greeted Iohannes enthusiastically into his disheveled and dusty personal quarters. Everything was neglected, as neglected as the commander's appearance, noted Iohannes. It was a far cry from the way it was when he needed permission from his assistant for even an audience, an assistant now nonexistent.

"As you see, my son, we are a skeleton of our former selves." Ouramos read his guest's mind as Iohannes kept surveying the once bustling quarters now occupied by one old man commanding ghostly cobwebs of the past. "I am left with just delivering messages and settling disputes the bishop cannot settle with God's persuasion."

"But what of the bandits that will accumulate in the hills?" Iohannes pondered on his commander's ghosts flitting from the garrison in the dead of night to unsuspecting bandits in the hills.

"We are hoping for the Romanoi to return before the Franchoi come back," said Ouramos with a tone that betrayed his reservations.

"But Count Roger is just over the hill in Mileto. Calabria is lost. The Greeks may never return."

"Yes, but to ask the Franchoi for help? They are bandits themselves, regardless of the Pope's investiture granted to them." Ouramos still held his Greek skepticism toward the Normans. "Besides, one brother is fighting Saracens in Sicily while the other is putting out fires in Apulia."

"Have you any news of Father Nicholaos?" Iohannes turned the subject.

"The bishop thought a monk entering the gate a while back may have had some news. We searched all over, but we could not find him. Maybe he has found the monk," Ouramos suggested.

"He didn't say anything about a missing monk. He did say he believes he is in Stylon."

"And you want him back?" How can I help?

"You've done enough, the rest is up to me. Thanks anyway."

The next morning, Iohannes left before daybreak and did not see light until he reached the Via Apulia along the shoreline. With the Ionian on his left, he made his way south, pushing the horse in a comfortable gait but slowing down to a jog on steep terrain. When he arrived in Stylon (11) he headed straight to the local commander and stabled the horse. And with the commander's directions he headed to the Episcopal church.

Iohannes found the priest in the sacristy laying out his clean vestments for the next mass. As Iohannes handed over the scroll, he introduced himself and explained the personal purpose of his visit. The priest, young with penetrating eyes, responded that he had heard of a Father Nicholaos, who was part of a laura—hermitage—on Mount Consolinum. But since it was late in the evening and the caves were located far up the mountain past the *katholikon*, a parochial church hugging the mountain, the priest offered his residence for the night.

"Thank you, Father." Iohannes adopted a humble patience as he watched the priest break the seal and studiously peruse the message on the parchment, squinting in concentration.

"Did the bishop say if he is coming here this spring?" the priest asked, turning his eyes upward toward Iohannes and then back down again to read.

"He didn't say," Iohannes responded flatly, and waited patiently.

Stylon-Katholikon

After having digested the gist of the message, the priest neatly rolled up the parchment for further reading and motioned for Iohannes to follow him to his residence near the church.

Once inside, they were confronted by a short and bald monk, with a constant smile and functioning as the priest's assistant; his duty was, among others, to care for the residence. The priest politely introduced Iohannes. "He is here for Father Nicholaos."

"Oh, yes. The monk from Saint Elias," said the monk. "It's an arduous trek up that slope to where his cell is located."

Mount Consolinum, has about sixteen natural caves in the limestone rock used by the hermits. Father Nicholaos occupied one small cavern that overlooked the Katholikon where they received mass. The cavern sat below the Stylon fortress, the citadel by which the Greeks gallantly protected the town.

Since the bald monk knew the mule paths to take, the next morning he led Iohannes up the proper trails. They stopped at the katholikon, which his guide insisted on showing to him, a quaint little church that seemed to hug the mountain for protection from the countless raids.

Stricken by the humility of its exterior, composed of simple clay bricks, Iohannes was equally awestruck by the contrasting rich spirituality of its interior, with the walls and apses covered in heavenly frescos of saints, Christ, and the Virgin Mary. "It has five cupolas or domes, four representing angels, while the center one, the largest, represents Christ," elaborated his guide.

The genuine humbleness outside with its spiritual wealth inside was like Father Nicholaos, Iohannes reflected. This was humble on the outside but overflowing with spirituality from within. He recalled his words, "The path to true spirituality begins with humble steps."

Up above the church, the path became more craggy, indistinguishable from the surrounding irregular terrain, but both men were able climbers and never missed a step. They climbed higher and higher. As they pushed through the growth, Father Nicholaos' cavern appeared. The bald monk stopped suddenly and pointed to an overhanging rock that cast a shadow just below it.

"Father Nicholaos should be there," he said, and quietly went on his way, probably to another cavern. Iohannes worked his way toward the dark shadow, being careful not to step on loose rock. Once there, he paused to catch his breath leaning against the outside wall of the cave.

While stretching his neck into the dark and dank cavern, he felt a tightening in his chest that reached to his throat, his heart beating faster. It was like going into hallowed ground without permission. In its depths, when his eyes adjusted, he discerned a figure quietly seated and transfixed on the blue sky greeting him from the opening. His garment was tattered, his eyes were glassy.

"Father, is that you?" Iohannes yelled eagerly, his heart wanted to jump out of his chest.

"Who is it?" rasped the monk.

"Me, Iohannes." He pushed the words through his throat. They embraced each other, but Father Nicholaos' embrace was weak. Iohannes had embraced skin and bones, a frail, emaciated body closer to its end than its recovery. Exposure and fatigue had compromised his body.

"Did you notice the laura on the way?" asked the former tutor softly, while adjusting his aging, glazed eyes on Iohannes whose heart had settled down to normal.

"Yes, it resembles the grotto back home with its walled entrance," volunteered Iohannes, happy that Father Nicholaos was well enough to talk.

"Indeed, it does," concluded his holy mentor and stopping for a moment. Iohannes could hardly hear his mentor's breath then the whispering voice returned. "My intentions have been to send word that I wish to be with my spiritual brothers in my remaining days, but the frailty of old age and this fever left me immobile here."

"We have received news of some sorts, but Flavia and the orphans miss you; they wish you to return," insisted Iohannes.

"My son, I've never left you. During sleep, my dreams whisk me away to the Cathedral of Skylletion, Saint Elias, and the grotto." Father Nicholaos cleared his throat. "I am at peace here; my communion with God is strengthened besides I'm close to my end."

"Your loved ones can help you heal; many men have lived longer," protested Iohannes, as a tear escaped from one eye.

"The solitude here is my friend. It releases me from the earthly shackles. I witness the glory of God and His eternal truth in my meditation. My deteriorating body is of no consequence in its majesty."

Iohannes nodded in a silent acknowledgment out of the respect for their long relationship as he tried hard to grasp the meaning in the Father's words. He wondered if there was enough time in the world to digest the monk's wisdom. But time, now he had little, just enough daylight to avoid the rocky dangers of the return to the episcopal residence for the night. "Father, I must go now. We will talk tomorrow."

When at the residence, he was confronted by an anxious air hovering over the monk and priest, who also wanted news of

Father Nicholaos and his intentions. "I understand the need for solitude and meditation," said Iohannes, "but why here? They can meditate anywhere." He looked inquisitively at the other two. The monk and priest glanced at each other, waiting for the other to speak first. Finally, the priest sighed deeply and began to talk.

This is a special place for the Basilian monks. "The holy migration began long ago with the iconoclastic persecution and continues through today."

The bald monk elaborated further: "The final waves came from Sicily during its Arabic conquest, initially in abundance and then in spurts depending on the latest turmoil between Greeks and Arabs. They reinvigorate their spirituality here in a community of mutual help as they fulfill their vows. They are like the swallows which perch here to rest for their final journey."

"You mentioned that you will try to return the monk home; does he wish to go?" asked the priest, concerned.

"He shows no inclination to leave, just smiles sadly in his refusal. I will try again tomorrow," Iohannes answered.

"Tell me, my good man. Do you want the monk back for your own regard or that of his?" The monk's wise remark penetrated a little too deeply.

Iohannes fished for a response. "But he is so wan and sickly. He needs nurturing attention. If a man encounters a sick man in need of help, is it not that man's Godly obligation to tend to him regardless of his refusal? A good Samaritan would stay by his side doing what he can, would he not?" His longed desire shared with Flavia to bring Father Nicholaos home now seemed less objectional in his mind.

"I believe you have a point," affably said the priest, "but if nothing can be done and he is most comfortable where he is?"

"I know Father Nicholaos well; he has been through worse and still has recovered."

"Then you must first bring him here to rest for the trip. In the meantime, I'll prepare the report for Bishop Mesimeros."

"By the way, was it really a miracle?" asked Iohannes.

"All I can say is that the leper did heal, my son," the priest said warmly.

The next day, he found himself at the small cave trying to persuade Father Nicholaos once more. In the past, it had been always the monk who offered enlightenment and wisdom, but this time he was ill. Iohannes asked him, simply, "Is your health not God's gift? If so, is it not your responsibility to nurture it if it goes awry?"

Father Nicholaos' fever had relaxed its tentacles during the night, allowing pleasant visions of Flavia, the family, and laity to seep into his sleep. The presence of Iohannes had teased out that palette of feelings for his flock and renewed his strength.

"Yes, I will come home," he said, softly.

After a week of convalescence at the episcopal residence, the Father's frail body satisfactorily recovered for the journey home. And the priest's report was ready for consignment.

With his mentor on horseback, peaceful and self-absorbed, Iohannes tugged on the reins in front, ruminating over his decision. He wondered if he had denied Father Nicholaos something, something greater than the two of them.

"Father, remember the story of Diogenes? You remind me of him." Iohannes struggled to keep upright, in his walk, on the steep path.

"Uhm." Gravity pulled the monk's torso precariously forward on the saddle.

"He lived in a barrel-like shelter. You, Father, prefer the same."

"But it was not to hide from the world," replied the monk.

I understand that it was to mock the onlookers, a way of saying, "I have been denied uttering the truth, so see what you have done to the truth." Iohannes remembered the monk's explanation.

"Yes, indeed." The monk was impressed.

"Father, you were tucked away in the crevices of that rocky mountain. Was it your symbolic statement to the world, the last expression of your soul?"

He turned around to receive an enigmatic smile before the Father answered, "Diogenes of Sinope, a humorous withdrawal on his part, but serious in depth."

"Father, you have an unusual humor in your mannerisms and speech." Iohannes waited for a response but felt only the enigmatic smile beam on his back instead. A means of expressing the Truth that wails in your heart silenced by an arrogant and unscrupulous authority, thought Iohannes.

The times were indeed brutal, so much so that Truth itself had taken refuge in those caves and crevasses. It was nurtured and kept alive in the fertile minds of the Basilian monks.

They slept, ate, and meditated in their makeshift homes in the manner of Diogenes in which Truth was allowed daylight only in their deeds and way of living. Their tattered attire reflected the tattered institutions about them with their arbitrary powers. They saw the arrogance of power as an obstacle not only to Truth but ultimately to God. Father Nicholaos' life fit this narrative, for he was a Basilian monk.

All these thoughts churned and churned in the mind of Iohannes on the grueling return but finally settled into a realization of the monk's resiliency and strength of character. He had not denied the Basilian monk his wishes; if anything, he had extended them. His passion to practice his meditation, *hesychia,* was not deterred. Only its venue would change, from Stylon to his beloved grotto, that original hallowed ground.

During the spring of the following year when the shepherds bring their sheep to the high country, Eugenius

Junior discovered Father Nicholaos in a state of eternal sleep. He seemed to have chosen the timing of his death to coincide with the arrival of Eugenius Junior, for the body was still warm to the touch.

But Father Nicholaos' story did not end when he passed to the other world alone in the grotto practicing his hesychia. It was given immortality by God and merged with the other countless stories of Basilian monks. As it happened while Father Nicholaos was on his last journey to Nicoptera, Eugenius Junior had by then fallen completely in love with Iris, whom he had known since childhood.

His attraction to the skinny, freckled girl whose face resembled a radiant sunflower only grew with age, and by the time of Father Nicholaos' death, their betrothal was written in stone. They saw the world through the same eyes. Their destinies were one, and to separate one from the other was the death of both. It was a playful, innocent love that in its own natural way matured and bloomed like the pretty flowers in the nearby meadows.

However, Iris, poor little Iris, was twelve when it had all started. She began to lose that lively prance, that hopping and skipping so amusing and delightful to Eugenius Junior whenever they met. Her leg muscles were shrinking in size and strength, such that the joyful prance was replaced by a waddle. She was not in real pain, just a discomfort that restricted her movements and cut short their walks together.

But the skinny, freckled girl held his heart even tighter as the illness progressed. Saverina, who had consulted with her mother, said this sort of thing happens more often with males, and with girls it is less severe. Her only remedy was to stretch the legs, and if need be, brace them to prevent further contractions. What the illness took away from their lives, their love for each other restored.

They were in their late teens when Father Nicholaos returned to his beloved grotto. The illness had not lost its slow progression, and Iris was still struggling to be ambulant, but the monk brought with him the soothing protective magic which he had so often dispensed to his orphans. His uncanny, gentle air seemed to put everyone at ease, including the illness itself, and when he died, Iris' limp mysteriously became less noticeable.

After Father Nicholaos was interned next to Helena at Saint Elias, Saverina and Flavia began talking of miracles surrounding the lives of the Basilian monks. Could Iris benefit from a pilgrimage to Father Nicholaos' grave site? The two debated among themselves.

Encouraged by the talk of miracles that the adults alluded to, the couple went there and knelt before the two graves in homage to the dead, quietly praying and pleading for the Father's blessings. When she got up, Iris felt a renewed strength in her legs, barely noticeable at first, but the walk back verified her hunches.

The next day and the days afterward, her muscle tone began to return to normal, no longer withering away but increasing in size and function. By the time they were to get married, two years later, she had turned into a wholesome, healthy, freckled bride, full of life and ready to tackle motherhood. Their first child was a baby boy they promptly named Iohannes after his grandfather, their second, a healthy girl, and the third was a boy again, whom they baptized Nicholaos. And many more came after that, four more to be exact.

Epilogue

The Florus holding never grew into an actual hamlet, for each subsequent generation found its own path and direction; some went to Sicily, and others went north. Since the Normans had, by the time Eugenius Junior and Iris began their family, completed their hold on Southern Italy with the fall of Bari and later Sicily, a type of peace emerged, allowing increased mobility for the inhabitants. Exceptions to this peace were two Saracen raids on Nicoptera in 1074 and 1085.

At the end of the eleventh century, Bishop Mesimeros passed away, and was replaced by Giovanni Niceforo, a Latin deacon from the church of Mileto who began to utilize the Latin Rite. It ushered in linguistic mutations in the everyday language of the people. Their cherished vernacular began to shed its Greek inflection and acquired an Italic sway already prevalent in the rest of Italy, further bolstering movement to other parts. The last Iohannes from the Florus family holding became known as Giovanni Floro, and his descendants found their way to the lower Sila region overlooking the Catacen Isthmus.

END

Historical Notes

CHAPTER III Orphans

(1) Under Michael IV, 1035 Peace Treaty between Constantinople and al-Akhal, Sicily becomes a vassal state under the protection of Constantinople.

(2) The oratory was built near the ruins of a Roman theater, and rumors claim that an ancient monastery, Cassiodorus' Castellensis, was located nearby. The ruins along with the monastery once comprised the old Skylletion, Scollacium, which then moved to higher ground for protection.

CHAPTER XIII The Patrol

(3) Inland from the Capo Zeffirio (Cape Zephyr) is Bruzzano and the Rock of Armenia, a sandstone mountain 377 feet high on which stands a fortification, built in the eleventh century for defense against the usual Saracen wave. The area was also inhabited a time before Islam, in the 600s, by Christian Syrians, Christian Armenians, and even Jews who escaped the Persians in the Middle East. Basilian monks joined them as well, and one can find hermit holy caves in its sandstone. Further back in time, the settlement is attributed to the ancient Greeks when part of the colonizers moved inland (800–700 BC).

(4) Rhegium was surrounded by a protective wall, and a citadel sat in the far corner, built by no other than Justinian himself on top of the ancient Greek ruins after defeating the Ostrogoths. Five hundred years later, the bulwark was reinforced, made higher, and the citadel rebuilt to become a proper Byzantine fort by order of Boioannes just before he attacked Messina.

Rhegium's Saracen woes started in the summer of 901 when it was taken, plundered, and the inhabitants enslaved. The Arabs called it Rivah while the Byzantines called it Rhegion, and the names alternated between Rivah, Rhegion, Rivah, Rhegion and so on and so on for the entire century. No less than eight of these changes have occurred as far as is recorded. Each change is not just academic; it is written with the blood of innocent Christians who dared to try to divest themselves of the Islamic yoke when the tribute became too heavy. Finally, in 1006 under the great Basil II and with the help of a Pisan fleet, it was restored to its rightful owners, reaffirming itself as an episcopal center for the Greek Orthodox Church formally instituted by Justinian centuries earlier.

CHAPTER XIV The War

(5) Within the two prior centuries, the Byzantines have made attempts to regain Sicily by taking Messina first. Apart from the role that fortune may have had or may have not, there has been mostly venality and ineptitude in the background of these endeavors. A maladroit leadership was a common denominator in each failure where the highest price was paid by the lower rank men with their blood.

The first of these attempts, shortly after the fall of Syracuse, in 878 AD, the able Syrian admiral Nasar managed a small victory between Messina and Taormina, towns still controlled by Christians. Fortune and Arab defenses proved too much but he did have success on the mainland.

The second occurred two years after Taormina fell for the second time in 962 AD. It had an initial success when they controlled Messina for nine days. However, it had a disastrous end. Emperor Nikephoros II put 40,000 men under the command of Niketas. Manuel Phocas, the emperor's nephew, oversaw the cavalry, and even Saint Nikephoros participated. The failure was due to Manuel's follies and imprudence; he brazenly attacked without the proper support and was defeated at Erymata (Rometta). The forces then retreated to Messina, where they tried to cross the strait to Calabria but were intercepted by the Arabs. The survivors were taken prisoner along with Niketas.

The third attempt was also short-lived, and little is known of it, but in the fourth in 1025 AD, a year after the Illyrian campaign, the elements of ineptitude, skill, and corruption all clashed in one performance on the Byzantine stage. As usual, corruption and folly won out. The brilliant Basil Boioannes, who was sent to Italy seven years earlier by an equally brilliant emperor, Basil II, easily took Messina. He was followed by a fleet headed by the incompetent Orestes, a eunuch whose forces were decimated by al-Akhal, the emir of Sicily. With the death of the great Basil II late that year, the Sicilian campaign languished and came to a final stop in 1029 AD by orders from Zoe's father, Constantine VIII, a man of little strategic ability.

(6) Prince Guaimar, in exchange, later annexed three duchesses to his domain, Amalfi, Gaeta, and Sorrento.

(7) Before the Arabs, Syracuse boasted a wealth in the culture, arts, science, and architecture rivaled only by Constantinople. The Byzantines Greeks had inherited this treasure from the later Romans and slowly continued its conversion into a Christian metropolis. Churches were erected, where once flourished temples such as the temple of Apollo or the temple of Athena. The Euryalus castle with its seventeen-mile protective wall that surrounded the plateau of the Syracuse, built by

Dionysius 400 years before Christ, for the most part still challenged the friction of time. Only the northern wall section was neglected under the Pax Romana.

These cultural icons embraced the Byzantine hegemony like an orphan who has discovered his true parents. The inland quarters of Neapolis, Tyche, and Acradina, before the Arabs still basked in the daylight of history demanding recognition. After the Arabs, the city was unrecognizable, stripped of its wealth, razed to the ground, and its citizens killed and enslaved. Only the island section, called Ortygia, separated from terra firma by a shallow isthmus, was still heavily fortified. They later decided to fortify it, and inside they transformed the cathedral into a mosque. But the scattered debris once called the Basilica of Saint John, the Greek Theater, Roman Amphitheater, and the altar of Hieron are still seen today.

(8) The people in this area of Sicily (Valdemone) refused to sever their ties with their Christian brothers across the strait, and the constant ebb and flow of people and news from Calabria kept their spirits alive. However, the heavy lifting in preserving the Christian identity fell on the Basilian monks. They retired in the nearby caves and crevasses, not only to practice their faith, but to also service the local laity. The caves surrounding Erymata, still found today, are a perfect example of the monks' stamina before an oppressive authority.

CHAPTER XVII The Northern Wave

(9) Uprisings, such as in Neocastrum in 1058 where the Norman contingent occupying it was annihilated by the former displaced Greek garrison, did not stop them. This revolt was short lived, for under Robert's orders his brother Roger managed to squash the rebellion. And when word of the atrocities also reached the Byzantine stronghold of Saint Giriaca, the local Prefect, and the bishop of Cassano confronted the Normans in the open fields of the Valley of Salt. Once again Roger was victorious, and the remaining Byzantine forces fled to Rhegium.

CHAPTER XX The New World

(10) The peninsula of Tropea, on which sets Nicoptera, is abundant in granite and calcareous formations mined from the beginning of time and ideal for building. The early Greeks were the first to mine the material for their temples scattered all over Southern Italy. Then the Romans followed suit where the ancient Greeks left off, only to be replaced once again by the Greeks or Byzantines. Tropea's coastline is an archeological treasure trove of their footprints. Neat, square cuts into the rock, some submerged, others on dry land, reveal human activity of mining, beginning from Pizzo all the way to Nicoptera. Even

partially completed columns, grain millstones, and basins for fountains can still be found in the quarries.

CHAPTER XXIII Stylon

(11) Stylon had been an episcopal center since Christianity surfaced here, and its importance as such prevailed up to the death of St. John Theristis in about 1054. The city's episcopal church at the time was typically Greek in its layout, with obvious structural members stolen from classical ruins, and frescos on either side of the nave. On the left was Christ dividing up the communal bread, and on the right, the Virgin Mary and the adolescent child looked on, while further on closer to the apse, Christ reigned over his kingdom with a scepter in his right hand. A few centuries later Il Duomo or La Chiesa Matrice di Stilo was built on top.

Glossary

Abdullah- son of the caliph of Kairouan.

Adranos- Adrano, Sicily.

Al-Akhal- emir of Sicily and vassal for Byzantines, 1019-1037.

Anatolia- Area in modern day central Turkey.

Anchorites- Monks living in seclusion, not part of a monastery as opposed to coenobitic.

Andirons- during ancient Greek time.

Anteri- A simple inner garment, can be worn alone.

Anxanon- Today it is Lanciano, Abruzzo.

Arabs- Arabs were the administrators of Sicily.

Arduin-a Milanese adventurer, interpreter, opportunistic fomenter.

Astolfi- is Italic for Haistulf, a Lombard surname.

Aurelius Cassiodorus- ~490 to ~583, statesman and monk, born in what was then Scollacium, which afterward it became Skylletion, in Greek, now thought to be located at Rocecelletta di Borgia, Calabria.

Avars- nomadic warriors, brought in use of stirrups, originally from Asia. (John Haldon, Warfare and History).

Ballista- huge crossbow.

Basileus Boioannes- catepan of Italy, 1018-1028, very successful, wins battle at Cannes.

Basileus II- 976-1025, conquered Bulgaria.

Basilian monks- played an important spiritual and cultural role in the Roman and Byzantine Empire.

Battle of Cannae- 1018, Catepan Basil Boioannes defeated 3,000 Normans and squelched a rebellion against the Byzantines in their province of Longobarda or Southern Italy.

Battle of Ostrovo- summer of 1041, Michael IV had an army of 40,000 men.

Bruttium- Latin name for Calabria.

Bucolic Verse- pastoral poetry, shepherds would engage in a type of singing about their lives. Sometimes they would compete.

Cala- name of the Bay of Palermo.

Catepan- title of governor, in this case of Southern Italy, based in Bari.

Cassiodorus Castellensis- a monastery founded by Cassiodorus.

Catacen- Catanzaro, Calabria.

Chorion- singular for Choria- small hamlets or towns whose inhabitants were grouped

together for protection and tax purposes. They shared equipment, often had their own

militia, and were required to provide military service to Constantinople.

Clio- Greek muse of history.

Dative- grammar form; here dative means to and genitive means from.

Dhimma- treaty made with non-Muslims who had no political rights and paying the gizyah.

Dinar- is about four grams of gold, a hefty amount for those days.

Disticha Moralia- ancient collection of moral principles in Latin. It was used as a teaching tool for the Latin language all the way up to the 17th century.

Dromons- Byzantine war ships.

Drungar- leader of about 1,000 men as a tactical unit.

Dyrrhachium- Durres, Albania.

Episkopos- the bishop sometimes was also the civil and military authority.

Euryalus- Northeast quarter of Syracuse.

Franchoi- Byzantine name given to the Franks; the reference here is to the Normans.

Gallia- modern day France.

Gidad- same as Harat al Gsadida or Quartiere Nuovo.

Giovanni di Niceforo-replaced Bishop Mesimeros of Shylletion (Squillace).

Gizyah- per capita tax on non-Muslims. tax imposed on infidels in Islamic domains.

Guaimar V- prince of Salerno, 1000-1052.

Gynaeceum- during ancient Greek time.

Harat-al-Hadid– an area south of present-day Corso Tukory, stretching to the sea.

Hesychia- orthodox meditation.

Hippagogon- ship constructed for horse transport.

Hipponion- became Vibo Valentia, then Vibona, then Monteleone, finally Vito Valentia again.

Ilyrian Expedition- 1024, led by Catepan Basileus Boioannes, he used Calabrian and Apulian militia.

Iohannes Cassianus Massiliensis- Saint John Cassian or John the Ascetic, born 360, founded the Abbey of St. Victor at Marseilles.

Italoi stratiotoi- Lombard and Italo Greeks.

Kairouan- Al-Qayrawn, Tunisia.

Karknios- named after some long-forgotten village nearby—if the historians are correct.

Kastron- Greek for castrum or fort, at times they were simple towers, turris.

Kataphracts- fully armed horsemen, horse also armed.

Katholikon- La Cattolica, Byzantine church in Stilo. A small Greek temple on the slope of Mount Consolino, Stilo.

Kentarch- in charge of 40-100 men.

Komes- captain.

Konterati- infantry lance throwers.

Laura- a group of hermits occupying a single cave or caves; they share common rules for meditation and prayer.

Leo Opos- catepan of Italy- 1034-1038, sent to Panormos in 1037 by Michael IV to establish Byzantine control under the Peace Treaty.

Maniakes, Georgios- ~998-1043, Sicilian operation, died in battle fighting the emperor.

Medma- Little is known of the city after the Punic wars.

Melfi- it was an early Norman stronghold. A town Located in northern Basilicata.

Modios- weight measure, 8.7 kg.

Mons Consolinum- Monte Consolino at Stilo.

Murabitum- Medieval Latin for mujahideen. They were both religious as well as military officials entrusted to maintain the frontiers of Islam and provide safe hospitality to their own.

Neapolis- center quarter of inland section, housed the Temple of Apollo.

Numisma- coin whose value is 72 numismata to one Roman pound (320 g) of gold; in this period, they were devalued by about 80%.

Opsikion- theme in Anatolia, south of the capital.

Oratory- a small chapel called Monasterium Beatae Mariae de Rokella.

Orthodox weddings- are in two parts, sometimes done on the same day.

Panormos- Byzantine for Palermo, Sicily.

Pathos Argiro- Catepan 1029-1031.

Peloritan Mountains- a ridge of mountains running north-south in Eastern Sicily, they loom over Messina.

Pentecost- celebrated 50 days after Easter.

Pikeman- carried a long, heavy spear used to neutralize a cavalry attack.

Plows- they were transported upside down.

Purple- sign of power, as born in purple, i.e., royalty.

Qiblah- direction of Mecca.

Quarters- city was divided into various zones, 5 total, Al Qasr, Al Halish, Harat al Gsadidà, Harat al Masgid, Harat As Saqalihà, respectively- Cassaro, Calsa, Quartiere Nuovo (merchant area), Mosque area, Quartiere Shiavoni.

Rape of Proserpina- Greek mythology.

Rhegium- Reggio, Calabria.

Ring of Gyges- according to the legend, the ring can make one invisible.

Rivers- city had two rivers, Kemonia and Pepyritus, that flowed into the bay.

Robert de Grantmesnil or *Robert II-* Abbot of S. Euphemia, later became bishop of Troina, Sicily.

Robert Hauteville- La Guischard, 1015 to 1085, duke of Apulia and Calabria.

Roger Hauteville – Il Bosso1031 to 1101, count of Sicily.

Romanoi- Romanos- Byzantines called themselves Romans. I use the term mainly for the Byzantine army.

Ruba'i- Arabic coin contained about one gram of gold, also called tari.

Rum- Arabs referred to the Romans and Byzantines by this term.

Saint Elias of Enna- 823-903, born in Enna, Sicily, captured and made slave, later freed, founded a coenobium in Valle dell Saline, Calabria.

*Saint Elias-*The Byzantine name for present day Vallefiorita, Calabria.

Saint Speleota- 863-960, born in Reggio, Calabria.

Saint Giriaca- Byzantine name for: Gerace, Calabria.

Saint Nicodemus of *Mammola-* 900-990, died at Kellerana, just above Mammola, Calabria

Sandalia- small boats, used for various purposes such as tenders, scouting, etc.

Santa Euphemia- also isthmus of Catanzaro.

Saracen- General term for Muslim invader no matter of his origin. Moors, Berbers, Arabs, etc.

Schema- Last article of clothing acquired by a monk during tonsure. It drapes down from the shoulders and is decorated with symbols. Last monastic vesture showing rank.

Sgrafitto- technique of decorating pottery with alternating slips.

Skita- small group of monks.

Skylletion- Squillace, Calabria, under the Romans it was called Scollacium.

Slavic area- Quartiere dei Schiavoni, emir had his mercenaries here, dock area.

Spathion- sword.

Stephen Kalaphates- brother-in-law of Michael IV and John Orphanotrophus, emperor's adviser.

Strategos Autokrator- given complete power in a campaign apart from the emperor.

Stratiotoi- local recruits, used for local defense and foreign campaigns.

Stridula- Scribla, Calabria.

Strongyle- Stromboli, a volcano still active today.

Stylon- Stilo, Calabria.

Suq- markets.

Tagmata- professional paid army, not local.

Tauriana- Gioia Tauro, Calabria, a coastal city on the west coast.

Termah- Termini, Sicily- near Palermo.

Terra d'Otranto- lower part of Puglia.

Thema of Calabria- Thema (Greek) became the Byzantine equivalent for province. At this time, Calabria was a province of Constantinople headed by a catepan at Bari.

Transubstantiation- the turning of the bread and wine to the actual blood and flesh of Christ.

Treaty of 1035- The internal conflict between the Arabs and Berbers in Sicily allowed for a peace treaty between the emir of Sicily and the Basileus Michael IV.

Tryoros- Tiriolo, near Lamezia.

Turma- an area of civil and military control with fortified towns, like a county.

Tycha and *Acradina-* both quarters surround Neapolis on its west side.

Valdemone- Eastern section of Sicily, also Val Demone.

Valle del Crati- long valley, north of Cosenza.

Valley of Salt- Valle delle Saline, Calabria, located just above Scilla on the same coast.

Varangian Guards- normally guarded the emperor, led by Harold Sigurdsson (Hardrada), 1015-1066.

Wolf's Pass- Passo Fosso del Lupo.

Zatrikion- a type of chest played on a circular board. Very popular at the time. This one had simple wood carvings for the pieces.

Zoe Porphyrogenita- 980-1050, Byzantine empress.

www.ingramcontent.com/pod-product-compliance
Lightning Source LLC
Chambersburg PA
CBHW051234260626
47162CB00002B/431